LEATHER
& LARK

Previous Books in the Ruinous Love Trilogy:

New York Times bestseller *Butcher & Blackbird*

LEATHER & LARK

BRYNNE WEAVER

SLOWBURN

A zando IMPRINT

NEW YORK

zando

Slowburn is an imprint of Zando.
zandoprojects.com

First Edition: June 2024

Text design by Pauline Neuwirth, Neuwirth & Associates, Inc.
Cover design by Qamber Designs

The publisher does not have control over and is not responsible for
author or other third-party websites (or their content).

Library of Congress Control Number: 2023948985

978-1-63893-179-9 (Paperback)
978-1-63893-180-5 (ebook)

10 9 8 7 6 5 4 3 2 1
Manufactured in the United States of America

CONTENT & TRIGGER WARNINGS

As much as *Leather & Lark* is a dark romantic comedy and will hopefully make you laugh through the madness, it's still dark! Please read responsibly. If you have any questions about this list, please don't hesitate to contact me at brynneweaverbooks.com or on one of my social media platforms (I'm most active on Instagram and TikTok).

- Eyeballs but not eye sockets, so you're welcome
- Teeth and tooth byproducts
- I might have ruined pizza and beer. Also smoothies. Still not sorry
- Snow globes
- Autocannibalism . . . ? Welcome to a debate you never thought you'd have
- Numerous weapons and sharp objects, including darts, scissors, guns, saws, knives, grinders, an edger, and a little implement called an enucleation spoon
- Severed fingers
- You might have new thoughts about crafting with epoxy resin
- Vehicular collisions
- Drowning in various forms

- Terminal illness of a loved one
- Detailed sex scenes, which include (but are not limited to) adult toys, choking, rough sex, mild degradation, sexual acts in public, pegging, praise kink
- References to parental neglect and child abuse (not depicted)
- References to child sexual assault (not depicted)
- Religious references/trauma
- Explicit and colorful language, including a lot of "blasphemy." Don't say I didn't warn you!
- Injured dog (cause of injury not depicted, and he's okay, I promise!)
- There is a lot of death . . . it's a book about a contract killer and a serial killer falling in love, so I feel like that's probably a given

For those of you who came here after the *B&B*
ice cream and just read the *L&L* triggers and thought,
"She's not really serious about the pizza . . . right . . . ?"
This one's for you.

PLAYLIST

Click on a QR code to listen:

APPLE MUSIC

SPOTIFY

PROLOGUE: Ignite
  "I Only Have Eyes For You," The Flamingos

CHAPTER ONE: Submerged
  "TUNNEL VISION," Melanie Martinez
  "444," Ashley Sienna

CHAPTER TWO: Bull's-Eye
  "Underground," MISSIO
  "Pulse," Young Wonder

CHAPTER THREE: Guillotine
  "Cuz You're Beautiful," Kiyashqo
  "BITE," Troye Sivan

CHAPTER FOUR: Germinate
  "November," PatrickReza
  "Shutdown," Hudsun

CHAPTER FOURTEEN: Retreat

"Superstar," MARINA

"Love Me," Jane XØ

"Front to Back," Buku

CHAPTER FIFTEEN: Signals

"Can't Forget You," NEVR KNØW

"Too Deep," Kehlani

CHAPTER SIXTEEN: Hymns

"Fears," MTNS

"Never Enough," TWO LANES

CHAPTER SEVENTEEN: Ascend

"Fight!," Ellise

"Soft to Be Strong," MARINA

CHAPTER EIGHTEEN: Spotlight

"Don't Dream It's Over," Kevin Olusola

"TALK ME DOWN," Troye Sivan

WATCH FOR SPECIAL BONUS TRACK "RUINOUS LOVE" BY T. THOMASON THAT WILL BE ADDED TO THE PLAYLIST FOR THIS CHAPTER!

CHAPTER NINETEEN: Exposed

"Close" (feat. Tove Lo), Nick Jonas

"Tranquilizer" (feat. Adekunle Gold), TroyBoi

CHAPTER TWENTY: Crawl

"Make You Mine," Madison Beer

"Make Me Feel," Elvis Drew

CHAPTER TWENTY-ONE: Enucleate

"Arms of Gold" (feat. Mia Pfirrman), Tape Machines

"Dangerous" (feat. Joywave) [Oliver Remix], Big Data

"Back to the Wall," TroyBoi

CHAPTER TWENTY-TWO: Wanderer

"Alone" (Slow Edit), BLVKES

"New Religion," MARGARET WHO

CHAPTER TWENTY-THREE: Last Defense

"Immortal," MARINA

"Dizzy," MISSIO

CHAPTER TWENTY-FOUR: Apparition

"Triggered," Chase Atlantic

"We Appreciate Power" (feat. HANA), Grimes

CHAPTER TWENTY-FIVE: Scorched

"Twisted," MISSIO

"Work," ionnalee

"Locked," Welshly Arms

CHAPTER TWENTY-SIX: Renew

"Liabililty" (feat. Astyn Turr), Tape Machines

"My My My!," Troye Sivan

"Believe in Love," MARINA

EPILOGUE: Magic Trick

"Afterlife," Hailee Steinfeld

BONUS: Strapped

"Troublemaker" (feat. Izaya), OMIDO

"Love U Like That," Lauv

IGNITE

Lark

"This is called the consequences of your actions, sweetie," I say as I unravel the fuse to the fireworks strapped between Andrew's thighs.

His cries reach a fever pitch only to die in the tape strapped across his mouth.

You wouldn't look at me and think it, but it's true . . .

I love the sound of his distress.

Andrew sobs and thrashes in his chair. I give him a bright grin and continue backing away through the meadow and toward the tree line, close enough that I can see the fear in his eyes, just far enough that I'll be protected by thick trunks when I leave him alone in the clearing. His muffled pleas are desperate. His rapid breaths billow from his nose in plumes of fog that reach toward the starlit sky.

"Do you know why you're there with fireworks strapped to your dick and I'm over here with a fuse?" I shout.

He shakes his head, then nods as though he can't decide which answer will stop this torture. The truth is, it doesn't matter what answer he lands on.

"If I ripped that tape off your mouth, you'd probably tell me you're *oh-so-very-sorry* about fucking Savannah in our bed while I was away, wouldn't you?"

He nods wildly, his predictable bullshit caught in the glue. *I'm sorry, so fucking sorry, I'll never do it again, I love you I swear* . . . blah, blah, blah.

"I'm afraid that's not really why we're here."

Andrew blinks at me, trying to decipher what I might mean as my grin turns feral, and when it does, his true panic sets in. Maybe it's my words, or perhaps it's the delighted gleam in my eyes. Maybe it's the way I watch him, unblinking. Or maybe it's the way I laugh as my thumb strikes the flint wheel of the lighter clutched in my hand. Maybe it's all of these things combined that make him piss himself. The urine shines in moonlit rivulets as it streams down his naked, shivering legs.

"That's right, sweetie. I know your secrets. *All of them.*"

My eyes stay locked on Andrew's as I slowly bring the fire closer to the fuse.

"Oh fuck—I almost forgot." I let the flame extinguish. Andrew's body sags with hope and relief.

Hope. It's cute, really.

I guess I can't judge so harshly—I had hope once too. Hope for *us*.

But I was naive to think Andrew was right for me with his hint of a bad boy edge. Those two well-placed tattoos seemed hot. That perpetually disheveled hair gave off a *no-shits-given* attitude.

Even his inability to stick to a job seemed legit, though I don't know why. Somehow, I'd convinced myself that he was a real-deal rebel.

Then he fucked our friend Savannah while I was out of town and I realized, he's not a rebel.

He's a loser.

And not only that. Once I discovered he'd cheated, I stole his phone, and I learned just how wrong I'd been all along about my so-called boyfriend. I found messages to girls, some of whom were too young to know better than to trust a hot drummer who called them beautiful and promised them all his attention. I found more than just a bad boy.

I found a fucking predator.

One who had slipped right under my defenses. And years ago, I promised myself one thing:

Never again.

When I lift my gaze to the night sky, it's not really this moment that I'm seeing. It's not even memories of the anger and disgust I felt when I looked through Andrew's phone. It's a memory of the gray stone spires of the prestigious Ashborne Collegiate Institute, their copper-capped points taking aim at the stars. Even now, years later, I can still summon the sense of dread that lurked beneath every breath I took there. It was a palace of shadowed rooms and sickening secrets. A castle of regret.

Predators like Andrew abound on this beautiful earth like a fucking locust invasion. Sometimes it seems like no place is free of infestation, even fortresses that are meant to be sacred, like Ashborne. Beautiful and grand. Secluded. *Safe.* Just like in nature, the prettiest things are often the most poisonous.

And Mr. Laurent Verdon, the artistic director of Ashborne? Well, he made some very pretty promises.

Regret washes over me. Regret about the death of Mr. Verdon. But not in the way you might think.

I should have been the one to kill him.

And now my best friend, Sloane, will carry that burden and its repercussions on her shoulders for the rest of her life.

I see glittering flecks of white light as I press my eyes closed, tighter and tighter. When I open them again, the past is safely stored away. Back then I had no power. But things are different now.

Predators might make beautiful promises, but mine is simple and unfussy.

Never.

Again.

It might not make for a pretty vow, but I do my best to make the execution of my promise fucking *spectacular*.

I take a deep, cleansing breath of the autumn air. Then I grin at Andrew and rummage in my bag until I find the portable speaker and connect my phone.

"Atmosphere is so important in these moments, don't you think?" I ask as I bring up "Firework" by Katy Perry and turn it up to full volume.

Predictable? Yes.

Perfection? Also yes.

I sing along and don't bother to hide my broad smile. There might be no chance for Andrew like Katy suggests, but he's definitely gonna have a spark inside.

"Well, I guess it's time to get this show on the road. And you know what you did. So do I. We both know I can't let you go. Like I said, baby," I call to him over the music with a shrug. "Consequences."

I light the fuse to the sound of Andrew's renewed desperation.

"Ciao, sweetie. It's been . . . something," I call over my shoulder as I duck into the safety of the forest.

Andrew's screams are a delightful harmony to the crescendo of music and the percussion of fireworks that crack and burst in the night. His suffering is a grand show of colorful sparks, a salvo of bright light and thunderous sound. Honestly, it's more majestic of an exit than he deserves. Everyone should be so lucky.

It's fucking magnificent.

I can't be sure when Andrew's wailing stops, not once the Triple Whistler bottle rockets start to go off. Those things are *loud*.

When the eruption dies and the last sparks are little more than falling stars, I step into the clearing. The scent of saltpeter and sulfur and singed flesh wafts from the blackened, smoking form in the center of the meadow.

With careful steps, I walk over to him. I can't tell if he's still breathing, and I'm not about to check for a pulse. It won't make a difference for him anyway. Even so, I watch for a long moment, music still blaring behind us from where I left the speaker in the tall grass. Maybe I'm looking for signs of life. Or maybe I'm waiting for signs of life in me. A normal person would feel guilt or sadness, wouldn't they? I mean, I loved him for two years. I thought I did, anyway. But the only regret I feel is that I didn't see the real Andrew sooner.

Even that tinge of remorse is dulled beneath a feeling of accomplishment. One of relief. There's power in finding secrets and blowing them up in a beautiful, bright light. And I've kept my promise. No one else suffers but the ones who deserve it. I took care of it myself. If a soul will be marked for this life taken, no one will carry that mark but me.

Never again.

A low moan pierces through the music. At first, I don't believe it, but then it rises again in a puff of smoke.

"Holy shit, baby," I say on the heels of an incredulous laugh. My heart sings beneath my bones. "I can't believe you're still alive."

Andrew doesn't answer. I don't know if he can even hear me. His eyes are sealed shut, his skin charred and raw, blood seeping from warped edges of seared flesh. I don't take my eyes from the fog that spills from his parted lips as I rummage in the depths of my bag until I find what I'm looking for.

"I hope you enjoyed the show. It was a great performance," I say as I unholster the gun and press the muzzle to his forehead. Another quiet moan escapes into the night. "But I didn't bring enough fireworks for an encore, so you'll just have to use your imagination."

I squeeze the trigger, and with a final explosion, there's one less locust in the world.

And there's only one thing I feel.

Fucking invincible.

SUBMERGED

Lark

"Don't hold your breath," I yell to the man in the sinking car as he pounds on the window and begs for my mercy. "Get it?"

I don't think he heard me. But that's okay. I just smile as I wave with one hand, my gun trained on him with the other in case the window budges and he manages to slither his way out.

Fortunately, the pressure of the climbing water makes it nearly impossible for him to escape, and in mere moments, the vehicle is submerged. Bubbles burst in the black water as the car slides beneath the gentle waves of Scituate Reservoir. The headlights point to the stars, flickering as the electrical connections succumb to the flood.

"Well, *shit*."

This isn't good.

Actually, it's kind of amazing. But it's also a giant pain in the ass.

I chew my lip and watch until the lights blink out and the surface goes still. When I'm sure everything will stay silent, I pull out my phone and open the contacts. My thumb hovers over Ethel's number. She's always been the one I've called when things have gone tits up. Admittedly, a car casket at the bottom of a lake might be a little beyond the usual definition of *tits up*, even if the timing wasn't already making it impossible to ask for Ethel's help.

With a sigh, I select the number just above hers instead.

Two rings and he picks up.

"Meadowlark," my stepdad chimes on the other end. I roll my eyes and smile at his use of my childhood nickname.

My wary tone is his first indication that something might be amiss when I say, "Hi, Daddy."

"What's wrong, sweetheart? Is everything okay?"

"Sure . . ."

"Did someone puke on the carpet?" he asks. It's safe to assume he's had a few drinks at his own Halloween party if he hasn't already clocked that there's no thumping bass or raucous voices in the background from my end of the line. "I'll have Margaret arrange some cleaners for you first thing. Don't worry about it, honey."

A final, damning bubble erupts from the lake like an exclamation point. "Umm, those aren't really the cleaners that I need . . ."

The line goes silent.

I swallow. "Dad . . . ? You still there?"

A door closes in the background on his end of the line, muffling the laughter and voices and music. My stepdad's unsteady exhalation is the next thing I hear. I can almost picture the way he's probably rubbing his fingers across his forehead in a futile attempt to channel some chill energy. "Lark, what the fuck? Are you okay?"

"Yeah, I'm totally fine," I say, as though this is just a minor inconvenience despite the balled-up, bloody T-shirt I press against my hairline where a deep gash throbs. My smile must be bordering on deranged. The Harley Quinn costume and twenty layers of makeup I'm wearing probably don't help either, so I guess there's more than one reason to be grateful that no one is around. "I can sort it out if you just give me the number."

"Where are you? Did Sloane do something?"

"No, not at all," I say, my voice firm, my smile instantly gone. Though I hate that he would jump to the conclusion that my best friend is at fault, I swallow my irritation rather than unleash it. "Sloane is probably holed up in her house with a smutty book and her demonic cat. I went away for the weekend. I'm not in Raleigh."

"Then where are you?"

"Rhode Island."

"Goddammit."

I know what he's thinking, that I'm too close to home for a fuck-up of this nature. "I'm sorry, truly. The car just . . ." I reach for the right words to explain, but only one surfaces. ". . . sank."

"*Your* car?"

"No. Mine is . . ." I glance over my shoulder toward my Escalade, the smashed headlights glaring back at me. "Mine has seen brighter days."

"Lark—"

"Dad, I can sort it out. I really just need the number for a cleaner. Ideally one with a tow truck. And maybe some scuba gear."

His laugh is hollow. "You've got to be joking."

"About what part?"

"All of it, hopefully."

"Well," I say as I lean over the rocky drop to peer down at the water, "we might be able to get away with someone who can snorkel. I don't think it's *that* deep."

"Jesus Christ, Lark." A long-suffering sigh permeates the line. I loathe the feeling of disappointment. It's as though he's standing right next to me with that look I've seen so many times before, the one that says he wishes I could do better but he just can't bear to break my heart by saying it out loud. "Fine," he finally says. "I'll give you the number for a company called Leviathan. You'll need to give them an account code. But *do not* give them your name. Not over the phone, not when they arrive. They might be professionals but they're dangerous people, honey. I want you to send me a text every thirty minutes to let me know you're okay until you get home, understand?"

"Of course."

"And *no names.*"

"Got it. Thank you, Dad."

A long silence stretches between us before he finally speaks again. Maybe he wants to say more, to call me out, ask some uncomfortable questions. But he doesn't. "I love you, sweetheart. Be careful."

"Love you too. And I will."

As soon as we hang up, I receive a text from my stepdad with a phone number and a six-digit code. When I call, a polite, efficient woman answers and takes down my details. Her queries are direct and my answers are minimal. *Are you injured?* Not really. *How many dead?* One. *Any special requests to facilitate cleanup?* Scuba gear.

When she's relayed all the terms and conditions and payment details, I hang up, then turn back to my Escalade where the cooling engine ticks beneath the crumpled hood. I could wait inside the vehicle, where it's warm, but I don't. This crash is going to take a toll on my already fucked-up sleep schedule, so it's not like I need to sit in the wreckage and conjure more nightmares. Even still, it was worth the consequences to watch that piece-of-shit predator sink to the bottom of the reservoir.

Another locust exterminated.

When a friend from back home in Providence mentioned rumors of a pervy teacher at her little sister's high school, it didn't take long for said pervert to take the bait on my fake social media accounts. Before long, he was asking for photos and begging for a meetup with "Gemma," my teenage alter ego. And I thought, *Hell, why not? I can come home for a visit, party for Halloween, and get rid of some vermin.* Technically, I guess I was successful, though I hadn't really intended to run Mr. Jamie Merrick into the water. I was hoping to force him to the side of the road and shoot him in the face, find a worthy trophy to take, and then leave him there like the piece of trash he is. Unfortunately, he seemed to catch on that he was in trouble and nearly got away. I guess I gave him a big clue with my failed attempt to shoot out one of his tires when he refused to pull over. Cackling maniacally as I waved the gun out the window probably didn't help either.

It might sound surprising, but it's actually not that hard to get away with shooting someone on a deserted road and driving away. Problem is, it's a little harder to cover your tracks when part of your car is imprinted on part of theirs.

On the plus side, ramming that asshole's vehicle into the lake does have more theatrical flair.

"Everything will work out better in the end," I whisper as I use a coin to loosen the screws from my rear license plate. The front plate is a crumpled sheet of metal—I already picked it up from the road. When I'm finished, I drag my coat out of the Escalade and pull on a pair of gray sweats over my tiny shorts and fishnet tights. With my gun safely holstered in my bag, I gather the paperwork from my glove compartment before I toss the strap over my shoulder and close the door.

For a moment, I just stand at the steep bank of boulders where Jamie's car flipped and catapulted him into the afterlife. His face is so clear in my mind, illuminated by my headlights in the instant before the crash. Wide, panicked eyes. Curly blond hair. His mouth agape in a silent scream. He was terrified. He knew he was about to die and had no idea why.

Shouldn't I feel bad about it?

Because I don't. Not at all.

I blink away the determined fury that still lingers in my veins and grin at the watery grave ahead. "Sometimes karma needs a backup bitch, don't you think, Mr. Merrick?"

With a satisfied sigh, I stride toward the rocky shore.

I text my stepdad to let him know I'm okay and set a timer for the next message. Then I climb the jagged rocks until I find a spot out of view from the road. With my hood tugged up over my pigtails and my body aching from the crash, I lie down on one of the granite boulders and stare up at the sky, a perfect place to wait.

And wait I do.

For almost three hours.

The occasional vehicle passes by during that time, though they can't see me where I'm wedged in the shadows of the boulders. None of them stop to check the Escalade. I managed to park it next to the ditch perpendicular to the lake before it thoroughly died, and unless you're on the lesser-used road and really looking, the damage is hard to see. So when a vintage car with a rumbling engine approaches slowly and rolls to a halt next to my SUV, I notice right away. My heart thunders beneath my bones as I remain crouched between the rocks to watch.

My phone buzzes with a text from an unknown sender.

| Here.

"Short and to the point," I say to myself before pushing to my feet. My head spins a little and my legs seem wobbly at first, but I manage to keep my shit together as I approach the car.

The engine cuts out. I hold my bag to my body with one hand inside, my fingertips resting on the cold handle of the gun.

When I hesitate in the center of the road, the door creaks open and a man steps out, his muscular body sheathed in a black wet suit. A mask covers his face so that only his eyes and mouth are visible. His build is powerful but every movement is graceful as he approaches.

My hand tightens around the gun.

"Code," he growls.

I rub my head with my free hand as I try to remember the numerical sequence that I've repeated to myself several times since my stepfather gave it to me. With this strange guy staring me down, it takes a moment longer to remember than it probably should. "Four, nine, seven, zero, six, two."

I can barely see the man's eyes in the moonless night, but I can *feel* them as they slide from my face to my toes and back again.

"Injured," he half-whispers, as though he's purposely trying to make it sound as though he's swallowed gravel.

"What . . . ?"

He strides closer. I back away but I don't make it more than three steps before he's caught my wrist. Thoughts of my gun evaporate as his palm warms my cool skin, his touch unyielding yet gentle as he flicks a flashlight on and points it at my hairline.

"Stitches," is all he says.

"Okay . . . well, those weren't readily available," I reply.

This earns me a grunt, as though it's *my* problem that I haven't stitched up my own head wound.

I give my arm a swift tug but he holds on. My attempt to twist free of his grip is futile too—he only holds my wrist tighter before he shines the light in my left eye, then my right, then back again.

"Unconscious?" he asks.

When I narrow my eyes and crinkle my nose in an unvoiced question, he taps me on the head with his flashlight.

"Ouch—"

"Unconscious?" he says again, his tone commanding even though it's barely more than a whisper.

"You mean, did I pass out? No."

"Nauseous?"

"A little."

"Concussed," he declares, his voice a gritty stamp of two syllables. He drops my wrist as though I'm contagious and then turns away, striding toward the intersection where I sped through a stop sign to T-bone Jamie Merrick's car.

I wobble after the man as he keeps the light pointed to the asphalt. He doesn't tell me what he seems to be looking for, but I assume it's pieces of the vehicles left behind from the impact.

"I've never had a concussion before. Could I fall into a coma?" I ask as I catch up to him, following close on his heels.

"No."

"Do you think I have a brain bleed?"

"No."

"But how do you know for sure? Are you a doctor?"

"*No.*"

"Oh good, because your bedside manner sucks."

The man scoffs but doesn't turn around. When he lurches to an abrupt stop, I nearly face-plant into his back. I'm so close that I can smell the lingering scent of the sea on his wet suit. It doesn't take much effort to imagine the broad span of muscle hiding beneath the thin layer of synthetic rubber that separates us. Should I be wondering if he also surfs, or what he might look like peeling off the saturated fabric at the beach? Probably not. But I am.

I pull my imagination away from picturing his irritatingly athletic body and focus instead on the slow sweep of his flashlight as it pans across the road from one ditch to the other and back again.

He points the light toward his feet and goes still, as though he's been snared by a thought that won't let him go.

And the longer he stands there, the easier it is to remember that he's kind of a dick.

My mind might be a little disjointed and slow right now, but all too soon I come back around to the facts—this guy is a single-word asshole who's dropped some unqualified, grunted diagnosis on me as though it's totally nothing to worry about.

Concussed, he'd said.

"What if—"

"Drunk?" he snarls as he whirls on me.

I blink at him. Rage kindles in my chest. "Excuse me?"

"*Drunk?*"

He leans forward. Our faces are inches from each other. My simmering fury becomes fucking pyroclastic when he sucks in a deep breath through his nose.

I shove him with both hands. *Christ*, it's like trying to topple a marble statue. He leans back from my personal bubble but only because he wants to, not because I made him.

"No, I'm not drunk, you one-word asshole. I haven't had any alcohol at all."

He huffs.

"Well? Did you smell any when you were all up in my face sniffing my breath like a fucking psycho?"

That earns me a snort.

"Exactly. So thank you for your totally unnecessary judgments, Budget Batman," I say as I flick a dismissive hand toward his neoprene unitard, "but I would never drink and drive. I'm not much of a drinker, actually."

He rumbles what might just be a relieved growl. "Right."

"And I'll have you know that I'm an adorable drunk. Not an accident-inducing drunk."

"Accident," he grunts, and though it's only one word, the sarcasm in his tone is undeniable. He gestures around us with the flashlight. "No skid marks."

I snicker. "Wh . . . what marks . . . ?"

A frustrated sigh spills from his lips. "Skid. Marks," he snarls, and I clear my throat in a failed attempt to contain my amusement. "There should be skid marks from where you tried to stop."

This time I can't hold it in—I laugh out loud. And even though Budget Batman is wearing a mask, I can feel his flat glare on my skin.

"I know you've probably been living under a rock with all your other salamander kin, but it's from a movie. *Hot Fuzz*. Skid marks. You know, the one with Simon Pegg and Nick Frost . . . ? Timothy Dalton ends up impaled on the church spire in the miniature village? So funny."

There's a long beat of silence.

"*Come on.* The longest sentence you string together in your whisper-growl Budget Batman impression is about skid marks and you expect me not to laugh?"

"He's not big on talking," another voice calls out in the night.

There's a flash of movement to my right. Before I can even turn, Batman's arm wraps around my waist, pulling me behind him. My bag drops to the ground and my face smacks into the neoprene-coated brick wall that is Batman's back.

"*Motherfucker—*"

"Put the gun down, bro. It's just me," the new voice says, interrupting the barrage of expletives I was about to unleash. New guy chuckles and Batman loosens his grip on me. Now that my head has stopped spinning, I make sense of what just happened. As though on instinct, he put himself between me and danger, keeping me out of sight.

I peer around Batman's shoulder to see another masked man standing a few feet away. His hands are raised in surrender and his stance is nonchalant despite the gun my protector points at his chest.

My gun.

"You fucker, that's *mine*. Give it back."

Budget Batman scoffs when I tap his bicep as the gun lowers to his side.

"No," he says, then walks away.

He leaves me in the dark as he approaches the new guy, my bag discarded at my feet, the contents of my unzipped makeup pouch strewn across the asphalt. The two men speak in hushed tones and I catch the occasional sentence as I gather my belongings in the dim light. *Tow her vehicle . . . Body's in the lake . . . Was probably on her phone. Just a dumb accident . . .*

A dumb accident.

My cheeks heat beneath the cake of white makeup. The urge to snap back with the truth is so strong it chokes up my throat, but I swallow it down and drop to the ground to gather the contents of my spilled bag, shoving everything inside as I shoot glares toward the two men that they don't see.

And would it really matter if I set them straight? These guys are professional *cleaners*. They fix messes for people much more creepy and dangerous than me. I'm sure they've seen it all, from legit accidents to torture to everything in between. What harm would it do if they knew the truth?

But it's a confession I can't risk getting back to my family. They might not be the squeakiest and cleanest of people, but I have a role to play, and while *chaos agent* might fit the bill, *murderer* definitely does not.

So I plaster on a sunshine smile, hoist my bag up my shoulder, and stride over to them.

"I'd hate to interrupt this little budget superhero whisper party, but we should probably get this show on the road, don't you think? It's four hours and twenty-two minutes to sunrise," I say with a flick of my focus to my watch. When I look up, the new guy's head tilts as though he's surprised by my quick calculation. Probably justified, given the dubious first impression. When I shift my gaze to Batman, his eyes are a narrow slash behind his mask. But I square my shoulders and raise my chin beneath, armoring myself against his judgment. "Well? The sooner we fix this, the sooner we never see each other again."

"Works for me, Blunder Barbie," my wet-suited Dark Knight snaps. I catch the cadence of an accent despite his attempt to hide it, though I can't place its origin.

"Don't drown, Budget Batman. What would Rhode Island do without your exemplary customer service skills and your empathetic medical diagnoses?"

The new guy snorts as I cross my arms and engage in a staring contest with Batman that feels about six years long. He finally relents and shoves my holstered gun at his sidekick with strict instructions to not give it to me. Then he turns on his heel with a huff and stalks toward his car to retrieve his scuba gear.

The new guy and I watch in silence as our disgruntled companion checks his tanks, hauls the gear to the shore, exchanges boots for flippers, and descends into the black water.

"I'm Conor," my new companion says, not taking his eyes from the lake as he extends a hand in my direction.

"Badass Barbie," I reply, accepting the handshake. "Also known as Harley Quinn, here for one night only."

"I figured. Cool makeup."

"Thanks. Not sure your friend would agree. Is he always such a dick?"

"Most of the time. Yes."

"Great."

"Usually he's more of a piss-taking, button-pushing kind of dick. Tonight he's just more of a dick-dick."

"Multifaceted in his ability to be a dick. Good to know."

Conor snickers and passes me the gun, but he holds it until I meet his eyes. "Don't do anything stupid."

"Cross my heart."

"And if anyone gives you trouble, shoot them," Conor says. I nod and he relinquishes his hold on the weapon. I pull it from his grasp with a slow and careful hand. With a final, assessing look, he turns to stride away down the deserted road.

"What about if it's your friend who gives me trouble?" I call after him.

"Definitely shoot him. Just aim for the kneecaps. The rest of him might still be useful."

I smile and slip the gun into my bag before I turn my attention to the lake. I can see the soft glow from a waterproof flashlight beneath the rippling surface. It's not long before the sound of an engine approaches and a tow truck pulls up to my Escalade. Conor works efficiently to get it hooked up, and as soon as he finishes, he heads to the shore to wait for his companion.

It's only a few moments after that when a body rises to the surface, followed by my disgruntled Dark Knight.

My heart rate spikes as he spits out his regulator and folds an arm around the corpse to tow it to shore. I find myself fiddling with the strap of my bag as I watch his progress. In this brief meeting, the scrutiny in his eyes has been like a brand on my skin. Even now, though I can't track his gaze from this distance in the night, I can still feel it carving me up, a slice from an unseen blade.

Why should I care how he looks at me? What he thinks? He knows nothing about me or what this is or why it had to be done. He doesn't know about the promise I have to keep.

"He's a fucking stranger," I tell myself out loud when my thoughts just aren't enough. "After tonight, you'll never see him again."

I take a few steps forward to watch as Conor helps to heave the body ashore while Batman climbs out of the water to ditch his gear on the rocks. When he's done, they hoist Merrick's corpse into their arms, Conor grabbing hold of the limp legs while Batman takes the arms. With a few grunts and minor stumbles, they make it to the road, dropping the body at my feet.

For a long moment, there's only the sound of their panting breaths.

The two men watch me. I watch them back. A thick curtain of silence descends. It's as though they're waiting for me to break out in a song and dance routine, but I've forgotten all the lyrics. I can't remember this choreography or what I'm supposed to do.

Conor's head tilts, and the epiphany strikes me in the face.

I press a hand over my heart and gesture toward the body sprawled across the road.

"Oh . . . my God . . . that's so horrible . . . what have I done . . ."

More silence. An owl hoots from the shadows of the forest.

"Such a tragedy . . ." I continue as I dab at my dry eyelashes. "So sad . . . I will never forgive myself."

"Feckin' Christ Jesus," Batman whisper-growls. "Typical."

"Excuse me?"

"*Typical*," he says again, striding forward to stare down at me. "You're somebody's perfect little princess who gives literally no shits about some innocent guy who got caught in your path of destruction."

The protest I start making about Merrick's "innocence" is lost as Conor slides a hand across Batman's chest in an attempt to diffuse him. "Hey man, come on—"

"Always depending on someone to come and clean up your feckin' messes for you," Batman continues, growling his way through Conor's wary protests, his accent surfacing once again. "Sailing through life with barely a mark, no matter who gets in your way."

I surge forward and eliminate the distance between us, stopping so close that I can smell the sweet mint of his breath above the scent of the lake water. My expression is nothing short of lethal as I glare into his masked face. "Would this be a good time to remind you that I am your client? Or later? This is your *job*, remember?"

"No, it's not."

"But I thought you were a fucking cleaner."

"You thought wrong, Blunder Barbie."

"Then why are you here?"

"I have no feckin' choice."

Batman gives me his back as he bends to pick up Jamie's slack arm, hoisting the corpse onto his shoulder with a grunt. When he draws close to me with a glare, I don't flinch, though my heart etches my bones with every hammered beat.

"You don't know me," I hiss.

His glare sears my skin. "And I don't want to," he says.

I watch him walk to the tow truck with the body slung across his shoulder. My eyes never stray from his form as it slips into shadow, not even when Conor stops at my side.

"I'm sorry about him," Conor says, his voice low and quiet as he clutches the back of his neck with a gloved hand. "He's just . . . yeah. It's not been a good night for him. I know it's probably hard to believe, but it's nothing personal. And he's just been doing this too long, I guess."

I nod and peel my gaze away from the tow truck where Batman is busy wrapping the body in plastic and then a blanket. Though I hear his labored grunt as he hoists Merrick into the back of the vehicle, I keep my attention on the forest. The trees beckon me to find a quiet place where I can sit with my thoughts. Maybe I could find some peace, if the world fell silent, just for a little while—

"We'll come back with the boom truck tomorrow night and get the car out of the lake. I'll clean up anything left on the road tonight," Conor says, interrupting my fleeting fantasy. I can feel his eyes on the side of my face, but I don't look his way. "Batman there . . . he can be rough around the edges, but he's as solid as they come. We'll get it done. We'll make sure nothing links you to this place. No records. No evidence. Soon it will be like the whole accident never even happened."

"Right," I whisper, but my smile is fleeting. If it was supposed to reassure him that I'm totally fine, it failed. When I glance in Conor's direction, I can see the concern flicker in his eyes, even though the rest of his features are obscured by his mask. I try a little harder with that smile of mine. "What accident, right?"

"That's right," he says with a laugh. He probably thinks it's just a half-hearted, lame joke when he walks away to help the disgruntled Dark Knight fetch his scuba gear from the rocks and place it in the car. And though a faint trace of a smile lingers on my face, waiting for when they both pass by, I feel more alone than ever beneath it.

Budget Batman tosses the wet suit into the open trunk of his vintage Dodge Charger. He's gotten changed into a pair of black jeans that hug his muscular thighs, a long-sleeved black shirt, and a fresh ski mask. He pulls on a fresh set of leather gloves and strides toward me as I resist the urge to clutch the gun that hides in the confines of my bag.

"Time to go," he grits out as he draws close to where I plant my feet in the center of the road.

I cross my arms. "How about, 'Time to go, *please*.' Or, 'Shall we depart? My Batmobile awaits, fair maiden.'"

There's a steady rumble on the cool breeze. For a moment I think it's a distant vehicle approaching. Maybe one with a shitty muffler.

But no.

It's him. *Growling.*

I back away but he plows into me. In a nausea-inducing flash of movement, he tosses me over his shoulder and spins, and then my guts are bouncing against his bone and muscle as he stalks toward the vehicles. I catch my belongings before they fall, and the urge to shoot him in the ass is nearly as irresistible as the one to vomit down his back.

"*Let me the fuck down.*" My efforts to whack him are just as futile as everything else I try, from squirming to swearing to attempting to trip him with my giant bag.

"Sure thing, you feckin' catastrophe."

In one swift motion, I'm plopped down hard on my ass with my legs dangling out of the trunk of his car.

"Absolutely not," I snarl. I try to shimmy out of the trunk but it feels like my brain has been sucked out of my head and replaced with soup. Everything sloshes. My thoughts. The world. The contents of my stomach. It takes too long to remember how to make my limbs work. By the time I do, Batman has me caged, his gloved hands braced against the base of the trunk on either side of my legs. The edges of his thumbs touch my thighs. He takes up all the space around me, and even though I close my eyes, his presence is everywhere. I smell him, mint and lake water. I feel the warmth of his breath on my face. When I meet his gaze his marine-blue eyes are the first thing I lock on to, their intensity amplified by the black ski mask that frames them.

A lump lodges in my throat. The tremor starts in my arms and creeps toward my hands. "Please, you don't understand," I say.

"In."

"No."

"Now."

"*Please*," I whisper. "Not in here. I'll go with the tow truck."

"No, you won't. Not with the mountain of evidence my colleague will be taking out of here. And I'm not going to risk you being seen sitting up front," Batman grits out.

"That sounds extreme and more like you just don't want to sit next to me."

Batman shrugs and leans an inch closer. There's barely a thread of space between us. His eyes drop to my lips, which are smeared with thick makeup, painted crimson and black. "I guess you'll never know," he says, his voice a low rumble. "But there is no other option."

My nose stings but I refuse the sudden temptation of frustrated tears. I'm not going to cry, not in front of this asshole. If he feels my knees shaking, he doesn't acknowledge it. He just leans closer, his eyes hooked to mine. I know he won't back down. And he can see it too, the moment the realization truly settles in my veins.

My shoulders drop. "I'm begging you," I whisper.

"You're not doing a very good job of it, I'm afraid."

"You really are a dick."

"And you want to get out of here as much as I do. This is your only ride out, so you'd better keep quiet," he says, and then his hand is on my head, pushing me down with gentle pressure as the other guides the lid down behind me, forcing me into darkness until I squeeze my eyes shut. "When we get to Providence, I'll let you out and you can cause havoc on your own time. Until then, try to behave yourself."

The trunk clicks closed. My eyes open to the total darkness. My heartbeat thunders in my ears. The tears I hid from him come full force now as I curl my body into a tight ball and hug my bag to my chest, Batman's discarded wet suit damp against the top of my head. I pull the arm of it down to rest across my forehead where a film of congealed blood and white makeup and sweat begs to be scraped from my skin.

You're okay. You're okay, you're okay, you're okay. You know what to do.

I repeat my mantra until my panicking breaths slow just enough to pick up the sound of the muffled words exchanged between Batman and Conor. It's a clipped and pragmatic conversation. My hope that Conor will talk some sense into his friend is a fleeting one, because a moment later the driver's door creaks open and slams shut. The engine starts with a growl, and then we're rolling away.

I need a new plan.

I harness my fury to stay focused as we maneuver around a couple of gentle turns and settle into a steady speed. When I'm sure Batman must feel confident that I'll *behave myself*, I bang my fist on the roof of the trunk in a riot of flesh against metal.

"Not sure if you've heard this before, but *you're a total asshole*," I yell, tears still leaking from my eyes. My banging becomes a percussion to punctuate my chant. "*Ass-hole, ass-hole, ass-hole.*"

"Pipe down," he snarls before applying more pressure on the accelerator.

"Come make me, I fucking dare you." I bang again, and he finally turns the music up to drown me out. The moment it's on, I soften my blows and protests, and then I let them fade away.

When I'm satisfied he thinks he's won this round, I turn on my phone's flashlight and rummage in my bag.

My maniacal cackle is drowned out by the engine and music as I pull out the screw-in whammy bar for my Jackson guitar with my sweaty, shaking hand. I may have been born a Montague, which comes with its own set of batshit-crazy history, but I'm a Covaci too, and my stepdad taught me all kinds of useful tricks, like how to break free of cable ties. How to tie a hangman's knot. How to load a gun.

And how to escape the trunk of a vehicle.

The vintage latch is a little tricky, but on the plus side there's probably no warning light on the mechanical dashboard to tip my crusty chauffeur off when I manage to pop it free on the third try. I hold on to the mechanism to keep the trunk's lid open just enough that I can watch the road fall away behind us. We're still in the middle of nowhere—no traffic, no pedestrians, hardly any houses. It's just the forest. Me and the dark and the red taillights that bleed into the black night.

The car slows. The driveshaft disengages as Batman shifts gears and brakes. The taillights brighten. One blinks, signaling a right-hand turn.

I pop the lid just enough to slip free of the trunk before we've rolled to a stop. It's not a graceful dismount. I smash a knee on the asphalt and tear a hole in my sweats. The exhaust fumes spill across my face when I kneel behind the bumper. I gently hold the lid down so that he won't notice it in the rearview. The old hinges are stiff enough that it doesn't spring open when I lessen the pressure. I can't close it completely, but if Batman doesn't spot me as he turns, I might have enough time to disappear.

The lights dim as he takes his foot off the brake. With a growl and a puff of gray smoke, the engine revs. The car coasts around the turn and rolls away.

I linger for just a breath of time, crouched on the empty road. And then I rise, wipe the cooling tears off my face, and walk away in the opposite direction.

You don't know me, I think when I cast a final glance to the car before it disappears around a bend.

And he's right.

He doesn't want to.

BULL'S-EYE

Lachlan

. . . ONE YEAR LATER

"We haven't had a happy hour like this in years," Leander says as he tosses a dart. An instant later, a garbled cry bounces off the concrete walls as the metal point lands in Robbie Usher's cheek. A few more darts quiver in his face as he shakes with fear and pain. His sobs escape from the gag that stretches back the corners of his mouth to reveal his swollen, bloodied gums. His top and bottom teeth are gone all the way to his molars. Bleeding gums aside, the dart hanging from his lower lip looks especially painful. Naturally, that one is Leander's favorite.

So far.

Can't say this is the life I imagined for myself, pulling teeth with pliers and playing darts with some guy's face in my boss's basement on a Friday night. Who does, I guess? Come to think of it, I probably didn't spend much of my childhood imagining what I wanted to be when I grew up. I was too busy figuring out how to survive. I don't remember dreams of being a firefighter or a police officer or a teacher or anything at all. The most vivid daydreams I can recall were how to get away with murder. I even *wished* for it on my thirteenth birthday, when my brothers cobbled together enough money to buy ingredients to make me a cake.

And we all know what they say about wishes.

Leander offers me a fresh dart on his upturned palm. I stare at it. Swallow my distaste. Catch an irritated sigh in my chest. Try to keep my apathetic mask from slipping. But Leander Mayes has known me since I was seventeen, when he appeared like an angel in my darkest hour.

Little did I know that angel would turn out to be the devil in disguise.

"Come on now, Lachlan. You know how much I love darts."

"Right . . ." I say, taking my time to raise my glass to my lips and down a long sip of water. *Goddammit.* I wish it was something stronger, but I learned the hard way to not indulge in Leander's extensive supply of thirty-year-aged whiskey on a Friday night when he's in the mood for a "happy hour." Last time that happened, I came to three days later, stuffing my face with watermelon as I sat on a curb in Carlsbad, New Mexico, with literally no recollection of how I got there. *New Mexico.* Motherfucker.

Leander grins like he's crawled into my feckin' brain as I pick up the dart and toss it in Robbie's general direction without taking my eyes from my boss. Judging by the clatter of metal against concrete, I've missed and hit the wall.

Leander sighs and drags a hand through his silver hair. His eyes twinkle with amusement even though he tries to look disappointed.

"You know," he says as he lays another dart on his open palm, "I've always kept my promise to you. I've never given you an innocent person to kill. And you know as well as I do that Robbie is no saint."

He's right. I do know. I've heard Robbie Usher's name pop up over the years. My brother Rowan even brought him up once as someone he wanted to kill before the reckless little shit started his annual murder competition with Sloane and lost interest in drug dealer assholes like Robbie.

"Yeah, I just prefer to get these things done and over with. *Cleanly.* Not like . . . this," I say, waving a hand in Robbie's direction. When I glance his way, he tries to beg for freedom. Tears and snot collect blood in their rivulets as they streak down his pale skin. "My job is a contract killer. Not a cleaner. Not a torturer."

"Your *job* is whatever I need it to be."

When I meet Leander's gaze once more, the amusement in his mossy eyes has burned away. Only a warning remains.

"As I recall, the last time you forgot your job and your manners, it ran you into a little bit of trouble. I definitely don't recall instructing you to piss off one of our most valuable customers, did I?"

Though I often think I should be impervious to emotions like shame or embarrassment, sometimes they sneak up on me and burn in my cheeks. Just like now, when I remember the aftermath of the cleanup job he sent me to do last year on Halloween night. That particular contract shriveled up after that night, along with my hopes of getting out from under Leander's thumb.

And the part that annoys me the most? I'm not even sure *why* I acted like such a prick to that woman whose mess I was sent to fix.

Maybe I was already annoyed that I had to leave Fionn behind at that goddamn party when he was a blubbering mess to do cleanup when that isn't my job. Maybe it was the way she acted like the death and chaos she'd just caused were no big deal. Maybe it was even the fact that she was clearly injured when I'd been told she was fine. She was definitely *not* fine. And that inexplicably made me almost as irate as being called out to scuba dive in dark and frigid waters on Halloween night. I'm not really sure what it was that tipped me over the edge. I just know that Blunder Barbie slipped right under my skin. And I fucking let her. Worse still, she slipped away and I don't even know *how*.

I shake my head.

We stare at each other for a long moment before Leander's expression softens. He lays a hand on my shoulder, the other still holding the dart aloft like a precious offering.

"Robbie's the one behind that latest batch of rainbow fentanyl that the cops discovered in a raid last week. *Rainbow fucking fentanyl.* He made his drugs look like candy," Leander whispers, a dark melody that rings in my ears. Leander's brows raise as Robbie squeals his protests from across the room. "He's purposely targeting *kids*, Lachlan. And this time, he just happened to reach kids whose parents can hire the kind of people who will actually deliver justice where it's needed the most. People like you."

I turn my attention to Robbie as he struggles against the cable ties that trap his wrists and ankles to a metal chair. His wide eyes are not innocent. His muffled protests are selfish pleas, not words of remorse. Though I didn't bother looking up the details on Robbie's latest escapades before we grabbed him, I know Leander isn't lying. He never does.

My eyes don't stray from Robbie as I pluck the dart from Leander's palm. There's no need to turn and look at my boss to gauge his reaction. I can feel it. His smile is a breath against my skin before he steps back.

I take my shot. Robbie cries out as the dart hits his forehead and ricochets off bone to land in his lap.

"Oof, good try. Almost a bull's-eye. But I'm winning," Leander declares as he lines up to take his next shot. He's about to let the dart fly when a security alert dings through the speakers. We turn in unison to the screen hanging behind the bar. A rugby game is on mute and the security feed in the upper right-hand corner shows the front gate of Leander's estate. There's an old Honda Civic waiting to be let in.

A second later, a call comes through to Leander's mobile. "Let him in," he says in lieu of a greeting. He hangs up without a goodbye and I watch the screen as the gates open. The car rolls forward on the driveway, which snakes through pines.

I exchange my glass for my gun and stride toward the fortified basement door as Leander lets another dart fly. "Be right back," I grumble. Robbie's shrill cry snaps at my heels as the heavy steel slams shut behind me.

The silence in the rest of the house is a balm, soothing and sweet after suffering. The October sun is already so low behind the woods surrounding the house that all the expensive furniture and curated decorations are coated in shadow. Leander's wife and teenage kids are gone for the weekend. Even the security guards are keeping their distance. Sometimes, the boss wants to pretend he's just a simple guy with an uncomplicated life. The kind of guy who has a few beers on a Friday night. Has fun with his tools. Orders some takeout. Maybe plays a round or two of darts.

But in his typical high-functioning psychopath style, Leander puts a bloody spin on pretty much everything he does.

I open the front door and keep my gun hidden behind the thick mahogany, the muzzle pointed toward the kid. At Leander's house, one can never be too careful.

"One pepperoni and one meat lover's?" he asks as he checks the receipt.

My stomach flips uncomfortably. Pizza is never a good sign. Leander is always better behaved when it's Thai—he doesn't like to waste the good food. "Sounds about right."

When I've tipped the kid and locked the door behind me, I holster my gun and take the boxes back down to the basement, casting a longing glance at the wall clock as I go. Nearly five-thirty. Thank fuck I have an excuse to get the hell out of here tonight.

Robbie has three more darts stuck in his skin when I enter the room.

"Fuck yeah. I'm starving. This is a sport, you know," Leander says as he tosses a dart in a high arc, probably in the hopes of getting it stuck in the top of Robbie's head like a little flag. It lands in his thigh instead, the metal point lodged deep, the sound of our captive's distress a grating accompaniment to the music that plays through the speakers mounted on the walls.

A headache surges behind my eyes. "Mmhmm."

"Hard work."

"Yeah, you're really breaking a feckin' sweat there."

Leander grins and follows me to the counter of his copper bar where I set the boxes down next to the blood-spattered pliers and discarded incisors. "Hungry?"

"Shockingly, not at all."

"Just one slice?"

I shake my head. "Saving myself for tonight."

"Ah yes. Is Rowan all set for the grand opening of his new Butcher & Blackbird place?" Leander opens the box of pepperoni and pulls a slice free. My molars clamp together like they do every time he mentions my brothers by name. Leander's never been anything but kind to them on the rare occasions when he's come face-to-face with my boys. But kindness is an insidious mask. A lure in the dark. I've seen the grotesque creature that lies behind the pretty light.

"As ready as he'll ever be."

"Wish him luck for me, yeah?" His grin is luminous as he takes another bite of pizza and washes it down with a long sip of beer. "*Two* restaurants. Who'd have thought you'd all be where you are now. Rowan a successful chef. Fionn a fucking *doctor*. And you with your own studio. Bet you never could have imagined it that first day I found you boys."

"Yeah," I say, my voice thin as the haze of memory descends to battle with the present.

"I still remember it like it was yesterday—Rowan some gawky teenager with blood running down his chin. Looked like something from a zombie film. At first I thought he'd bitten a chunk out of Fionn until I realized Fionn was stitching up Rowan's lip with a fucking sewing needle."

I nod, or at least I think I do. Leander keeps talking, but I don't really hear him.

The memory is untarnished. It's like I've stepped into that moment. Every image is so sharp. So clear. I can recall every detail, from the minute to the monumental. I still feel the phantom throbbing beat in my fingertip that had been sliced off. I can see the precise shade of crimson that poured from a deep slice through Rowan's upper lip. I picture Fionn's face as he pulled the thread through the torn flesh, the concentration in his eyes. I remember the way the moonlight poured through the window and reflected off the broken shards of glass and the last of my mother's porcelain plates scattered on the floor.

And most vividly, I recall my father's lifeless body lying at my feet, my belt wrapped around his neck, one end still curled around my sticky, shaking fist.

Rowan had turned to me, the thread pulled taut between his split lip and the needle clutched in Fionn's fingers. His eyes were soft, so soft that I realized that maybe it was the first time I'd ever seen him relaxed. "You can let go, Lachlan," he'd said as his gaze flicked down to my hand.

It was only a moment later when Leander strode in and changed *everything*, even the things that had already been irrevocably changed. That belt was still wrapped around my fist. And when Leander looked down at me, he grinned.

" . . . and then Rowan said, 'I swear it was almost an accident,' and I thought, yeah, these kids are all right," Leander says with a low chuckle. I blink away the memory, realizing I missed part of what he was saying . . .

. . . and all of what he was *doing*.

"What in the feckin' hell are you making?"

Leander takes a slice of meat lover's pizza and stuffs it into the blender where a first slice is already folded, grease and condensation smeared across the glass. "Smoothies."

I look from the pizza box to the blender and back again. "What?"

"*Smoothies.* You know, drinkable food."

"A . . . pizza smoothie . . . ?"

Leander simply grins as he pours half a can of beer into the blender.

"*Why?*"

"Robbie doesn't really have teeth anymore. How else is he going to have a last meal?" Leander shifts his attention to Robbie, who cries in his chair. "Didn't anyone tell you that candy will rot your teeth out, dickhead? Speaking of which . . ."

Leander slides the teeth off the counter and onto his waiting palm before he plops them into the blender and turns it on. The beer froths. The melted cheese sticks to the glass. It takes a few stops and starts, but eventually he gets the mixture whipped into a thick, bubbly brown paste.

"Feckin' Christ Jesus. That is truly horrific."

Leander shrugs. "Still just pizza and beer, but with extra calcium."

"Didn't he have a gold cap on one of them?"

Leander sloshes the mixture around and peers into the jug, but there's not much to see in the brown sludge. "Yeah, he did. So, it's got *fancy* calcium. Anyway, I'm sure it tastes pretty much the same."

"Doubtful. You should try it. Test your theory and let me know."

"*Fuck* no," he says on the heels of a barked laugh as he pours the mixture into a pint glass. "I have a thing about teeth."

I groan and Leander cackles again, clearly delighted with himself. He runs a hand through his silver hair and then rummages in drawers behind the bar until he pulls out the funnel with a sound of triumph. "Christ Jesus, man. I'm leaving."

I turn on my heel but don't make it even a step away before his words stop me dead.

"You know, kid, I could *make* you stay."

I stare at the door for a long, unblinking moment before I pivot to face Leander. He's still smiling as he walks past me with the funnel in one hand and the full glass in the other. But there's always a threat beneath his bleached smile and the creases that fan from the corners of his eyes. There's a predatory edge to Leander that cuts through that mask like a razor.

Leander jerks his head toward Robbie in a bid for me to follow, and I do. "Good thing I'm all benevolent and shit. I wouldn't want you to miss your little brother's special night. And I *definitely* wouldn't want him spitting in my meal the next time I pop in for a visit. Word is that while he might have scaled back on his Boston Butcher theatrics around town, he's still a bit unhinged. I understand he was recently up to no good in Texas with that girlfriend of his. That's where they went, right? Texas? And . . . oh, where was it before that . . . ? I remember now. California. Calabasas, specifically. And West Virginia—"

"What do you want from me?" I snap.

Leander grins. "Just hold him steady."

With a flash of a lightless glare, I step behind Robbie and press my palms to either side of his head. He trembles in my grip.

"Open wide, fucker." Leander pushes the end of the funnel past Robbie's gag. Robbie tries to thrash free of my grip, but there's no escape. "Last meal down the pipe. Did you know the Nelsons' kid had to be tube-fed after he OD'd on your fentanyl candy? This is kinda the same thing," he says as he pours the first thick dollops of pizza smoothie into the funnel.

"Not really the same at all," I grumble over the sound of Robbie's gurgling cough.

"Close enough." Leander pours more mixture in, but it only ends up dribbling from the corners of Robbie's mouth. A frustrated sigh leaves my psychotic boss's lips. "He's not swallowing it."

"Can't imagine why."

"It's just pizza and beer, Robbie."

"And teeth."

"Just imagine it's protein powder. Come on, man. Down the hatch," Leander says as he tries again. Robbie whimpers and whines, but still doesn't swallow. A petulant sigh leaves my boss's lips as his shoulders fall. "Pinch his nose."

"Hard pass."

"That wasn't a question, kid."

"Leander—"

"*Do it*, Lachlan, and then I'll let you head off to your party."

Our eyes lock for a moment that feels endless.

I could snap Leander's neck. With one punch to his throat, I could crush his trachea. I could shove the heel of my palm into the base of his nose with a satisfying crunch. Or I could take the easy way out and shoot him. Leave him to bleed across the floor like so many others before him who have found themselves in his basement on a Friday night.

But revenge for my betrayal would be swift and merciless. His equally batshit brothers would hunt me to the ends of the earth, just like I would do for mine. And their vengeance wouldn't start or end with me.

My fingers curl around Robbie's nose and pinch it tight.

"The Nelsons wanted him to suffer like they have suffered. This is not torture, Lachlan. It's not murder. This is *justice*," Leander says, his eyes not straying from mine as he fills the funnel.

This time, Robbie has no choice but to swallow. Not all of the liquid makes it down his throat, of course. But Leander doesn't stop, not until the pint glass is empty. And even then, he keeps his unwavering stare on me.

When he's satisfied, Leander gives a single nod.

I release Robbie from my grip, whip my gun from its holster, and shoot Robbie in the head.

The pressure and pain behind my eyes subsides now that Robbie's gurgles and sobs and pleas no longer drone on around us. It's just the music, and now the steady *drip, drip, drip* of blood that falls to the floor.

I slide my gun back into its holster. There can be no threat when I let my next words loose between us. "I want to retire."

A slow, predatory grin creeps across Leander's face. "You don't say," he says, turning his back to me. "I'm totally shocked."

"Leander, I'm grateful for everything you've done for me and the boys. Covering our asses back in Sligo. Bringing us here, setting us up. You know how much I appreciate it. I've put in the years to pay it back, you know I have. But this . . ." I say, trailing off as I cast a glance down to the slumped body next to me. "I don't think I can do this anymore."

Leander lets out a deep sigh as he sets the glass and funnel next to the sink and turns to face me. "I'm going to be straight with you, kid. I always am."

I nod when he raises a single brow.

"When you pissed off Damian Covaci last year, that didn't just kill our contract with him. It had ripple effects on other contracts as well when gossip spread in certain circles. And you know what, kid? That pissed *me* off."

Blush crawls into my cheeks. "So I acted like a feckin' eejit *one time*. This seems extreme."

"You put a Covaci in a fucking trunk, Lachlan."

Shit. I really did.

Leander leans against the counter and folds his arms across his chest. He might be closing in on sixty, but he's still built like a brute, and his thick biceps strain against the confines of his black sweater. "We talked about this. Like it or not, we're in the customer service business. You should know what that means, you do it every single day at your studio. If some client comes into Kane Atelier to buy leather saddlebags for their motorcycle or some shit and they piss you off, are you gonna lock them in the fucking closet? Chrissakes, I hope not. Because that would be terrible *customer service*."

"So, what, I've gotta keep doing this indefinitely?"

Leander shrugs. "Unless you magically find a way to fix the damage you caused, yeah. I guess so."

A suspended moment lingers between us. Leander might feign disappointment in me, but sometimes I wonder if this mistake of mine worked out to his benefit, even if the jobs tapered off like he claims. As though he can see these thoughts turning over in my mind, Leander pivots away before I can read too much into his expression.

"Go on, get out of here," he says as he cracks open a fresh beer. "Say hi to the boys for me."

I wait for him to meet my eyes, but he doesn't.

Without another word, I stride away. The steel door slams shut behind me with a reverberant thud.

I leave Leander behind.

But I know I'll never really get away.

GUILLOTINE

Lachlan

I buzz the intercom for my brother Rowan's apartment for the second time and take a step back from the panel to stare up at the brick building toward the third floor. My grip is tight around the bottle of Athrú Keshcorran whiskey as I tamp down the urge to hurtle it at the window. With a curse, I surge forward to jam my finger down on the little black button when a voice crackles over the speaker.

"If you're selling farts in a jar, I don't want them."

My eyes narrow. *Fionn*. I love our younger brother dearly, but he's a right little shit.

"You and I both know you order them on the internet in bulk. Let me up, ya gobshite," I say, pulling the neck of the bottle free of the brown paper bag as I hold it toward the camera above the door. "Unless you don't want any of this."

The door buzzes and I step inside.

When I arrive at the third-floor landing, Fionn is there with a devious grin, leaning against the threshold of the open door as he picks at a bag of trail mix. I can hear music, bits of conversation, and laughter trickling out of the apartment.

"Good to see you, ya little shit," I say as I wrap my arms around him. He's an inch taller than me, built of lean, powerful muscle that's solid beneath my arms. He claps me hard twice on the back as though proving his strength. "How long will you be gracing us with your presence in Boston?"

"Just until Monday."

"Or you could just stay permanently."

"Hard pass."

We part enough to press our foreheads together, something we've done since the very first moment I held him in my arms in the hospital room back in Sligo the day he was born. When he takes a step back, Fionn scrutinizes the details of my face with clinical intensity. "You look miserable."

"And you look like a dickhead with your feckin' bag of birdseed."

"Omega fatty acids decrease inflammation and LDL choles-terol," he says as I pass by to enter Rowan's apartment, a space that takes up the entirety of the third floor in the narrow building.

"I'm sure they do. They also increase your chance of looking like a dickhead, Dr. Kane."

Fionn chatters on about fatty acids and brain inflammation as he trails behind me down the hallway that opens to the living space of exposed brick and industrial windows. Our friend Anna casts me a wave from the kitchen, where she's making a pair of martinis. There's a small but fierce-looking woman sitting on the couch with a broken leg propped on the coffee table, her black cast adorned with a single gold star sticker. I realize she's the one

Rowan has been texting me about, the injured motorcycle circus performer who's somehow found herself staying at Fionn's place in Nebraska and who he says Sloane befriended after a crutch-wielding incident. Fionn introduces her as Rose but seems unwilling to provide any context for their relationship, which I file away for later so I can take the piss out of him. Judging by the snarky smirk on Rose's lips, she's thinking the same. Rowan and Sloane's demonic cat, Winston, sits next to her raised foot, his tail flopping from one side to the other as though he's contemplating how quickly he could bite off one of her exposed toes. My attention lands next on Sloane, who rises from her chair to approach me with a wary smile.

And then she moves aside and my breath catches as the most beautiful woman I've ever seen steps into view. Her bright-blue eyes lock on me, her plump lips curved in a sly but warm smile, her glossy, honey-colored waves cascading across her shoulder. I think I should say something, or do something, but I can't seem to do anything but stare.

"Lachlan," Sloane says.

I swallow and replace my shock with a forced smirk as I tear my attention away from the unfamiliar woman and focus on Sloane. "Spider Lady. How are your crafting hobbies going these days? Made any new projects?"

Her eyes narrow. Even though she could pry my eyeballs out of my head, she's still so fun to antagonize.

"What about sketches? Leave any more bird drawings behind for my lovesick little brother?"

Sloane's cheeks flame crimson and my smile spreads as I hold the bottle of whiskey out for her to take, but before she can grab it, Fionn whips it from my hand as he passes between us. She doesn't so much as glance at Fionn, her attention locked on me as though she's trying to communicate a warning in her lightless glare. "Lachlan, this is my friend Lark."

I shift my focus to Lark and hold out a hand. When she takes a step closer, the details of her face blur and I curse myself for leaving my glasses in the car. I might not be able to see the finest features of her smile at this distance, but I can *feel* it, her energy a lick of warmth on my skin. My gaze drops to our hands. An electric hum zings through my flesh at her touch.

"Lark Montague. Pleased to meet you," she says. There's a devious edge in her, like a vibration that slips between our palms. "So, you're the notorious Lachlan Kane."

"Notorious?" I say, raising my eyebrows.

"Indeed. I've heard . . . things."

"Oh, you've heard *things*, have you? What kinds of . . . things?"

She giggles and slips her hand free of mine as she says, "Well, I think the word 'broody' might have been tossed around."

"Now, now," Fionn chides as he brings me a glass of whiskey on ice. "Don't mischaracterize my poor brother. I said he's a broody *asshole*."

"Ass*hat*," Rose pipes up. "You said he's a 'broody asshat whose only hobby is scowling.'"

Sloane snorts. "Accurate."

"*Hey*, I do more than just scowl." I lean closer to Lark and give her a lopsided, rakish smile. "I have *hobbies*."

She laughs when I give her a wink. "Oh yeah? Like what, crochet? I could see you being a big crochet guy. I bet you make a mean doily."

Rose cackles, her eyes dancing from one person to the next. "Nah, that's doc's forte—"

My brother chokes on a sip of whiskey. "Rose—"

"He's in a club, actually—"

"Fucksakes, *Rose*—"

"They meet every Sunday. It's called the Suture Sisters, and he's the—" Rose's next words are lost to the palm my brother clamps over her mouth, her diabolical laugh replacing whatever would have come next. The look that Fionn gives me is both horrified and pleading.

"Don't tell Rowan," he begs. "I finally got the upper hand by resurrecting his Shitflicker nickname when he came to Nebraska."

I bellow a laugh and shake my head. "My sweet, adorable, naive baby brother. *Of course* I'm going to tell Rowan. It's my job to promote the maximum amount of conflict between you two. That's the only way I can get any peace." I clap a hand to his shoulder and slip past him to take a seat on one of the leather armchairs. "Hate to break it to you, kid, but you're still in your peak Sadman Cinderwhatever era with this doily shit. Rowan is going to love this."

Fionn tosses out some nonsensical explanation, something about a flyer and a simple misunderstanding, but I don't really pay much attention. Not when Lark follows to sit across from me on the end of the couch. Sloane's psycho cat curls in her lap the moment she's settled.

I can see her much clearer at this distance, from the mole on the edge of her upper lip to the ripple in the skin near her hairline, a cut that must have been left unmended and healed with jagged edges. But even though I couldn't see her clearly, she'd be impossible to miss. All the energy in the room seems to siphon through her and concentrate before it radiates through her bright blue eyes and her glowing skin and her easy smile. It pours through her laugh and warms the notes of her voice. And even though I'm not listening to the good-natured argument between Fionn and Rose, she is. She interjects just frequently enough to bolster the person she seems to think is losing in a given moment, which is mostly Fionn. *Do you take commissions?* Or, *I bet you could make a killing on Etsy.* She focuses every ounce of her attention on the person talking while her hand trails through Winston's fur, his purr rumbling beneath the conversation. It's as though nothing and no one else in the world exists, even me. If she can feel the weight of my gaze on her face, she never lets on.

Lark Montague is *beautiful.*

And I have to stop staring like a feckin' creep.

I look down at the drink in my hands. Scars hidden beneath ink. The missing tip of my index finger. Tattoos on my knuckles. Silver rings. I tap one against the glass before I raise it to my lips. My hands would look so good on her perfect skin. Folded around her soft thighs. The image of my tattooed fingers gripped around her smooth flesh has me shifting in my seat in a failed attempt to alleviate the strain of my hard cock against my zipper. Someone like me with someone like *her*? Even imagining it feels wrong.

Yet so deliciously *right.*

When I look up again, the doily argument is still going, but Lark's eyes connect with mine, her smile conspiratorial. It's just a flash of camaraderie before she turns her attention back to Fionn and Rose, but there's something in that brief grin that sticks with me. A silent conversation. A familiarity I can't explain.

Even after the conversation takes other turns, that feeling stays with me. It's like there's a thin thread binding us together. And as Lark seizes the opportunity to slip away to the balcony when she seems to think her absence won't be noticed, that connection tugs at my chest. Though I spend a few minutes trying to snip it free, it still pulls, and it doesn't loosen even after I follow.

When I slide the balcony door open, Lark doesn't move from where she leans against the railing, as though she's been expecting me.

"Hey." It's not my most slick opening line, I know. But Lark still smiles when she glances over her shoulder at me.

"Hey. You're not coming out here to be an asshat, are you?"

I chuckle, shutting the door behind me. "No, that's only weekdays from nine to five. The rest of the time I just brood."

"That just sounds so wrong," she says through a tinkling laugh. "It's like you spend your evenings in a chicken coop sitting on a clutch of eggs. But somehow it kinda makes sense with your brother's doily vibe."

"You're right, scratch that."

She snorts. "*Scratch?* You're really wedded to the chicken puns, aren't you."

"Oh my dear Christ. This is the least smooth opening I've ever had. Let me start again." I turn around and head inside. I can hear her laughing through the glass as I open the door again and step back out onto the balcony. "What a lovely evening. Mind if I join you? I know nothing about chickens, by the way."

"That's good. The last guy was way too into poultry."

"He sounds like a feckin' asshat. Feather fetishes aren't really my thing."

"Such a shame, I do love a bit of feather play—"

I turn around again, opening and closing the door for a third time before she's even finished laughing. "Hi. My name's Lachlan and I don't know anything about chickens but I do like feathers under the right circumstances."

Lark is still giggling, her eyes shining and bright in the ambient glow of the city lights. "Well, you sound like my kind of guy. The first dude had a chicken obsession and the next guy hated feathers. I'm batting oh for two here. But you're welcome to share my little perch."

I step just close enough to catch the scent of perfume on the autumn breeze, the fragrance of sweet citrus. Lark studies the drop below us and I follow her gaze even though I've stood out here many times before. It's not the greatest view from here. Just a dark alley, a brick apartment building next door that feels too close on the other side of a black chasm. But somehow she makes even this seem like more than a narrow wedge of space suspended over darkness. Her keen interest in everything she observes makes me want to pay more attention, like maybe I've been missing something in the details.

"First time in Boston?" I ask when she lifts her focus to sweep across the buildings in the distance.

Lark smiles and shifts her golden hair over her shoulder so she can get a better look at me. "Not exactly. I grew up not too far away."

"Whereabouts?"

"Rhode Island."

I hum a note and nod, then take a sip of my drink. "Sloane says you've been friends a long time."

"Yeah," Lark says. Her smile wanes, but only for a moment. With a blink, she reins in the blip of emotion beneath a brighter smile. "We met at boarding school, actually. Took me a while to wear her down, but now we're best friends."

"That doesn't take much imagination."

Lark shrugs and twists her interlaced fingers. "Sloane's not as sketchy as she seems. She might have a crusty exterior but she's gooey in the middle."

"I meant you," I say, giving her a smirk as a chuckle escapes me. A crease flickers between Lark's brows as her gaze lands on my lingering, lopsided smile. "I could see you wearing her down. Doubt she could have withstood you for long."

Lark rolls her eyes and turns to face me, leaning her weight on the wrought iron railing. She tries to look fierce but she can't help the smile that stretches across her lips. "And why is that, exactly? You're going to say my sparkling personality? My happy-go-lucky charm?"

"Pretty much, yep," I admit, and this earns me a breath of a laugh. "It's working on me."

"Working toward what, exactly?"

I hold her gaze. She seems so endearing and sweet that I'd expect a woman like Lark to back down the longer I stare. At least give me a blush. A nervous nibble of her full lips. An unsteady breath. But she doesn't do any of those things. Her half-smile remains unchanged.

I lean closer. If anything, her eyes glitter with amusement.

"Maybe toward me kissing you. Or, more accurately, you ask-ing me to."

"How bold," she says with a *tsk*, but I can tell by the bright glimmer in her eyes that she likes it. "You think I'd want that?"

I grin and look down into my glass as I swirl the liquor across the ice. The image of my hands on her skin returns, my tattooed fingers gripped tight around her flesh. I take just a moment to indulge in that fantasy before I lift my gaze to hers and shrug. "I do own an impressive collection of feathers."

Lark laughs and I take a long sip of my drink, my eyes soldered to hers over the lip of my glass. She glances away, but her attention returns as though drawn back to me despite her best efforts to sever the energy that crackles between us. I hear the moment she gives in to it, the way she sighs. I even see it in the fog that escapes her lips and rises on the cooling breeze.

"Despite the rumors, you don't seem like too much of an ass-hat," Lark says as she unlaces her fingers to grip the railing.

"I might be a little bit. Sometimes."

"That's probably not a bad thing."

"You think?"

Lark lifts a shoulder. "Sure. If you're too nice, you might get roped into making doilies on Sundays."

"Feckin' Fionn," I say, my lip curled in a derisive grin. "What I wouldn't give to find out what Rose was about to say before he cut her off. He's probably the treasurer of their little club. It's defi-nitely the kind of thing he'd find himself sucked into. He's always been a sweet kid. Too feckin' sweet for his own good." Lark smiles but her brows flicker as though she's working out a complex prob-lem. "What is it?"

"Nothing," she replies as she shakes her head, her expression smoothing as her gaze bounds between mine. "I just . . . I dunno. Something about you seems familiar. It's probably just because I'm getting to know Rowan and I see the likeness in you."

I chuckle and nudge her elbow before I take another sip of my drink. "Now there's an asshat. Don't compare me to that reckless little shit."

"Oh stop," she chides, giving me a gentle backhanded whack on my arm. "He's great. So perfect for Sloane. Don't be an asshat."

I grin, my eyes locked to her full lips. "Whatever you say, ma'am."

She snorts. "'Ma'am.' Please don't."

"Miss?"

Her nose scrunches.

"Madam?" I offer. Lark shakes her head. "Yeah, that's not much better than 'ma'am,' I guess. Wait, I've got it. *Duchess.*"

"Ooh I like it. Somehow it works with the feather thing. Regal, yet saucy."

Saucy. I don't know why that word does something to my blood when she says it, as though she's plugged herself into my veins and hit them with a jolt of electricity. Images fly through my mind of Lark in all kinds of *regal, yet saucy* scenarios, and even the ones that inexplicably involve Marie Antoinette wigs are sexy as fuck.

"You okay there?" Lark's voice is soft but the amusement still colors every note. "You look like you've gone full brood mode."

"Yeah," I say as I clear my throat and force my hand to relax around my glass before I crush it. "I, um . . . I'm good."

"You sure . . . ? Maybe you're not so bold after all."

The heat of Lark's body creeps into mine as she steps closer. When I turn to face her fully, a faint smile plays on her lips. Even though I can't see the details of her features clearly at this near distance, the crystalline shade of her eyes is still piercing, cutting through the dimmest light.

"Seems like something I said has you a bit . . . flustered," she whispers. Her head tilts as she regards me, her gaze falling from mine to fix on my mouth. "Was it the 'regal' comment I made? Maybe you have a thing for corsets and tulle to go with the feather fetish."

Christ Jesus. Now *corsets*. "Not really—"

"Shame, that would have been super hot."

"I mean, not really *just* corsets and tulle. Also wigs."

Her rich, melodic laugh surrounds me.

Lark Montague crawls right into my brain and injects unexpected, wild fantasies into my thoughts every time she opens her feckin' mouth. She's taken control of some part of my mind I'm not sure I even knew existed, and I have no idea where she's going to send me next. I just know I'm going to follow whatever trail she lays down. It's unnerving. But it's also irresistible.

"I think you could pull off a waistcoat and breeches," Lark says with a grin as she takes a final step, closing any space between us. Her fingers curl into my shirt, one after the next, each touch a gentle rasp against my chest until she's balled the black fabric in her delicate fist. "Those tattoos on your neck would look pretty hot peeking out from beneath a cravat."

I swallow, my breath caught in my lungs as Lark rises on her toes, her eyes locked to my lips, my heart a hammer beneath her hand. Every one of her exhalations pours an electric warmth into my flesh. "Rakish, yet debonair," I finally say on a gravelly whisper.

"Goes pretty well with 'regal, yet saucy,' don't you think?" Her head tilts, and it feels like the whole world distills to this moment. "Maybe you're not the bold one after all."

Any clever reply I'm about to attempt is lost the moment Lark's lips press to mine.

My brain is a black void behind my shuttered eyelids. Lark's citrus scent floods my nostrils. She runs the tip of her tongue across the seam of my lips and I taste the echo of the orange soda she was drinking. The softest moan vibrates from her mouth to mine.

And I come undone.

My tongue plunders her mouth. Lark's fist tightens in my shirt. The glass clutched in my hand is in danger of being crushed to dust or thrown over the balcony. I'm desperate to mold her flesh in my palms, but I settle for laying one hand to the side of her neck instead. The second my palm touches her skin, she whimpers with need. My erection is painful against my zipper as she presses her body against mine.

Our teeth clash. The kiss grows brutal. Within seconds, Lark has ripped through any restraint I thought I had. She kisses me with the kind of fevered desperation that makes me feel not just wanted. Or needed. It's as though she *craves* me. She grips onto the back of my neck as though she'll fall apart if she doesn't hold on. When she sucks in a breath, she dives deeper, towing me into the dark with her. Every time I think I've gotten control of the kiss, she tears it from me. With a touch. With a bite or a suck or a moan.

Lark's tongue sweeps over mine and then she pulls away, taking my bottom lip with her before she lets it slide from between her teeth, her bite the perfect balance between pain and pleasure.

"Lark . . ."

Her breathy laugh eradicates any thoughts of whatever plea I was about to make. She trails a line of open-mouthed kisses along my jaw. My fingers thread into her golden waves when she nips at my earlobe hard enough that I hiss. I tighten my hold on the strands in my grasp and she moans, her mouth dropping to my neck where she sucks on my inked flesh.

A growl rips free of my chest as I grip her hair. "Feckin' Christ Jesus," I groan.

Her lips go still on my pulse.

. . . *Shit.*

I immediately loosen the fist tangled in her locks. Did I do something wrong? Something definitely *seems* wrong. It's obvious in the way she stiffens.

"What did you say?" she whispers, her breath hot on my skin.

Fuck. *Fuck.*

What did I do? Was it the whole *thou shalt not use the Lord's name in vain* business? Maybe Lark is super religious. I can't remember if she or Sloane mentioned if the boarding school was some strict Catholic thing. Nuns. Were there nuns?

I swallow. "Uh, I said 'feckin' Christ Jesus.'"

"Growlier," Lark snaps.

"*Feckin' Christ Jesus.*"

There's a single heartbeat of stillness in the world.

And then Lark has backed away out of reach, the heat of her body gone, a chill left behind on my skin. Both of her hands cover her mouth but they can't mask the shock in her eyes.

Shock and . . . *fury.*

"Oh my fucking *God*," she hisses into her fingers.

"What . . . ? Was it the Jesus?"

"No. No, it was not '*the Jesus*,'" she says with air quotes and a sneer as she leans close enough to jab a single finger into my chest. "It was 'the Batman.' The *Budget* Batman."

Lark takes a step back. Crosses her arms. Raises a single brow.

My eyes narrow to thin slits. The words come out as a venomous hiss when I say, "Blunder Barbie."

"Oh. My. God. *Ohmygodohmygodohmygod*," Lark says, flapping her hands like she's trying to get any residue of me off of her. "You had your *tongue* in my *mouth*."

"I'd hate to remind us both, Blunder Barbie, but *you* kissed *me*."

"And you *let* me. You fucking *knew* it was me."

"Clearly, I did not, or I would have taken my chances with the fire escape."

"There is no fire escape."

"Pre-feckin'-cisely."

Lark rolls her eyes before they sharpen on me in a lethal glare. "You are such a liar. You were all up in my face that night. With a *flashlight*. One that you smacked on my head."

"Your face was *plastered* with makeup. And I didn't smack—"

"My *concussed* head. Where I needed fucking stitches which I never got because I had to walk home, *thankyouverymuch*. And then you growled at me like some rabid trash panda that was about to gnaw my leg off and tossed me in the trunk of your car, you fucking psycho."

"Oh *I'm* a feckin' psycho, am I? *You're* the one who jumped from a moving vehicle after you rammed some poor bloke into a lake and then fake teared up when I dropped his blimmin' body at your feet. And they weren't even good fake tears. They were *sarcasm* tears," I snarl. I take a step closer and bend to meet her eye level, dabbing my eyes as I clear my throat for my best candy-sweet vocal impression. "Boo-hoo, I'm Blunder Barbie and I just *feckin' killed a man*. My bad. But don't worry, I'll just get someone else to fix it so I can toddle on back to my perfect little life."

"That is the biggest pile of hypocritical bullshit I've ever heard. How's the contract killer gig going, by the way? Raking in some good cash with your murder-scuba skills, Batman?" Lark snorts and steps toward me, drawing a giant circle in front of my face with a dainty finger. "What you think you know about me, or *anything*, frankly, is *this*," she says as she continues the circle. "But what you *actually* know is *this*." She stops abruptly to hold her finger and thumb close together, only a whisper of space between them.

"What I *actually* know is that you're a huge pain in the arse."

"And what *I* actually know is that you're a monumental douche-bag." She lets out an exasperated sigh. "Is this some kind of cruel joke? Why would you let me kiss you, you fucking nutcase?"

"Like I said, I didn't feckin' recognize you. It was Halloween, for Chrissakes. You were in a costume. With makeup. *Thick* makeup."

Her jaw drops. Then closes. Then drops again. "Seriously?" When I don't reply, she balls her fists at her sides, and I find myself wishing she would try to throw a punch just so I could have the satisfaction of catching all her fury in my calloused palm. "You are *unbelievable*. You were wearing a full-on mask and I recognized you by your grumble whisper and ass-backwards Christ Jesus–ing. All I had on that night was some white face paint and colored eye shadow. Hardly the same thing as your thrifted super-hero disguise."

Deciding it's time to throw her off-kilter, I shrug and lean against the railing. My sudden nonchalance seems to infuriate her as much as I'd hoped, so I take a long sip of my drink before I give her the truth. "It was dark. I wasn't wearing my glasses."

"*Your glasses*," she parrots after an incredulous snort. "Forgive me, dickhead, but that sounds like complete bullshit."

"Forgiven. Well, for that, anyway."

"You're not wearing them *now*."

"Highly observant of you, *duchess*. It's probably all well and good too. I imagine you'd be ripping them off my face to smash them underfoot, am I right?" When I narrow my glare at her, Lark smirks, unable to hide her agreement. "Maybe now is a good time to inform you that you got me into *so much shit* at work. Or have you forgotten the part where you managed to single-handedly decimate a very important contract for my employer? You have no idea the shit my boss has put me through."

"*Me?* You think it was *me* who fucked your contract?" she shrieks. "First of all, I did no such thing. But I can't help it if rumors of your abysmal customer service skills worked their way back to your employer. Deserved. You were being a dick. Even your friend Conor agreed."

Goddammit, Conor. He should know better than to give out his name. A low growl escapes my throat and a feckin' demonic little grin creeps across Lark's face. Oh, her dart hit the target and she knows it.

My foreboding expression doesn't seem to scare her, not even when I lean a little closer. "This is not the kind of industry where you demand to see the manager and leave a shitty review, princess."

One perfect brow flies up. Her smile stretches and her eyes glitter in the dim light. "Oh, it's not?" she says, her voice saccharine. She saunters closer, one slow step after the next. "Because it certainly sounds like that's *exactly* how your industry works, and you're butthurt about being called out for acting like a prick. You've decided to take it out on me under the erroneous assumption that I'm the one who got you into trouble, instead of you looking in the mirror and giving yourself a stern talking-to."

Lark stops so close to me that my chest will touch hers if I take a deep breath. Her eyes drop to my lips and linger there. Heat tingles on my flesh. I can still taste her kiss, the sweetness of soda on her lips. I don't take my eyes from her face as she touches my sternum and walks two fingers toward my neck.

"Erroneous assumptions are kind of your forte, aren't they? But this time I guess it's just the consequences of your actions coming back to haunt you, sweetie."

I catch her hand in a tight grip and guffaw a laugh. Even with its vicious edge, this still feels like the first true moment of delight that I've had in a long while. Well, at least since the kiss we just shared, though that particular event now seems like it happened to another man. "That is precisely the kind of oblivious, hypocritical horse shite I expected to come from someone like you."

There's a flash of hurt in her blue eyes, more fleeting than a lightning strike. "'*Someone like me*'? You have no fucking idea who I am or what I know about consequences."

The rage on her face is fuel. I want to find every one of her buttons and hammer them until she blows, just to see what she'll do next. But this time, she doesn't push back. Instead, her spine straightens. Her chin tips up. She slips her fingers free of my fist with a swift tug. I fight the strange urge to pull her back closer to me. I'm unsteady. Unmoored. Like I've been hit by a rogue wave and lost my balance. But I shove the feeling away.

Lark gestures to the glass door. "That is my best friend in there," she says, her voice low and menacing, her eyes pinned on me. "And she deserves to celebrate with the love of her life. Your brother." Lark's face scrunches as though she just tasted something bitter. In an instant, she's smoothed her mask out again and takes a step closer. "So I'm going to be nice to you. For *her*. And you can continue being whatever scowling, smirking, asshat jerkoff you want, but you're not getting anything more from me."

Without so much as a blink, she whips the drink from my hand and downs it. Her eyes water as soon as the liquor hits her tongue.

"Thought you didn't drink, duchess," I say with a smirk.

"I guess your stimulating company has that effect," Lark retorts before shoving the glass against my chest, nothing more than chips of ice left behind. "And fuck off with the 'duchess' shit. That bitch has met the guillotine."

"Whatever you say," I snarl after her, but she's already slid the glass door open and stepped over the threshold. She doesn't even acknowledge the way I close the door after me with a thud that's just a little too abrupt, a little too loud.

Lark is striding toward the kitchen when Sloane intercepts her from the corridor that leads to the home office. "Hey, I was about to come find you." Her faint smile disappears as she scans the details of Lark's face. "You okay?"

Lark wraps an arm around Sloane's shoulders, not breaking her stride. "Yeah, of course. You look so beautiful, by the way. Have I told you that?"

"You might have said that once or twice when you tried to put gold star stickers on my tits."

"They deserve it. That dress is smokin' hot."

"Uh, thanks."

"I could really use a glass of wine, or like, maybe a bathtub of tequila so let's get to the restaurant *tout suite*, we're running late. I don't want Rowan to be worried about you."

"Okay . . ." Sloane glances over her shoulder at me, her eyes narrowed in scrutiny. I raise my hands and saunter after them with a smirk tugging on one corner of my lips, something about my forced grin seems off this time, and with the way a crease flickers between Sloane's brows, I think I'm not the only one who can sense it.

And that feeling of being pushed off my axis? Well, it doesn't leave. Not as we arrange for two Ubers to the restaurant, Lark ensuring she doesn't ride in mine. Not as we eat our meal and celebrate the opening night of Butcher & Blackbird, and she spends the whole time beaming her smile everywhere but on me. Not even when she slips away shortly after Rowan and Sloane. Much like the first night we met, she disappears, only an unfamiliar void left behind.

Even after she's gone, that feeling remains, like something has shifted in the world that surrounds me. Like I've been displaced.

Like I'm standing in the shade.

GERMINATE

The Phantom

I slide the tension tool into the bottom of the keyhole. Next, the needle of the snap gun. When it's positioned beneath the pins in the lock, I strike the trigger until they give way. Five quiet ticks of metal friction. A moment later, I'm standing in the home of my adversaries.

Behold, I am coming soon, bringing my recompense with me, to repay everyone for what he has done.

Pocketing my tools, I close the door behind me and check my notebook. I've memorized the details already. I checked it again just before I walked here. But there must be no room for errors.

August 2nd. 13:00. Tattoo appointment, Prism Tattoo Parlor. Estimated time of absence: two hours.

I put the notebook away and cast my eyes across the details of the room.

The interior is familiar to me. I've seen it many times through the windows. I know where the Orb Weaver sits to do her work. What times she has recurring phone calls. What time she enjoys a morning coffee. The Boston Butcher's habits were initially more difficult to track. Easier now that I've obtained access to the restaurant schedules. But I have observed long enough that patterns have emerged.

A growl emanates from beneath the coffee table. I bend at the waist until I meet the eyes of the cat.

"Ah yes," I say with a slow smile. "Hello, you."

The feline hisses at me, and I fold my gloved hand into a fist. My heart rate spikes as dark urges threaten to take over. The memory of my mother's anger calms them.

Let the wicked change their ways and banish the very thought of doing wrong. Let them turn to the Lord so that he may have mercy on them. Yes, turn to our God, for he will forgive generously.

I turn away from the animal and walk to the sliding door leading to the balcony. I open it and step outside. Many times, I've seen the Butcher and the Spider here. They share coffee in warm weather. A glass of wine in the evening. They commit lewd acts, as though no one else can see them.

But I do. I have been watching.

For my suffering and servitude, my Lord has rewarded my dedication. One evening, he showed me my true prize here, standing right where I stand now. The brother. The assassin. The eye for an eye.

But he gave me an even more precious gift. He showed me the best friend. The one so close to the Spider that they could be sisters. The singer.

The tooth for a tooth.

I reenter the apartment and slide the door closed behind me. The hand of the Lord guides me. His voice whispers and I follow.

I stop at the sideboard in the dining room, where framed photographs face away from the window. The Boston Butcher and the Orb Weaver. Faces I recognize. Faces I don't. Among the pictures, there's one at the restaurant in a booth. Rowan Kane and Sloane Sutherland sitting next to each other. Lark Montague smiling at the camera. Lachlan Kane, killer for hire, the deadliest serpent in a nest of snakes. His gaze is caught on Miss Montague. Hate and desire are often indistinguishable to me. But I know what I saw on the balcony the same night that the restaurant opened. I know what I heard. There was anger between them. But beneath it, there was *need*. It burned in Kane's eyes like twin flames as he watched her walk away.

My focus returns to Lark Montague. The cherished daughter of two empires of sin. The beloved friend of the Orb Weaver. The coveted object of Lachlan Kane's desire. And divine inspiration strikes. A new idea. The seeds of a magnificent plan. A plan to not only avenge, but to debride their rotting souls with the cleansing, righteous fire of pain. Of suffering.

The worst suffering is not death. It is in living, day after day, knowing you've forever lost that which you most cherished. Most loved. Most desired. It's being forced to continue existing in a world indifferent to your pain. To realize how powerless you are against the tide of God's wrath.

So I will bring them pain. The Butcher. The Spider. Lark Montague. And what is the worst fate for a man like Lachlan Kane?

To ensure anyone left behind believes *he* is the cause of Lark Montague's destruction.

With the pure you will show yourself pure. And with the devious you will show yourself shrewd.

Step one. *Destabilize.*

I smile and turn to leave, the cat taking a swipe at my leg as I go.

But know this: in the last days, there will be suffering.

For he shall then repay each person according to what he has done.

An eye for an eye.

And a tooth for a tooth.

THREADS

Lark

. . . ONE YEAR LATER

I let myself into my great aunt Ethel's sprawling home, the familiar rhythm of waves following on my heels from the nearby rocky shore until I close the door behind me. The scent of lavender and roses greets me in the foyer from the large bouquets that line either side of the entryway. There's a framed photo of Ethel and my great uncle Thomas resting between two of the vases, a picture I took at their wedding anniversary party six months ago. I'm staring down at the photo when my older sister, Ava, appears from the direction of the kitchen, the cadence of her footsteps so familiar that I don't need to look up to know it's her.

"That was a great party, wasn't it?" I say when she stops at my side to admire the warmth of our aunt and uncle's wrinkled faces, their smiles forever frozen as they dance against the backdrop of friends and family.

"Yeah, it was. Aside from that jellied carrot salad. What the fuck."

"It's Ethel. She likes what she likes."

"Apparently, she likes making the rest of us gag at the table. How she can be so good at muffins and so horrible at literally everything else, I'll never know." Ava shudders in my peripheral vision before turning to embrace me. "Hey, Meadowlark."

"I missed you," I reply, and she squeezes tighter before letting me go. "Are you still good to drive Ethel to the venue this weekend if everything with Sloane's surprise elopement goes to plan?"

Ava sighs, my biceps gripped in her hands as she appraises me. Something about her expression seems drawn now that I have the chance to really look at her. Maybe it's just the stress of recent travel from California. She's not the type to chill, and it's probably starting to catch up to her along with everything she's been organizing here. I give her a bright smile and hum a few bars of the "Wedding March," but it doesn't crack her stoic mask.

"Sure, I can get her there, but I can't stay for the wedding, unfortunately. You'll have to give Sloane my best if she ends up saying yes to this crazy elopement plan," Ava finally says as she lets go of my arms.

"Where is Auntie Ethel anyway? She wanted me here at eleven o'clock *exactly*, for some reason," I say as my gaze pans across the living room. Normally, when my aunt demands a specific time, she's already at the door, ready to bark her orders.

"She's upstairs. Mom and Dad were in the sitting room with Tremblay the last time I saw them. I'll be in the office going through the eighty million pieces of fucking paper that are still left. If you don't see me, I've chosen to end things by paper cut rather than read through another ledger of flour and sugar orders."

♪

"I know what will cheer you up."

"Margaritas?"

"Jellied salad."

"In the most loving way possible, fuck off."

My sister gives me a sardonic grin before she presses a kiss to my cheek and then marches away, disappearing down the corridor past the boxes of paperwork she's set out in the hallway. A sense of unease settles in my chest like a thick syrup that sticks to my bones.

My watch buzzes with an incoming text from my aunt.

You're not late, are you?

I roll my eyes but smile as I pull out my phone to tap a reply.

Right on time, Auntie. Just arrived.

Good. Take the rear steps. And bring me the hand lotion from the bathroom down there, would you? Take your time.

My face scrunches. I'm not unfamiliar with my aunt's strange demands. Hurry up. Then take your time. Bring me a random thing. Even still, it's a little odd.

I shrug it off and send her a simple "okay" before I head toward the bathroom next to the stairway that leads to the wing where my aunt's bedroom looks across the sea. I'm nearly there when I hear tense voices floating out into the corridor. It's the familiar tone and cadence of my stepfather speaking, followed by another man's voice I recognize to be Stan Tremblay's. His deep baritone summons goose bumps on my skin.

Normally, I would leave my mom and stepdad to their secrets and plans and the never-ending machinations that keep their respective businesses running and their family happy. I've overheard meetings like this for as long as I can remember. They're part of the murk rippling beneath the pristine surface that gives the appearance of a flawless life.

" . . . the name of the one who worked for Leviathan?"

My steps falter. My mother's voice evokes memories of the night I crashed Merrick's vehicle into the reservoir. I mean to grab my aunt's lotion and keep walking like I can simply ignore this is part of my life. This is none of my concern, this constant scheming, these endless battles. But it's the next two words that root me to the floor.

"*Lachlan Kane.*"

I look toward the sitting room at the end of the corridor. One of the double doors is ajar. With just a moment's hesitation, I follow the flow of voices, slinking into the empty office across the hall.

"The fact is, there could be a hundred different people who want a pound of flesh from either one of us. We can't go around killing everyone who does." My stepfather lets out a sardonic laugh. "There would be no one left in Rhode Island."

My mother's irritated huff escapes the room. I imagine her silvery-blue eyes are likely sharp enough to flay the skin right off my stepfather's face. She might love him with every beat of her steely heart, but when it comes to work, there are lines they don't cross, even if their businesses bleed into each other more and more as time goes on. "Damian, we're not just talking about someone wanting to fuck up a factory and make your life miserable for a few months. We're talking about someone deliberately targeting *both* of us. Kelly Ellis was on my board. Cristian was your fucking *cousin*. Every month there's another murder. It's clockwork. Forty days. It's not some coincidence."

"And every forty days we're right back at square one. We have no witnesses and no evidence. Certainly nothing that points concretely to someone from Leviathan."

"Kane has the skill," Tremblay says as I hear the sound of thick paper slapping a wooden surface. "He worked for Leviathan for sixteen years. Perhaps he's taking revenge for being cut loose."

Pages rustle. A thoughtful hum resonates in my stepfather's warm tone. "Are we sure he was even fired? For all we know, they kept him on. I scrapped their whole contract—it's not like I told them to get rid of Kane."

"All the more reason for him to be going after us if the wrong people are taking advantage of the situation. How do we know Leviathan hasn't been hired by a competitor?"

"We don't. Because this is all just conjecture. We have no proof that points to anyone or anything specific." A heavy sigh escapes from my stepfather and I hear him shift in his chair. "Look, I agree it's possible that Kane or perhaps Leviathan have something to do with this . . . pattern. They certainly have the means. But it could just as likely be a competitor like Bob Foster—"

My mom snorts.

"—or someone *paid* by one of our competitors or a hundred other options. I don't believe it's prudent to go after an organization like Leviathan or one of their maybe-employees without being completely sure."

"And if we don't remove the most likely threats, we invite harm to our doorstep," Tremblay says, another paper slapped down on a table. "Kane has two brothers. One appears to be . . . normal. A doctor, living in Nebraska. But the other . . ." Papers shuffle. "Rowan Kane. He's volatile. He will back up his brother and has done it before."

No. No, no, no.

My hand covers my mouth to trap the desperate sound that begs to escape. It feels as though the world has flipped over, like I'm falling off the edge.

My mother sounds just as shocked as I feel when she says, "Rowan Kane . . . ? The same Rowan that Sloane is marrying?"

"Yes. I've been digging into him, asking around. He had a history of violence, some juvenile citations shortly after immigrating to Boston but the details appear to be missing from police records and nothing ever resulted in charges. And there was something in his early twenties as well, a fight at a bar that put Lachlan in the hospital. Word from my connection is that Rowan beat the man who injured his brother and left him in the alley. There's record of Lachlan's medical treatment, record of the other man who ended up dead in the hospital, but nothing on Rowan."

My blood rushes in deafening waves in my head, dulling the hushed conversation between my parents as pages rustle. But I catch their brief questions. *Is Sloane safe? What about Lark? We need proof. But can we take the risk to wait . . . ?* Every word feels like a sharp blow.

♫

"What you're suggesting, Stan . . ." my stepfather says, letting his thoughts trail away. I can picture the stress on his face, the way he's probably shaking his head. "We could eliminate the Kanes and still not solve the problem and then what? Then we've got Leviathan breathing down our necks for real, that's what. We need *proof.*"

"We cannot sit back and wait for proof to drop into our laps. If we do, more of our people will die. You're telling me you've not done worse for Covaci Enterprises?"

"Stan—" my mother barks.

"And this is why not everything should be outsourced," Tremblay says. Pages shuffle and then slap against the wood. "Nina, we should discuss this with Ethel, look at handling this kind of thing the way the Montagues always have—"

"No," my mother interrupts, her tone firm. "Leave her out of it. She's got enough to worry about right now. Damian and I will sort this out. Give us a week and we'll let you know what we want to do. Thank you, Stan."

Standing in the shadows, I watch through the crack between the hinges as Stan Tremblay leaves the sitting room. He doesn't glance in my direction as he strides away with sure and powerful steps, his head bent, papers tucked beneath his arm. He might be nearing his seventies, but he's still one of the most formidable people I know. A specter of my childhood.

My parents leave a few moments later, talking about mundane things. Lunch and liquor. Where they might go for dinner. Things that seem so far removed from the conversation they just finished, and yet this is the way it's always been. Deals in dark corners. Life in the light.

I let them pass by and wait until my heart calms enough that I can hear clearly before I leave my hiding place and grab the bottle of lotion from the bathroom, then take the stairs by twos.

Hands trembling, I make it only a few feet down the hall before I set the lotion down and press my palms to one of the decorative tables lining the corridor and stare at my reflection in the gilded mirror. My cheeks are flushed as waves of adrenaline wash through my veins.

I can't let them take Rowan from Sloane. I need to find a way to stop them. I *must*.

But I don't know how.

I don't have some family enforcer on my side. No one who can rally for my position. I've always been the one to protect, not the one to scrap with the other apex predators for a slice of prey or territory.

"I don't know how to do this," I whisper to my reflection as tears well in my eyes.

My watch vibrates against my wrist and I look down to see Rose's name flash up on the screen.

> Hello Boss Hostler! I'll be ready to make a dukey run soon!

My nose scrunches and I wipe my eyes as I try to decode Rose's circus lingo, pulling out my phone to blink down at her message as though it might help to see it on a larger screen. It doesn't.

> Boss Hustler . . . ?

Boss HOSTLER. The dude in charge of
the show. That dude is you.

Okay . . . And I'm supposed to
make what now?

A dukey run, you know? To Leytonstone
Inn to take all the wedding shit to the
venue? How about we meet at 3pm at
your place. Got the dress? I can't wait to
see it!

I glance down the hallway toward my aunt's favorite wing of
the house and bite down on the inner edge of my lip until blood
washes over my tongue. Though I might not know how to fix
this situation that seems as inevitable as an avalanche, I can't let
Sloane down on the most important day of her life either. We've
still got a handful of days until the surprise elopement that
Rowan has been planning for the last few weeks. Maybe I can
convince her and Rowan to run. They could get out of Boston.
Get out of the *country*. Live some other paradise life far away
from here. But as fast as these ideas come up, so too do the
thoughts that whisper about how this will never work. Because
families like mine, we don't get to where we are by letting shit
go, or by allowing such simple things as borders and geography
to stand in our way. Not when we have every resource at our
fingertips to do what we want.

I need to find another way.

I clamp down on my panic. I just need to get the dress and get the fuck out of here so I can find a safe, quiet place to figure it out. Breathe. Plan the next steps and then take them one at a time, just like I've practiced.

With a single deep breath that fills every crevice in my lungs, I wipe my eyes a final time.

> I'll be there.

I slide my phone into my pocket and turn my attention back to the mirror. I take another deep breath.

Smile, I tell myself.

Keep smiling.

I smile and smile and smile until it looks just right, until everything beneath it is stored away. Only when I'm sure I look just the way I'm supposed to do I take a step back from the mirror and head down the corridor.

I find Ethel not in bed, where she often is just before lunch, but in her craft room, where paints and threads and yarn and canvases line the white shelves and tables, everything laid out with impeccable precision and kept clean despite frequent use. She's sitting at her favorite wingback chair, which faces a window overlooking the sea, her hair a cloud of white curls resting on her hunched shoulders, her focus honed on the needlepoint in her hands. With a sudden swear and a hiss, she puts a finger in her mouth and for a second my smile is genuine.

"You should take a break from stabbing yourself so you can visit with your favorite niece," I say with manufactured brightness as I enter the room.

Ethel gives a sharp, startled inhale that spills out with a rumbling cough. "Sweet baby Jesus, girl. You'll scare me to death before I make it to the nursing home."

"That's one way to piss Mom and Ava off. They've been packing for days."

I set the bottle down on her table and press a gentle kiss to my aunt's cheek, her wrinkled skin dusted with powder and blush, the scent evoking my childhood memories of sitting at her vanity as I played with her makeup. The comfort of those moments isn't enough to mask the worry that burns in my chest and threatens to ignite into panic.

"Ava should go back to California. She's got enough to worry about at home, she doesn't need to be here," Ethel says as I turn away and face the black garment bag that hangs from the top edge of the closet door.

"You know she won't, not until she's got everything packed up at least. She's stubborn. Wonder where she got that from."

"Not me, if that's what you're implying, my girl."

"No," I deadpan. "I would never, Auntie."

My aunt glances up and I flash her a bright, fleeting smile. I take a step closer to the closet, but I can feel her scrutiny on me, Ethel's watchful gaze sharp enough to cut through any armor I try to put between us. I should have known better than to try to fool the woman who built an empire out of flour and sugar—details are kind of Ethel's forte. It's better to grab the dress and get out of here so I can figure out what the hell I should do.

The only problem is, I'm just a little bit too late.

"What's wrong?" Ethel asks, no hesitation in her tone. "Are you unsure about Sloane's wedding?"

My eyes don't stray from the garment bag, even though I feel my aunt's gaze drilling into my head. I have the most powerful urge to rescue the dress from its black cocoon, as though Sloane's happiness will suffocate in there if I don't let it out.

I shake my head as I walk toward the bag and grab the hanger. "No, Auntie. Absolutely not."

I'm unzipping the first few inches of the garment bag when Ethel says, "Well, that's a bit of a shame, dear, because it would make solving the Kane problem a little easier if she were to suddenly dislike those boys."

When I spin to face her, my aunt is pulling a thread through her canvas, a devious grin on her lips. "How do you know about the Kanes?" My eyes narrow. "You set me up to overhear Mom and Damian."

"Maybe."

"Why didn't you just tell me?"

My aunt shrugs. "Better for you to hear it from the horse's mouth. Your sister thinks I'm senile. Who knows what I'm making up?"

Fair point. I know as well as anyone not to trust half the shit Ethel Montague comes out with. It's part of her power, to always keep you guessing. "How do you even know about all that?"

"Meadowlark," she says with a cluck of her tongue as she pins me with a flat glare above the acetate rims of her glasses, "this is still *my house*. And this family's business is still *my concern*, whether your parents think it should be or not."

My throat tightens as I take a few steps closer to my aunt, the partially opened garment bag draped across my raised arms like an offering. I open my mouth to say something, but words die on my tongue when my aunt smiles and turns her attention back to the embroidery hoop clutched in her hand.

"Have a seat, my girl."

I do as she commands and sit across from her as she pushes the needle through the canvas to create stitches of crimson. "I don't think the Kanes are involved in whatever is going on," I say. She keeps her eyes down on her work but nods. "Definitely not Fionn. Rowan would never do anything to inadvertently hurt me by harming people I know, no matter how thin those connections might be."

"And Lachlan?"

Would he? Is this retaliation on behalf of his boss like my parents and Tremblay were saying downstairs? Could Lachlan be the type to take revenge on us for dropping the contract? For him being sucked deeper into a life he never asked for? He's certainly sharp around the edges with a giant and jagged chip on his shoulder. But it just doesn't sit right. "I don't think he would take a risk that would jeopardize his brothers' health or happiness. No."

"I don't either. Personally, I think Bob Foster is finally making his move, that slimy little shit. Leave it to him to kick a dying dog when it's down. But Tremblay has a different opinion, and your mother is leaning in his direction." Ethel looks up at me as she pulls the thread taut. "Damian doesn't seem wedded to the idea that Lachlan is involved in these murders, no pun intended," she says as she momentarily drops her gaze to the dress spread across my lap. "But it's one of the reasons I love her as much as if she had been born a Montague. She's just as bossy and conniving as me."

A deep sigh fills my lungs. "Maybe there's some way to prove it, like a solid alibi that would take Lachlan out of consideration."

I know as much as Ethel does that there's no such thing as a solid alibi when people like Lachlan are involved. "He is a professional. People like him with access to the right resources can make up any excuse, fabricate any believable story and evidence."

"What if I just talk to Mom and Dad, convince them he wouldn't do it . . ."

"It's going to take more than a conversation to sell that story, Lark."

"But I can't just let this happen to Sloane. *I can't.* Not after everything that happened when we were at Ashborne—"

My aunt's hand darts out and catches mine, squeezing with surprising strength. "I know where you're going with this, Lark. But you cannot blame yourself for the things that happened at that school. None of it was your fault, you hear me?"

Though I nod, the tears still blur my vision with a watery film. Although I know that what Mr. Verdon did was not my fault, I can never seem to shake the guilt I still feel. It's a sense of shame that drapes across me like a veil. I've questioned myself thousands of times, blamed myself for being strung up in the fear he injected into my thoughts with his whispered threats and promises. And just as I've questioned myself over and over, I've reassured myself too. *It wasn't my fault.*

But maybe if I'd acted sooner . . .

"You can't second-guess the decisions you made to survive." Ethel lets go of my hand and coughs, a rumble of discomfort that creases her face with pain. When I reach out to lay a comforting hand on her arm, she waves me off.

"We could get nurses here for you. Get a room set up just the way you want it. You don't have to go to a care home," I say as her cough continues and her face pinks with strain. My heart squeezes as Ethel raises a tissue to her mouth and wipes away a smear of bloody saliva from her lips. "I can arrange it all for you. I don't mind."

"*I* mind," she wheezes out. It takes her a moment, but she regains her composure, though her cloudy eyes are still glassed with a thin film of tears from the mere effort to breathe. "I won't have you all scurrying around this house like deranged little hamsters while I slowly wither away into the afterlife."

"Well that's . . . bleak. And kind of weird."

"Maybe it's time you learn that power can be found in unexpected decisions." Ethel picks up the hoop with one hand, her needle with the other, and levels me with a serious look. "I'm the one who decided to go to Shoreview. No one will watch me deteriorate in my own home. It won't stop it from happening, of course. But it's even worse to fall apart in full view in the symbolic heart of the empire I built. Besides, I'll be closer to you. And you never know," she says with a wink before her eyes finally drop to her work, "I might need to hang on to a little power for a final scheme or two."

My head tilts, but Ethel doesn't look up, not even when we descend into an extended moment of silence. "Scheme . . . ?"

"Indeed. You know," Ethel says as she pierces the taut canvas to pull a red vein of thread through the fabric, "something I love about your mother and Damian is that they are so steadfast in their beliefs. Family first. Promises made must be kept. Vows, honored."

My gaze drifts out the window toward the sea as I nod. I expect my aunt will say something about how it's our shared duty in this family to make hard decisions to look out for one another. *There's a lesson in this*, she'll say. *Sometimes, we all need to sacrifice a little happiness to protect the ones we love and keep our promises to look after one another. And nothing is more important than that.* But the hollow pit in my stomach will only grow deeper. More desolate. More insatiable.

"Back at the school, when Sloane protected you, did you promise to look after her in return?"

I blink at Ethel, only now realizing my cheeks are damp. "Yes."

"Yes," my aunt echoes. "You did. And you can keep that promise by making another. The kind of promise that your parents would not interfere with. At least, not if they were . . . convinced."

"I don't understand . . ."

Ethel lets my confusion linger in the air as she pulls her thread through the fabric. Pierce and pull. Pierce and pull. Maybe she's waiting for me to find a solution myself, or to divine her thoughts from her simple motion, but I don't. "Do you know what my favorite thing is about your mother and stepdad?"

"Their ability to obliterate their competition and take out their opponents while maintaining the image of a perfect, happy family?"

"That too," Ethel says. "Mostly, though, it's their loyalty. Their deep love of each other. Their deep love of you girls." Ethel pulls a final crimson stitch through the canvas before she knots the thread and clips it with scissors. "Their unwillingness to break promises to the ones they love."

She's right, of course. I know that for all the darkness in their lives, my mom and stepfather love us deeply. Just like my mother loved my dad, Sam. And long before she met my dad, she loved Damian. Her childhood sweetheart. A young love that burned bright but couldn't survive the demands of time. Or so they must have thought, until my dad passed away and those embers slowly came back to life.

"So you think I can talk them out of killing Lachlan because, what . . . my parents love their family . . . ? That doesn't make any sense, Auntie."

Ethel turns to me, and I meet her eyes, the color of fog, a mist over the sharp mind that grinds away beneath the gray film. "Do you remember going to Damian's father's funeral when you were little?" I shake my head. "You were about five. It was the first time your mom and stepfather saw each other after so many years apart. I'm sure I'm not the only one who could feel that electric charge between them. But your mother had you girls. She had Sam. Life had moved on. And no matter how much love Damian and Nina still had for each other, they would never break your mother's vows or wound your dad. Had we not lost Sam, that never would have changed."

I swallow, trying to conjure a memory of the funeral, but it doesn't come. Neither does the meaning of what Ethel is trying to tell me, though she watches my reactions closely as though imploring me to catch on. "I really don't understand. Are you saying you think they won't make a move against Rowan once he and Sloane are married, because they won't interfere with her vows . . . ?"

Ethel chuckles and shakes her head. "No. They care about Sloane, of course. But they care because you do. They took Sloane in because of what she did for you at Ashborne. But it's *your* happiness that is their priority. *Your* heart they can't bear to break."

"So, what . . . if it was me getting married . . . ?"

Notes that felt discordant suddenly blend together. A chord that rises from chaos.

"Look down at your lap again, girl," my aunt says, and I drop my gaze to the wedding dress draped across my legs. "And tell me more about Lachlan Kane."

LEYTONSTONE

Lachlan

The doors of Leytonstone Inn swing open to reveal the ocean and a curving walkway lined with flowers. An angelic melody of piano and guitar rolls toward us along with the scent of the sea.

Sloane's grip on my arm tightens and I glance down at her from the corner of my eye. Her black hair is pulled away from her face in loose waves that lift on the breeze entering the room. A blush creeps into her cheeks as she smiles, her dimple deepening next to her lips.

She glances up at me with sharp hazel eyes. "Are you staring at my tits?"

I sputter and choke on the sea air.

"Christ Jesus," I hiss as she tosses me a devious grin and takes a step forward, prompting me to match her stride. "Just when I thought my brother was the biggest pain in my arse, you came along."

"I'm trying to keep you humble, Lachlan. An impossible job, quite honestly," she says, her smile only widening when I mutter a weak protest. "But in all seriousness, don't forget what I said."

A groan works its way up my throat. I remember.

Don't be a dick. Dance with the maid of honor.

I take a breath to ask why it matters or to make another attempt to get out of it, but Sloane cuts me off.

"Bride's orders," Sloane whispers as though she's crawled right into my brain. "Or I'll take an eye."

"I'd like to see you try."

"What did I say about threatening me with a good time?" When Sloane looks up, a little tremor quivers in her lip and the grumbles I want to shoot back at her evaporate. Her teasing bravado falters and she knows I can see it, the nerves beneath the mask, the glassy sheen at her lash line.

"Hey," I say, patting her hand. "You remember when you came into the restaurant that first time and I was there?"

Sloane nods as she keeps her gaze trained away from me.

"I whispered something to my brother. Want to know what I said?"

She pauses, then nods again.

"I said, 'That girl is too good for you, asshat, but she loves you anyway. Don't fuck it up.' And he won't. One thing I know for sure, Spider Lady. You and Rowan are meant for each other."

Sloane's face crinkles as she fights her hardest to hold back tears. With a few deep breaths and a pass of a tissue beneath her lashes, she composes herself. "Thank you."

"Sure. Just keep my brother out of the whiskey. He'll start singing 'The Rocky Road to Dublin' and it's bad. It's so feckin' bad. He's got a voice that'll make Satan weep."

"Give Rowan all the whiskey. Got it."

"Christ Jesus."

An anxious giggle bubbles from Sloane. By the time we reach the open door she's vibrating, her arm unsteady against mine.

And then we pass the threshold.

I can feel the exact moment when she sees my brother waiting at the end of the long aisle beneath an arch of flowers, the sea a shimmering backdrop lit with the morning sun. Sloane's talon grip on my arm relaxes. The tremors fade. Her smile grows bright.

And as for Rowan?

He's a feckin' blubbering mess.

Rowan presses a handkerchief to his eyes, but it doesn't stop more tears from replacing the ones he catches. He shifts his weight from one foot to another until Fionn claps a hand on his shoulder and whispers something in his ear. Whatever it is earns Fionn a backhanded smack to the side of his head, but Rowan never takes his eyes off Sloane.

"Do you boys *ever* leave one another alone?" Sloane whispers to me as Fionn grins and Rowan returns to his state of crumbling disarray.

"Not usually. No."

"Of course you don't."

We fall into silence as we draw close to the limited seating. There are only a handful of guests, mostly Rowan's friends and a few of Sloane's closest work colleagues and Lark's elderly aunt, all of whom stand to watch our progress with warm and encouraging smiles. They block our view of the musicians seated somewhere to the left near the flower arch, but even without seeing them, I recognize the singer's voice.

My eyes narrow. My smile feels more like a grimace.

I try to resist the urge to glance in the direction of the guitarist and pianist, nodding to the few guests I recognize as we near the archway. But it's futile.

My gaze slices to the musicians. To the source of the voice that crawls into my chest and twists like barbed wire beneath my bones.

To Lark Montague.

Her sparkling blue eyes connect with mine for only an instant, just long enough for us to glare at each other and look away. An electric charge surges through my heart. I want a thousand things. To leave. To stay. To pick up where we left off on that balcony. But which moment would I choose? The one where I pressed my lips to Lark's, her hair gripped tight in my fist? Or the argument that still feels unfinished, one I want to reopen like a festering wound, a cut across my memories that refuses to heal? No matter how many times I try to ignore it, that conversation still bleeds into my thoughts. My stomach twists when I remember that brief moment where my sharp words struck a mark. I can still see the flash of hurt in her eyes.

You have no fucking idea who I am or what I know about consequences, she'd said as she submerged her pain beneath fury.

Her words echo through my mind as Sloane and I slow to a halt and stand before my disintegrating younger brother. The music fades into the final bars of the song.

"You okay, pretty boy?" Sloane whispers to Rowan as he replaces his damp handkerchief with a fresh one.

"You look . . ." Rowan trails off and clears his throat to try again. It's an admirable attempt, but his voice remains little more than a gravelly whisper when he says, "You look so beautiful, Blackbird."

"You kind of cleaned up okay yourself. Though I'm a bit disappointed you're not in a velveteen dragon onesie."

"It could use a wash," he squeaks out.

Rose cackles off to the side and buries her grin in her bouquet. Fionn grumbles something unintelligible about sports as a blush creeps from beneath his collar. Lark joins the bridal party now that the song has finished. She's beaming. Tears dampen her cheeks as she takes Sloane's flowers alongside her own. And by Christ it takes me a long moment to realize that Conor just asked who was giving the bride away and it's up to *me* to respond. Sloane catches the delay, of course. Her pinch on my arm is what pulls me away from trying to decode Lark, a woman who can ram some poor bloke into a lake with zero remorse, yet cries so hard at her best friend's wedding that one of her fake lash clusters falls off. *Seriously.* That fucker slides right down her cheek and she swipes it into her hand, not giving two shits about anything but Sloane and Rowan.

I set Sloane's hand in Rowan's and try to keep my attention on my brother as he sniffles his way through his vows. Maybe there's a sting in my nose when Conor declares them legally wed by the laws of Massachusetts. Maybe it burns a little in my throat when Rowan frames Sloane's face between his palms and just stares at her, making sure she knows this is the most monumental event in his life.

"You'd better kiss me, pretty boy. You're not my husband until you do," Sloane whispers as a single tear breaches her lashes and slides toward her lips.

Rowan does kiss her, of course. He slides an arm across her back and dips her as the small audience cheers. Lark is the loudest of all.

We have a few drinks at Leytonstone Inn, where Lark's aunt Ethel has arranged for canapés and cases of champagne, far more food and alcohol than could ever be consumed by such a small group of people, even with three rowdy Irish brothers in the mix. When everyone is sufficiently buzzed, we file into chauffeured vans and head to town. We wind up at a tavern down the road, an unfussy place filled with seaside knickknacks and wood paneling and jovial locals. A dinner of barbecue ribs and fries and beer is served with napkins printed with a logo of a melting ice cream cone and the words BUTCHER & BLACKBIRD ANNUAL AUGUST SHOWDOWN. The surprise detail makes Sloane first laugh and then cry as Rowan presses a kiss to her cheek. When the DJ starts the music and declares it's time for a first dance, we surround my brother and his wife, and though I try not to let it show, I marvel at how far he's come from the reckless kid who was always on my heels or making trouble for me to fix. Somehow, watching Rowan now, with his life right where it needs to be, mine feels a little empty, even though I couldn't be happier for him. And though I mull that over as I watch, I can't settle on a reason *why*.

"Asshat," Fionn says, interrupting my thoughts as he stops next to me at the edge of the dance floor, which is filled with a combination of our little wedding party and locals who have been swept along in our celebrations.

"Doctor Doily." I smirk when he shoots me a side-eye that's equal parts menacing and pleading. I give a nod toward the small crowd. "Nice *craic* this, isn't it?"

"Yeah. Though you might have more fun if you weren't such a dick and asked the maid of honor for a little spin on the dance floor."

"Ahh. The bride put you up to this?"

Fionn scoffs. Rolls his eyes. "I'm a doctor, you wanker. Observational skills are kind of my thing."

"So are crochet and a shocking inability to say no to dumb shit."

"Stop deflecting from the issue at hand."

"Oh, so you mean there's a point to this conversation?"

"Damn straight there is. And the point is this: What the fuck is your problem with Lark Montague?"

Something unnamed and unexpected tightens in my chest. "What do you mean?"

Fionn grins and lets my question linger as he pulls a long sip of his beer. It takes more concentration than it should to not look to where I last saw Lark talking to the DJ and flipping through his music options. She was splashing her sunlit smile all over him, and the fucker was basking in it like he was trying to catch a feckin' tan. Not that I was paying that much attention.

"You think you'd have learned how to be a bit smoother, seeing as how you've spent the last decade going through the women of Boston faster than you change your fucking socks," Fionn finally says.

My blood heats and I tap one of my rings on my glass as I take a drink, resisting the urge to swallow the whole lot, ice and all. "I don't know what you're feckin' on about."

"I've been watching you look at her all day. One minute you're glowering, the next you're staring at her like a lost kitten, then you're glaring at her like she ripped the head off your teddy bear."

"Fuck you," I snarl. "And leave Mr. Buttons out of it."

Fionn chuckles, nonplussed. We turn our attention back to the dance floor and though I don't look over, I can feel the amusement fade from my youngest brother. Honestly, I'd rather it stay, because the jabs I can take and give back tenfold. It's what comes after that I can't navigate.

"Seriously though. You all right, brother?" Fionn finally asks. I can feel his eyes on me, but I keep mine focused on the dancers. "It's not like you to be so miserable about a woman. Or *to* a woman, for that matter."

"I'm not feckin' miserable, you *bellend*."

"What's gotten into you?"

"Nothing. Absolutely *nothing*."

"Then why are you being an arse? Like, more of an arse than usual?"

"I'm not being an arse."

"No. You're right, you seem perfectly charming. I'm sure she finds it endearing."

I growl and turn enough to pin Fionn with a menacing frown. He looks straight back at me but his eyebrows knit together with worry. "I'm just standing here, having a drink, trying to survive my overanalyzing little brother, minding my own business. I have no clue what the hell you're talking about."

"Right. Well you'd better figure it out soon, because I have a feeling the bride noticed you trying your best to avoid Lark all day. Kinda hard to miss your shittier-than-usual attitude, brother. And if there's anyone in this room scarier than you," Fionn says as he claps me on the shoulder, "it's *her*."

He gives me a gruff laugh and walks away.

Fuck.

Though I try to keep my attention on his back, I can feel it, the weight of Sloane's murderous stare on the side of my face.

With a heavy sigh, I finally meet her eyes across the dance floor.

Sloane jabs a pointed finger in my direction.

Me? I mouth, my palm pressed to my chest, my expression one of sweet innocence even though my guts twist in my belly.

Sloane points at me again and nods her head in Lark's direction, though I don't dare look that way. *Dance,* she mouths in a silent command.

I pretend to be confused.

She *does not* pretend to be infuriated.

Sloane mimes the saddest little choreography I've ever seen as she makes another voiceless demand. *Dance with Lark. Right the fuck now.*

I point to my ear and shake my head. *Can't hear you.*

Sloane rolls her eyes, then pivots on her heel and marches away, her glare not breaking from mine until she arrives at the bar. When the bartender leans across the polished wood to take her order, a sense of dread sneaks into my veins.

"Ah *shit*," I whisper as he passes her a full bottle of Teeling whiskey. She tosses me a dark and devious grin. My hands raise in a truce. "Okay, okay."

Sloane shakes her head and points to her ear before her expression shifts into a sarcastic pout. *Can't hear you,* she mouths.

"Feckin' pain in the arse." I'm about to stride across the dance floor and beg her not to give the bottle to Rowan when Sloane's face transforms. A slow smile plays on her lips and her eyes move to something just over my shoulder.

Tap, tap, tap.

Three gentle taps land on my shoulder and I turn just enough to find Lark's crystalline eyes latched to mine. They're still beautiful and bright. But *cutting*.

"Dance with me."

Whatever she feels about this demand she's just made, I have no feckin' clue. Her voice is nearly monotone, her expression a neutral patina. It's unnerving. This isn't the vibrant woman I kissed on Rowan's balcony, nor is it the fiery one I argued with moments later. It's not the one I've met a handful of times since, who might have been displeased to see me, but who still held warmth within her, as though she can't stop its radiant heat. This version of Lark is none of those things. This woman before me is cold, her edges jagged.

I glance toward Sloane as though she might be able to shed some light on the situation, but I don't think she's even blinked.

"Sloane will just stand there staring until you dance with me," Lark says.

"Christ. You're probably right." A heavy sigh passes my lips as I continue waiting for Sloane to at least blink, but she doesn't. "I guess we might as well."

"That's the spirit. Just the enthusiasm every woman is dying for."

I hold out my hand. "Ready, duchess?" I ask. She doesn't answer, just stares at my palm like she has to work herself up to touch me. Maybe it's my missing fingertip? Does it freak her out? Maybe she never noticed the first time we met and shook hands. She doesn't seem like the type of person that would be put off, but the longer she hesitates, the more I grow unsure. "It's not that bad," I grumble.

She cocks her head to the side. "What isn't? Dancing with someone who hates you?"

Lark watches as I swallow and try to smooth my surprise beneath an apathetic mask. "I . . . I meant the finger."

Confusion deepens the crease between Lark's brows until I change the angle of my hand so she can better see the missing end of the digit. Now she just looks . . . *insulted*. She scoffs and slides her palm onto mine, not taking her attention from my face when I curl my inked fingers around her hand. "I'm sorry for whatever happened to you," she says as we face each other, "but you really are a dumbass."

"Just the compliment every man is dying for."

With a wink that earns me an eye roll, we start dancing, just a slow sway of movement in a gentle arc across the polished parquet floor. Though we don't talk, I sense there's something Lark is eager to say. It's as though she doesn't know how to start, so she presses her lips together and hums instead. At first, it's so quiet that I'm not sure if I've imagined it, but then it grows louder. Soon she can't seem to help but sing the occasional word, her gaze trapped somewhere beyond my shoulder as she loses her focus to the melody.

"I don't hate you," I finally say in the hope the tension between us will break, my tone low and quiet, barely more than a whisper. Her eyes snap to mine and her cold edge is back.

"Sure you do. And I don't think I like you either."

"Would you really give a shit if I did?"

"Yes, but not because I'm desperate for some dickhead guy to like me."

"Thanks."

"It's just weird. So yes, I do give a shit." There's no hint of hesitation in Lark's voice. Her honesty isn't just surprising, it's refreshing. She must notice that she's caught me off guard with her reply, because she lets her eyes rest on me for a moment before she looks away and shrugs. "Despite what you think, I'm pretty nice, most of the time. People like me. Even the ones who betray me."

"*Betray you?* That's dramatic," I scoff, though an irrational spike of anger still flares and dissolves in my chest. "They can't like you that much if they turn on you."

"I said they like me. I didn't say they respect me. There's a difference."

I turn her words over in my mind, reflecting on my interactions with people in my past and the times I've felt betrayed and disrespected. "Maybe you're on to something there, duchess. I'm not sure how many people like me, but most respect me, I think."

"Most people don't like you? What a shocking revelation."

Lark's hand leaves my shoulder and I glance down to catch her bright smile and her flicker of a wave in Sloane's direction. In just an instant, she's transformed, from cold and cutting to bright and blinding. I can actually *feel* it, her love and adoration for Sloane, like rays of sunlight that slice through a cloud. But it doesn't feel forced or disingenuous. Her warmth seems just as real as the icy unease that descends as soon as she faces away from Sloane and back to me.

"How's work? Still going swimmingly?" she asks. "Many glowing reviews?"

A mirthless chuckle escapes and I scan the patrons around us. Her words a trigger for an automatic response to check my surroundings. "It's feckin' fantastic," I deadpan. "I get all the fun jobs, thanks to a certain former client of mine."

I glance down to watch the pulse pound in Lark's neck where the skin blotches with a deep crimson flush. She glances at me but can't seem to hold my gaze. "What if I told you I could fix that?"

I bark a laugh. Glare at her. Laugh again. "*Fix it?*"

"That's right. And since your sense of intuition is about as functional as tits on a rock, I'll tell you this plan makes me fucking miserable, if that's any consolation."

"Well, that does hold a certain appeal. Do continue."

Lark chews her lip for a long moment, and I remain silent this time, determined to wait her out. "I've heard you're looking to retire from your . . . freelance . . . escapades."

"You mean my contract killer side gig and all the other bollocks that I get roped into on a regular basis for my psycho boss?"

"Yeah," Lark says after an audible swallow. "That."

"Sure, retirement would be the goal, but I don't think that's ever gonna happen."

"You're right, it won't. Not unless you have a little help."

"And you think you can help me?"

Lark's ice-blue eyes would slice into me if they could. "I'm the only person who can."

My snort becomes a barked laugh as silence rolls on between us, Lark's hard stare unblemished by my dismissive huff. "I highly doubt that, duchess. Besides, why would you want to? You don't like me, remember?"

She lifts one shoulder. "True. But I need your help as much as you need mine. And if I get it, I can make sure your boss wins the

Covaci contract back. Plus, I'll get him the Montague contract too."

My brow creases as I consume every micro-expression that flickers across Lark's face. "Your family had a contract? Never heard of it."

"The Montague side didn't. We've always handled our own shit. But things are changing." She looks up at me, then glances at something over my shoulder. When I turn to follow her line of sight, I watch Sloane gather the skirt of her wedding dress so she can sit on Rowan's lap. His arm wraps around her waist, the sleeves of his dress shirt rolled to the elbows, his recent tattoo a burst of black and color across healed scars. They whisper to each other as they pass the bottle of whiskey between them. "The Montague side of the family is going to need to outsource soon," Lark says, drawing my attention back to her. "Protection. Fixing. Cleaning. It won't be as much work as my stepdad's contract, but still enough to be of interest to your boss, I'm sure."

"What's the business? If it's drug smuggling, I won't do it."

Lark rolls her eyes. "It's not drug smuggling."

"What then, weapons? Shipping logistics? Investments?"

Lark takes a deep breath and squares her shoulders. "Muffins."

"Muffins . . . ? Your family's big bad business is feckin' *muffins*?"

Lark jabs a finger into my chest. "Do you not know the mass market food industry is full of sociopaths and murderers and dodgy-as-fuck behavior?" Lark hisses as I dissolve into laughter. "Have you never heard of the history of literally any food and beverage franchise or producer? Montague Muffins can psycho with the best of them."

"And you need contracts. For your *muffin* business."

"It's a highly competitive industry. Don't you know Bob's Banoffees? That guy's always riding my aunt's ass."

I briefly raise my hand from her waist in a gesture of surrender. "Okay, okay, I believe you. Anyone who feels the need to argue that point clearly fits the bill."

"Fine. Maybe sometimes weapons might get shipped with a batch or two, but mostly it's just about the muffins." Lark rolls her eyes and shifts her attention to the other couples on the dance floor. Her steps become smaller as she watches them, her movements stiff. Maybe it's just nerves that I sense in her. She's clearly worried about getting to the point of what she wants out of this proposed deal. But when her eyes linger on Conor and his wife, Gabriela, as they dance nearby, it isn't just anxiety that I see in Lark. It looks like loss. Like surrender. Like she's trying to wrap herself in tight armor, when all she really wants, all she really *needs*, is just a deep breath of cool air.

I know what that looks like, because I know what it *feels* like. "What is it you want from me? Because I'm not going to gnaw my leg free from one trap just to find myself caught in another."

"Spoken like a true trash panda," Lark says with a fleeting, melancholy smile. When she tugs her gaze away from Conor and Gabriela, she keeps her eyes away from mine, her face pale. "It seems as though someone is killing off my mother and stepfather's business associates. It's spilling into my extended family. And this isn't really the kind of thing where we want the police nosing around in our shit. I'm sure you can understand wanting to keep law officials away from the people you love, right?"

"Right," I reply, my voice grim. I automatically scan the room to find my brothers. "Do you have anything to go on?"

"Nothing concrete yet aside from a set schedule. The killer seems to be targeting the victims when they're alone and leaves nothing behind. But I'm hoping you'll be able to help me put the pieces together. From what I understand, that kind of thing is in your skill set." Lark nods in Rowan and Sloane's direction. "You know how to investigate crime as much as you know how to cause it. I know you've put together information for their annual game."

"I guess I shouldn't be surprised that you know about that."

"Let's just assume from now on that I know more about you than you do about me, shall we?"

Lark's snide little glare isn't just a swipe at me, it's a warning. And though I try to keep my expression neutral, we both know she's right. Ever since the night we met, I've done my best to avoid anything that has to do with her, mostly out of sheer shame and stubbornness. The consequence? Lark Montague now has the upper hand.

"So my boss gets the two contracts, you get the murderer, and I get my freedom. Everybody wins. Does that sum it up?"

Fine lines crinkle at the corners of her eyes as Lark's face scrunches in a cringe. "Almost."

"What do you mean, *almost*?"

"There's a slight catch."

"Can't wait to hear this."

"We need to get married."

"*Bollocks.*" I snort a laugh, but nothing in Lark's expression changes. I laugh again and it's a derisive, mirthless sound, but she doesn't flinch. "Oh my feckin' Christ, you're bloody serious."

"Sadly."

"Why . . . ? Why the hell would we need to do that?"

"Because it's the only way I can guarantee your safety. My family sees you as a likely suspect."

"*Me.*"

"Disgruntled assassin with the means to exact precise revenge on the people who fucked up his contract killer gig? Kinda fits the bill, don't you think?"

I see what she means but I don't want to give it to her. "No," I say.

Lark sighs, exasperated. "Does it even matter if it's not you? You're a strong contender as a potential threat, so to them it's better just to put you down and see if that solves the problem. And me vouching for you won't fix it. My parents won't care if they think we're friends. They won't care if I tell them I hired you myself. And they won't care if we're just dating. But marriage . . . ?" Lark pauses. Her blue eyes glisten but she quickly looks away. "Marriage is different. It's a vow they both take very seriously, and they won't fuck with it if they believe it's what I really want. They wouldn't risk hurting me that way. Especially my stepdad. He's kind of old school like that when it comes to the people he cherishes."

I scoff and roll my eyes, trying to hide the growing sense of dread I feel. "This wouldn't be the first time I've had a target on my back. I can ride this out on my own. Sorry about the deaths and all, but I'm sure you'll be just fine." Though I say those words out loud, I immediately want to cram them back in my salty feckin' mouth. I resolve to look into the situation of the murders in Lark's inner circle without the additional burden of having her around.

"Right. I feel your concern for my well-being in my very soul. But since you're clearly not motivated by my health and happiness, which tracks, you should know that you and I aren't the only ones on the line." Lark's determination is a fortress when she nods toward Rowan and Sloane, and I can only break against her like a wave. "They know enough about your brother to think he's a risk. And they don't suffer risks, they mitigate them. To my family, it's best to put down all the strays."

It takes a moment for me to realize that we've stopped moving, or that I've stopped breathing. That other couples pass us. That the song has changed. We're suspended in time, and all I see are the variegated blues in Lark's eyes anchoring me in place.

Lark's hand slips from mine. My heartbeat thumps in my ears and dampens every other sound but her voice when she says, "Without me, Lachlan Kane, you're going to die. And I can't guarantee the reckoning will stop at you."

And then she backs away, just out of reach.

A round of hoots and applause shocks me out of my stupor as Rowan takes the small stage next to the DJ, microphone in one hand, whiskey in the other. He tilts his bottle in my direction and winks as he clears his throat and belts out the first lines to "The Rocky Road to Dublin."

"Let me know if we have a deal by the end of the night," Lark says, her voice grave as it rises above the off-key lyrics that leak from the speakers. "We don't have much time."

Lark plasters on a smile and turns away from me to join the crowd in front of Rowan. He beams as she cheers louder than anyone else and sings along.

One two three four five
Hunt the Hare and turn her down the rocky road
All the way to Dublin.

JUSTICE

Lark

"This is probably one of the worst days of my life," I say as I dispense a burst of spray adhesive onto the petals of a pristine white rose.

A string of swears and pleas and panicked exhalations accompanies the song that plays in the background.

"I mean, I can't say it's *the* worst, but definitely top five for sure. Probably number three. And considering that the top two spots have involved gruesome deaths and harrowing, traumatic experiences that carved indelible marks into my very soul, that's really quite the accomplishment for a wedding day."

My captive strains against his leather bonds. His bare toes squeak along the bottom side of his plexiglass casket as a ribbon of epoxy drops onto his legs from the tap in the barrel I've rigged on a stand above him. This old factory that I've been steadily transforming into my personal music retreat, an unused space gifted to me by my stepdad, came with all kinds of gadgets that have really spoken to my crafting soul. And this project is my most ambitious yet. Poor Dad—he probably gave me this old textile factory hoping that I'd have so much fun transforming it that I'd settle into a more sedentary lifestyle. Little could he know that the space would also prove useful to ensure no one will hear Patrick O'Neill's final screams.

I glance at Patrick's sweat-streaked face. The box has nearly filled to his ears. He won't be able to hear me soon.

With a pot of gold glitter in hand, I lean over the edge of Patrick's enclosure and tap the shining flecks onto the surface of the rose, the excess falling into the glitter-infused resin next to his head. "You're married, right? Were you nervous when you got married?"

"Fuck you, you psycho bitch," he snarls before his fury transforms into frustrated sobs.

"I think it's probably normal to be nervous, right? It's a big day. Like, the *biggest*." I set the rose aside to dry and grab the next one, this time leaning over the clear casket when I spray the adhesive so droplets land on Patrick's face. "Tell me a secret, Mr. O'Neill. In fact, let's call it your opportunity for repentance," I say as I smile down at his desperation and distress. He can't seem to decide on rage or fear as my smile takes on a devious edge. "Were you nervous the first time you groomed a student?"

Patrick's lips purse and I manage to dodge the lob of spit he fires at me. It falls and lands on his own cheek with a thick plop and slides into the resin that's creeping higher with every second that passes.

"Did you see what I did there? Weddings. Groom. *Groomed*. I thought it was pretty clever for literally no sleep." I shrug and twist the flower between my fingers, the thorns sliced free. "I always wondered why you married guys aren't a little bit more careful. It makes sense for the single guys. But you're just as gullible. It only took, what? A day or two of baiting you online before you were trying to meet up?"

"What do you want from me?" he hisses.

"For you to die, obviously." I roll my eyes and spill the rest of the pot of glitter across the rose, the excess landing in a thin film that adheres to Patrick's skin. "I like to think of this as justice, but make it sparkly. Also, I need a coffee table."

"Just g-go to Target."

"But I like DIY," I reply with a shrug, setting my rose next to the others. "My fiancé—God, I hate that word—is moving in tomorrow and I wanted a bold statement piece so he doesn't think he can just bring in some shitty bachelor pad furniture. And since I like to take a little trophy from every pedo shitbag I delete from this beautiful world, I figured two birds, one stone, you know? I need a coffee table, you're a pedo shitbag—it's kismet."

"You have the wrong m-man," Patrick begs as I open a new pot of glitter and start on a fresh rose.

"No, I don't."

"I never meant to hurt anyone."

"Yes, you did."

"If you let me go, I swear I'll never go near another school again."

"Well, at least we can agree on your last point. You'll definitely never go near another school again." With a faint, menacing smile, I lean into his enclosure and blow across the surface of the rose, dispensing a fine cloud of sparkling dust across his skin.

"You'll never lure another student. Never touch another child. Never steal another future. Never break another soul." I hold Patrick's eyes for a long moment, the gray-blue shade of his irises contrasting with the network of tiny red blood vessels that lace through the whites of his eyes. Not for the first time, I wish Sloane knew about this side of me. Her talent for removing her victims' eyes is maybe a bit gross for my tastes, but there are some people who simply deserve to be relieved of their body parts, and this Patrick O'Neill is certainly a good candidate.

But as tempting as it might be to clue Sloane in on my hobby, one that was in fact inspired by her, it would also be unsafe. So I tell myself the same mantra I always repeat when the urge to confess rises:

The more Sloane knows, the more danger she'll be in.

I take a deep inhalation of a fresh rose and the petals whisper against my skin, the scent almost strong enough to mask the fumes from the resin. For a little while, I just watch the epoxy ripple from the tap. A sense of calm washes over me, despite Patrick's endless swears and begging. There's a rightness to the sweet fragrance of the rose and the shimmer of gold. There's beauty in terror when it sparks to life in dark souls.

My watch alarm goes off, cutting through my momentary peace. Eleven in the morning. Sloane will be ready to pick me up by one, and the wedding is at two sharp. And I'm truly hoping that this adventure in table-making will help calm me down, not just for my upcoming nuptials, but for facing Sloane. It kind of went down like a lead balloon when I told her two days after her own wedding that I was going to marry Lachlan Kane, and she's been hounding me for details in the few days since then, details

I've avoided sharing. But I guess it's time to face the music, as they say.

"Well, Patrick, this has been fun and all," I say as I spray the final rose and dust it with glitter to set it on the table with my other flowers that I'll tie in a ribbon, "but I really have to get going. Big day and all. I want to look my best, you know? These overalls probably won't cut it, even though I am marrying a certifiable asshat."

Patrick's never-ending pleas grow louder as I stand and dust off my overalls. "You can't do this," he says as he struggles to keep his head lifted above the viscous liquid that fills his box.

I smile as I turn the tap fully open on the barrel of epoxy and change songs on my playlist. The heavy beat pumps through the speakers mounted on the walls. "I *can* do this, actually," I reply as I walk back toward Patrick's head and grasp the metal handle of the cart his casket rests on. "And I will."

Hands gripped around the cold steel, I push the cart forward. The caster wheels squeak as they spin on the polished concrete.

"P-please, I'm b-begging you," Patrick sobs. His eyes bounce between me and the golden liquid that sloshes around his body as I roll him closer to the tap. It coats his legs. His hips. His lower abdomen. Veins protrude beneath the pale, sweat-slicked skin of his temples as we roll closer, inch by inch. "I'll g-give you anything you w-want. *Anything.*"

"Mr. O'Neill. You probably should have figured it out by now." I push the cart until the tap of the suspended barrel hovers just over the notch of his throat. His hammering pulse disappears beneath shimmering waves of resin. "I want things that no man can simply *provide.*"

With a final shove, the cart stops where his mouth lines up with the viscous stream. Patrick squeezes his eyes shut. Thrashes his head side to side. Sputters and spits, shooting spatters of resin against the plexiglass. He begs for help, for a God who will not answer.

"Don't bother asking Him for help," I say as I pull on my long leather work gloves and slip my hands into the pool. Palms pressed against his temples, I hold his head steady beneath the stream. "He never answered me either."

Patrick fights and shakes and holds his breath until he can't anymore. Air escapes his lungs in a rush. There's only liquid waiting to fill his mouth on the next inhale.

I know he can't hear me beneath the resin as I list the names of every girl I know he harmed. But I say them out loud anyway. I name every child he made into a survivor as his lungs seize in a rhythmic pulse. And when his body goes still, I pull my hands from beautiful swirls of gold and watch until his face and body disappear beneath the shimmering surface.

With a final, satisfied look at the golden block, I turn up the heaters and fans to help cure the epoxy, pick up my flowers, and leave.

My dog rises from his favorite spot on the floor of the craft room and follows in my wake as I walk down the corridor, heading to the main floor of what was once a textile factory. I pass the old steel elevator that still works but freaks me the fuck out and head toward the metal staircase on the far wall instead, taking the steps by twos until I reach my apartment, with exposed brick, tall windows, and eclectic decorations—photos and sculptures and wall hangings and posters—mostly things I've collected from the times I've spent performing on the road.

♪

There might even be a few souvenirs of sparkly justice, and though they're mostly hidden from view, their presence still makes this space feel like home.

I thought my furniture project downstairs would make me feel better about what's to come, and though it helped, the effect is more temporary than I expected. The nerves creep back in with every second that passes, like an infectious melody that takes over my thoughts note by note until it's all I can hear. I turn up the volume on my music in the hope it will drown the anxiety. I dance as I roll my hair in curlers and sing as I do my makeup. I even pick up my guitar and play along with a few songs before I get dressed in an ivory satin pantsuit with a strapless lace corset. When I'm finished and every detail is in place, I take a moment to twist side to side in the floor-length mirror in my bedroom. It probably comes as no surprise to say I always thought I'd have a big white wedding. A princess dress and a flowing veil. Five hundred guests and fireworks and a fairy tale.

But that's not my reality and I'm not upset about it. Am I still nervous? Sure. But I also feel fierce. Destined to defy expectations.

By the time Sloane texts that she's arrived, I'm as ready as I'll ever be.

And I know the instant I slip into her car that I'm doing the right thing.

"What the fuck is going on?" Sloane asks, worry etched in her features, the green hues of her hazel eyes more vibrant against the bloodshot evidence of the worried tears she must have shed during her drive here. "I thought you hated Lachlan. You can't be serious about marrying him."

"What gave you the impression I hate him?"

"You saying, 'Lachlan is a dickhead, I really hate that guy,' might be one reason."

I let out an unsteady laugh as I try not to fidget with the bouquet clutched in my iron grip. "Well, he can kind of be a dickhead, sure, but *hate* might be a bit strong."

Sloane turns toward me, the car still idling in park. "Tell me what the fuck is going on, Lark. You're my best friend. You're the most impetuous person I know, but *this*? A random-as-fuck wedding to Lachlan Kane when you've spoken to each other what, like, five times? And all those times have been some kind of miserable? There has to be a reason for this sudden one-eighty." She shakes her head as fresh tears well at her lash line. Her voice is barely more than a strained squeak when she says, "The math. It ain't mathin'."

I grab Sloane's hand across the center console and stare into her eyes. It takes more force than it should to remain steadfast, to not cave to the temptation of saying *to hell with this insane plan* before I run away to fuck-knows-where. "I promise you, sweetie, everything will be okay."

"But—"

"I love you," I whisper as I lay a hand to the side of Sloane's face. There's no measure of relief in her expression when I give her a reassuring smile, one that feels discordant with the sting in my nose and the vise that grips my heart. "You don't need to look after me this time, Sloane. I really just need you to trust me, no questions asked. I've got this."

It takes a long moment, but Sloane finally reins in her tears. "Okay," she says. "But if he hurts you, I swear to God I will take his fucking eyes."

"Sounds good to me."

"Slowly. With a rusty spoon. Like, a full-on gouging. Rough edges. Amateur-looking shit. Really shoddy work."

"Okay. Well, you could leave me one eye."

"I'm serious, Lark."

"Yeah, me too. I think I'd probably enjoy having you teach me your tricks," I say with a grin.

After a final, scrutinous look, Sloane shifts into drive and we pull away, headed for downtown Boston.

I connect my playlist to Sloane's car on our ride to the courthouse for this auspicious day. "Chapel of Love" by the Dixie Cups. "Marry You" by Bruno Mars. It's got a fun vibe that I'm hoping will buoy my mood. "Single Ladies" by Beyoncé, because *obviously*. Though I sing and have a smile ready whenever she glances my way, Sloane is having none of it.

"What about your mom and Damian?" she asks, turning the music down as we crawl closer to Boston City Hall through the midday traffic.

My heart squeezes. "What about them?"

"Won't they be upset?"

"Maybe," I reply, picking at the hem of my white satin jacket. My gaze shifts out the window and I squint at the passing buildings. "I think they've got plenty to worry about with Ethel though."

"Not doing so well?" Sloane asks, and I shake my head. When I don't look her way, she pulls my hand from my lap and holds it on the center console. "I'm sorry, Lark."

"Thank you." My brittle smile does little to reassure Sloane, judging by the way her brow furrows when she glances my way.

"Maybe this will give them something to focus on instead of Auntie Ethel."

Sloane's face scrunches. "You think your elopement to a man they've never met will help with that?"

"Sure," I say with a shrug. "Entertainment, you know? Something to take their minds off . . . stuff."

"What kinds of stuff?"

"Like, Ethel dying stuff."

"That's not what you meant."

"What else would I mean?"

Sloane sighs and her grip tightens on the steering wheel, her knuckles white across the bone. "Something such as, I don't know, the real reason behind what is clearly a sham marriage to a man you loathe?"

"Sloane, I thought we just agreed. I've got this."

"We didn't agree to shit. You just told me not to worry, which makes me exponentially more worried."

"More worried than if I'd suddenly said, 'Sloaney, I just realized I'm madly in love with Lachlan Kane and we're going to get hitched'?"

Sloane blinks. Tilts her head. Calculates. "No. All options are shit."

"Even the one where we're officially sisters-in-law?"

"Okay, that is the upside. But the *only* one."

"Well, just take that for the ray of sunshine that it is." I pat Sloane's leg and she glares at me, coaxing out the first genuine smile I think I've made in days. I love poking Sloane's lethal side, especially knowing I have complete immunity from her retribution. "Honestly though, I'm not sure how I'm going to tell them

all yet. Was thinking I might just wing it. Goes with the elopement theme."

"I'm shocked. Truly."

"Maybe I'll just send a pic to Ava. No context, just me and
Lachlan and the officiant. Then turn off my phone."

"Didn't you tell me once that Ethel was the only person who
loved to poke your sister more than you?"

"Yeah . . ." I say, tilting my head to the side. "Why?"

"Well, I think sweet ol' Ethel has it covered today."

Sloane nods toward the sidewalk. I follow her line of sight and
my gaze lands on a familiar elderly woman, her hair curled in a
halo of white waves, her floral dress billowing beneath a glossy
black fur coat even though it's a mild October day, an ebony cane
clutched in her hand.

Her other arm is looped with that of none other than Lachlan
fucking Kane.

"How in the ever-loving fuck . . ." I hiss.

"Looks like she enjoys poking you, too," Sloane says, giving my
shoulder a playful nudge.

We slide into a parking spot right next to where they're walking, which would probably have gone unnoticed if Sloane didn't
beep-beep them a joyful little honk. My aunt grins at me from the
other side of the tinted glass.

"I hate you both," I whisper through a fake smile before my
gaze shifts to Lachlan. "But I hate him most of all."

Ink climbs Lachlan's skin from beneath the collar of his black
suit. His hair is slicked back, a cocky smirk lifting one edge of his
lips when his eyes connect to mine. He pats my aunt's gloved hand
as though proving a point, and my eyes narrow to thin slits.

"Really? You hate him? Because you look like you want to climb him like a tree."

I whip around to face Sloane. "I do not."

"You're right. You don't. You look like you want to decapitate him and parade around town with his head on a pike." Sloane leans closer as my mouth drops open and my flesh flames crimson. "Piece of advice, Lark. If your intention is to convince anyone that this isn't just some sham marriage, you should probably at least pretend to want to fuck your husband on your wedding day."

"Shit. You're probably right." My shoulders lift and drop with a heavy sigh. "He does look pretty good. I just have to pretend he's not just a sexy skin suit over a completely shitbag interior."

"That's the spirit," Sloane deadpans.

I give her a weak smile and turn my attention back out the window where my aunt and Lachlan linger on the sidewalk. Rowan waves at them, walking faster to catch up, but his attempt at enthusiasm does little to disguise his worry. He probably thinks this is just as batshit crazy as everyone else does, myself included. Well, everyone except Ethel, who looks like she's having the time of her life.

I lower the tinted window just enough to be heard clearly through the crack. "Hi, Auntie."

Ethel's eyes glimmer despite their cataract haze. "Hello, dear. Lovely day for a wedding."

"Sure."

I shift my attention to Rowan and give him a wave. Then I look to Lachlan, whose grin has become diabolical. For someone who probably hates this idea as much as I do, he certainly looks like he's enjoying himself nearly as much as my aunt.

Not to be outdone, I put on my most vibrant smile. "Darling."

Lachlan's smirk brightens. "Duchess."

"It's bad luck to see the bride before the wedding ceremony."

"Is it? Huh." Lachlan runs a hand over his freshly shaved face, rings glinting in the October sun. "You mean it can get worse?"

"In the most loving way possible, fuck off," I say, flashing Lachlan a sardonic grin as I roll up the tinted window.

"Yeah, so . . . we might need to work on that a little bit," Sloane says, and then she pats my leg in a wordless command to stay seated. She gets out of the car and waits by my door until the others disappear around the corner. Only then does she help me out of the vehicle. But even when I'm steady on my pointed stilettos, Sloane still holds on. She gives my hand a squeeze. Offers a promise in her stern expression. "We can still turn around."

"I know," I say but I take a step forward. She gives me a resigned smile.

I hate seeing her feel this way, so worried with no way to fix it because I've kept her in the dark. I hate being the one to do this to her. I hate everything about this plan, except that it gives me my best chance to keep her safe and to figure out what the hell is happening to my family.

Never again.

I square my shoulders and grip Sloane's hand tighter. "Let's get this done. The sooner we do, the sooner we can go drinking at the Dubliner as official sisters."

"Wedding night, Lark," Sloane says as we walk hand in hand toward the city hall entrance. "You're supposed to go fuck your husband, remember? Not have two martinis and start crying on a stranger."

"I do not do that. I'm an adorable drunk."

Sloane snorts as we pass through the doors and into the lobby. Our heels clack against the floor and echo off the stark walls and vaulted ceiling. "Either adorably happy or adorably weepy. Fifty-fifty chance of happy Lark or sad Lark. One hundred percent chance of singing and tears."

"All right, *fine*, maybe a little crying happens on occasion. But I think I get a free pass this time. It is my wedding day. Tears are warranted."

I meet Sloane's eyes with a cringe, and she reflects an equal amount of discomfort back to me. "I don't think you're supposed to make that face every time you say 'wedding,' or 'married,' or 'husband.' Just FYI."

"Right," I say as we enter the elevators to the city clerk office. "Smile. Pretend I want to fuck him. Got it."

"At least he looks damn good. He's kind of like a combination of *Constantine*-era Keanu with *Mad Max*–era Tom Hardy. Hot and kind of sad."

I turn and glare at Sloane. She tries not to smile but her dimple gives her away like it always does when she's up to no good. "That is the most profane thing you have ever said. I am disgusted, Sloane Sutherland."

Sloane's grin breaks free as the elevator dings and the metal door slides open. "You're only salty because you know I'm right."

When we step out onto our floor, Lachlan's at the end of the hallway, standing next to Rowan with his hands in his pockets. My aunt is seated in one of the chairs lining the wall. And though I don't admit it, Sloane called it perfectly—he is a bit Keanu-Hardy, all hot and dangerous and sad. Though Lachlan smiles at whatever my aunt is saying, there's something haunted in his eyes, something missing.

And when he turns to me, that chasm fills with fire.

I don't know what he's thinking, whether it's hatred or determination or suspicion. I can't interpret his hard, dark stare or his furrowed brow. All I know for sure is that no one has ever looked at me the way he does now.

I shove my shoulders back. Chin up. If it's butterflies in my stomach, they've come armed, because it feels like I'm being hollowed out. Scraped clean.

The crease deepens between Lachlan's brows as I draw to a halt in front of him. He takes in the details of my face, from my eyes to my lips, where his focus lingers, then the flush that heats my cheeks, then the scar at my hairline. A faint smile lifts one corner of his lips as his gaze reconnects with mine. "Thought we weren't supposed to see each other before the ceremony, duchess."

"That's it? That's all you've got?" I roll my eyes and take a step forward to move around him and greet my aunt, but Lachlan catches my wrist. His expression has turned serious, any trace of amusement burned away.

"You look beautiful," he whispers, his attention fixed to my lips. It resurrects a memory I keep trying to bury, but one that claws its way into the light more often than I wish it would. I'd like to say this is the first time I've thought about our kiss on Rowan's balcony, but that would be a complete lie.

I swallow the phantom taste of whiskey on my tongue as I pat Lachlan on the chest. "Better not say that too loud. Someone might hear you. Wouldn't want them to get the wrong impression and think you're actually pleasant."

"Don't worry, we know he's not," Rowan pipes up from behind Lachlan's shoulder, which earns him a sharp kick to the shin from his older brother. Rowan winces and walks it off in a circle that ends at Sloane's side. "Looking great, Lark."

"Thanks."

"Yes, you look so lovely, dear," my aunt says, and Lachlan finally breaks his gaze away from my face to turn and help her up from the chair. When she's steady on her feet, she extends an antique red velvet jewelry box in my direction. "Here, I want you to have this. Consider it your something old."

I take the box from her with a tentative hand, casting a glance toward Sloane, who lifts a shoulder, her expression as puzzled as mine must be. I open it . . .

. . . then snap the lid shut.

"No." I thrust it in Ethel's direction as I shake my head. A fist lodges in my throat, sudden tears burning my eyes. "I can't take that."

My aunt's wrinkled hand folds over mine and pushes the box back in my direction. "Yes, you can."

"You can't give this to me."

"I can give it to whoever the hell I please."

The first tear slides down my face. "Ava should have it."

"Why?"

I try to push the box away again, but for a dying octogenarian, Ethel is pretty damn strong. She digs her fingernails into the back of my hand just enough to cause discomfort. My voice is a breathy plea when I say, "Because she's my older sister. And this would make her happy."

"But giving it to you will make *me* happy."

I glance at Lachlan, who watches us with a crease between his brows. He seems more pensive than usual. Maybe it's the suit paired with his glasses that's giving a calculating edge to his already intimidating presence. I feel like I'm being studied. Measured. Probably deemed to be falling short, because it is Lachlan Kane after all. When he catches my eye, he seems to suddenly realize his attention is too intense. He looks down to my hand and relaxes his stance, but the notch between his brows remains.

Ethel opens the box and takes out the ring. It's a huge dark yellow diamond flanked with baguette-cut white diamonds on each shoulder. "When Thomas proposed to me with this ring, it was the happiest day of my life. But I was naive, of course. I knew nothing about how to build a successful marriage. It took a while to learn that being in love is not enough. *Choosing* love is what it takes," she says as she slides the ring onto my finger. Ethel's hand folds over mine and she flicks a glance not to Lachlan, but to where Rowan and Sloane stand behind me before she leans a little closer. "You are choosing love, Lark. And I am so proud of you."

My aunt lifts her hand away and I stare down at that diamond. There are so many beautiful memories of my aunt and uncle reflected in the familiar facets that glint in the light. I press my lips tight and try to smile at Ethel through the haze of tears. It earns me a rogue lash cluster that drops onto my cheek, and after a brief but fierce embrace with my aunt, Sloane pulls me away to fix my makeup in the washroom, and we rejoin the others just as we're called into the office for the ceremony.

"You ready?" Lachlan asks when I stop in front of him as the others lead the way into the room. Hands shoved deep into his pockets, his suit perfectly pressed, that goddamn smirk—he looks so calm and collected, and I feel like such a mess beneath a forced smile.

"It was my idea, wasn't it?"

It was. It was my insane idea that I'm one hundred percent not regretting now. *Oh my God, what am I doing? I've literally lost my mind. I'm marrying Lachlan Kane, Boston's biggest asshole. This is probably crazier than blowing someone up with fireworks.*

"Sure was, duchess," Lachlan says with a fleeting grin. He leans a little closer, his voice low enough that only I can hear him when he whispers, "It's not too late to change your mind."

I allow myself just one deep breath. One moment to live on the razor edge between two futures. "I've made my choice."

With a single nod, Lachlan extends his arm and I take it, and we follow our loved ones into the room.

Rowan FaceTimes Rose and Fionn so they can watch the ceremony. We stand in front of a glass bookcase. Lachlan holds my hands. He watches me as though he expects me to ditch and run. But I don't. Maybe he thinks I'm going to cry. I don't do that either. I repeat the vows after the officiant and my voice is clear, never wavering. We slide our wedding bands onto each other's fingers, and in only a few minutes, it's over. The officiant declares us married. A union under the laws of Massachusetts. *You may kiss the bride.*

I don't know what I expected from this moment. Maybe for Lachlan to quickly press his lips to mine and stalk away. Maybe even a kiss to the cheek. Hell, I'm not even sure I expected us to get this far. But I know I didn't expect Lachlan to look so intently at me as though he's savoring the details of my face and this bittersweet moment. I didn't think I'd see longing hidden away in their dark blue depths. I never imagined he would sweep the end of my high ponytail away from my shoulder and let his fingertips graze my neck, or that he'd lean in slowly.

"*Geallaim duit a bheith i mo fhear céile dílis duit, fad a mhairimid le chéile,*" Lachlan whispers before his lips press to mine in a kiss that blankets my heart with an electric charge. Need and denial. Heartache and loss. I feel everything as his mouth slants over mine and I drown in his scent of amber and mint. He kisses me like I'm exactly what I am. His key to survival.

And I kiss him back as though I'm saying goodbye to something that was never mine in the first place. Because I'm choosing love.

Just not my own.

FRICTION

Lachlan

There's a steady tension in the air, the shearing whine of friction and an electric motor wrapped in the melody of music that echoes down the concrete corridor. Lark's voice mixes with the mayhem, a pure and precious sound, the one thread of calm within a cacophony. When I stop at the doorway, her back faces me, head bobbing in time to the song as she guides a sander across the surface of a long golden block of a coffee table on a raised cart. A huge dog rests a few paces away from her slippered feet. Its thick coat is a mix of white and dark, patches of brindle and splashes of dots, as though the universe said *fuck it* and just mixed all the options together. The beast senses me above the racket and stands, raising its bearlike head to let out a single, authoritative *woof*.

The room is plunged into sudden silence as Lark switches off the sander and music, then turns to face me.

I cross my arms and resolve to keep my eyes on Lark's face and not on the thin sliver of exposed skin I can see between the sides of her overalls and the cropped shirt that skims her ribs. "Hi."

Lark doesn't smile. If anything, she looks a bit disappointed when she lowers her mask and raises the safety glasses onto her forehead to eye me as though I've ruined her hopes by showing up at her door. "Hi." The dog rises to stand between us, its posture stiff as though the stocky legs have been cast in steel beneath the fur. If she gives the right command, I'm pretty sure Lark could ask the beast to rip my throat out and it would happily oblige. "Go lie down."

The dog gives me a dirty look and takes a step closer before it drops to the floor with a huff, its legs askew.

"What is it?" I ask, shifting my attention to Lark as the beast drills its glare into the side of my face.

"Some would call it a dog."

"What *kind* of dog."

"American Akita."

"He looks . . . broken," I say, taking in his wonky legs that seem bent at uncomfortable angles.

"He's an Akita. It's what they do."

"What's his name?"

"Bentley."

"*Bentley?*" I snort a laugh. "Let me guess, the last car you crashed before the Escalade?"

Lark glares at me then turns away, smoothing her hand across the table. "Bentley Beetham." The dog lets out a long sigh as though he's heard this explanation a thousand times before. He's clearly just as done with me as she already is. "Ornithologist. Mountaineer. He climbed Everest in 1924. But my dad was more interested in how he'd rappel down cliffs with a rope around his waist so he could photograph gannets with a camera that probably weighed half as much as he did."

"Bit of a twitcher, is he?" I ask, and when Lark casts me a sharp glance over her shoulder I smile. "Your dad. A bird watcher."

"Yeah. What was your first clue?" Larks says, her voice dripping with sarcasm.

"When do I meet him? I'll bring some binoculars and birdseed. Fionn should have some to spare."

Lark shakes her head, her eyes trained on her hand as she sweeps the dust from the table's surface. She doesn't answer at all, so I take a few steps into the room with a wide berth around the dog, absorbing the details of what seems to be her hobby space. There are unopened cans of quick-curing epoxy resin stacked beside a steel counter where tools lay next to folded fabric and boxes of hardware. Nails. Screws. Crafting wire in gold and silver and copper and pink. Paintbrushes in mason jars stained with a rainbow of dried splashes. And glitter. Pots and pots and pots of glitter, in every color glitter can possibly be made. Gold most of all.

"Big fan of sparkles?" I ask as I pick up a pot of gold flecks and twist it in the light. The glitter sticks to the walls of the jar like a threat.

"You came down here to harass me about glitter?"

"Actually, I came to talk about the plan. We have a lot to figure out. Where do you want to start?" I set the pot down and pull a worn metal stool from beneath the table. When I'm seated facing her, I undo my custom stropping belt and loop the metal ring around my middle finger to pull the strip of leather taut.

"Umm, not with getting naked, that's for sure."

"You wish, duchess," I say with a wink and a grin as I take my switchblade from my pocket and start to run the edge across the leather, sharpening the polished steel. "I mean for real. Where do you want to start? Probably best to not Blunder Barbie our way through this situation of ours, don't you think?"

Lark eyes me over her shoulder and I feel the burn of her gaze as it slides across my face, down to the ink that covers my arms, to the new wedding band on my finger and back again. "I guess you had a point about meeting my family. We'd better get that done first before they slit your throat and cremate you in an industrial batch oven."

"That . . . that escalated quickly."

Lark shrugs. "Wouldn't be the first time they tried that, according to my auntie Ethel, anyway."

"You mean the sweet old lady Ethel from yesterday? *That* Ethel?"

With a dismissive flick of her hand, Lark lowers the safety glasses onto her nose. "Yeah but like, who knows with her. I don't think the rotary batch ovens get hot enough to cremate someone. But they'd do a pretty good job at the killing part." Lark shoots me a bright, untroubled grin before she pulls the mask over her nose and turns on the sander to scour the surface close to one end of the table. "We should go over to my parents' place on Sunday though," she says over the whine of the sander. "Family brunch, rain or shine."

"Nothing like diving into the deep end. Maybe we should practice before then? You know, to be convincing and shit?"

"If you mean, 'maybe we should have sex,' you can fuck right off."

I snort, though the image of my tattooed hands on her soft thighs unexpectedly bursts through my mind. "I mean, maybe we should try pretending we can stand each other in a public setting. I like not dying."

"You're not the one whose family is being actively killed off," Lark says. A spike of protective rage instantly replaces the desire I just felt. "So yeah, I also don't think it's wise to leave it longer than we have to. For my sake or for yours."

"Right. The batch oven."

"Exactly." Lark glances over her shoulder at me as she continues swirling the sander across the table. Her gaze lingers on me for a long moment and I should probably mention something about how she's about to make the table surface uneven, but it feels like the words have slipped right off my tongue. "We'll need to be convincing with my family," she says before I can cobble a sentence together. "Do you think you're capable of that?"

One corner of my mouth turns up in a cocky grin. "Are you?"

Lark rolls her eyes. My smile spreads. Something about getting under her skin is addictive. Every time I do, it feels like I've sneaked beneath her defenses to run amok in a place most people never even see.

But as I've quickly learned, she's never one to be outdone. "Bitch, *please*. I've had years of practice," she says.

My laugh seems to startle her. The sander growls against the table to accompany the lethal look she gives me.

"I can't wait to see how quickly this whole thing will be feckin' banjaxed."

"I'm guessing 'banjaxed' is bad?" she asks, and my brows raise in affirmation. "Well then, if it all goes tits up, it won't be because *I'm* the one who couldn't pull it off. And I can guarantee it won't be me in the batch oven. So I guess you'd better not fuck it up."

Lark gives me a saccharine smile beneath her mask, one I can see in her eyes, the way they narrow and crinkle at the corners. I reply with a dark smirk of my own. If she thinks I can't play this game with her folks, she's wrong. I'll make this the best goddamn parental first meeting she's ever had, so good that even she'll think she's fallen in love with me.

. . . Probably.

Fuck.

Lark pulls me out of my spiraling doubts when she says, "What about your boss? I'm assuming we'll need to meet him too."

All that amusement I felt while teasing her only moments ago snuffs out as though she just flipped a feckin' switch. The thought of taking Lark to meet Leander has slithered around in my mind since Sloane and Rowan's wedding. It's swum in the murk of all the other worries that came along with this insane plan, but this is the first time it's landed a bite.

"Yes," I reply, my grip on the blade handle so tight that my hand aches. "He doesn't expect to see an actual romance—"

"Thank God."

"—but he will want business assurances. Likely a financial commitment."

Lark gives me a single sharp nod. Her gaze doesn't waver from mine. "Give me the paperwork. I'll get it done."

"Leander Mayes is seriously fucked up, Lark. Even if he wants something from you, you can't count yourself as safe, yeah?"

"I'll be fine," she says, her eyes narrowing behind the safety glasses. "I said I'll get it done, and I will."

Though I hate to admit it, I admire her determination. Lark doesn't falter, even when I expect her to. But I don't know why I keep thinking she'll break apart when she never has, not once since the first time I met her. She could have cowered from me that night, but instead she got all up in my face with her Budget Batman shite. I trapped her in my trunk and she feckin' escaped. The moment I realized she was gone, I double-backed and zig-zagged the country roads, searching for her until dawn. Every time I've argued with her since then, she's either hit back just as hard or let my barbs slide over her shoulders like they were noth-ing more than silk.

"All right, duchess. Once you sign your soul to the devil, we'll use Leviathan resources to track down this killer of yours. We'd better get on with meeting Leander as soon as we can after your family. He travels a lot, so I'll get the details of what he wants and when he'll be around so that you can have it ready in advance."

Lark nods before she pulls her attention away from me. The moment she looks down at the table, she jolts as though shocked, her gasp audible despite the sound of the machine.

I've taken two hurried steps toward her before I even realize what I'm doing, my blade forgotten on the floor and the belt tap-ping against my thigh. I'm nearly at her side when that giant dog jumps to his feet, again putting his body between us.

"Are you okay?" I ask as she switches the sander off. Lark has the machine still clutched in one hand as she slaps the other down on the table, her gaze caught on the surface. She lets go of the sander to pull her safety glasses and mask off, but she doesn't look my way. "Did you hurt yourself?"

"No. Nope. Totally fine."

She doesn't sound fine at all. "You sure about that, duchess?"

"Very sure."

"Something wrong with the sander? I can have a look." I take a few slow, careful steps around Bentley, but Lark tries to wave me off. "I'm pretty good with taking things like that apart, I can probably fix it—"

"*No.* I'm good. I just . . ." Lark's entire body is tense, from the palm she presses her weight into, to her tight shoulders, to her lips that are set in a grim line that traps whatever words she was about to say.

"You just . . . ?"

"I just realized I should put a star right here." Lark nods down to her hand where it's splayed across the scoured epoxy, but she doesn't lift it away, not even when I edge into her space to stop at her shoulder. "Yep. Right there. A big black glittery star."

"Okay . . . well . . . go for it."

"I will."

"Then what's stopping you?"

"I don't want to lose my place. It has to go right here. Yep. This exact spot. I can feel it." A grimace flickers across her face before it transforms into a smile that's both pained and a bit . . . deranged. "There's a star-shaped cake tin in the kitchen, second cupboard to the left of the stove. Can you please go grab it for me?"

"You have a cake tin shaped like a giant star? Why does that not surprise me."

"Just please go and get it, would you?"

"What's that smell . . . ?"

A sudden blush ignites in Lark's cheeks. "Bentley. He farted."

I shift my attention to the dog, who looks toward Lark at the sound of his name. He lets out a disgruntled huff and glares at me as though I'm the one who passed wind. "Are you sure he's not sick or something? It smells like he ate something rancid. You should change his food."

"I'll take that under advisement, Lachlan, but for the love of all things holy, pretty please with a glittery cherry on top . . . *cake tin?*"

"All right, all right. I'm going." With an eye roll that Lark doesn't see, I turn on my heel and leave the room, but not before I give her a final glance over my shoulder. Head bent, shoulders slumped, I can almost feel her relief.

I fasten my belt as I head toward the stairs and up to the apartment, where my two suitcases lie unopened next to the door. The cake tin is exactly where she said it would be, which for some reason I find surprising. Lark seems chaotic, yet when I peek in a few cupboards, everything is highly organized. Mugs lined up by size and design. Tea organized by color. Every tin of soup or sauce in neat rows, labels facing forward.

Storing that observation away, I take the cake tin downstairs and enter the room where Lark hovers over the table as she free-pours a thin stream of black epoxy on the surface. When I pass the star to her and wait to see what she'll do next, she mutters a thank-you but doesn't take her eyes from the table surface. She sets the star down to surround the small dollop she's already poured and then speeds up the process until she's filled all the angles and points with glittering black resin.

I lean against the table edge and cross my arms. "Everything good?"

"Mmhmm. Great." Lark falls into silence, all her concentration on the edges of the metal as she checks the boundaries for any bleeding black edges. When she seems satisfied, she sets a UV lamp over the star and turns it on before wiping down the rest of the table. She hums as she works, a melody I don't recognize until she lets the lyrics start to slip out. The tone of her voice is both haunting and pure, both light and shadow, like you can take what you want from her and hear the song the way only you need to.

"You're a fan of the Smiths?" I ask. Lark's singing fades to silence, the wiping slows, and she regards me for a long moment. "'How Soon Is Now?,' right?"

"Yeah. You like them?"

One of my shoulders lifts in a shrug before I bend to retrieve my wayward knife. "I like that song. Not all their stuff."

"Same." She turns her attention back to the table but glances over her shoulder at me as though she can't keep her gaze away. "You listen to a lot of music?"

"Yeah, at the shop."

"The leather studio?"

"That's right."

"You made the wing above Sloane's booth," Lark says, and I nod. "It's beautiful."

"Thanks."

Lark watches me for a moment as though expecting me to elaborate. I could tell her how it was the largest piece I've ever made, or how I hand-tooled every feather individually before laying them all together. Or maybe she hopes I'll ask her if I've heard her sing before today, whether I know any of her music. And I have, but I don't say that either. I sure as hell don't need more connections to Lark than the legal ones that already bind us. I want them easy to snap when the time comes. So I remain silent.

I see something in her eyes. Disappointment. Maybe a little bit of hurt.

Lark goes back to her project, and before long she resumes humming as she cleans the table surface and examines the edges.

She says nothing more as she works, not until she casts a glance to the clock above the workshop sink and then her watch, her lips moving in a silent calculation. She turns the UV lamp off and sets it on her workbench before turning to face me.

"Help me get it upstairs?" Lark asks, and I eye the table before lifting my gaze to her.

"You're done?"

She nods.

"Fine," I say, "but only if we're using the elevator. I'm not carrying this feckin' thing up eight million stairs like we did with your couch when I helped you move in last year."

Though Lark rolls her eyes, she looks nervous, the most nervous I think I've seen her about anything. "Okay," is her only reply before I take position to push the cart, and she begins to steer the leading edge, Bentley following behind us down the corridor.

When we reach the century-old Otis freight elevator, the doors are already open, the floor covered with a thin film of dust. It's the first untouched area I've seen so far in this massive building. Granted, I haven't been to every hidden room or storage area, but it's hard not to notice how clean this place is despite its size and former purpose. Even the windows are perfectly streak-free, no spiderwebs wavering in the drafts from their corners, no desiccated insects gathered on their sills.

Lark moves out of the way as I push the table into the elevator. She hovers by the door when it's in position, watching from the threshold while I head to the manual controls to figure out the simple mechanism.

Lark makes no motion to enter. "You getting in or what?" I ask. Her body seems to tighten as though she's ready to take

126

off running, but she steps inside instead, the dog sticking close to her heels. Though I give her a quizzical look, she just ignores me. I wait until her gaze shifts away from me before I flick on the overhead fluorescent light and she startles. "Up or down. Seems straightforward enough. You wanna get the door there, duchess . . . ?"

Lark blinks as though coming out of a haze and looks from me to the cord that will pull the two halves of the door shut. But she doesn't move.

"Got a thing about elevators?"

"No."

"You sure about that?"

"It's just . . . I don't trust this one," she says. When she looks at me again, her face is flushed. "My stepdad said they got stuck in it the first time he came to see the place with the realtor. He got it serviced when he bought it, but that was a few years ago."

"If it hasn't seen much use, I'm sure it's fine. It's all mechanical. And we're not climbing far."

Lark still doesn't move. "I'm not afraid."

I don't try to hide my grin and I can tell it irritates her. "Right. But for argument's sake, if you are, you can just take the stairs."

"And let you ride alone with my coffee table? Fat fucking chance. It has sentimental value to me and I'm sure you'd love nothing more than to *oh-so-accidentally* bust it up."

I blink at her. "A table . . . one you just made . . . has sentimental value to you . . . ?"

"That's what I said."

"And you think I'm going to break through three feet of epoxy resin with what, my bare feckin' hands?" I slap a palm on it and

Lark looks like she's going to pass out or rip my face off, and I'm not sure which reaction brings me more glee. "Why did you make it so feckin' enormous anyway?"

Lark's eyes narrow to thin slits. "If you don't like it, you can go hang out by yourself in your room." She pulls the rope to shut the door, then folds her arms across her chest and raises one brow in a challenge. Feckin' stubborn. She has the iron will of someone used to getting their way. It stokes my urge to find something to push her with, harder and harder until she's forced to relent. In fact, I'm not sure there's much right now that would give me greater satisfaction than seeing Lark Montague concede defeat at something. *Anything.*

Shaking my head, I let out a low chuckle as I turn my attention toward the mechanism. "All right, you feckin' catastrophe. Fingers crossed, yeah?"

I shift the lever to the up position and the elevator lurches as the motor comes to life and the cables begin to pass through the sheave. It's a shaky start, but the car lifts toward the upper floor. I turn enough that I can see Lark, who looks a little more relieved now that we're moving. "See?" I say. "I told you it would be fine."

But then there's a lurch. The motor goes silent and the elevator grinds to a halt.

Lark and I stare at each other, unmoving. I can actually watch the panic creep into her body, her pulse surging in the tiny veins that swell next to her temple.

"Are we at the second floor?" she asks, and I glance around at the box we're in as though it might cough up an answer.

"Not quite."

"Then why are we stopped?"

"I assume one of the electrical wires in the motor burned out."

"I thought you said it was mechanical."

"It *is* mechanical. With an electrically powered motor." When I give her a *shit happens* shrug, Lark's eyes narrow to a slash of menace in reply. "Let's just be glad the lights are still on, shall we?"

The fluorescent bulb flickers.

My hand hovers over the switch. "For fucksakes."

"*No*, don't touch it." Lark's hands are out, her gaze darting between me and the ceiling as the bulb hums and pings with the effort to say on. Her chest rises and falls with heavy breaths. "Please . . . I don't know how to get out. I need the light—"

The utter terror in Lark's eyes claws at my heart. I take a step toward her . . .

And then we're plunged into darkness.

Lark lets out some kind of sound I've never heard a person make despite having thought I'd heard them all, something between panic and powerlessness and despair. The dog whines. There's a crash against the steel wall.

"*Lark.*"

She doesn't reply, but I hear her increasingly rapid breathing from the corner of the pitch-black box. And then I hear her whispering, though I can't make out what she says.

"Lark," I say again as I pull my phone from my pocket and turn on the flashlight. I keep it pointed to the floor and pan toward where she sits curled in the corner like someone trapped in a horror film, hands over her ears and eyes wide but unfocused. Bentley stands next to her and lets out another whine, his tongue lolling with every panting exhalation. I step around the table and the dog gives me a single woof of a warning bark. When I drop to a crouch and try to look as nonthreatening as a bloke like me can, the dog stays plastered to her side, but seems to relax a little. "I won't hurt her."

I shift my attention to Lark. She's shaking. Her brow is misted with sweat. She whispers a string of numbers. *Two twenty-four three eighteen five thirty-nine six twelve six fifty-two.* The sequence repeats twice before I manage to creep close enough without upsetting the dog that I can put a hand on her ankle.

"Lark . . ."

She still doesn't respond. A chill washes over me. I've seen this look before. It was when I dumped her in the trunk of my car the first night we met. There was a plea in her eyes despite her defiance. I'd thought it was petulance.

I was wrong. *Very fucking wrong.*

I try to ignore the feeling in my chest like I'm sinking, caught by an anchor that's pulling me to the darkest depths of the ocean. "Hey, duchess." I squeeze her ankle, just a little, my wedding band an unfamiliar point of reflection in the dark. When Lark's whispering slowly fades and her eyes focus on the patch of light on the floor, it feels like the first breath I've taken since the lights went out. "It's okay."

Lark doesn't reply, just blinks at me for a moment until something seems to settle in her thoughts and she breaks her gaze away. Her cheeks flush a deeper crimson. She draws her legs in even closer to her chest and I let her go, though I don't want to. It feels wrong, somehow. But she seems embarrassed to let me see her in distress. I shouldn't want to touch her at all, even if I think she needs it.

I clear my throat and lean back to put some space between us without really moving away. "I'm good at fixing things," I say for the second time tonight. "I can lift you out the roof hatch and then have a look at the mechanism."

Lark turns her head toward me only slightly. Her inhalations are still uneven, her tears a continuous stream that she can't seem to stop. "What about Bentley?"

"He'll be all right in here for a little while."

"How long?"

"I dunno, duchess. Maybe twenty minutes. Maybe an hour. It depends."

Lark shakes her head and wraps a shaking arm around the dog, who sinks into her side. "No. I'll stay."

"Lark—"

"Go," she says, her voice unsteady though her tone brooks no argument. She shifts enough to pull her phone from the pocket of her overalls, switching on the flashlight. "I'll be fine."

"You can call me."

"I'll call Sloane."

That sinking feeling returns to fill my chest as I watch Lark bring up her favorite contacts, where my name doesn't appear in the short list. She presses Sloane's name but it goes straight to voicemail. Without glancing up at me, she tries Rose next, who picks up on the second ring.

"Boss hostler. How's married life, pretty lady?" Rose says for a greeting.

Fresh tears still glisten on Lark's skin and her shoulders tremble, but her voice is summer sunshine when she says, "Oh you know, lots going on. How are you, what's new? Teach the good doctor any new circus tricks yet?"

Rose cackles on the other end as Lark gives me a glance that clearly says *fuck off immediately*. And I should want to leave. I should not want to linger here. Lark would rather be in this metal box alone with her fears in the dark than sharing the shadows with me. And it's best that way. For *both* of us.

But when I back away from her pool of light, it feels like the wrong thing to do.

In the time it takes me to hop onto the table and open the roof hatch, I never hear a complaint from Lark, only her questions to Rose, anything to keep her friend talking or make her laugh. Their voices follow me as I force open the door to the second floor, which is not much of a reach from the roof of the elevator. I hop out to Lark's open-plan living and dining area and head back down to the first floor, and with a little scavenging of tools from her craft room, I manage to fix the faulty electrical connection within the hour.

Lark looks as though she hasn't slept for days when the elevator finally opens where it was supposed to. I roll the coffee table into place in the living room and we work together to get it just where she wants it. Lark stands back to look at her work for a long moment, her expression unreadable.

"It looks good," I say. "Like it's deserving of sentimental value despite being brand spankin' new."

Lark doesn't rise to my teasing, nor does she hit back. She only gives me a faint nod.

I face her and suck in a breath. "Lark, I—"

"No." She turns to me, her bright blue eyes are pink-rimmed from tears. "I'm done for today. Thank you for your help."

I want to say more. I want her to talk to me. I want to listen. But there's no give in her expression.

It's for the best . . .

I give her a nod and let her show me to the guest room. She takes Bentley out for his final walk of the night as I unpack my bags. I don't see her when she comes back into the apartment, I only hear her enter the primary bedroom with the dog in her wake. Though I cook enough for two and text her when it's ready, she doesn't appear for dinner. If it wasn't for the quiet music that slips from the crack beneath her door, I'd be convinced that I'm alone. Even the gentle melodies fade away before midnight, and I go to sleep wishing I'd said more than I did.

I wake from a nightmare shortly after three in the morning and head to the kitchen for a fresh glass for water. The last thing I expect to see is Lark sitting curled in a round chair by the windows, a guitar nestled in her lap and headphones on her ears, papers spread before her and a pen discarded on the pages.

She doesn't see me. But I see her clearly. Puffy eyes. Blotchy skin. Swollen lips. The sheen of tears on her cheeks, as though they haven't stopped. She's stripped down to her raw edges, to the bloody knuckles from battling with life. I've lost skin in this fight to survive too, and though I've tried to cover the physical marks with ink, the ones in my memory never seem to heal. Sometimes old scars still ache, an echo of sharp moments.

Have I wounded her? I know I have. But maybe not with a fresh, shallow strike that would soon be forgotten. No, I think I sliced through thin tissue that first night we met. And there is something still bleeding deep beneath the wound.

"Two twenty-four three eighteen," she sings, her gaze disconnected from the world around her as she stares out the window. *"Five thirty-nine six twelve six fifty-two . . ."*

I turn and leave before she can see me, feeling like I've finally settled at the bottom of the sea.

BANJAXED

Lachlan

I need to ask you a question.

SLOANE: Go for it.

Lark, her thing about dark
enclosed spaces, what's up
with that?

SLOANE: Why don't you ask her yourself?
She's your wife in this weird ass marriage
that neither of you will tell me about, so if
you want to play the part of husband, how
about this novel idea: TALK TO HER.

I don't think she'll tell me. Was
hoping you could give me some
insight . . . ?

Sloane's reply takes a moment to come through, which I soon realize is because she spends that brief time yelling at Rowan about why I'm such a dickhead.

> **SLOANE:** You think I'm just going to cough up my best friend's history on a platter for you? Lachlan Kane, be so fucking for real right now.

> **ROWAN:** Hey dickhead. My wife wants to know why you're such a dickhead.

> **ROWAN:** Should I give her the long version or the short version?

> **SLOANE:** Do you honestly think I would tell you that? Seriously? GO FUCK YOURSELF.

> **ROWAN:** Secure your eyeballs. Repeat. Secure your eyeballs.

> **SLOANE:** If you're having trouble with your "marriage" and talking to your "wife," why don't you crack a fucking book. A ROMANCE book, not more of your "history of leather" bullshit. It's literally an instruction manual for dumbasses like you.

| **SLOANE:** And get fucked.

| **SLOANE:** METAPHORICALLY

| **ROWAN:** If you can find insurance for
eyeball enucleation, now would be a
good time . . .

"Feckin' *bollocks*." I drop my phone on my desk and rest my pounding forehead on my arms as I try to work out what the fuck I'm supposed to do.

After that first night we met, I tried to push away every thought of Lark. I never looked into her. Never hunted her down. Though I spent until dawn searching for her once I realized she'd escaped from my car, shame had stopped me from trying to find her beyond that day. I didn't even realize she was related to Damian Covaci until Leander ripped a strip off me for ruining the contract. I didn't want to care about Lark Montague. But every moment that passes seems to upend my ideas of the woman I thought I married. And lately, it feels like I haven't looked into Lark because I'm afraid of what I'll find.

But I think she needs help. It feels like I'm the only one who can see it. And I'm at a total feckin' loss at how to *do* it.

Since I moved in two nights ago, Lark has barely slept. The first night when I woke in the morning, she was still in that chair that faces the windows, headphones on, guitar in her grip. She was asleep, but it seemed restless. When I tried to move the guitar off her lap, she woke with a vicious glare, then padded off to her room without a single word. Last night, she didn't appear in the living room, but the light stayed on under her door. Sometimes her voice followed it as she sang or hummed. She's spent the last two days running around, only settling long enough to play a few minutes of a movie, something with Keanu Reeves, but she turned it off with a muttered "*Constantine*" when I asked the name of it. Otherwise, she's either heading to Shoreview, where her aunt has just been moved and where she'll start a new job as a music therapist next week, or taking her dog out, or cleaning with a precision that borders on obsession, or rehearsing with a band she's supporting. I can already tell she's exhausted.

I might not know her well, but she doesn't seem the same since that experience in the elevator. And I need to know why.

Also, I am now unequivocally sure that I am an even bigger dickhead than I ever imagined.

The image of Lark sitting in the trunk of my car replays on a vivid loop in my mind. There was fear in her eyes. Determination too. Though they welled with tears, she blinked them away. She *begged*.

And I pushed her down and closed the lid.

"*Feckin' eejit*," I mutter, barely aware that I've said it out loud.

If Lark and I are going to figure out what the hell is going on and get what we both want out of this marriage, we're going to have to work together. And we can't do that if she's falling apart at the seams. If I want to figure Lark out, I'm going to have to do it through her, not around her. And I'm way out of my feckin' depth.

I've done a lot of dodgy shit in my life. Life has worn down most of my emotions to little more than smooth and polished stone. But every once in a while, I find a long-neglected feeling that cuts like broken glass. Such as, for example, the intense discomfort of the realization that I need to ask my sister-in-law for help.

I pick up my phone and start a new text to Sloane.

> Eyeball spider lady, I humbly request a truce.

Didn't I just tell you to pick up a fucking book?

> Christ Jesus. You are so acerbic.

Thank you. What the fuck do you want now?

> Are you and Rowan free for lunch today at B&B? I want to invite Lark, but maybe she'll be more comfortable if you're there.

There's a long pause before the three dots start dancing on my screen.

OMFG I KNEW THERE WAS A GOOEY CENTER IN THERE SOMEWHERE

YES WE WILL BE THERE. Rowan is off at 2pm, let me know if that works.

> You're still an asshat though. Just so
> we're clear.

I try not to smile, but it happens anyway.

I need a few deep breaths before I manage to type out my next message. It takes me a surprisingly long time to come up with:

> Hey.

At first I think she's not going to respond, and I'm almost about to tap out a second message when Lark's reply comes through.

> What's wrong?

My brows feel too tight as I stare down at the phone in my hands.

> Nothing . . . I just wanted to see
> if you'd like to come for lunch at
> B&B at 2pm? Rowan and Sloane
> will be there.

> I can give you a lift. Or we could
> meet there if you want. You have
> a break then, yeah?

The dots of Lark's reply flicker at the bottom of my screen. They stop. They start again. They stop another time and finally, her message comes through.

> Okay. I'll meet you there.

My heart claws its way up my chest, resurrected from where it seems to have fallen into my guts.

> Okay.

I stare at my screen even after it goes black. Though my pulse starts to slow to a normal rhythm, the empty space between each beat still aches with a feeling I can't quite name. A disquiet that surges in my blood as I count down the hours between now and when I'll see her next.

My morning at the shop passes slowly. I leave early for the restaurant, and when I walk through the door, she's already sitting at the booth with my brother and sister-in-law. The wary smile she casts my way sparks an unexpected hope in my chest, one I didn't ask for. Yet somehow, it's not enough.

Lark is effervescent with Rowan and Sloane, and if I didn't know otherwise, I'd think she was as well-rested and happy as my brother and his wife. She laughs and teases and smacks a gold star sticker on Sloane's dimple when she makes a joke I don't get about cookies-and-cream ice cream that drains the color from Rowan's face. And maybe they're too busy trying to figure out the status of our "weird ass marriage," with their occasional prying question or scrutinous look. But I can see what they don't notice. The way Lark's smile falters when she thinks no one is watching. The way she presses two fingers to her temple before she digs an ibuprofen out of her giant bag. The yawn she hides in a fist. Lark is exhausted, operating on caffeine and sheer determination to keep her mask from slipping.

The longer it goes on, the more I regret asking her to this feckin' lunch. She could have tried to catch a kip. Maybe she could have curled up with Bentley on the couch in the sun. I just want to get her home. She won't care about trying so hard if it's just the two of us. Out in the world, it's like she needs to be everything to everyone, with nothing left for herself at the end of the day.

But it seems inescapable, even from the people who love her.

"I saw the first posters for your gig at Amigos," Sloane says, and I know by the way Lark smiles and nods that she hasn't shared what a drain it's been trying to boost up the band she's playing with. She's only mentioned the show to me in passing, as though it's no big deal, but I can see the effect it has on her when she has to rearrange her schedule to fit in everything, from social media posts to rehearsals for their upcoming gig. It's yet another favor for a friend who likely doesn't appreciate the effort she's putting in. "I'm sorry I won't be able to make it, I'll be away that week for a meeting."

"Where are you off to this time?"

"Singapore. The client is a pain in the ass, but worth it for the trip. I'm going to build in an extra day for some sightseeing."

"That's amazing, Sloaney." Though Lark's smile is genuine and warm, I still find myself shifting in my seat, eager to suggest she tag along even though I know she never would. No matter how hard I remind myself it's none of my feckin' business, and I shouldn't care, and it's better for me to just stay away, it doesn't work.

As if sensing my unease, Sloane zeroes in on me with the precision of a falcon diving for its unsuspecting prey. "You're going, right, Lachlan? I need photos. I never miss a show when we're in the same town."

Beyond the mundane scheduling conversations and minimal details, Lark and I haven't talked about the show. She hasn't invited me. I don't know if she's as uncomfortable as I am about Sloane's question, but I don't dare glance her way to find out.

My hand finds the back of my neck and I look to my brother, but he's no feckin' help, grinning at me like the bloody saboteur he is. When I put on a gruff, don't-fuck-with-me expression, his smile only grows. "I dunno. I—"

I'm cut off by the sound of a familiar voice. "Lachlan Kane."

Right when I think it can't get any worse, it feckin' does.

My eyes press closed for a heartbeat. When I open them and turn, I catch Lark's watchful and wary gaze before my attention lands on the source of the familiar voice.

"Claire."

Claire Peller looks just the same as I remember her. Hair scraped away from her face in a high ponytail. A bleached, predatory smile. The minimalist lines of a black suit. It's all a pristine veneer over a deeply hidden desire to make everything messy.

Claire grins and turns her attention to Rowan. "Hi, Rowan."

He gives her a single nod, but there's no warmth in his simple response. Claire doesn't give a shit. In fact, she feckin' loves it. She turns her gaze to Sloane and Rowan preempts whatever she's about to say when she sucks in a breath. "This is my wife, Sloane. Sloane, Claire."

"It's a pleasure," Claire says. Sloane only gives a tight smile but Claire barely notices, her focus already shifting to Lark.

"And this is Lark," I say as I bow my head in her direction. "My wife."

An incredulous laugh bursts from Claire and my blood turns to fire. She looks between us as though waiting for the punch line, one that doesn't come.

"You're *married*?"

"Yep."

"Lachlan Kane," she says and shakes her head. "I never thought I would see the day. A lot has certainly changed since that Halloween party two years ago." There's a cutting edge to Claire's voice that's meant to leave wounds. But when I meet Lark's eyes, there's only an unreadable mask watching me back. I should probably feel relieved that she seems unscathed, but part of me is a little disappointed, as much as I don't like to admit it.

"Yeah. Well, see you around," I say with finality as I turn back to my food.

"Yes, definitely," Claire says as her phone rings. "I'll stop by the shop sometime. We can catch up properly."

Before I can protest, Claire accepts the call and her heels clack across the slate floor as she leaves Butcher & Blackbird. I shake my head, focused on my food until I sense tension in the air and look up.

Lark and Sloane exchange some kind of silent conversation.

Sloane raises a single brow.

Lark's eyes narrow.

Sloane sighs and shrugs.

And then Lark is sliding off the booth. She stands and hikes her ridiculously huge bag up her shoulder.

"Well, this was fun. Gotta run," she says as she beams a smile bright as a feckin' laser at Sloane and Rowan. When it lands on me, that smile feels like it could slash my skin open. "See you at home."

And then she's striding out of Butcher & Blackbird, her energy trailing after her like a comet.

Rowan laughs and shakes his head before he takes a sip of his drink. "Unless you want to be bailing her out of jail, you'd better go get your wife."

I lean back in my seat and tap the ring on my index finger against my glass as I try not to look toward the door. My focus lands on Sloane instead, who masks her smile with a bite of food.

A sinking feeling coats my chest. "What are you on about?"

"Go get her before she knifes Claire, you *bellend*," he says.

"Nah . . . she . . ." I look toward the door and then to Sloane, her eyes full of sparks. "What . . . ?"

"Listen," she says, laying her palm flat against the table as she finally meets my eyes. That bloody dimple flashes next to her lip. It's like her bat signal for mischief. "Lark Montague might be cute as a button, all *shiny happy ra-ra cheerleader* shit, but bitch is fucking vindictive. I love her to death and beyond, but let's just say that particular unicorn doesn't shit rainbows."

I still can't reconcile her words with the woman I think I know. "*That* Lark . . . ? *Let's cover everything in sparkles and sing a song* Lark . . . ? You're telling me she has a legit spiteful streak? Like . . . she's not just a walking catastrophe but *on purpose* malicious . . . ?"

They both laugh. Fucking *laugh*.

"Lachlan," Sloane says, shaking her head, "I'm going to give you this one because you're hopeless and I pity you."

"Thanks . . ."

"Lark Montague doesn't just have a 'spiteful streak.' She takes the idea of retribution and makes it into a full-on glitter parade of vengeance."

Rowan points his fork toward her. "She rigged a glitter bomb in my car for the time I made Sloane cry and told her to go home. I spent a grand getting the car detailed and I still find glitter on a daily basis."

"When we were in boarding school, this girl named Macie Roberts called one of Lark's friends a 'skanky cum bucket.' So Lark got into Macie's room and spent an entire night writing *I'm a skanky cum bucket* in fabric paint on literally every item of clothing Macie had, even her underwear."

"Tell him about the sequins."

"Sequins?" I ask as the two snicker.

Sloane's brows hike as she pushes a bit of food around her plate. "A few years ago, Lark was living with her boyfriend at the time, a guy named Andrew. One weekend while Lark was out of town, he and their mutual friend Savannah hooked up at Lark and Andrew's apartment," she says as an irrational tidal wave of anger sweeps through me. "A couple weeks later, Lark broke into Savannah's house while she was sleeping and spelled *cheating bitch* on her face with Gorilla Glue and sequins. She stole Savannah's bottle of nail polish remover and her phone and computer so she had no choice but to go out and buy more to get the glue off. Even once the sequins were gone, you could still see the marks. It was pretty awesome."

I can't deny I kind of love the ballsiness of that plan. I almost smile, but then I catch the exchange of a dark look between Sloane and Rowan. "What is it?"

"Well . . . Lark will neither confirm nor deny her involvement, but two months later, Andrew died in a freak fireworks 'accident,'" Sloane says with air quotes.

"You think Lark . . . murdered someone . . . ? *That* Lark?"

Sloane shrugs.

"Don't know why you're still sitting here when she's probably slicing Claire's face off to make into a kite, but it's your bail money, I guess," Rowan says, and in a heartbeat I'm halfway to the door.

The sound of Rowan and Sloane's laughter follows me out to the street.

I lurch to a stop on the sidewalk, craning my neck to look past pedestrians. I listen for Lark's voice, which always carries like chimes on the wind.

Nothing.

I pivot a single spin before I follow my gut and head east.

Phone clutched so tight in my hand it might snap, I bring up Lark's number where it's saved to favorites and tap it.

Straight to voicemail.

"Feckin' banjaxed *bollocks*," I hiss, and the memory of her laugh slaps me. She would make fun of me for saying that. Tease me until I'm forced to turn away to hide the smirking grin that begs to break free every time she pushes my buttons. Then she'd fire some snarky comment at me about Budget Batman and put her walls back up, just like I try to keep mine from falling.

But this time, the problem isn't the barriers between us. It's not what will happen if we let each other in.

It's what she's letting *out*.

I take off running. *She can't be far.*

I don't know if it's instinct, or fate, or dumb feckin' luck, but I glance down an alley and catch a glimpse of her just before I speed right past it. Lark is storming down the narrow passage, her bag whacking against her round arse.

My heart rate spikes with the thrill of chasing her down. Fortunately, it's not hard to sneak up on her with the slew of expletives she mutters to herself as she stalks down the alley.

I grip Lark by the throat and break the cadence of her marching steps. Air whooshes from her lungs when I push her back against the brick wall, her eyes locked with mine, shocked and fierce.

"What the *fuck*?" Lark grips my arm and tries to pull my hand away, but I don't budge. "Let me go."

"I don't think so, duchess."

"Stop with the fucking *duchess* already."

"Stop with the chasing down random women to kill them and slice their faces off."

"Random my ass," she snarks. Lark's nose scrunches, her pulse a fierce thrum beneath my palm. "And she could live without a face."

My head tilts as I take in the details of Lark's expression, from the outrage in her narrowed eyes to the blush of her full lips to the scar at her hairline, a memento of our first meeting that carves a slice of regret into my memories whenever I look at it too closely.

"I find it interesting that your first objection is about the randomness and not the face-slicing."

"I was arguing sequentially."

"Sure you were. And what was your plan, exactly? Because something makes me think you weren't about to invite Claire over for popcorn and a Keanu movie marathon."

The glare Lark drills into my eyes is nothing short of lethal. "Do. Not. Say her name. In the same sentence. As Keanu Reeves. *Ever.*"

"You seem to be glossing over the main point of what I said."

"You have a point? I just thought you were being a bossy asshole."

I manage to repress a frustrated growl, but only barely, and Lark can tell. I'm convinced there's little more that gives Lark Montague true delight than slithering her way beneath my self-control and snapping my restraints free. "What the hell was your plan, Lark?"

"I don't know," she says with a dismissive flap of her hand. "Maybe follow her home. Break into her house—"

"Christ—"

"Rig up a few cans of spray adhesive and put a glitter bomb in her closet I guess." The devious glint in Lark's eyes becomes downright maniacal. "Can you imagine that woman with a tricked-out, sparkly wardrobe? I think that would be her personal hell."

"Actually, I can, since my brother said that you did something similar to his car recently. Seems like you have a bit of a glitter psycho streak going, duchess."

Lark glares at me.

"Okay, so I get why you would do that to Rowan. It was probably deserved, given it's my dumbass brother. But why would you give a shit about Claire?"

Lark blinks, her throat working beneath my hand as she swallows. I'm not sure if she was purely running on instinct and is now struggling to connect the dots, or if she doesn't want to tell me why she was about to hunt down a woman she's met only once.

"Spit it out, duchess." I lean in closer and try not to make it obvious when I take a deep breath of her sweet scent. My gaze drifts across her features and her breath hitches, her eyes locked to mine. "What's your issue? Just talk to me."

"Kind of hard to do with your hand around my throat."

I loosen my grip, but I'm unwilling to let go when I catch the way her eyes dart toward the end of the alley, as though she's ready to resume her hunt. "Give it a try. Somehow, I think you can manage—"

"She's the reason, right?" Lark's lash line glistens with furious tears that she blinks into submission. "That night. Halloween. You didn't want to leave a party and you had no choice because of me."

My grip on her throat relaxes as I remember that night with perfect clarity. Fionn was a feckin' mess, as much as he pretended not to be. I'd nearly convinced him to move home the month before and Claire was ruining everything. And then that call came in from Leander. I ignored his first attempt. The second too. But I picked up on his third try and he sent me to the Scituate Reservoir with my scuba gear to clean up some woman's careless accident.

Or so I thought.

"I ruined your chance," Lark whispers. "I'm the reason you left the party. And Claire is the reason you wanted to stay."

"No, duchess. *Fionn* is the reason I wanted to stay."

Lark's mouth opens on a sharp breath that's intended for words that never come. I wait in silence as she weighs her options before she lands on a single one. "What . . . ?"

It takes cobbling together every scrap of self-control to not smile at her confusion, but it fades when I lean a little closer and the heat of her body shreds other layers of my restraint. "Claire broke Fionn's heart. He was a mess at that party, it was the first time he'd seen her since they split."

"She was with Fionn . . . ?"

I nod, and Lark's cheeks flush pink. "They'd been together for a few years. They met when he was in medical school and she was doing her law degree. He'd nearly finished his residency and was ready to propose. He carried that feckin' ring around for weeks, just waiting for the right moment. When he finally got down on one knee, Claire cut him loose. It shattered my brother. It's why he moved to Nebraska, to get as far away from her as he could. I'd almost convinced him to come back, until that party ruined it all."

"But . . . the way she said—"

"Yeah. I'm sure she wanted to hook up. Of course I would never indulge Claire, but she doesn't take the rejection well. Not really her personality type."

"So . . . it wasn't because I ruined your shot with Claire . . . ?"

"No, Lark."

It takes more effort than it should not to let my thoughts run away with the meaning behind her words. I don't know why she would care about Claire. And I don't know why it suddenly matters so much to know the history there.

Lark's gaze drops to my lips and narrows as she seems to work through her thoughts. "You hate me because you think I busted your chance to bring Fionn home. You had to come for me, and you couldn't look after him."

Something uncomfortable twists in my chest, a little snake that grips my heart and squeezes. "I don't hate you. But I sure would like to talk about your plan to cut off Claire's face."

Lark rolls her eyes and smacks my arm, my grip on her throat releasing. "Right. I have to go."

In a flash of motion, she slides free between me and the wall. The space left behind is cold and lifeless. Her scent lingers, a temptation that beckons me, sweet and dark. I blink to try to clear Lark from my senses, but it's futile.

"We need to talk," I call after her as she nears the mouth of the alley.

"Hard pass," she yells back, and flips me the bird before she disappears.

I stand in the narrow passage for a long moment, watching her absence as though she'll return and fill it with revelations as I replay everything Rowan and Sloane said in the restaurant.

And then I turn in the opposite direction and head to my car to drive straight home and get my shit together. To do what I should have done months ago.

To hunt Lark Montague.

TROPHIES

Lachlan

When I enter the living space of our apartment, I stand for a long moment in the center of the room, trying to see it through a different set of eyes. Bentley watches from the couch in stark judgment of what I'm about to do.

"I don't like it either," I say to him, though he doesn't seem convinced. "But she's going to get herself into the kind of trouble I can't bail her out of if I don't find what she's hiding."

I don't even take off my jacket before I start looking. For what, I'm not sure. I just feel as though if I've been missing pieces of this woman for so long, maybe there are treasures she doesn't want anyone to find.

I open cupboards. I pull out drawers and run my fingers over their underbellies. I hunt in places I've purposely avoided the last two days out of respect for Lark's privacy. Her en suite. Her bedroom. If she believes I despise her, maybe she thinks I'd never want to see her lingerie drawer? I could easily prove her otherwise as I shift through lace and silk and thin dangling straps. My cock feckin' aches with every piece of material I touch as I picture Lark in each one. I get a little derailed by a certain deep blue corset that ignites all the fantasies of Duchess Lark that I've been trying and failing to suppress. I stare at that fabric in my hands for longer than I probably should, imagining how it might skim Lark's curves, how her skin might look covered with lace.

Though I have the urge to steal it to fuel my fantasies in the privacy of my room across the hall, I set the corset back down and press my eyes closed as I shut the drawer.

With a deep breath, I turn and head back to the living room.

"Feckin' hell," I say to the dog, who heaves a disinterested sigh. "What does she see?"

She sees the city from her round chair as she counts the hours between dusk and dawn. She sees photos of friends and family and places she's traveled. She sees the gold table she made and a macrame wall hanging of tiny stars. She sees huge movie posters printed on canvas. *The Life Aquatic. Beetlejuice. Sharknado. Constantine.*

Constantine.

I inhale a sharp breath and march over to the poster, lifting it gently from the wall. Behind it, I finally find what I was looking for. A thin sheet over a ragged hole in the drywall.

By the time Lark returns to the apartment an hour later, I've cleared out the hole and replaced the poster on the wall. But now I'm left with a small cardboard box containing far more questions than I started with. I want answers. And the only woman who can give them to me walks in with a cutting glare, suspicion a heavy note in the tense beat of quiet between us.

"Hey," I say when the silence in the room grows to the size of a black hole.

Balancing a covered tray with one hand, Lark glances up and places her bag down with the other. She says nothing, just casts me a brief, exhausted look as though she knows something is coming but is too weak to avoid the collision.

"We need to talk, Lark. Really."

She sighs and rubs her forehead with her free hand. "Lachlan, honestly, I don't want to talk about Claire right now or any of that shit. I just want to exist in a place of caffeine and butter and sugar." Lark sets a tray of muffins onto the counter and lifts the plastic lid. The scent of apple and cinnamon drifts toward me. "I volunteered to teach music lessons this afternoon and this kid Hugo literally tries to gnaw on the cello every single time. He is so fucking weird."

"This is important."

"Is it about the mystery murderer?"

"Not exactly."

"Then it's not more important than the caffeine I need to survive Hugo's mouth-splinter fixation."

"It's about *you*."

Lark glances at me, wariness filtering into her eyes. "Since that is your least favorite topic and I've made it a personal life goal to cause you the most misery humanly possible," she says as she takes a little bow and gracefully sweeps her hand before her, "please, do continue."

Normally, I would reply with a diabolical grin. Maybe a jab or two to rile her up. But this time, my stomach flips uncomfortably as I reach into the cardboard box tucked beneath my arm to pull out the first item in question.

"What's this?" I ask as I hold up a flat disc of fabric.

The flash of shock in her expression snuffs out as quickly as it appears. She clears her throat. "It appears to be a coaster."

"Not quite," I reply as I take a step closer. "It's a coaster made from an extra-thick, aftermarket, corded boot lace. One with a suspicious stain on the fibers."

Lark huffs a dismissive laugh, but there's a spark of trepidation in her gaze when it flicks from the string in my hand to my face. "An aftermarket boot lace? Did it come with a spoiler and muffler package?" She rolls her eyes and pads away toward the kitchen as I trail behind her like a joyless specter. "It's a wine stain on a coaster, Lachlan. You could have gotten it anywhere."

"I could have, but I didn't. I got it from right here in the apartment."

She scoffs but doesn't look at me.

Next, I take two sticks with brightly painted bulbous ends from the box. "And what are these?"

Her focus darts to the items in my hand. She avoids my eyes. "Maracas, clearly."

I clear my throat for dramatic effect. "Maracas . . ." Lark nods. "And what would they be made of, exactly?"

Lark turns to the fridge for butter. "How am I supposed to know?"

I rattle them, the objects inside hitting the lacquered walls of what looks suspiciously like skin. "You know I'm a leatherworker, Lark. Want to try again?"

She refuses to acknowledge me.

"What do you think would happen if I . . ." My words evaporate as I crush one of the bulbs in a fist. Human teeth fall into my waiting palm, several falling to the floor as Bentley rushes over to

156

investigate the possibility of wayward food. "Somehow, that's what I expected, and yet I'm still surprised. What a feckin' conundrum."

Lark pretends to focus on the muffin she pops into the microwave.

"Okay . . ." I tilt my hand and let the teeth fall into the box. "We'll come back to that one. In the meantime," I say as I hold up my final prize, "what is *this* . . . ?"

Lark's eyes flick from the item on the table and back to the microwave as it dings. She shrugs. "A ring . . . ?"

I let the weight of my gaze hammer into the side of her head, and even though she fidgets, she resists the urge to turn around. "A ring," I repeat.

She nods.

"Did you happen to notice it's *attached to a finger in a feckin' jar*?"

A nervous laugh trails behind her as Lark moves toward the sink. She grips the stainless-steel edge as though she hopes it might suck her down the drain. When she finally turns to face me, she's biting her lower lip, unable to control the cringe that creases her features.

"Ha . . . yeah . . ." Lark's half-hearted laugh disintegrates as I set the mason jar down on the table with a damning *thunk*. A little shiver racks her body as she shores herself up and raises her head, readying herself for a confrontation. "Well, there's a very straight-forward explanation."

"Which is?"

"I couldn't get it off. His fingers were too thick."

I clear my throat, every carefully curated word a proclamation when I ask, "So you took the whole finger?"

A flare of irritation bursts in her eyes. "Seems to be the case, genius. I see your observational skills haven't improved with the presence of glasses."

I let out a long, slow breath. "Let's try this another way. Why did you feel compelled to take this combination of finger and ring and then save it in a jar? It was shockingly easy to find, by the way. For future, I suggest a safe, not a literal hole in the wall."

"It's not like I asked you to go nosing around in my business."

"Protecting you *is* my business. That was part of the deal you proposed at the wedding, remember? And I draw no distinction between keeping you safe from outside parties and keeping you safe from yourself." I take one step closer and raise the jar between us. "So? Any explanation . . . ?"

"He didn't deserve to wear it. *Clearly.*"

I haven't had time to look up the crest on the signet ring, but obviously it has significant meaning to her that I don't yet understand. Perhaps there's even a clue on the inner surface, and I start to spin the lid to open it up so I can try pulling the ring free of the waxy gray flesh.

"*No,*" Lark says. There's utter panic in her eyes. Her skin goes instantly pale. "Don't open it, *please*, Lachlan." When I raise a brow in a silent question, she shakes her head. "Seriously. The formalin. I hate the smell. I nearly puked like five times just pouring it in there. If you open it, I'll definitely hurl."

"Well, I'm glad you managed at least long enough to put glitter in the jar."

Lark mutters something that sounds like *snuffluk* as she scratches her head and trains her gaze toward the floor.

"Didn't quite catch that, duchess."

"Snowflakes," she repeats a little louder, then flicks a hand in my direction without meeting my eyes. "Shake it."

I glance from her to the jar and back again before I pick it up to give it a shake. The ring clanks against the glass and the finger taps the steel lid. When I set it back down, tiny, glittering snow-flakes swirl around the severed digit before they slowly fall toward the base of the jar.

"A snow globe," I say slowly, waiting for her to look up, which she doesn't do. "You made a severed finger into a feckin' *snow globe*."

"It was almost Christmas," she says with a shrug. "It felt . . . festive."

"F . . . fest . . ." I blow out a long, thin stream of a breath and set the jar back down with numb fingers. "I just . . . *what the fuck*, Lark . . . Are you . . ."

Lark tilts her head, her brows raised as she waits for me to continue. Her shoulders go rigid, and I know she's arming herself for battle, so I might as well just spit it out before she puts the last of her psychological chain mail on.

"Are you a serial killer?"

"No." She scoffs. It's entirely forced. "Of course not. *No*. I'm more like a . . ." She drifts off into thought as she seems to weigh several possible responses. Dread sinks into my guts as her brow furrows and then smooths. A heartbeat later, a vibrant smile erupts on her face. "I'm more like a *multiple deleter*."

Lark gives a single, decisive nod, the glossy blond waves of her ponytail bouncing across her shoulder. I don't think I've even blinked yet but she looks like she's just had ten shots of espresso when she beams a bright smile and says, "Honestly, it feels so much better to finally tell someone."

Lark pivots on her heel to face the espresso machine.

Silence descends. Unsurprisingly, she fills it with humming.

She grinds beans. Grabs a pink mug shaped like a skull. Pours milk into the stainless-steel pitcher and turns on the machine. She doesn't seem to notice that I'm staring at her the whole time with my mouth agape.

"'*Multiple . . . deleter*'?" I finally say. Lark doesn't look up as she grins and nods. "A '*multiple deleter*,' Lark? What in the Christ Jesus is that?"

"What in the Christ Jesus is 'Christ Jesus'?" she fires back on the heels of a giggle as she presses a button and the espresso machine whirs to life. "Is this Jesus's roll call in school? 'Christ-comma-Jesus, please put your hand up if you're in class.'"

Dumbfounded. I'm bloody *dumbfounded*. I don't even know what to say.

Not that it matters, because Lark just keeps going.

"*Bueller . . . Bueller . . . Bueller . . .* nope, he passed out at Thirty-One Flavors last night. *Christ . . . Christ . . . Christ . . .*"

"The fuck . . . ?"

"Oh my *God*, have you never seen *Ferris Bueller's Day Off*?" Lark's crystalline eyes shine with amusement. "Oh, a classic comedy marathon, that's what you need to pry that broomstick out of your ass. I need to get popcorn. *Immediately*. I have such a great lineup in mind—"

"Back the fuck up," I interrupt, my voice low and stern as I take a step closer. The change in Lark is instantaneous. Amusement evaporates from her expression.

No, I realize. *The other way around.*

It's like a sudden fog that rolls in from the sea to obscure the sun.

Light dulls in her eyes as she squares her shoulders. She holds the pitcher clutched between her palms, the milk not yet frothed, her knuckles bleached with the force of her grip. By the look of determination on her face, I figure I'll be wearing that milk if I take another step closer.

But it's not just determination. I can see it in the way her pulse drums within the smooth column of her neck.

I know fear. And I know it better than most.

I try to relax my stance, though judging by the way her eyes dart from my face to my shoulders to my balled fists and back again, I'm not very feckin' successful at coming off as reassuring.

When I struggle to keep my hands loose, I slide them into my pockets, then say, "How about we go back to the 'multiple deleter' part for a second."

Lark swallows.

"How many . . . deletions . . . are we talking about, exactly?"

"Umm." Lark's gaze shifts to the ceiling. "I think . . . seven?"

"*Seven?*"

"No, eight. Definitely eight."

"You cannot be serious."

"Well, there was this one guy who died in the hospital maybe, like, four days later. Does he really count?"

My reply is a silent, dead-eyed glare.

"He could have died from medical incompetence," she barrels on, tapping her calloused fingertips on the metal jug. "Or maybe he choked on a bagel. The food in the hospital is pretty bad, you know? Could have been anything, really. Yeah, I don't think he counts. Four days has gotta be past the grace period."

"There's no grace period, Lark."

She sighs. "Yeah, you're probably right. Make it nine."

"You're telling me you've killed—"

Lark growls.

"Fine, you *deleted* nine people," I say, pulling a hand from my pocket to wave it in her direction. "*You.* Lark feckin' Montague."

Eyes molten with a dare, she gives me a sardonic smile. "Kane. Lark feckin' Kane."

Her words smack me like a fist to the face.

Whether our vows were real or not, whether she *believes* them or not, whether she uses her name or mine, she's deftly reminded me of the ultimate truth: for better or worse, we are stitched together.

The Montague and Covaci dynasties have kept her safe, at least from law enforcement. I might have experience traversing her world, even thriving in it, but I don't have the means to offer the same protection. Even worse, I come with another set of targets and vendettas and baggage that could put her in danger. If someone else finds out what she's done . . .

I'm still caught in the grip of this new fear when she tilts her head and inhales a sharp breath.

"So there was this guy—"

"*Lark.*"

"Ten," she whispers.

We stand in silence as I try to pick through the thousand questions that compete for top spot in my short-circuiting brain. She watches me with wide, innocent eyes, and even hearing it from her own mouth, I have a hard time believing it's possible. The Lark Montague I know is annoyingly kind, at least to everyone but me. She's unfailingly loyal. Empathetic to her own detriment.

And she's . . . a serial killer . . . ?

One question finally works its way to the top.

"*Why*, Lark? Why would you kill ten people?"

She swallows, her lips pressed tight in a resolved line. I've seen her fierce. I've seen her determined. I've seen her full of light, beaming with joy. I've seen her bite and tease. Adoration and defeat, resignation and heartbreak and hope. I've seen them all in Lark. But there's something in her eyes now, buried deep beneath all her layers, hidden in the shadows of music and chaos and movie quotes and all the sunshine she wears like blinding armor.

The armor is the Lark I thought I knew.

And though I've glimpsed it before, this is the first time I've truly looked beneath her shield and I see someone else entirely. I see pain that festers in the dark.

Lark might fear me, but she doesn't back down, doesn't let her eyes shift from mine when she says, "So that no one I love has to do it for me ever again."

Her words are a blade that slips between my ribs.

"Sloane . . . ?" I ask, my voice low. "Did she . . . is that what happened at the boarding school . . . ?"

Lark's only admission is the shine in her eyes, and I stop myself before I push her too far.

When was the last time I felt this way? I can't even remember. I've left only enough room to worry about my brothers and business and my psycho boss and nothing else, no one else. And suddenly there's Lark, who was never meant to be here, was never meant to shine light into places I thought could only stay dark. But with those words she manages to reach right inside and ignite something I never thought I'd feel. Pain and loss and heartache for someone standing on the outside of my tiny sphere.

I clear my throat. "Lark . . ."

All it takes is one bright smile, and everything I think she wants to say disappears.

"Anyway," she chimes as she thrusts the jug in my direction, "I should probably get going."

"But—"

"Gotta run." In a single spin she grabs her bag off the couch and steps toward the door, the dog trailing at her heels. She stumbles and I instinctively take a step closer but she puts her hand up and I stop short.

"Goddammit, woman, where—"

"Bye."

The door slams shut.

I stand for a long moment in the space between the rooms. Not quite the kitchen. Not the dining room or den. The void.

Whenever she leaves the room, it's as though the warmth disappears. It's like returning to a version of myself that isn't me anymore.

Well, fuck that shit.

I stride toward the door and pull it open with more force than necessary, a crash of metal against the wall. Lark is already two thirds of the way down the stairs.

"Stop right there, Lark Montague," I call after her.

"Not sure who you mean," she yells back.

"Lark *Kane*." My voice echoes through the open warehouse space and bounces back toward us. Lark halts with one hand gripped to the railing, but she doesn't turn around. "We need to talk about this."

"Actually, Lachlan, we don't."

"Discovering you're married to a serial killer—"

"Multiple deleter."

"—'*multiple deleter*' probably warrants a conversation, don't you think?"

Lark shrugs. "Not particularly."

"Then why in the bloody hell would you admit that to me?"

Her grasp tightens around the railing as Lark turns just enough to cut me with her glare. "What was I going to say when you shook the finger jar? 'Oops, not sure how those snowflakes wound up in there with a severed digit but I'm sure it's nothing to worry about'?"

I swallow my irritation and stay planted to the landing, unwilling to approach her even though I want to. But I can't. I can't bear that flash of fear in her again. Not of me.

"Just . . . just come up here and talk to me."

Bentley plops down between us on the metal stairs with a disgruntled huff like I'm the dumbest feckin' eejit to walk the earth. I swear his eyes roll as Lark lets out an incredulous bark of a laugh. "*Talk* to you? Since when have you made it fun to do that? You cannot wait to judge the shit out of me again. You really are an asshat, Lachlan Kane." Lark shakes her head, and the smile that should be so bright it's blinding only comes off dark and lethal. "You asked me once if I really cared what you thought about me, and I said yes. Well, go ahead and judge me all you want, because I got over that. Fucking fast too, I might add."

"That's . . ." That's *what*? Good? Bad? Fuck, I don't know. I shake my head and wrap my hands around the railing, but the cold metal does nothing to soothe the heat that courses through my palms.

Lark watches. Waits. But I feel like something is broken inside me. Like I keep pressing a piano key and no sound comes out.

For a moment, the look in Lark's eyes is pitying. "I haven't told Sloane because I love her, Lachlan. I haven't told Rowan because I love him. They expect me to be a different person than the one I am. Everyone does. And I don't want them to be disappointed. I don't want them to think the worst of me. But you already do. You have from the first moment you laid eyes on me. So what does it matter if I tell you? What is it really going to change about living with you? You'll like me less?" With a sardonic snort of a laugh and an eye roll, Lark turns away. "I've got bigger things to worry about than how much less you'll like me."

Her footsteps echo against concrete walls and steel beams as she descends the stairs, Bentley a ghost in her wake. And I just watch. I don't call after them, and they don't look back. The door is an exclamation of metal, and then silence.

I'm still here. Standing still. Holding on. Holding on to *what*?

I release the railing from my grip and turn my palms upward. Tiny flakes of rust stain my skin.

It's only now that she's gone that the realization truly settles in my thoughts.

Even with these secrets revealed, I still know next to nothing about Lark Montague.

"Kane," I say aloud. "I know nothing about Lark *Kane*."

I enter the apartment, determination growing with every step I take. Then I grab my keys and jacket and leave.

HOLOGRAM

Lark

My eyes are still closed as one thought plays on a loop in my head, a song on repeat: I have many regrets. And most of them are related to this fucking chair. Maybe one or two related to Lachlan. But mostly the chair.

It was shortly after midnight and I'd just torn myself away from cleaning to sit in this round wicker chair by the windows. This is where I can almost convince myself that I'm out in the open, the city lights spread before me like a blanket of stars, a view that feels endless. Lachlan had gone to see his boss after our argument and came back with the details memorized of what Leander wants from my family. It's a pretty simple list. A minimum of four jobs per contract per year. A five-hundred-thousand-dollar retainer fee. Muffins homemade by Ethel herself.

"Are they really that good?" Lachlan had asked.

I gave him a suspicious glance as he loomed in my periphery. "You've never tried one?"

When he shook his head, a little sliver of disappointment wedged into my thoughts. If the situation were reversed, I'd have tried every flavor by now so I'd know my adversary better. Just like I've googled everything about his studio, Kane Atelier. I've seen every photo in Lachlan's portfolio and read every testimonial for his business. I scoped out his social media posts too—they're mostly about his different leather projects, with the occasional scuba diving photo dump. I mean, I only really care that he knows fuck-all about me because it'll make it that much harder to convince my family that we're truly in love. That's one hundred percent the only reason.

"Well," I'd said with a shrug, "I'd like to think so. But if you ever decide to try a Montague Muffin, go to the flagship store on Weybosset Street in Providence. It's always better than the mass-produced stuff."

Lachlan lingered as though he wanted to start another conversation, probably about the elevator, or Claire, or maybe my cache of trophies, all of which are absolutely the *last* thing I want to discuss with him. So I shifted my headphones over my ears and tried to concentrate on the sheet music in front of my folded knees. I strummed my guitar until Lachlan finally disappeared.

It must have been nearly five when I finally fell asleep in the round chair, and it was just after six when I awoke with the guitar still resting on my lap.

And now I'm trying to unfold my legs.

I can't feel my feet. Or my ass. Or one of my hands, which spent the last hour trapped between my leg and the body of the guitar. I pull my headphones off and groan, a sound that dissolves into an exhausted whimper as I rub my eyes.

When I open them, a cup of coffee hovers in view, clutched by a tattooed hand.

"Didn't want to wake you with the espresso machine," Lachlan says as I give him a single eye, the other still unwilling to face reality. "This is the freeze-dried shite, but I thought it might help while you get your bearings."

As I accept the cup, I study him. He seems serious today. There's not a single teasing note in his voice. He looks down at me like I'm dying and he doesn't know what to do. A deep crease has formed between his brows and even after I take a sip of the vile brown liquid that I refuse to call coffee, he still hovers, some kind of pent-up anxiety rolling from him in waves despite his attempts to cover it. He even whisks the guitar from my grip when I try to set it on the floor.

"You didn't go to bed last night?" Lachlan asks, his eyes flicking across my face.

"No. Guess not."

"You didn't go the night before last either."

"Your observation skills have finally improved since the first time we met."

Lachlan sighs. "I already told you. I wasn't wearing my glasses."

I snap my fingers and give him a devious grin. "And I was wearing makeup. An infallible disguise," I say as I place the mug on the side table and heave myself out of the chair.

Lachlan's eye roll nearly rivals Sloane's and warmth spreads in my chest. Irritating him is even more energizing than the disgusting sludge I take with me to the kitchen.

"Thank you for this attempt," I say as I pour the coffee down the drain, "but it's basically the devil in liquid form and now we have to exorcise the sink. *In nomine Patri, et Filii, et Spiritus Sancti.*"

"You know Latin?"

I snort and rinse out the mug. "I know 'Constantine, John Constantine.'" As expected, when I glance over my shoulder at him, Lachlan seems clueless. "You haven't actually seen *Constantine*? I thought you were joking when you asked the other day, but honestly that does not surprise me one bit that you have no idea what I'm talking about. Batch oven for you."

"I thought you were going to say you learned it at that boarding school where you met Sloane. Ashborne, right?"

"Yeah." A brittle smile forces its way across my lips. I'm surprised he didn't rib me back. "Ashborne."

"You didn't graduate there though," Lachlan says as he sits and smooths a hand across the surface of my new coffee table. I give him a suspicious look as I start grinding a fresh batch of espresso beans. "Sloane told me a while back."

"That's right. We finished school at my aunt's home with private tutors."

"Why?"

I bark a laugh. "None of your business."

"You don't think that's something I should know? We're going to your parents' place in what, six hours? And we barely know anything about each other. I'd kind of like to be convincing, yeah? I like the idea of not dying in the batch ovens."

"Trust me when I tell you the subject of my Ashborne education will not be discussed at the dinner table." The espresso machine hums and hisses as I make two drinkable Americanos. I take them back into the living room and sit across from Lachlan, absently remembering that I probably look like a reanimated corpse. I shrug it off and slide him a mug across the glittering resin. "You're supposed to know stuff like my favorite movie. *Constantine.* Or if I get stage fright. I don't, by the way. Or where I'd like to go on our honeymoon. If this was real, it would be Indonesia. I like orangutans."

Lachlan lets out a little huff, a sound of surprise. "I want to go there too, for the diving."

I nod and sip my coffee. Even with my eyes trained on my mug, I can feel him watching me like I'm something broken that he doesn't know how to fix. It's been a long time since anyone has looked at me like that, so long I've forgotten how it used to make me feel. Damaged. Irreparable. *Weak.* But for some reason, I don't want to put in the effort to cover it over with a fresh veneer, a glossy surface. I guess that's the irony of being married to someone I have absolutely no desire to make happy. For once, I don't have to try so damn hard to project one thing while I feel another, and the realization of how exhausting that is settles into my thoughts. But with Lachlan, I can turn the hologram off and just exist.

. . . Well.

That's a fucking terrifying epiphany.

I take a long sip of my coffee even though it's still too hot, then leave the rest behind. "I'd better go walk Bentley before he starts getting all dramatic," I say as I stand. But Lachlan catches my wrist as I pass, holding it just long enough to stop me before he lets go.

"I did that already while you were sleeping."

"He let you put a leash on him?"

Lachlan shrugs like it's no big deal. "I did bribe him with chicken."

I look over at Bentley, who keeps his head down on his folded paws and watches our exchange with guilt-ridden eyes. "Traitor."

"If it's any consolation, he stayed as far from me as he could at the end of the leash."

"That does make me feel marginally better."

I'm still standing, my eyes glued to my dog, unsure of where I should look or what I should do next when Lachlan grazes my hand with one of his knuckles. "Hey," he says. My attention shifts back to him, but I say nothing in reply. "Just . . . sit down."

I raise a brow and bite my lip, trying not to smile. "Are you bossing me around in my own home?"

Lachlan blushes. "No . . . but . . . please?" he asks, fidgeting with his glasses. "I'll make breakfast. We can talk a bit longer before we have to go."

"Talk about what?" I ask, making no move to sit.

"I don't know. How about we start with Indonesia?"

Our eyes lock once more and I let myself really look at Lachlan. Deep blue eyes, the color of a cold and treacherous sea. His dark hair swept into place. Tattoos that flow down his neck beneath the collar of his gray Henley, scrolling Irish script and an intricate triquetra on one side, a weeping angel on the other. I don't know what they mean or the story they tell, but I do know a lot about pain and grief. Sometimes, you need to carve the things you've lost right into your skin so you remember what you left behind.

I sit back down across from Lachlan, and his shoulders drop with relief.

"I'd love to volunteer there, if I could find a good place to do so. I guess working with orangutans in the Borneo jungle for a few weeks probably isn't everyone's idea of a fun honeymoon though," I say with a shrug. "Not really a romantic beach getaway."

"I don't like lazing around either. Love the water, not the beach. Gets boring after a day or two. Your idea sounds fun to me."

I look up at Lachlan and the faint smile on his face might be the most genuine of his I've seen. And I know he's still an asshole. I'm not going to forget that. It's not like he's ever apologized to me for being a dick or stuffing me in the trunk. Not going to let that one slide either. But he's kind of okay to listen to when he gives me that smile, or when he gets up and makes breakfast and it's actually really good—and bonus: not poisoned. There's maybe a decent guy buried in there somewhere. Deep, deep, *deep* down. Not that I want to find out, but learning a little bit about him doesn't hurt, I guess.

The question is, will it be enough to convince my family?

That, I don't know. But before long, we're on our way to find out.

We stop first at Shoreview Assisted Living to pick up my aunt, and despite Lachlan's multiple offers to assist, I head into the facility on my own. I find Ethel in her room already waiting to go, hair coiffed, lipstick on, cane polished. When I escort her out the doors, Lachlan is standing outside his Charger in the bitter wind, waiting with the seat flipped forward so I can slide in the back before he helps my aunt into the passenger seat. Ethel's cough is vicious with the transition from warm to cold to warm again, but she fights her way through the persistent rumble to ask Lachlan a million questions about the vehicle. They chatter for almost the entire hour-long drive to my parents' home in Providence.

When we pull into the driveway and Lachlan cuts the engine, my aunt turns to me with a wicked grin. "Ready to stir some shit up, my girl?"

I shake my head. "No. No, I am not."

"Too bad." Ethel shifts her attention to Lachlan and whacks his arm with her purse. "What about you?"

"Yes, ma'am. Ready to stir shit up."

"That's the spirit." Lachlan lets out a quiet chuckle before he gets out of the car to retrieve the gift he brought for my parents from the trunk. I asked him what it was, but he wouldn't tell me.

"I like him, Meadowlark," Ethel says.

"*You* should have married him then."

"Too late now," she declares as Lachlan opens her door. With a delighted cackle, she takes his waiting hand and steps out of the car.

I start to follow her, trying to steel my nerves for what's ahead, when Lachlan's hand reaches into the back seat. I take it, feeling an unexpected reassurance from sharing warmth with the only other person who could possibly feel what I'm feeling right now. When I'm out of the car and standing next to him, he doesn't let go like I thought he would.

"You okay?" he asks.

I feel like I'm coating myself in layers of papier-mâché when I smile. "Yeah, of course."

But Lachlan isn't buying it. "You sure?"

"I'm nervous," I blurt, and I don't know why.

My internal reprimand is immediate. He shouldn't see any

weakness in me. Lachlan Kane does not like me. He's only going through this whole insane escapade to save his ass.

I lock my spine and pull my shoulders back. "I'm nervous for *you*. If they suggest taking you for a tour of an industrial facility in Portsmouth, you should politely decline. And then *run*."

Worry flares in Lachlan's expression before he smothers it beneath a smirk. "All right, you feckin' catastrophe. Let me show you how it's done."

I snort. "If they don't throw you in the batch oven, I'll do it myself."

With a final glare at each other that doesn't really sting, we follow my aunt to the front door, our hands still clasped together.

IN NOMINE PATRI

Lark

My aunt rings the doorbell and we wait. She can't help but bash her cane against the door a few times when it takes longer than it should for someone to fetch us. When the door swings open, Ethel is already grinning, ready enough for the both of us to set off a few bombs at what is normally an uneventful weekly brunch. She gives Ava a kiss on both cheeks, then stands aside in the foyer to watch the first drops of chaos hit the hot pan that is my sister's volatile temper.

"Meadowlark," Ava says, suspicion laced in her voice as she gives me a weak hug.

"Good to see you," I say. "I thought you'd be heading back home soon?"

"Another week. Edward is too busy with work right now to miss me anyway." She lets me go and scrutinizes my face with the razor-sharp precision only a sister can. She looks at Lachlan then back at me. But I'm no rookie. Show no fear to the devil—*in nomine Patri*, and all that. I keep my shit on lockdown. "So,"

Ava says as she slowly pivots to face Lachlan. "Are you going to introduce me?"

"Of course." I grin and rest a hand on Lachlan's rock-hard bicep. I barely resist the urge to poke it and see if there's any give. "Lachlan, this is my sister, Ava. Ava, this is my . . . Lachlan," I say, chickening out at the last minute.

"*Husband*, dear," my aunt pipes up.

Ava lets out a deafening shriek that echoes up the vaulted ceiling of the foyer.

"Husband . . . ? Husband. *Husband*. What the fuck?" Ava grabs my hand and shrieks again as she turns toward my aunt, her mouth agape. "The *fuck*?"

Ethel is having the time of her life watching my normally cool and composed sister spiral. And in true Ethel style, she loves nothing more than to hasten the descent. "I believe the proper response is 'congratulations on your elopement,' dear."

"What is happening? You're *married*? When? I don't understand."

"What's all the commotion?" my mom asks as she enters the foyer, the uneven cadence of her steps announcing her presence before her voice does. "Oh, hello, Lark darling, I—"

My mom's voice cuts short the instant she sees Lachlan, but Ava is there to fill the void. "She's married, Mom. Lark. Is. *Married*," Ava says as she grabs my wrist and thrusts my hand toward my mother. Mom immediately recognizes the ring and shoots Ethel a shocked glare.

Ethel grins.

"Fucking hell," I whisper to Lachlan when my mother, Ava, and Ethel start talking over one another. "We haven't even made it into the house yet."

Lachlan snickers and glances down his shoulder at me. "Watch and learn, Blunder Barbie."

He winks at me. Fucking *winks*. And then he steps into the fray holding out the black bag with the gift he brought. "Perhaps we should crack this open and I can explain," he says as he reaches into the cloud of tissue paper and pulls out a bottle of 2018 Château Pétrus. "Or there's a bottle of Springbank whiskey if that's your preference. Figured we all might want to share something a bit stronger, given the circumstances."

The arguing stops momentarily as all three women eye him.

"I promise this story is not quite as wild as it seems."

No one says anything for a beat and I begin to think we're going to have to slink back out the door and give up on this plan. But then Ava whips the bottle of whiskey from the bag with a glare and leads the way toward the back of the house.

My mom lingers for a moment with a long, grave look in my direction then locks her silver-blue eyes on Lachlan. "I'm looking forward to hearing this 'not wild' version of events. Please, do come in," she says before she follows my sister, my aunt trailing after her.

Lachlan extends a hand for me to take. I cross my arms and he shrugs as if to say *suit yourself.*

"Were you making your accent thicker to appeal to my mother and sister with your nonexistent Irish charm?" I hiss.

Lachlan's smile is nothing short of devious. "Ye wound me with yer accusations, me darlin' wife."

"You just did it again."

Lachlan twinkles his tattooed fingers in my direction, and I heave a dramatic sigh before taking his hand again. "Told you I would be fine."

179

"Shut up. It's been like, five minutes. Plenty of time for you to fuck it up."

The sound of heated conversation greets us as we head toward the kitchen, where my mom and sister try to simultaneously explain to my stepdad that *yes*, I am indeed married and *yes*, his name is actually Lachlan Kane. Thankfully, my sister just looks confused when my parents shoot each other knowing glances. If Ava knew about their concerns regarding Lachlan, I'm pretty sure he'd be dead already. She's always had over-protective sibling energy and I'm ninety-nine percent sure she's spent her adult life looking for an excuse to activate her Montague murder genes.

I put everything into radiating what I know they need to see. Happiness. Contentment. Adoration for the man whose hand I hold a little too tightly. I introduce Lachlan to my stepdad and stay Velcroed to his side until I'm sure my new husband won't be murdered on the marble island. The barrage of questions starts, of course, and they don't let up as we bring the food over to the dining table and take our seats. Some moments of the inquisition are more painful than others. *When did this happen? Where? Why weren't we invited?*

"Because I told them not to invite you," my aunt declares, silencing the bombardment. "You all have enough going on lately with the businesses. With me. So when Lark told me she'd met someone and wanted to marry him before I pass away, I asked her to do it this way. She wanted something intimate, and I wanted to be there. And now it's done."

As if to rub it in, Ethel coughs, at first a gentle rumble that I'm not entirely sure she's not conjuring into existence, but one that quickly turns into a lengthy fit. My mom rubs my aunt's shoulder while my sister fetches a box of tissues, and when it finally subsides, the first thing my aunt says is, "Do you know how these two met? It'll be a great story for the grandkids. He tossed her in the trunk of a car."

Oh dear God.

"You *what*?" My sister drops her cutlery and rounds on Lachlan, and it's the first time since he walked in here that I've truly seen him thrown off his axis. "You put her *where*?"

"It's not as bad as it seems," I protest, though in reality, it's worse. "I was in a . . . situation. And it was the only way to safely get out."

"A situation."

"Yep."

"Care to elaborate?" Ava asks, her eyebrows raised.

"Not really."

"And it involved putting you. Lark Montague. In a fucking trunk."

"Well, I did get out, so . . ." I shrug and force my way through a bite of roast beef that I would normally decimate. "We worked past it. All turned out well in the end. Like Auntie said, it makes for a funny story." Lies. So many lies and half-truths that I feel like they're clinging to my skin, like all the masks I cover myself with will slide off in the oily muck of my deceptions.

"The trunk wasn't my best idea at the time," Lachlan says as a hint of blush creeps into his cheeks, "but our options were limited and, fortunately for me, Lark has a very forgiving heart."

I cough around a sip of water, nearly spitting it back into the glass.

My mom and stepdad exchange weighted glances. I see fury in my mom, but disappointment in my stepfather, and somehow the latter is worse. I lay my hand on his, waiting for him to meet my eyes. "I'm sorry, Daddy," I whisper, my throat suddenly tightening around my words. "I've always wanted you to walk me down the aisle. But I fell in love with Lachlan so fast," I say, gazing over at Lachlan in a way I hope is convincing. "And it just . . . happened."

Part of me wishes my stepdad would challenge me on this. Dig a little deeper. Call me out. But to him, this is probably just another example in a long line of *Lark doing her own thing, fuck the consequences*. What else would he expect from someone who phones him in the middle of the night to cover up a fatal accident? Or who drops her job to go touring for six months, or packs up on a whim and moves closer to home because her best friend did?

He never calls me out, not really. Instead, he plasters on a weak smile and gives my fingers a gentle squeeze. "It's all right, Lark. I'm just . . . very surprised. It's a big shock."

"I understand. But I just want you to know that I'm happy, truly." I smile and shift my gaze to where Lachlan sits across from me. I probably should have asked him if he's ever been in love, because honestly, if this is his attempt to look smitten, it sucks. He seems more pained than anything. Like he's trying, but there's too much worry and anxiety fizzing just beneath his surface.

His eyes narrow at me, just briefly. With the slightest bob of his head, I realize he's communicating with me. Asking if I'm okay.

My smile grows a little brighter. *Of course I'm okay.*

There's a slight tilt to his head as he studies me. He doesn't look convinced.

My eyes widen until I know they'll look a hint deranged. *Play the fuck along, unless you want a tour of the batch ovens.*

"I have to thank my brother, really," Lachlan pipes up. "If it wasn't for his wedding and all the preparation that went into it behind the scenes, I don't think Lark and I would have spared each other the time."

At least his lie is pretty convincing, because we sure as hell didn't spare each other a single fucking second. Every time Lachlan was suggested as a companion for a run to the florist or the venue, I made every excuse possible to take someone else or do it solo. I'm sure the same was true for Lachlan, though I made a point of never asking about him, even though I remember every detail that fell into my lap. I can still recall the satisfaction I felt but pushed away when Rowan said Lachlan wasn't bringing a plus-one to the wedding. I don't analyze that thought.

My aunt jumps on the mention of the wedding to redirect the conversation to Rowan and Sloane's nuptials, and I finally feel like I can take a breath. When questions come back around to Lachlan, he handles them with ease. Questions about his studio. About Ireland. About his parents, which has him shifting in his seat. He calls his father "a troubled man" and focuses on his mother instead. I know most of this from Sloane and Rowan, at least at a surface level. It's different to not just hear it from Lachlan, but to *see* it in him. The haunted depths in his eyes where secrets thrive in shadow. His smile when he speaks about his brothers with pride that was earned by the pain he must have endured to raise them when his mother passed away. Every once in a while, Lachlan catches my eye as he talks, especially about the harder topics. He leaves the details unspoken, but I can hear them, the ghost notes in a melody.

And by the time we've finished the main course, I'm a little more at ease. Not just with myself, or because I know my family is at least trying to make sense of this situation, but with Lachlan too. When Ava clears our plates and returns with coffee and dessert, I feel calmer. We may not be in the clear yet, but we're on our way.

Which is, naturally, *exactly* when Ethel chooses to strike.

"Now that you've harassed the poor boy with your inane questions, why don't we address the elephant in the room? The contract with Leviathan."

My stepfather wipes a hand down his face. My sister chokes on her coffee. My mother tries to chastise Ethel, which seems to delight the old matriarch. I groan and lean back in my chair as a headache needles my sleepless eyes. And Lachlan? He looks like he wants to melt into some other dimension, which brings me a single sliver of joy to realize I'm sitting across from a deadly assassin who's out of his depth with family drama.

"There is no contract," my parents say in unison.

Ethel grins. "There will be for the Montagues."

"I haven't signed anything," my mother declares.

"That's because I haven't given you the power to do so. Nor will I. I've appointed Lark as chief security officer." Ethel takes a thick envelope from her purse and slides it across the table toward me. My face heats and the rest of the family stares me down as though I've orchestrated a coup. I throw my hands up and shake my head, which seems convincing enough as they all refocus on Ethel.

♪

"Conflict of interest. She can't hire the company her husband is working for."

My aunt snorts. "'Conflict of interest' my wrinkled old ass. We're not doctors or lawyers. We make *muffins*, Nina. Since when have we cared about a conflict of interest?"

"Since now. She cannot hire Leviathan."

"Lachlan is retiring. Problem solved," I interject. Everyone is as shocked as I am. I don't know where this is coming from, but holy fuck, it's too late to stop now. "Thank you, Auntie. I hope to make you all proud. I'll award Leviathan the contract, this family will be protected, Lachlan will retire, everyone will be happy."

"No one will be happy," my sister says.

"I'm happy," Ethel protests.

"You're dying and half-crazy. No offense."

"I'm dying and perfectly sane. Certified by three doctors and my lawyer," my aunt says as she slaps another stack of papers onto the table. "Ironclad, by the way. Just in case you try to overturn my decision."

"Great. Then it's settled." I smile at each one of my family members, leaving Lachlan for last. His face looks like I imagine it would if he were stalking his prey from a distance. It's like he's shut off every part of himself so that only instinct and skill remain.

My mother's gaze bounds from one person to the next before it lands on me, her hand gripped so tightly to her napkin that her knuckles bleach. "You don't know what you're doing, Lark."

"I do. I chose love," I say, unable to bear the weight of a lie about something so precious. "We are married. This is the life I chose. He is the man I chose."

185

"He is a killer," my mother hisses, throwing the penultimate grenade.

My heart cracks when I softly say, "Maybe we should all be transparent for once and admit that when it comes to this family, he's not the only one."

There's a brief second of stark silence. I can feel the disbelief like an entity that hovers above our plates, a ghost caught between our rigid bodies as we sit unmoving in its midst.

My stepfather's sharp inhale breaks the spell. "Lark Montague—"

"*Kane*, Daddy." I set my fork down and cross my hands in my lap. Everyone else is still suspended, trapped in time, Lachlan included. Even Ethel doesn't move, her face frozen in a moment of repressed and scheming glee. "Lark Kane. I'll keep Montague for the stage, for now. But I've already started changing it everywhere else. Got my new driver's license on Friday, actually."

I toss the plastic card down on the table. The final bomb.

A sheen coats my mother's eyes, but she blinks it back before straightening her spine like she does when she's pissed and preparing for battle. "Well. That's just—"

"That's just lovely, dear," Ethel says, and gives me a demure smile that fades into melancholia. My chest aches when she studies me. "You've always been a feather in the wind, my Meadowlark. You deserve to be happy on your own terms. But I never wanted you to be alone. And now, you're not." She raises her forkful of cake to me in a toast before sliding it into her mouth. The last word, punctuated with a dark chocolate stamp.

I bury my short nails into my palms. The weight of Lachlan's gaze lies heavy on my face, but I can't look up. I don't know what will happen if I do.

My stepfather takes a sip of his coffee and clears his throat, and though he forces a smile, all I see is the torn heart beneath it. "Lachlan must mean so much to you."

His words summon a mist across my vision and an ache in my throat. I glance at Lachlan. He studies me before his attention flicks to my stepfather and back again. It's as though he knows there's so much more that's been left unspoken, but he can't see his way through the fog.

"Of course he does, Daddy," I whisper, my voice unsteady. "I wouldn't have married him otherwise. He is a good man. And you'll see it too, in time."

"I am . . ." My mom glances toward my stepdad, who gives her a warning look. She starts again, "*we* are happy that you've found someone, Lark. This is just not what any of us expected."

"You can always have another celebration here or at the beach estate, we would of course love to host it," my stepfather says. He gives me a weak smile. "We would love that very much."

I nod a little too enthusiastically. "Thank you. We'll think about that when things settle down a little bit." I can't look at them, so I look everywhere else. My watch. The half-eaten dessert. My empty coffee cup. Finally, I catch Lachlan's eyes and take a breath. "We have to get going, I'm sorry. We need to take Auntie Ethel back and then I've got rehearsal." I don't take my eyes from Lachlan as I shift in my chair. He's faster than me, fluid and graceful as he comes to my side of the table and pulls back my chair. "Thank you for brunch. I'm sorry it went a little sideways, but just know that I love you."

I give my mother and sister swift kisses to their cheeks before my stepfather leads us to the door. His embrace is long and tight.

His familiar smell is both a comfort and a burning ache in my chest. My eyes sting when he kisses the crown of my head. "You look tired, Meadowlark," he whispers. "Try to get some rest."

I squeeze a little tighter before I let him go and step back. Lachlan is there with a hand extended, and after a brief hesitation, my stepfather takes it.

"I know you don't have any reason to trust me, Mr. Covaci," Lachlan says. He lets the handshake go so he can interlace his fingers with mine. "And I know there's more going on than what we discussed today. But my word is worth my life. I made a vow to Lark. I will protect my wife."

An electric charge hits my heart. *This isn't real*, I remind myself. But the way Lachlan looks at me, *really* looks at me, I believe him. I might be his wife on paper only, but I know what he's trying to tell me in a simple glance. He will keep his word.

"I'm counting on it," my stepfather says. And with a final, melancholy smile shared between us, we leave.

We walk in silence to the car, Lachlan escorting my aunt, who seems to move slower now after so much excitement. But he doesn't release my hand either. He keeps hold of it even when we can't be seen from the house. He doesn't let go until I get into the rear seat, and even then I sense a momentary reluctance. A reluctance that, for some reason, I share.

It's just camaraderie, I try to remind myself when the moment passes and he pushes the seat back before helping Ethel settle into the passenger side. And then we're off, my heart still beating too fast in my chest.

"I don't know the first thing about being chief of security,

Ethel," I say when the house is out of view, as though they might be able to hear us.

"I know you don't. That's why you outsource."

"We didn't secure anything about the Covaci contract. Dad's not going to sign shit. I have no influence there." My sigh is unsteady. I press my fingers to my eyes, and when I open them once more, I catch Lachlan's uneasy gaze in the rearview. "I'm sorry. I promised you both contracts, and I'll get it done."

Lachlan turns enough to give me a brief glance. "I know, Lark. It's all right."

"We'll find a work-around," my aunt says.

"Do you think we convinced them?" I ask as my aunt turns to cast her smoky stare at me. "Do you think they believe we're in love?"

"You didn't need to convince them. You needed to give them enough doubt to stop them from acting. I'm sure they'll send someone to keep tabs on you both over the next while, so if you want to go necking in public it wouldn't be the worst idea—"

"*Auntie*," I hiss, but she merely laughs at the embarrassment in my tone. Lachlan chuckles and I catch his eyes in the mirror. I know he can probably see my deep blush, the heat of it burning in my cheeks. "'Necking'? Seriously?"

"*What?* I'm old." When I let loose a heavy sigh, the levity slowly evaporates in the car and Ethel reaches toward me to take my hand. "Don't worry, my girl. Sure, they will likely have lingering doubts. We presented them with a difficult situation to accept. But as for giving your parents enough reason to rethink any plans they might have been brewing to go up against Mr. Kane?" Ethel lets go of my hand to give Lachlan's leather-clad sleeve an affectionate pat. "I'm quite sure you did that. The license was very clever, Lark."

I blow out a long breath and look out the window as the familiar neighborhood slips past. I gnaw at my lower lip until I taste an iron thread of blood. "Maybe."

"You did a good job, Meadowlark. I know it hurts now, but his heart will mend. Damian loves you dearly, always."

"What was that about? With the license?" Lachlan asks, but I don't reply. I don't take my eyes from the suburban streets. Places I've felt lost in. Places where I've been found. The paths and passageways that my stepdad walked me down. The ones where he taught me how to ride a bike. The ones where he taught me how to drive. He spent the time to make this home *my* home. He did all the things my dad would have taught me how to do, had he lived.

"Lark never took the Covaci name," Ethel says, her voice low and quiet. "She always said she would never leave that piece of her dad, Sam, behind. But she did it. For you."

I can feel Lachlan watching me in the rearview. But I can't bear to meet his gaze.

"Your wife just broke her family's heart," Ethel says. "And she did it to save your life."

NETWORK

Lark

How can we come back from this when you left me in the dark?

You left me in the dark.

But I can't stop myself. I can't stop wanting you.

I scratch through the last few lines of text and close my notebook, placing it back in my bag as I watch through the window of my aunt's room. I've never been so blocked with a song before. It's like I just can't figure out what to say. I can't hear the notes that should come naturally. I'd like to think it's because I'm tired. *So fucking tired.* But I know it's not just that. In the last ten days since we went to my parents' place, Lachlan has crept into my thoughts, into my daily life. He makes coffee and breakfast every morning. He brings me little things every night, as though he thinks they might help me sleep. A silk eye mask. He blushed when he gave me that. An incense diffuser. Tonight, he'll make me a cup of chamomile tea and hand it to me with a haunted look in his eyes, just like he does every night. He'll disappear into his room and then we'll do the whole thing all over again tomorrow, over and over until we die.

But one thing Lachlan hasn't done? *Apologize.* And I can't seem to let go of those first moments we met. My hurt still festers, and maybe I just need him to open that wound. But he won't.

"Well, fuck him," I whisper and lean back in my chair.

"Yes, fuck him. I need to live vicariously through someone and Ava's love life is boring. I'm half-convinced that husband of hers is a robot," Ethel says.

A surprised gasp leaves my lips as I sit up straighter and look toward my aunt. She shoots me a devious grin before she raises the back of her bed.

"I'm sorry. I didn't mean to wake you," I say.

"You didn't. I've been watching you stare out that window for the last ten minutes. That Kane boy getting under your skin?"

Though I roll my eyes at the teasing spark in my aunt's voice, heat still creeps into my cheeks. "He's trying."

Ethel nods and coughs but waves me off when I rise to help her with water or tissues. This time her cough takes a long while to subside. Unease burns in my guts. Guilt creeps into my veins. She's been so lively with all the scheming lately, but maybe it's taken too much out of her. She suddenly looks so frail, pain etched across her crinkled skin.

Despite her protests, I press the call button for the nurse, who enters a moment later, followed by a doctor, who comes in while the fit still rumbles on. The doctor maintains her professional detachment when she tells me they're going to administer an IV for pain relief and antibiotics to prevent secondary infection, but I've been around facilities like this long enough to know that the prognosis of Ethel's cancer is grim, and this might be the fast deterioration of a disease my aunt refuses to treat.

Ethel's cough dissipates as they ready the fluids and prepare the cannula. "I don't like needles," my aunt says, her eyes darting toward the door to her room and holding there. I'm about to follow her gaze when she grabs my hand. "Sing to me for a distraction, girl."

"What would you like?"

A melancholy smile lifts my aunt's lips. "The one you sang at our anniversary party."

It's hard to believe it wasn't even a year ago.

My aunt and uncle danced beneath the patio lights we strung up in the tent. They looked into each other's eyes as I started to sing and I thought, *I wonder how much love is out there like that, really. I wonder if I'll ever find it. And if I do, I hope I deserve it.*

And now I think, *Maybe we don't find it. It doesn't just appear. It's not fantasy, not a fairy tale. We make choices, note after note, chord after chord, until we create it.*

I lean down and place a kiss on my aunt's cheek before I clear my throat and sing:

I can't give you anything but love, baby
That's the only thing I've plenty of, baby
Scheme awhile, dream awhile
We're sure to find
Happiness and I guess
All those things you've always pined for
Gee, I'd like to see you looking swell, baby.

The nurse slides the cannula into the vein and my aunt never flinches. She keeps her eyes on me and I don't even finish the song before she says, "Doll, go and get me a candy from the reception desk, would you? I like those hard caramels."

I scrunch my face in a question but my aunt just pulls her hand free of mine to flick me away.

"All right, Auntie," I reply with a shake of my head. "You're so demanding, you know that, right?"

"Less talk. More candy."

I give Ethel a bemused grin and slide off the bed as the nurse checks the pump and the doctor reviews her chart.

And when I turn from the room to join the corridor that leads to the reception desk, Lachlan is there, head lowered, one hand raised to his forehead as he strides toward the doors like he can't get out of here fast enough.

"Lachlan."

He halts instantly, but he doesn't turn around. I've stopped too, waiting for something, maybe a reaction or a word or even movement, but Lachlan remains tense and still.

"Hey, Lachlan," I say, and take a few steps closer. He shifts his head enough to show that he's listening, but not enough for me to see his face. "Everything okay . . . ?"

There's a long pause before he nods.

"You sure?"

Lachlan clears his throat, but he doesn't turn around. He only gives me the corner of his eye before he looks away. "Came in to say Leander needs me. You can come too if you're free. I can give you a ride, if you want. Or if you want to stay, I can take your guitar so you don't have to carry it."

"I'm fine, thanks," I say, though I immediately regret it and take a step closer. "I'll stay awhile. I'm leaving the guitar here today so the therapist on shift tomorrow can borrow it."

"Oh." Lachlan sniffs and nods, and a little fissure in my heart splits open.

"Are you sure you're—"

"I've gotta go." He grips the back of his neck, the missing tip of his finger more obvious against the collar of his cream knit sweater. Tattoos and rings cover his scars, ones that I've felt when I've taken his hand. Lachlan gives me a nod, but it seems like more of an affirmation to himself than it does to me. "Leander will get impatient. And impatient Leander turns into weird Leander."

"Okay. Text me the address. When I'm done here, I'll get an Uber and meet you there. We can talk to him about . . . stuff. My family stuff."

One final nod, like that's all he's capable of, and then Lachlan strides through the lobby and into brisk autumn wind. I watch as the Charger departs, and then I grab a fistful of candies for Ethel.

When I take them back to my aunt's room, she's pretending to be asleep.

"You're hilarious," I deadpan as I dump the candies on her blanket. "I know you're faking. You snore when you sleep. Loudly, I might add."

"Do not," she says without opening her eyes. "You didn't go with him."

"Obviously."

"Why not?"

"I'm busy here."

"Well I don't want you, girl. I need my beauty rest. And I'm assuming your husband needs something if he came in here."

I cross my arms and glare down at Ethel, though she still hasn't opened her eyes. "He said I can go to his boss's house today, but he hasn't sent me directions."

One cloudy eye cracks open and scrutinizes me before Ethel reaches beneath her pillow and pulls out a phone.

"What are you doing?"

"Texting your husband so I can get some peace and quiet."

"How do you have his number?"

My aunt glares at me as she puts her phone back and settles in deeper beneath her covers. "I get all the boys' numbers, missy," she says as she shoos me away, the IV tube dangling from the top of her hand. A heartbeat later, a text comes through on my phone from Lachlan with a dropped pin. "Now get out of here. And take the muffins for his boss with you. Made them fresh this morning with Nurse Lucy. They're at the front desk."

"How did you . . ." I shake my head, but still smile as I place a kiss on my aunt's cheek. "Love you, hell-raiser."

"Shh. Don't give the devil any ideas. I want to sneak up on him. And don't you and Lachlan go testing those muffins. Those are all for Mayes."

Ethel blesses me with a cheeky grin, and then with a deep, contented sigh, she closes her eyes. With a shake of my head, I grab my bag and order an Uber, and before long I'm headed to the sprawling estate home of Leander Mayes with a box of my aunt's muffins on my lap.

When we pass the fortified gate and the house comes into view, Lachlan is waiting for me at the entrance. We roll to a stop and he comes forward to open my door, his hand outstretched in an offer. I hesitate only briefly before taking it.

"Thanks for coming," he says as we wait for the Uber to depart. He seems suspicious of my driver's intentions until the taillights disappear around the curves of the winding driveway. I wonder how long he's been doing that, studying everyday things and people, making sure nothing is amiss. I've seen it in him before, the way he scans a crowd, searching for threats. He's vigilant, wary of enemies hidden in plain sight, an instinct that's been carved into him, as indelible as the ink in his skin.

I wonder how tiring that must be, or if he even notices at all.

"Of course," I say. I offer a smile he doesn't return. "I promised I would."

Lachlan's face remains grim as he opens the door for me. His hand finds the small of my back as I pass the threshold, his touch igniting a hum in my belly. "Remember what I said."

"That Leander's a bit nuts?"

"Yes. And I don't recommend accepting any hard alcohol. It rarely ends well."

"Got it."

"And pizza. If he orders pizza, we're feckin' leaving."

"Okay."

"Basically, don't take anything he offers," Lachlan says with a shudder as we walk through the foyer and down a wide corridor.

"Sounds super fun."

Lachlan ushers me through another door, this one leading to a set of concrete stairs that descends to the basement. I can hear a man's jovial voice talking over loud music. Before I can take my first step down, Lachlan presses a hand to my stomach to stop me.

"Let me go first," he says. His touch is gentle, just his fingertips graze me, but somehow it sends a tingle along my skin. I clutch the box of muffins a little tighter. I don't think he notices how my breath stops or my lips part. He just looks right into me with an expression so wary it looks like pain. "Just . . . be careful."

He lifts his hand away and turns to lead our descent, leaving an empty ache behind.

No. No ache. That was definitely a hunger pang. It's just all that talk about pizza. Probably.

And even if it wasn't the pizza and it *was* an ache, it's still just simple biology. I'm on a very long dry spell, that's all. And Lachlan's being extra broody and weirdly protective, and he's hot, and I have eyes. I can appreciate hot. It doesn't mean I want to fuck my husband.

I snort a laugh.

Lachlan's head whips around as my outburst echoes across the concrete. He looks at me with both confusion and fear, as though Leander could come storming through the door at the bottom of the stairs to blow our heads off.

And that's pretty much what Leander does.

"*Bang bang bang.*"

I'm looking down the muzzle of a gun.

At first it's all I see, a snapshot etched into memory. Lachlan's hand darts out and he yanks me up onto the step behind him. The movement takes just long enough that I capture the image of Leander on the threshold of the open door, gun raised, a welcoming yet terrifying smile on his face. And then all I see is Lachlan's back, my body sheltered by his.

"*Christ feckin' Jesus*, ya psycho. Put that away before you kill yourself and then the rest of us," Lachlan says, his accent thicker with his irritation.

Our host laughs and lowers his gun before stepping back from the doorway in an invitation to pass. "Can never be too careful."

"You were just trying to scare her."

"He'll have to try harder next time," I say even though my heart is pounding its way up my throat. I try to maneuver around Lachlan but he slides an arm around my waist, gluing us together. I extend a hand toward Leander. "Lark Kane, pleased to meet you."

Leander grins as he shakes my hand. There's something off about this guy, just like Lachlan said. A disconnect between his sharp green eyes and cutting smile. "Kane, huh? You don't have to keep that up here."

"I'm not." My smile has an edge when I pull my palm away and pass him the box of muffins clutched in my other hand. "Per your request. These were made fresh this morning by my aunt herself. Her famous brown butter apple cinnamon muffins."

"Oh, you spoil me. I like you already," Leander says, and I know with the way he beams at me that it's not the butter or sugar or apple cinnamon he craves. It's power. To bend the dying matriarch of Montague Muffins to his will.

Rather than return my hand to my side, I take Lachlan's arm instead, a detail that Leander absorbs before he ushers us inside.

Leander welcomes us into a room that's meant to look like a pub, with a stocked bar and a big-screen TV and a dartboard. He offers us drinks that we decline and directs us to a set of leather couches and chairs. I don't feel any comfort in this space that's meant to feel familiar. All I feel is out of my depth.

But he can't know that. And neither can Lachlan.

I might not know what the fuck I'm doing negotiating contracts in this underground world, but one thing I do know is how to play a part.

"I've come to discuss the Montague contract," I say. Leander is about to take a bite of a muffin but pauses. A slow smile stretches across his lips.

"Right down to business, hmm? I knew I liked you." That grin of Leander's reaches his eyes as he looks to Lachlan. He takes a bite of the muffin, leaving us in silence as he chews and swallows before he speaks. "I thought you said there would be *two* contracts in exchange for your retirement."

Lachlan is rigid beside me. He's sitting so close to me that I can feel the tension radiate from his coiled muscles. "I said my wife will make you a deal. The conditions are up to her."

"One contract now, I'll pay the full retainer, and I'll initiate one job immediately," I say, forcing myself to hold his penetrating gaze. "Once that job is done, Lachlan is out, and you'll have your second contract."

Leander's brows flick once, a reaction that feels too much like dissatisfaction for my liking. His head bobs with a pensive nod and he takes another bite of the muffin before he raises his eyes to me. "What guarantee do I have that you'll follow through on the second contract?"

"You don't," Lachlan says before I have the chance to answer. "So I won't leave until you have it."

I dart a sharp glance toward Lachlan before he can make any further promises. I know how much he wants out. He *needs* it. And I don't want him to stay on Leander's hooks longer than he has to. Something about that just doesn't sit right with me.

My focus returns to Leander as he washes the last bites of the muffin down with a long sip of beer. "I *will* get you the Covaci contract, but this job needs to be done first."

"Search, protection, and kill, is that right?" he asks, and I nod. "Lachlan mentioned the muffin business is darker than it seems. Certainly is delicious though." Leander finishes the last bite and brushes the crumbs from his hands before he sets the baking paper aside. "Some of the last ever made by Ethel Montague herself. Chef's kiss."

I watch as Leander kisses his fingertips in a dramatic *al bacio* gesture before his gaze settles on mine. With just a blink, he goes from jovial and amused to stern and shadowed. My eyebrows raise in a silent question. *What now?*

After another pull from his pint glass, Leander leans a little closer, steepling his fingers as he regards me. "One million for the retainer. Five jobs a year."

"You told me five hundred thousand," Lachlan says. "And she gets unlimited access to the office to use the investigational resources whenever she wants."

Leander's smile is predatory as it shifts from Lachlan to me. "She can have unlimited use. For double. And five jobs a year."

"Six hundred thousand, unlimited access to the office, and four jobs a year. And I initiate that job today with a one-hundred-thousand-dollar bonus if the aggressor is identified and killed before my aunt passes away." I feel the fleeting graze of Lachlan's knuckles across my wrist and turn, meeting the question in his eyes. Just like at brunch with my parents, I know what he's asking without words. "I want her to know her family is safe before she goes."

A smile sneaks across Leander's lips as he extends a hand across the space between us. "Done."

I take his hand, and as soon as I let go, he's writing in the agreed numbers and passing me the paperwork to sign.

Leander claps his hands together. With this business done, his demeanor shifts again. He starts poking Lachlan for details on the recent Kane weddings, information that Lachlan deftly keeps to a minimum. It seems second nature for Lachlan to provide just enough color for Leander to feel satisfied, and just enough shade to keep him at arm's length. By the time I've wired the retainer money, Leander seems relaxed, maybe even a bit drunk, though he's only finished one pint since we arrived.

I tamp down a grim smile.

"All right, kids," he says with a slight slur as he slaps his palms to his knees. "Feel free to get started in the office whenever you like. The sooner the better, right?"

"Right."

Leander stands. He takes two unsteady steps.

Then he falls flat on his face.

"*Shit*," Lachlan hisses as he bolts upright. I smooth my hands over my skirt as Lachlan checks Leander's breathing and taps him a few times on the cheek. "Well, that's a bonus. He's alive." When Lachlan's shocked gaze lands on me, I'm waiting with a sheepish smile. "What in the bloody feckin' hell, Lark?"

"Yeah . . . I kinda thought that might happen."

"Seriously?"

I shrug. "Ethel doesn't like to be bossed around. Especially when it comes to muffins. She gets a little vindictive."

"How about this, you feckin' catastrophe—clue me in next time before you give my psycho boss drugged baked goods, yeah?"

"To be fair, I wasn't *one hundred percent* sure they were drugged. Ethel was pretty vague about us not eating them."

"Were you going to tell *me* that?"

"I figured you wouldn't touch them out of spite."

Lachlan shakes his head and gestures toward the man sprawled at his feet. A rumbling snore rises from the floor. With a string of whispered curses, Lachlan rolls him into the recovery position then turns his attention to me, his expression incredulous.

"Don't worry. He'll be fine in like . . . four hours. And when he wakes up he'll remember that Ethel always gets the last word. The Montagues can psycho with the best of them, remember?"

"Christ Jesus."

With a wink, I stand and clap my hands. Leander's snore continues, undisturbed by the sudden sound. "Right. Let's go to the office then, shall we?"

Lachlan gives me a weary shake of his head, then gestures for me to follow as he leads the way to the basement door.

The house is empty and silent as we leave out the back door and walk down a curved path toward a separate building, one that feels utilitarian compared to the house. Stark white brick with a black steel roof, the darkly tinted windows giving no indication of what lies within. The single access point is a fortified steel door.

Lachlan places his left hand on a control panel, then leans toward a circular lens that scans his iris. A moment later, a set of cylindrical bolts disengages and the door cracks open.

"Pretty fancy," I say as Lachlan pushes the door wider and allows me to pass the threshold first. "I should get that for my glitter collection. I know you've been crafting when I'm not around."

"I have not." Lachlan pretends to look haughty. "If I was going to steal something, it would be gold stars. Gold stars are clearly superior to glitter."

I give him a teasing grin, and before either of us can get too sucked into a nonabrasive moment of levity, we break the connection between us and head deeper into the room.

The interior is as utilitarian as the outside of the building, no decorations on the waffled soundproofing that lines the walls. There are several screens that hang from the ceiling, nothing displayed on their matte surfaces. Four computer stations sit in the center of the room, each with three monitors. The desks are uncluttered, only a mouse and keyboard on each one. A metal staircase leads to a lower level from which a low hum resonates.

"What's down there?" I ask with a nod to the stairway as Lachlan leads us to one of the desks.

"Servers," Lachlan replies as he pulls a chair back for me to sit, then grabs another for himself before powering up our station. "Conor manages most of it on Leander's behalf. He's the real tech guy, but I can still get us started with the search. Normally, I'd go through whatever background files we have for the Covaci side of things at least, but since you're here we can skip a few steps."

"You mean the files are *in* the *computer*?"

Lachlan looks from me to the monitor and back again, confusion etched between his brows. "Yes . . . that's . . . how it works . . ."

"Oh my God, you have literally no idea what I'm talking about." I whack Lachlan's arm with the back of my hand and roll my eyes before clicking into the search field to type a name. "It's from the movie *Zoolander*. How are we even married?"

I'm met with silence from Lachlan. Ignoring his reticent expression, I pull the keyboard closer. "Can I look up anyone on this?"

"Yeah, it'll pull in data from multiple sources. Driving records, medical information, criminal history if there is one. Some sources are more expensive than others, so we start with basics and build from there. The more valuable information might go for auction, like if there's a specific person with a bounty on their head with multiple contractors mining the records, for example. FBI information fetches a high price so we'll only go there if we're sure we're on to something. Costs me a small fortune to find the info on serial killers for Rowan to play his little game with Sloane." Lachlan shrugs when I tilt my head and my brows knit. "Keeps him out of trouble around here. And it makes him happy."

I give him a brief smile that he seems to ignore before I turn back to the screen. The system looks slick but simple, and I start typing a name into the search field at the top of the page.

Louis Campbell. Location: Connecticut. Age, I leave that blank. Occupation: education. I don't bother with the advanced search fields, details I don't know or maybe I did once but have since forgotten.

I press enter. Seven Louis Campbells populate in a list below the search fields. Each has basic details—age, address, contact details, medical insurance, utility providers, job history. One contact card blares at me like a siren.

"Louis Campbell? Who's that?" Lachlan asks, and his question hangs like an ornament in silence. I don't reply as I hover the cursor over his name. "You think he has something to do with what's happening to your family?"

"No," I say as I return the cursor to the search box and clear the query. "I was just curious."

Though I feel Lachlan watching me, I don't turn toward him. "You sure—"

"Maybe we should start with the most obvious names and work our way from there." My fingers fly across the keyboard. "My aunt's nemesis would be the most likely candidate."

I have enough information about Bob Foster to enter into the search fields for the results to turn up a single contact card. When I click on it, a spread of more detailed data fills the screen. There's a row of locked queries at the bottom of the page, the information hidden behind paywalls.

"I doubt he would do the dirty work himself, but he's definitely the kind of guy to pay for chaos. Do you think we can figure out if he was involved?"

When I meet Lachlan's gaze, his brow is furrowed, his eyes dark as they sweep across my skin, leaving heat behind. "It's your contract, duchess. Do what you want."

I return my attention to the screen and gnaw at my lip.

"It's a good plan," Lachlan says as he points to one of the locked tiles. "Click on that one and enter your Leviathan account number. We'll check through his bank records and see if there are any recurring payments around the same time as the murders. That's where I would start."

I grin at Lachlan. And though it's soft and almost shy, he smiles back.

And we hunt through the records together.

RETREAT

Lark

Lachlan leans against the passenger side of the Charger with his arms crossed. The doors to Shoreview Assisted Living slide shut behind me and I take a few steps into the muted light of the overcast morning, my bag slung across one shoulder, the strap of a guitar case across the other. Though my eyes are hidden by sunglasses, I know he can see the surprise and trepidation in my wary stance as I draw to a halt. I don't know why I'm surprised when it's been just over two weeks now of Lachlan doing little things to try to chip away at the wall I try to keep between us. It's not the first time he's showed up somewhere unexpectedly to offer me a ride. But something in his expression seems different this time, even from a distance, and it keeps me locked in place.

Lachlan unfolds his arms, stepping to the side to open the car door. He flips the passenger seat forward so I can put my belongings on the back seat. When he faces me once more, I haven't moved an inch.

"Come on, duchess. Let's go."

"Go where?" I ask.

"Can't tell you."

I swallow and fidget with the strap of my bag but I don't come closer. A heavy beat drums in my chest as indecision and distrust root me to the ground.

Lachlan takes a small step forward and I remain still, my steady breath a fog in the cold air. "The . . . uh . . . the passenger seat is comfortable."

"Better than the trunk?"

He winces. "I thought it might be too soon for that joke."

"It was probably going to come up eventually."

His hand slides to the back of his neck. I cross my arms over my chest, waiting to see what he'll say. We've never spoken openly about that night—maybe we're both too stubborn, or are unwilling to fracture the fragile peace that's grown between us. But something seems different in Lachlan today. Like there's both heartache and hope in his eyes.

He takes another step closer. I stand my ground. "That night we met," he says, his voice soft with regret. "The way I acted, the way I took my shitty attitude out on you, putting you in the trunk . . . it wasn't right. I'm sorry, Lark. I know what I did was . . . it was cruel. I wish I could take it back. I wish I could take *a lot* of things back. But I can't. I can only tell you I'm sorry, and I'm not going to ask you to forgive me."

I square my shoulders and tip up my chin. "Well, that's kind of a half-decent apology, aside from the weird forgiveness part."

"I'm not going to ask you to forgive me because I want to earn it." Lachlan takes a final step closer. Gently, he takes the strap of my bag and slides it from my shoulder. "And when I do, you can let me know."

My cheeks heat beneath the cold bite of the wind. And he sees it. His lips curve in a faint smile before he turns and starts walking back to the car.

"You sound pretty sure of yourself," I call after him.

"Yeah, well, I'm not the type to give up easily. I'm not afraid of putting in the work."

"And what if we both get what we want and time is up on our marriage but I still haven't forgiven you?" I ask. "I guess you're in the clear then, right?"

Lachlan flinches from the sting of my words.

He lays my bag in the back seat and slides off his sunglasses as he turns to face me. The leather of my gloves creaks as my grip tightens across the strap of my guitar case. I clutch it as though it's a lifeline in choppy waters. "There's no end date, duchess. Get in," Lachlan says. "We've got somewhere to be, and before you ask again, I'm not going to tell you. It's a surprise. So please just get in."

I grin and draw closer, finally passing him the instrument. "'Please'? I didn't realize that word was in your vocabulary."

"I'm full of surprises," he says as he lays the guitar down and flips the passenger seat back into place. He turns to me and offers his hand. I stare at it, unmoving and suspicious.

"What are you doing?"

"Helping you into the vehicle. You know, like a gentleman. Believe it or not, I'm normally quite a well-mannered bloke and not a total heathen. You just caught me on an off day," he says, which earns him a snort. "Okay, maybe a few off days."

"Well, this chivalrous streak is weirding me out."

"Then I guess you've got two choices. Get used to the weird, or fight me every step of the process. Either way, I'm not going to stop."

"You do realize I'm not going to be dickmatized into Lachlan Kane's accelerated apology plan, right?" I say as I slide my palm onto his. He laughs as he lowers me into the car.

"I'll put that in my notes," he says. "'Do not dickmatize Lark into forgiveness.'"

When he starts driving, he grips the steering wheel too tightly, getting a little distracted when I connect my phone to the stereo. When I ask him about music he stalls the car at a red light. He grumbles a handful of swears and his cheeks flush crimson. When he glances my way, I turn to look out the window, hiding a teasing grin.

It takes us a minute to find our stride. But soon we're talking about . . . everything. By the time we reach our destination, we've been talking for a half hour nonstop about the band I've been rehearsing with, and I feel at ease.

At least I do until we turn down a quiet lane and roll to a stop at the end of a paved walkway.

"What is this?" My head swivels between Lachlan and the log ranch house at the end of the path. Its black and gold sign merely says ROCK ROSE LODGE. My eyes narrow with suspicion, all the comfort I felt in Lachlan's presence suddenly gone and replaced with an uncomfortable knot that tightens in my chest. "Is this some kind of place where you're going to leave me in an attempt to cure my—what did you call it—*glitter psycho streak*?"

"Christ Jesus. No, Lark." Lachlan reaches down and releases my seat belt, guiding the buckle away from my body and back to its resting place by my shoulder. "Rock Rose Lodge is a sleep retreat."

My breath hitches in my throat as I attempt to process his words. "A . . . what?"

"A sleep retreat. They specialize in treating insomnia." Lachlan pulls a brochure from the interior pocket of his jacket and passes it to me. "Sound therapy sessions. Yoga. Acupuncture. Light therapy. Meal plans. There's a sleep specialist here, Dr. Sargsyan. She'll help to make a personalized plan for you to follow."

"Sleep retreat . . . ?" I whisper, my words an echo, stuck on a delay.

"That's right. And you're going to stay for the long weekend and look after yourself. If it doesn't work, that's okay. We'll keep looking for something that does. The time off will be good for you regardless."

My eyes are narrow slits. "Did you just abduct me for nefarious purposes under the guise of sleep?"

"*No.*"

"But—"

"You need. Time. Off." His gaze holds steady to mine as though he hopes to somehow etch those words into my mind. I press my lips together as tears sting my eyes. Lachlan's hand folds into a fist as though he wants to touch me but stops himself. "Look, I know you could just call an Uber as soon as I drive off. But I want you to try."

"You're not staying?"

"No," he says as he slides a hand across the back of his neck. "I thought it would be better for you if I didn't."

"Um . . . yeah," I say with a brittle smile. "Makes sense." Though I drop my gaze to the brochure, I only skim the details, because the truth is, I really want to do this. But I'm needed elsewhere. I fold it and set it on my lap, turning my eyes to the lodge. "It's just, there's so much going on right now."

"And all that shit can wait. You can spare a little time."

Other than a faint nod, I don't reply. I just keep my attention fixed to the retreat as I fidget, playing a phantom song with one hand on the back of the other. Nobody's ever done anything like this for me before. "What about you?" I finally ask, still unwilling to look in Lachlan's direction.

"I'll be out for the rest of the day. But you can call me tonight if you need me, yeah? I should be back by eleven. I've got no plans to speak of for the rest of the weekend."

His words are met with silence as a thousand thoughts swirl in my head. A blush creeps up my neck as I look out the window and worry my bottom lip. I want to go. But what if something happens to Ethel? What about Bentley? My responsibilities? Band rehearsals? And most unexpected, what if Lachlan is trying to get rid of me for the weekend? Is there a woman he wants to take home? It's not like we're a real couple. We never talked about not being with other people. So why does a hole burn in my chest when I wonder if that's the real reason he's doing this?

"It's just a few days, Lark. If something comes up, it won't take me long to come and get you. Conor is looking through the information we pulled for leads on Foster's people and I've got him monitoring police investigations on the murder cases, so there's not much we can do until he finishes his work. And I'll drop in on Ethel. I'll take Bentley to see her. You can turn your phone off, I have the number for the retreat and they'll let you know right away if something happens. But everything will be fine, yeah . . . ?"

I'm not sure what I'm supposed to say. How am I supposed to tell him that I'm afraid of losing something that isn't mine to begin with? Why should it mean anything to me what he's doing or who he's seeing? It's not a real marriage. *It's not real.*

Silence stretches on in the car. And then I feel his touch. A simple graze of his fingers to the bones on the back of my hand.

My head whips around and I pin Lachlan with a lethal glare.

He pulls his hand away as though he's afraid he overstepped, but that just makes it even worse. Frustrated tears fill my eyes.

"Lark—"

"Why is this so hard?" I blurt out.

Lachlan shakes his head, confusion etched between his brows. "Why is what so hard?"

The first tear breaches my lash line and slides down my cheek toward my trembling lips. Lachlan's face creases with worry as I lose the battle to hold my emotions back. "You," I say with a flick of my hand between us as more tears escape my control. "*This.* It's so fucking hard. I don't want to care what you're doing or where you're going. It shouldn't matter to me at all. But it does fucking matter and I don't know *why*—"

Lachlan grasps my chin and stares right into me until I press my eyes closed. "Lark," he whispers. I try to bury the turmoil I feel, but it's unstoppable, a molten core that churns in the dark. I can feel it in the heat that radiates from my skin, in the hammer of my pulse beneath the finger that Lachlan lets rest against my neck. "Lark, look at me."

I open my eyes but can't hold Lachlan's gaze, not with the heartache and contrition that stare back at me.

"I know this isn't the type of marriage either of us envisioned for ourselves. I know it's not . . . ideal," he says as he lays his other hand over mine where it rest on my lap, my attention snagging on the simple touch. "But if you're worried about me stepping out on you and breaking our vows, that's not me. Doesn't matter that it's not a normal marriage. If I make a promise, I keep that promise."

Lachlan's thumb slides in a slow arc through the line of tears on my cheek as I take one steady breath in, letting it back out again in a thin stream through pursed lips. It takes more effort than I expect to bury my fears and insecurities and hopes back where they belong. In the shadows. I slip into familiar armor and raise my chin, and when I meet Lachlan's gaze, he tamps down a half-hearted smile. "I . . . I don't really care what you do in your spare time, you know," I say.

A grin tugs at his lips as his hand falls away from my face, the softness of his touch imprinted in my flesh. "Definitely not, no."

"And I don't forgive you."

"Trust me, I know."

"If you think you're going to . . . sleepmatize me . . . into for-giving you—"

"I think it's maybe just hypnotize—"

"—it won't work. You can't bribe me with pillows or some shit."

"I'm not trying to bribe you." Any hint of levity spirits away from Lachlan's expression. He leans a little closer and holds my gaze. This time, I don't look away. "I see how much you're doing.

I know what it's like to be so busy looking after everyone else that you forget how to look after yourself. You're going to burn yourself out that way. And I won't just sit back and watch it happen, Lark. Not if this place is *right here*, ready to help."

When he nods in the direction of the ranch, I follow his line of sight, swiping beneath my lashes with the hem of my sleeve. "Okay," I reply after a long moment. I say it once more and punctuate my declaration with a decisive nod before I finally turn my eyes back to Lachlan. "Thank you."

He offers a faint smile before he exits the vehicle, grabbing my belongings from the back seat and then a roller bag he packed for me from the trunk. I grumble at him about going through my panties, then about my retainer, and then about panties again, but I can't help but point out things I like too, from the sprawling log and stone building to Bantam Lake that stretches behind it and the walking paths that snake into the woods.

The staff at the reception desk check me in and describe the amenities and the plan for the next few days, and I feel Lachlan's focus on me the whole time, his attention unwavering and protective in the periphery. When an attendant takes my luggage and starts to lead the way toward my room, I pause in the center of the lobby and turn to face him. I know I look like shit. My eyes are puffy, my lashes damp with cooling tears, my skin blotchy. But Lachlan looks at me as though I'm beautiful. Like he can't bear to look away.

"Thank you, Lachlan," I whisper.

He nods. I should pivot on my heel and walk away and put some space between us.

But I don't. Not even when Lachlan steps closer.

I stand unmoving in the center of the lobby's stone floor as though I've been carved from it, my expression unsure as Lachlan draws to a halt in front of me. He runs a hand over my hair and gently pulls my head to his chest. "Get some rest," he whispers in my ear. "See you soon."

His lips press to my temple in a kiss that lingers just long enough for me to take a deep breath of his scent of leather and amber and mint, and then he lets go. With a final, melancholy smile, he shoves his hands in his jacket pockets and walks away. When he glances over his shoulder, I'm right where he left me, my cheeks flushed and the barest hint of a smile on my lips.

Before it can fade, Lachlan turns away and strides out the doors.

SIGNALS

Lachlan

I slide into the car and grip the steering wheel. One deep breath is all the time I allow myself to take before I key the engine and drive away from Rock Rose Lodge.

I plow through the next several hours, and even though I'm kept occupied, my thoughts always return to Lark. My pulse pounds faster with every second that ticks closer to eleven. Part of me hopes she won't call. That she'll be sound asleep. But a more selfish part of me needs to hear her voice.

It's two minutes after eleven when my phone rings.

"Hey, duchess."

"Hey." I can tell from that one word that she's wide awake. "I couldn't sleep. Still a bit wound up, I guess . . . Am I disturbing you?"

"No. Not at all."

There's a pause. "How was your evening?"

"It was busy," I reply, trying not to let excitement color my words. I know the mystery of my whereabouts this evening bothers her. "Saw some people. Did some shit."

"Cool . . ."

She wants to ask. But she won't. And I let the moment linger for a long beat before I finally say, "Want to see what I was up to?"

There's a rustling sound in the background. I imagine Lark shifting off her bed, darting to the window of her room. "What do you mean? You're *here*?"

"Maybe," I say, and she fails to muffle an excited squeak that sets my blood on fire. "Do you want to come with me? I might have another little surprise for you, but it can wait a few days—"

"No, I'm coming now."

My smile grows wider as I hear her gather her belongings. "Leave the giant bag there, duchess. And put on a sweater. Come out the back door of the lodge and try not to let anyone see you. Keep me on the line until you get to the car, I'm parked out front."

"Okay," she says, a little breathless.

In just a few moments, Lark is jogging down the path from the lodge and I key the engine as soon as she pulls the door open. In a whirl of motion, she's seated next to me, her familiar scent and her bright energy a balm to the unexpected anxiety I've felt in her absence.

"Where are we going?" she asks.

"Can't say." I glance over just in time to catch her teasing pout. *Those feckin' lips.* My cock aches with the sudden image of my erection gliding through the hot embrace of her mouth. I shift on my seat and refocus on the road ahead as we pull away. "Let's just say the sleep retreat is in a prime location. And it makes for a solid alibi."

I glance at Lark and meet her wary gaze. But she can't hide the excitement that glimmers in her eyes.

We hardly talk at all on the short drive to our destination, but Lark fills the silence with songs. Maybe she's as nervous as I am. I think back to the Scituate Reservoir and how I pulled up to the scene of Lark's "accident," how my flashlight illuminated a woman standing alone on the road, blood trickling from the deep gash on her forehead. I wonder if Lark goes back to that memory too. She's never told me about Jamie Merrick, the man I pulled from the lake, but I've been digging into him in Leander's office in my spare time during my recent quest to learn more about my wife. One day, maybe she'll be willing to tell me everything. Maybe even after tonight.

It's eleven thirty when we turn down a gravel driveway and park between a white van and a vintage Jaguar. There's an A-frame cabin in front of us, the lake shimmering just behind it, the black waves illuminated by the lights that spill from the tall windows of the cottage. Conor steps out onto the porch and gives us a wave. Lark takes hold of the door handle and moves to exit the Charger when I grab her wrist to stop her.

"You don't have to do this," I say.

"Do what?" Lark's eyes shift between me and the cabin. Confusion is etched between her brows. "To whom?"

"You'll see. But I'm telling you now. You can walk away."

Lark's eyes linger on me, falling to my mouth and resting there. She nods and I unfold my fingers from her wrist.

We step out of the car and I retrieve my toolbox from the trunk. I resist the urge to take Lark's hand as we ascend the wooden stairs to meet Conor on the porch. He holds a gun in one hand, sheaves of paper in the other.

"Everything okay?" I ask as I take the weapon and documents from his extended hands.

"Not much to report. He got a little vocal. I gave him something to take the edge off and taped him up pretty good so I could get some work done, but he's awake now." Conor's gaze shifts to Lark, and I feel the tension radiate from her as she tries to work out what's going on. A grim kind of hope settles in my chest as I turn my attention to the gun in my hand and check the magazine before I turn to face Lark. When she shudders in the cold, I set my belongings down and shrug my jacket off to drape it over her shoulders. Her eyes shine in the dim light as she watches me and the rest of the world fades into darkness. All I see is her. The way her lips part to spill her foggy exhalations into the night. The pulse that drums in her neck. My hand raises beyond my control and I sweep my fingertips across her cheek. Her breath hitches at my touch.

"Come in if you want to. You'll know when," I say, letting my hand fall away.

Lark's head tilts. "How?"

"I'll give you a bat signal." I grin when Lark rolls her eyes, then nod toward the toolbox sitting at my feet. "That's for you. See ya, duchess."

With a swift kiss to Lark's cheek, I give Conor a knowing look and then step inside Dr. Louis Campbell's cabin.

The lights are low, the living room dim. There are shelves of old books. Oil paintings in heavy gold frames. Diplomas and awards. Photos with politicians, Campbell's silver hair coiffed, his smile bleached, every suit finely tailored. Pictures of him with his wife, his nondescript children in school uniforms. I stop at a side table and glare down at a photo of his smiling face frozen in time. A whimper finds me from the dining room, and I meet the terrified eyes of the same man from the photograph, except this time he's strapped to an ornate chair. The headmaster of Ashborne Collegiate Institute.

I'm genuinely feckin' *excited*.

At first, I thought feelings like joy or hope or excitement had been dulled in me, worn down by the tides of an unforgiving world. But I was wrong. Since Lark came into my life, I've felt excited every day. It started when I followed Lark onto the balcony the night of Rowan's restaurant opening, and though it had a vicious edge at first, it gradually transformed. I realize now that I'm excited every single time I see her. The need to push her away has become a desire to pull her closer. I don't just want to hear her laugh, I need to earn it. Every time I gain a little ground, I want more. I want to break out of the shade and back into her light. Without even realizing it, I've become *addicted* to it. To *her*.

Lark's needs are my priority. Even the ones she doesn't know about.

Like the one bound before me now.

I close in on Dr. Campbell and tear the duct tape from his lips.

"W-what is this?" he sputters. His Cambridge-accented voice is tight with panic. He struggles, but Conor has bound even his head to the high back of the chair. All he can do is shift his eyes, and they flick in every direction with distress. "Who are you? What is this about?"

"What do you *think* it's about?"

Campbell pauses, weighs the options, then picks the most disappointing one. "Money. If it's money you want—"

"Wrong. Try again."

A flicker of panic brightens in his eyes. His pulse surges above the sharp edge of his pressed shirt collar. "This has something to do with a political connection."

"Pedestrian." A smirk tips up one corner of my lips. "For a man who runs a school for excellence in arts, your guesses are pretty feckin' uncreative, Dr. Campbell."

He says nothing as I set the papers before me on the table. I pick up the top sheet and hold it up so he can read it.

"I'm here for something much more fun than money or connections," I say.

Campbell's cheeks brighten with crimson blotches as his eyes dart between me and the words on the printed email.

I lean closer and hold his focus as my smile stretches. "I'm here for vengeance."

"I didn't do anything," he declares.

"Precisely. You didn't do *anything*." I pick up the next email and hold it up for him to read. "You didn't do anything when Ms. Kincaid raised concerns about the deteriorating mental health of a student who was working privately with Artistic Director Laurent Verdon on her college preparations." I toss the sheet aside and pick up the next one. "Ms. Kincaid again, raising questions about why Mr. Verdon was spending time with another girl outside of class. You didn't do anything then either and brushed it off as extracurricular work toward auditions." Another paper, another question, another girl. I force him to read one after the other until I get to the last two.

"I don't—"

"*Shut the fuck up*," I snarl, steadying my aim to keep the muzzle of the gun pointed at Campbell's sweating forehead. I hold up the penultimate paper close to his face. "Mr. Mehta this time. He brought you a concern about a student who seemed, what did he say again? Oh yes. 'Exceedingly withdrawn.' He had seen Mr. Verdon leave the art hall one evening as he was heading toward the staff room. On his way back to his office, Mr. Mehta heard someone crying. The withdrawn girl was there in the art room, alone in the dark. She was splashing black paint across a colorful canvas. When he asked her what happened, she wouldn't tell him, but Mr. Mehta suspected Mr. Verdon had something to do with it. So he asked you to look into it. He was worried about the girl." Panic drains the color from Campbell's skin. "She's my brother's wife. Sloane Sutherland."

Campbell tries to shake his head, but we both know his protest is futile. "I spoke to Miss Sutherland. She told me nothing. There was no reason to believe Laurent Verdon was involved in any inappropriate activities with her or any other student. There was no evidence to support those concerns."

"There was no desire to even *look* for evidence, was there? Because Laurent Verdon had just as many connections as you do, and you needed to mine every last one of those opportunities to ensure Ashborne Collegiate Institute remained a top-rated, exclusive private school so that you could secure a sizable donation from a certain wealthy benefactor's estate, a donation you intended to siphon from to line your pockets. Business is business, right?"

"That is categorically untrue."

"Watch yourself, Dr. Campbell. If I got hold of these emails, what more do you think I found in my travels through your sordid private life? How's your mistress, by the way?" I shake my head and *tsk*. "Fucking the nanny, how utterly unoriginal."

The silence is so thick that it presses against my skin. Campbell swallows, his lips quivering. "Listen, whoever you are. While I understand you're upset, the fact remains that allegations about inappropriate conduct are extremely serious and can have career-destroying implications, and they must not be pursued on rumor alone. Besides, Mr. Verdon is no longer with Ashborne."

"Oh, I know he's not," I say.

My hand trembles. My heart climbs up my throat with every beat. Rage paints my vision red the moment I hold the final message up between us.

"This one is about a happy girl. One who was well-liked. Talented. Effervescent. One who Mr. Aoki alerted you about when he found her shaking in a corner of the music room with her uniform stained and askew. He was sure something serious had happened, but she wouldn't tell him what it was. He was worried for her well-being. And just a day later, Verdon mysteriously disappeared."

Campbell goes rigid beneath his bonds as I take slow, predatory steps around the edge of the table until I'm standing next to him, my eyes fixed to the words on the page. To the name. To the image of the person it evokes, and all that must be hidden beneath what I can see.

"Her name was Lark Montague." The gun clicks as I release the safety. "And she is *my wife.*"

"No, please—"

"You were meant to keep her safe. But you *failed.*"

"Please, *please*—" Campbell begs as I press my weapon to his temple. "If you love her, you won't hurt me. I made a deal with the Montagues to help them cover up Laurent's disappearance. I recorded those discussions. If anything happens to me, the information will go straight to the FBI."

"You mean the information you stored in the safe of your home office and the copies you kept here at Bantam Lake?" A deep sense of satisfaction blooms in my chest when Campbell whimpers as I press the suppressor harder against his skin. "Since you have such a good streak of *not doing anything,* I didn't want you to start now by fucking up her life from beyond the grave. I have it all."

"I-I'm b-begging," Campbell says. "I'll g-give you anything, just please d-don't hurt me."

"That's not up to me."

I lower my gun and take a single step back.

The door opens. Campbell whimpers as slow footsteps approach.

Lark's voice is low and quiet when she says, "Hello, Dr. Campbell."

I see the exact moment he realizes who Lark is, and a misguided hope floods his watery eyes. "Miss Montague, *please—*"

"Kane," Lark says. "Mrs. Kane."

"Mrs. Kane, I'm s-sorry. Please, *help me.*"

Lark sets the toolbox down on the table and rests a hand on the lid as she turns to pin her glare to the trembling man at the end of my gun. My beautiful wife. An angelic devil, so wickedly innocent, her sweet and welcoming features contrasted by the lethal coldness in her crystalline eyes.

"My husband brought me a present," she says as she snaps open the clasps on the box. "I'm *dying* to know what's inside. What about you?"

Campbell sobs as Lark flicks the lid open.

A murderous squeak leaves Lark's lips as she claps her hands. She beams her smile at me and I can't help but grin as she pulls out a small glass pot. "You brought me glitter," she says, shaking the jar. I shrug and try to look nonchalant, but I can feel my cheeks heat with a shy blush. Lark has mercy on me and turns her attention back to the contents, taking her time to examine and announce each item, everything from gold star stickers to a brand-new set of polished knives.

Lark pulls a needle and gold thread from the box.

"You know, it was my aunt who taught me how to sew," she says as she threads the needle and knots one end. Campbell bucks against his bonds and whimpers when she sits on his lap. "I'm quite good at it."

With a steady hand, Lark pierces Campbell's lower lip. He wails in pain, but there's no one in the distance to hear his pleas for help as Lark slowly pulls the thread through his flesh.

"Did you know that's how I finally told Sloane what Mr. Verdon was doing to me?" Lark pushes the needle through his top lip and pulls the thread taut, closing the first suture. "He'd torn my uniform. I wanted to fix it. But I was shaking too much to thread the needle, so she did it for me."

Blood beads around the hole as Lark slides the needle through his lower lip for the second stitch.

"I told Sloane everything as she fixed my uniform," she says as she tugs the thread. "And the next day was the last time I ever had to wear it. Because she did what I wanted to but wasn't ready for. She made me realize it was possible to slay demons."

Tears stream down Campbell's face and I feel no pity. No remorse. Only pain for the suffering my wife has endured. Only admiration for her resilience as she makes another stitch. And another. And another, until his lips are sewn shut with gold thread.

"There." With a few vicious tugs, Lark pulls the thread taut and knots the tail before clipping the excess free. Then she pats him on the shoulder and stands back to admire her work. Campbell's lips are already swelling around the tight thread, blood smeared across his chin. His eyes beg when his mouth can't. "Now you can't say a word. Just like you always wanted."

Lark comes to my side, her palm held aloft. I lay the weapon onto her waiting hand.

She doesn't tremble. Doesn't waver. There's no fear in her voice when she says, "Enjoy hell, Dr. Campbell. Tell the devil that the Kanes send their regards."

There's a quiet pop. A crimson spray of blood. The room falls into silence. She passes me the gun, but says nothing. The only sound is Lark's steady sigh. And then, finally, I feel her hand on mine, a gentle squeeze, and the relief she feels finds its way into my veins.

"Conor will take you back," I say as I turn to face her. Disappointment flashes in her eyes, though she tries to hide it. But it lights up my chest all the same. "I'm going to clean up here. I'll take care of everything, yeah?"

"Okay." Lark hesitates, but then grips tighter to my hand and rises on her tiptoes to lay a swift kiss to my cheek. "Thank you, Lachlan. I . . ." Her gaze drifts to Campbell's body, but when it returns, she gives me a tired smile. "I needed that."

Her hand lifts away, and then I watch as Lark leaves the cabin, passing Conor, where he watches next to the door.

"You good?" Conor asks, pulling me out of a sudden desire to follow her into the night.

"Yeah. I'm good," I reply. I take a knife from the toolbox and start cutting the ropes and tape that bind Campbell's lifeless body to the chair.

"You ever heard of a place called Club Pacifico?"

"Don't think so."

"Well, I've got something you should check out from the records you pulled. Might be connected to what's happening to Lark's family."

A current slithers down my spine. "Oh yeah?" I ask as I bend to start cutting away the ropes at Campbell's ankles. "What's that?"

"Large payments are going through the club's books every month, but I can't figure out where they're headed. Fifty thousand dollars each time, three hundred thousand paid out to date. The guy who owns the club is named Lucas Martins. He's a second cousin of Bob Foster's."

"Payments for what?"

"Not sure. Couldn't find any details, just amounts. Might be worth checking at the club, maybe there's something on a hard drive there."

"Thanks. I'll look into it," I say, cutting the final bond free before I stand and kick Campbell off his bloody throne, his body falling to a heap on the floor. We stand for a moment in silence before I jerk a nod toward the door. "Keep her safe, yeah?"

Conor chuckles as I take the grinder from the toolbox and plug it in. "Of course, bro."

"What are you laughing about?"

"Nothin'. I'm just happy for you, man."

"Shut the hell up. Feckin' gobshite."

I turn the grinder on to drown out Conor's delighted cackle as he leaves the cabin. When he's gone, I turn it off again for just a moment to listen to the engine of the van start and the crunch of gravel beneath the tires as it departs. And then I get to work.

It's close to three in the morning when I make it home, and though I'm tempted to text Lark, I don't. Still too hyped up by the night's events to be ready for sleep, I walk Bentley instead, then take the toolkit with me to Lark's craft room, my trophy hidden inside. There's a wooden box there that will suit my needs perfectly, and several cans of unopened clear epoxy left over from one of her projects. I connect my phone to the speakers and start playing my latest book as I pour myself a drink. I then clean my prize at the sink and pat it dry before I bring out gold crafting wire and start bending the pieces into shape.

I've just finished forming the wire frame when I receive a call from Lark.

"Hey," I say simply as I put the phone on speaker and continue my work.

"Hey."

"Anyone see you come back?"

"Nope, I don't think so. I didn't see anyone."

"Good. You're like, a pro or something," I say, and she giggles and then yawns. "You sound tired. I was kind of hoping that our little excursion would have worn you out enough that you'd be asleep by now, duchess."

Lark huffs a laugh. "It did. But then again, I'm always tired."

She must be, I think. Always tired. Physically tired. Mentally tired. Stretched thinner and thinner until she's a warped and distorted image of who she's supposed to be. It fills the bottom of my stomach with something that burns. "How'd it go earlier at the retreat, anyway? Think you'll enjoy the next few days? I never got a chance to ask."

"It was great," Lark replies, and I hear the shuffle of sheets in the background. I imagine her settling deeper into a plush bed. She's probably wearing the lace-edged sleep shorts I packed for her and the matching spaghetti strap tank top. The thought of slowly dragging that delicate black fabric down her skin has my dick instantly hardening. "I went for a swim after you dropped me off this afternoon then did a Bikram yoga class after dinner."

"What's that?"

"The hot yoga where they pump the heat way up, you know? I was head-to-toe *covered* in sweat. Like, *dripping*."

My cock twitches, demanding attention. I shift on my seat. "Right. Yeah . . ."

"It was great though. I still feel all bendy. I even managed to do the Yoganidrasana pose."

"I have no idea what that is, but it sounds complicated."

"It's the yoga sleep pose. You lie on your back and fold your feet behind your head and your hands under your bum. I got my instructor to take a picture, I'll send it."

My phone dings and sure enough, it's a photo of Lark twisted into some kind of impossible shape, her shorts stretched tight across her ass, her strong, sweat-slicked legs trailing up the length of her body to where her ankles cross beneath her head. If she wasn't wearing those shorts . . .

Christ Jesus.

I take my glasses off and drag a hand down my face. "That's . . . awesome."

Lark giggles, and I wonder if she knows exactly what she's doing to me. I'll need to wank off for the third time today to yet another yoga-inspired fantasy of Lark if I have any hope of falling asleep myself.

"You should be asleep now yourself. It's super late. What are you up to?" she asks, and I pinch the bridge of my nose and take a deep breath before I slide my glasses back on.

Trying not to die of the worst case of blue balls I've ever had in my feckin' life.

"Nothing really," I say as I pull my fist free of a spiral cage of wire. "Just having a drink, listening to a book." *Waiting for you to call,* some hidden inner voice declares.

Fucksakes, no I was not. That would make me worse than Fionn.

Lark gifts me with an unsure breath of a laugh. "I feel like I should ask what you're reading."

"Please don't."

She laughs again, and this time I know it's for real. "Okay, Budget Batman. You keep your secrets stuffed in your neoprene suit, then."

"That suit is top-of-the-line, I'll have you know. Premium synthetic rubber. Hidden storage compartments. Very high tech." When Lark is done giggling and my smile slowly fades, I ask a question that's been worrying me, poking holes in my thoughts since we parted. "Do you think you're going to manage to get some rest before the sun comes up?"

"I hope so, yeah . . ." Lark trails off, and I catch the faint sound of her steadying breath. "But . . . I was wondering . . ."

I don't press her. I just let her come around to it, and it takes a moment of waiting that feels eternal.

"Can you maybe read something to me . . . ? I know that probably sounds stupid, but it can be anything you want. A gun manual, maybe, or *so-you-wanna-be-a-leatherworker*, or like, the history of dryer lint, or just . . . anything. I feel like maybe it would help to hear a familiar voice. Unless it's a pain in the ass, I know it's late, or I guess so late it's early, and you're busy and—"

"*Lark.*" I sit back in my chair and let my hands rest on the counter, my project momentarily forgotten. "It's not a pain in the arse. Okay?"

"Okay," Lark says on a long exhale.

"Just hold on, yeah?" I bring up the reading app on my phone and search for something I'm not sure the online store will have, but it does, and I grin like a feckin' fool when I find it. "You might like this. I hear the history of dryer lint is a riveting tale."

"I can't wait to fall asleep in record time."

At first it feels a little strange to read aloud to someone, but I quickly fall into the rhythm of a story that opens with an ancient city and a prisoner who finds a strange relic during a daring escape from his cell. I describe how the artifact seems to affect him. My tone is hushed and sinister when I tell her the prisoner hears voices when he holds it, and though he looks everywhere for the source, there's no one nearby. He breaks out in a feverish sweat. He seems compelled by a hidden force, driven to run. When the prison guards discover he's missing and chase him through the city, he's hit by a car, the metal crumpling around him, and yet he stands uninjured, the relic still clutched in his hand. The man looks down at his forearm where a symbol burns through his flesh.

"Is this *Constantine*?" Lark asks, her voice colored with awe. If I close my eyes, I can imagine the rare blush that must be sweeping through her skin. "You're reading me the script from *Constantine*?"

"Hmm. Is that what this is?"

Silence permeates the line.

"Seems like you might be right," I continue, and I wait for a beat for Lark to reply, but she doesn't. "I know it's not exactly the same as what ended up on screen, but I've gotta say, I kind of prefer the opening they went with for the movie. Makes it more unexpected when the bloke gets smoked by that car."

"You watched it . . . ?"

I lift one shoulder, though of course Lark can't see it. "Yeah."

"When?"

With another invisible shrug, I place the spiral wire into the box and start shaping the two ends so it will stand upright on a smaller spiral frame. "The first time would have been about two weeks ago."

"How many times have you watched it?"

"I dunno, duchess. Maybe one or two."

"Liar," Lark says with a laugh that dissolves into a soft melody of words when she adds, "Tell me the truth."

"Twelve, I reckon."

"Twelve," she whispers.

I grin as I lift my prize from the damp and bloody tea towel and place it in the wire cage within the box. With a few minor tweaks, the golden spiral will be a perfect fit. "I thought you were supposed to be falling asleep. You gonna let me keep reading or what? I haven't even gotten to the Keanu bit yet."

"Umm . . . yeah."

"You know, I've been told I'm like a tougher, buffer, generally better-looking version of *Constantine*-era Keanu—"

"Stop right there, Lachlan Kane. You will *not* Keanumatize me into forgiveness. That is fucking blasphemous."

"Worth a shot."

Lark laughs and I make a few digs at Keanu, which of course get her fired up. But then we get back to the story. I tell her about Father Hennessy and the holy water and the possession that he can't exorcise. I introduce *Constantine, John Constantine*, in my best Keanu impression, which she says reminds her too much of my "whisper growl" from the night we met. "Less whispering, more growling, but make it sound morose like you're so over this bullshit—so basically be you on a normal day but with demons," she declares, and soon enough I get her stamp of approval. And eventually, Lark goes quiet, staying that way even after I taper off into silence. When I take the time to wait and listen, I hear it. The muffled, steady cadence of her breath as she sleeps.

With a faint smile, I set my phone on mute and place it off to the side as I continue my work.

Just in case she wakes up.

HYMNS

Lachlan

The end of the day is my favorite time in the shop. It's serene. The studio feels comforting in the dim light as the sun slips behind the city buildings. Music drifts through my wall-mounted speakers. I resist the urge to change playlists so I can hear Lark's voice as I start my last project for the day. She'll be here soon and I don't want her to catch me with her music playing when she arrives. She'll think I'm lovesick and pining, though I've come to accept that's probably true. It's been a week since Lark was at the sleep clinic, and every day since she came home has been better and better, yet, in some ways, each day is more painful than the one before. I think about her every waking moment. I worry about her constantly. I'm particularly anxious about what we'll find when we check out Club Pacifico tonight, but I'm also counting down the hours until I see Lark. So I try to distract myself, but I still struggle to focus on the rhythm of my tools as I cut and shape and carve through hide.

I'm glancing at my watch when the brass bell rings over the door.

When I look up, an unfamiliar man steps over the threshold. There's a faint smile on his face as he looks around the shop. I lower the music and slide my glasses off, setting them aside on the worktop.

"Welcome to Kane Atelier," I say, walking toward him. "What can I help you with?"

The man shifts the weight of a heavy Western saddle onto his hip as he extends a hand for me to shake. He's a few inches shorter than me and a decade older at least, but his forearm is thick with the type of muscle that comes from hard, consistent labor. The bottom of a tattoo peeks from his sleeve, a simple cross with three waves beneath it like pages of an open Bible. "The name's Abe," he says in a faint Texan drawl as he tips the brim of his worn Carhartt ball cap in greeting. "Abe Midus. We have an appointment for tomorrow, but I was in the area, so thought I might drop in to see if you're free."

"Right. Abe, of course. Come on in, let's take a look and have a chat about what you'd like done." I lift the saddle from him and lead the way toward the work area. "Good timing, actually. I don't have any more appointments today, aside from drinks with my wife."

"Any recommendations for good places to eat? I'm kind of new to the area."

"Well, my brother is a chef at 3 in Coach and Butcher & Blackbird, so those would get my vote," I say with a chuckle. "You just move here?"

"I guess you could say so."

I expect Abe to elaborate, but he doesn't. His eyes pan across the shelves of materials, tools, and works in progress. I wait until he meets my lingering gaze then nod toward a chair but he declines to sit.

When I'm seated on my favorite rolling stool, I set the saddle on a stand and pull the fabric cover off to reveal the old leather. It's cracked and scuffed in some places, worn down from use in others. The elaborate scrollwork and flower tooling is faded, an echo of what was once a vibrant design. "Quite a piece, Abe. Why don't you tell me about it?"

"It was my granddaddy's," he says, and I look up to find him standing close, his expression wistful as he passes his hand over the pommel. "He was a rancher, bought it from a man who made custom rigs in Galveston. Paid a small fortune for it at the time, but he used it nearly every day on the ranch before he took sick. Eventually he stopped riding. Passed it down to my father."

Abe turns away, but not before I catch the sharp edge of darkness descend across his weathered features. He wanders to my workstation, bending at the waist to look across my tools and pieces of hide ready for various projects.

"My daddy . . . he wasn't a pious man, you could say. He was gone much of the time. Gambled away most of the livestock and horses, all the good machinery. Even that saddle," Abe says with a nod toward it. He pivots to face me, the WUTA edge beveler gripped loosely in his hand. He tips the shining silver toward the saddle before testing the sharpness against the pad of his thumb. "It took me some time to track it down. And a bit of effort to get it back."

He flashes me a brief smile, one I return as a faint echo of what I see.

"A sentimental piece, then," I reply, blinking away the images of my own father that flick through my mind. My focus shifts back to the leather as I lift the flaps to examine the tears and scuffs to the billet straps. "The repairs will take a little time. You said on the phone that you wanted a refresh on the design, but is there anything new you want added to it?"

Abe takes a step closer. He taps a finger to his chin, as though my question sparked an idea. "Yes, actually. I do."

Something about him sets off the alarm in my mind. Maybe it's his wolfish smile. He seems like a man who has secrets that want to claw their way free. Or maybe it's the way his grip tenses a fraction around the edger, like he's ready to make a tool into a weapon. It could be that easy if he's anything like me. He could lunge forward in a blink of movement, drive it into my chest, maybe spear me in the neck. Is that what he's thinking?

But a heartbeat later he sets down the tool with a pleasant smile, and I'm right back to wondering if my vigilance is becoming paranoia.

I clear my throat and push my stool away from the saddle. The caster wheels squeak in protest as I roll toward the nearest worktop where a pad of paper rests. "Great," I say, clearing my throat as though that will cleanse my thoughts. "Let me just grab a pen so I can take down exactly what you want."

I turn my back on Abe, and two things happen in the same instant.

His boot scuffs against the floor as he takes a step closer to me.

And the brass bell rings over the door.

"Hey, Budget Batman. If you're not ready to go, I'll drive you to Portsmouth and throw you in the batch oven myself," Lark chimes as I stand, pivoting so I can see both the door and Abe. But he's not where I thought he would be. I swore I heard him closer, but he's on the other side of the saddle, where he watches Lark enter the work area. She stops abruptly when she spots him. "Oh I'm sorry, I didn't know you were with a client."

Before I can reassure her, Abe strides forward, removing his hat as he extends a hand in greeting. "Afternoon, ma'am. It's no interruption. I was due in tomorrow, but I was close by and thought I might stop in. The name's Abe."

Lark beams a smile as she accepts his handshake. "I'm Lark," she says. I catch myself hoping she'll expand on how we know each other, but she doesn't. Instead, she lets Abe's hand go and nods toward the saddle next to me. "You're a rider?"

"Yes, ma'am."

"Me too. A little, anyway. It's more my sister's thing. Not Western though—I did a bit of hunter/jumper until I picked up a guitar, and that was that."

Lark flashes Abe a warm grin, and though he returns it, the smile doesn't meet his eyes quite right. The light seems off, as though it reflects at the wrong angle.

I tap my pen on the table and clear my throat. "So Abe, you said you wanted an addition to the design . . . ?" I ask as I settle back onto my stool and flip to a fresh page in my notebook.

"I do, yes." His faint smile fades as he casts his eyes across the cantle of the saddle. "Here. I'd like some scrollwork script. 'Nearer, my God, to thee.'"

I'm writing it down as Lark's singing voice cuts me short:

> *Though like the wanderer, the sun gone down,*
> *darkness be over me, my rest a stone*

My pen stops partway through writing *God,* I turn and look at Lark, her expression peaceful as the melody tumbles from her lips:

> *yet in my dreams I'd be*
> *nearer, my God, to thee;*
> *nearer, my God, to thee, nearer to thee . . .*

Lark's voice fades away. The instrumental music in the background is the only sound left, but it feels cold and lifeless.

"Sorry," Lark says. It's the first shy smile I've ever seen play across her lips, and I want to capture it and keep it somewhere safe. "The music just comes out sometimes."

"No," Abe says. He takes a step closer to Lark as my back stiffens. "It was lovely. One of my favorites."

"Thank you."

"You're a believer?"

The luster dulls in Lark's smile when she drops her gaze to the saddle. Her fingers coast across the embossed roses, the faded design lost to time. "My dad was. We all were, I guess. But I'm not anymore."

I pull my attention away from Lark and finish writing the lyric Abe requested.

"*The one who believes in me will live,*" Abe says. "John 11:25. We are meant to hold on to our faith in the absence of proof. The Lord rewards our perseverance."

I'm turning on the stool, about to interject, with what, I don't know. But as I pivot, I catch sight of Lark staring unwaveringly at Abe.

"I believe that proof can be found in perseverance," Lark says, her voice firm but not unkind. "Just not the proof you're hoping for."

Abe is about to say something further when I rise. "I think I've got what I need, thank you, Abe. If you think of anything else you'd like added or changed, please let me know. Now you'll have to excuse us." I grab my jacket from where it rests on the back of a nearby chair and shrug it on. I offer a hand to Lark, and I'm surprised when she takes it. "We have an appointment to get to, but I'll be happy to keep our time tomorrow if you want to chat through other ideas."

Abe nods once. "No need. I think you have the details."

I turn off the music, and Abe tips the brim of his hat to us both before he turns away. He whistles Lark's song as he strides through the shop.

A moment later, the bell rings over the door, and Abe is gone.

ASCEND

Lark

I lead the way out the door of Lachlan's shop just as a FedEx truck rolls to a halt along the curb. The driver waves at us. Lachlan salutes him, then turns to me.

"He's really leaving it to the last minute," Lachlan says as he checks his watch, frowning when he realizes it's already after eight p.m. He passes me the keys to the Charger. "I've got a couple of boxes to put inside. Go ahead and warm it up, yeah? I'll be there in a minute."

I head to the car and slip into the driver's seat. I have to stretch my legs to depress the clutch before I key the engine. It roars to life. The faded lights on the old dash glow a ghostly blue. The new stereo comes on.

But it's not music that fills the car.

"*I'm not done with you yet,*" a male voice coos through the speakers.

"What the *fuck*?"

I look toward Lachlan as the narration plays on, but he's busy picking up boxes and setting them down just inside the door.

"Do you want me to stop, love?"

"Holy shit." A sense of glee washes through my veins as I sit up straighter and turn the dial on the volume.

"If you want me to fill your ass, you have to say it."

I whip out my phone and open my last conversation with Sloane.

> I get it now.

> Get what?

> Your thing about books

> Okaaaay. I'm still not catching what
> you're laying down though . . . ?

I record the narration on a voice note and send it to her, catching enough of the audio to provide Sloane with a colorful segment of ass foreplay.

> Oh. My. God.

> I told him to crack a romance book. I
> didn't think he'd actually DO IT ahahaha

My head tilts. I reread Sloane's message.

> You told him to what . . . ?

I glance at Lachlan as he heaves the last box from the ground. I'd be lying if I said I didn't notice the way his clothes strain across his taut muscle, or the way my belly clenches in response.

> Crack a romance book

> Why? Now I'm not catching what
> YOU'RE laying down

> So he could learn how to talk to you
> without being such an asshat

> He wanted to know about the
> claustrophobia thing. I told him to go
> fuck himself and read a book. I think he
> just wanted to connect with you. Kind of
> cute, actually. Dumb but cute.

> Hold on a second . . . is it working?!

Sloane's question rattles around in my head. I lower my phone and notice in my periphery Lachlan locking up the shop.

> I've gotta go

Several texts buzz in my pocket when I shove my phone in my jacket, but I ignore them. Lachlan strides toward the car. He doesn't notice that the door is locked until he tries the handle, then meets my eyes with confusion as I hold down the push button lock for dramatic effect. A wicked grin creeps into my lips. With one finger still pressed to the lock, I reach toward the dial and turn it up until it's nearly deafening.

The look of pure mortification on Lachlan's face is *delectable*.

"*Fuck fuck fuck.*"

I can't hear him between the audiobook playing at full volume and my maniacal laugh, but I can certainly see the word repeated across his full lips as he scrambles for his phone. He pats down every pocket until he finally finds it. The recording comes to an abrupt stop, and I pout as he glowers at me through the window.

The moment I pull the lock button up, Lachlan whips the door open.

"Well. That was enlightening," I say as I rise from the driver's seat and block Lachlan's access to the vehicle. The heat in his gaze washes over me. I'm standing too close. I should step to the side, out of the radiant warmth that spills through me as Lachlan stares down into my eyes. His cheeks are still crimson with embarrassment and something else. Something hot and dangerous. Something that smolders in his eyes.

Desire.

I know I should move, but I don't.

"What was that one called?"

Lachlan swallows. He doesn't answer so I lean a little closer. Though I expect him to back away, he doesn't.

"Maybe I want to listen to it," I continue, letting my teasing smile mask the burst of need that coils low in my belly. "It would sound good through the speakers in my room. At night. With the lights down low."

What the hell is wrong with me?

What am I doing? This is insanity. Sure, Lachlan wants me to forgive him for our shitty first meeting, but pushing these kinds of buttons might just invite more suffering than either of us can bear.

My smile fades. He won't tell me, and I shouldn't want to know.

"Fine, Batman." I squeeze between him and the polished black metal. "Keep your secrets to yourself—"

Lachlan catches my wrist. His glasses do little to disguise the frustration in his eyes. I still think he's not going to tell me. But then he says, *"Death's Obsession."*

A faint smile plays on my lips as Lachlan releases my wrist and takes a step back.

"Get in, you feckin' catastrophe," he says, his voice gruff. "We've got places to be."

It takes a second longer than it should for my feet to start moving, but then I stride toward the rear of the vehicle, my steps a little lighter than I thought they'd be. "I think we should listen to it on the way—"

"Not a feckin' chance."

"Okay then."

Lachlan puts music on. We don't talk much, so I hum along and watch the city lights as they slip past my window. I feel safe in this bubble of steel and black leather. Lachlan's energy is as gravitational as an imploding star's. His thoughts churn, but never release. It feels like he has so many things to say but no means to let them loose, so they coil inside. More and more, I want to know what they are. I *need* to know.

"I'm kind of looking forward to this," I say, trying to break the tension that's crept into the silence. "I feel like a spy."

Lachlan lets out an unconvinced *hmph*. "Hopefully it won't be that exciting. Let's just grab the files we need and get out."

"But it's Friday night at the club. We should at least check it out a little. Who knows, you might actually have fun." I gasp theatrically and clutch a fist against my heart. "You do know how to have *fun* . . . right?"

"I'll have you know—"

"You don't. I already know that," I say flatly before I let go of a dramatic sigh as we stop at a red light. "I guess I'll just have to have enough fun for both of us."

I wink, stoking the flame that always seems to burn deep within Lachlan. He holds my gaze, unerring. "You'll be careful. That's what you'll feckin' do. The person we're looking for could be at that party."

"And what, you think they would do something in public?" I shake my head. "We're talking about someone who's obviously careful to kill in private and who keeps to a set schedule."

"I don't care, Lark," Lachlan says. "And if this is some barmy plan of yours to goad a killer out of hiding, don't even think about it."

My teasing smile falters and I turn my gaze to the road ahead. "It's not. Don't worry."

A honk sounds from behind us. Lachlan mutters a curse and the car surges forward. For a long moment, I think we'll be riding the rest of the way in silence, but after just a few blocks I feel Lachlan's eyes on me. The moment I glance in his direction, he catches my hand from my lap and holds on.

"I'm sorry I snapped at you. Maybe I'm overthinking it. But just be careful, yeah?" He squeezes my hand, my wedding set trapped beneath the pressure of his palm. "I want you to be safe. I'm worried about you."

An ache slides into my chest, burning hot and unexpected. When Lachlan lets go of my hand, I catch his before it reaches the steering wheel, and the responding surprise in his expression is unguarded, a reaction that I store away in memory. "I will. I promise."

I lift my palm away and offer an untroubled smile. But I can tell something is still roiling within Lachlan. It doesn't pass—definitely not when we park and he pulls a gun from the glove compartment to holster it at his back, nor when we head toward the entrance of the building. He keeps a hand on the small of my back as we walk through the lobby and head for the elevators. One arrives just as a small group enters the building and catches up with us, and they follow us inside with no acknowledgment that the elevator is beyond capacity. A tiny burst of anxiety flares inside me as my back presses to the wall, but at least we're not in the dark. Rather than face the doors, Lachlan turns toward me. We're so close I can feel his body heat. His eyes stay trained on mine. My heart knocks a stuttered rhythm when his hand presses to my waist.

"You okay, duchess?" he whispers as the elevator starts its ascension. The group around us talks and laughs, oblivious to the electric charge that seems to encase Lachlan and me.

"Yeah." My eyes fix on Lachlan's lips and I can't seem to tear them away. I'm caught up in the heat that rolls from his body. He's so close that I can smell a hint of the mint on his breath. "I'm fine."

I could so easily reach up and wrap my hand around his nape and draw his mouth to mine. I could discover where this current takes us, see if it ignites or destroys. Maybe I could confess that I think about our moment on Rowan's balcony every day. That when I do, I can't help but touch my lips and wish that it had been the first time we met. I could tell him how I wonder more and more about the hurt I'm still holding on to and question why I don't just let it go. I could tell him that I'm starting to see things in him that I tried to ignore—his fierce loyalty, his protectiveness for the few people he cares about, the way he remains true to the hardest of promises. I could admit that I forgave him when he stood next to his car and promised to work for my forgiveness. Maybe even before that. I know that saying these things would erase the heartache and regret in his eyes.

But I don't say anything.

The elevator arrives at floor seventeen and the group exits first. A heartbeat later, Lachlan's hand slips away from my waist and he leads the way to the entrance of the club.

Base thumps beneath the thrum of voices and laughter, the club already busy despite the relatively early hour. Jewel-colored lights flicker across the ceiling. At the far end of the club there's a wall of windows looking out over the shimmering city skyline. Some people dance, some stand with their drinks and mingle. There's an energy in the air, a sense of darkness and need that I struggle to define. Maybe that's just me—or us. Lachlan's fingers intertwine with mine as he leads me though the throng toward the bar. After we grab our drinks, we find a spot to stand near the windows where we can watch the crowd on the dance floor and the patrons who mingle at the high-tops.

"Do you see anyone you recognize?" Lachlan asks. I can feel him watching me as I scan the crowd. I spot a few familiar faces from the music scene, but not the kind of acquaintance he's referring to.

I shake my head. "No."

"Anyone you've seen around lately?" Lachlan edges behind my shoulder as though he can watch the club through my eyes. His breath warms my neck. Gooseflesh rises on my arms. "Anyone whose gaze lingers on you a little too long?"

When I turn my head to the side to meet his eyes, Lachlan's attention fuses to my lips. They curl in a smile. "Only you."

His lips twitch. There's that fire again—the flame inside him that if coaxed just right, becomes a beacon in the night.

My teasing smile might fade, but the flame between us doesn't. If anything, it brightens.

Maybe I'm torturing him. Or maybe myself. I don't know anymore. So I drag my focus back to the room before I can start something I don't know how to finish.

"There's nothing unusual," I say with a shake of my head. "But it's fucking packed, so it's hard to tell. Maybe we should get this over with now while everyone is more likely to be occupied."

His heat radiates through my back. I fight the urge to lean into him. I nearly lose it when his hand grazes my hip. "Follow me," Lachlan says, his voice low and rich, and then his warmth is gone.

I trail after Lachlan as we head toward the offices. He had me memorize the layout so I know exactly where to go. Lachlan slides his phone from his pocket, unaware that the crowd parts for him like a school of fish around a shark that swims through night waters. He texts someone, likely Conor. His eyes stay locked to the screen until it lights up with a reply. When it does, he pockets the phone, then reaches his hand back for mine. I take it and follow in his wake, and a moment later we pass through the staff door, music and voices dampening when it shuts behind us.

"Conor's got the cameras under control," he whispers as we stride down the hall. "Hopefully this will only take a few minutes."

My heart thunders with excitement and fear. When we reach the office door, Lachlan keeps his hand poised over the gun hidden at his back. He grips the curved door handle with his other hand and presses his ear to the wood. A moment later he pushes it open, and when he seems satisfied, he motions for me to follow.

We don't turn on the lights, using the flashlights on our phones instead. Lachlan goes for the laptop on the desk and plugs in a flash drive, while I look through papers for anything that might be useful. Notes, open mail, anything with a dollar amount—I take photos of everything I can, barely digesting the information I flip through. My hands shake as I turn the pages and try to hold my phone steady. The moments that pass feel stretched too long.

And then I land on an invoice.

"Lachlan," I hiss, holding up the piece of paper. He looks up from the laptop just as he pulls the flash drive free. "Fifty thousand, paid in cash. A contracting company."

Lachlan's eyes flash as a smirk claims his lips. Maybe I'm imagining it, but I think he looks a little bit proud, and my cheeks heat at the thought. "Get a photo and let's get out of here. Conor can follow up on it."

I snap the picture. I'm just stepping around the desk to Lachlan's side when a voice closes in on us from the corridor. There's someone talking on a phone. My body stiffens with panic but Lachlan is already in motion, his arm wrapped around my waist as he drags me with him to a storage closet.

He shuts the door, closing us in cramped darkness.

"Lachlan—"

His hand slides across my mouth and I try not to whimper as blood rushes in my head. "Shh," he whispers, his lips grazing my ear, his voice so quiet that even I can barely hear him. "I've got you, duchess."

And he does.

Lachlan holds me to his chest. His grip tightens when the office door opens and someone enters the room. He holds me tighter still as my body shakes with shocks of adrenaline. The man in the office talks about liquor orders and a drawer slides open in the desk. He can't hear Lachlan whisper to me, a steady current of solace, a pillar in the dark. *We're okay. Just close your eyes, if you want to. I won't let go, I promise.*

My panic surges when the man walks around the desk and heads to a filing cabinet.

"You're doing good. So fucking brave." Lachlan's voice deepens with a deadly vow when he says, "I'll kill him before he lays a finger on you, I promise you that. Understand?"

I nod, Lachlan's hand still clamped across my mouth.

"That's my girl."

My blood turns volcanic when his lips press to my temple and linger there.

Fear and desire. They war in my veins.

I wrap my trembling fingers around Lachlan's wrist and pull his hand down just enough that my lips are free. He leans back, his eyes following the contours of my face behind his glasses. Maybe he expects I'll put distance between us, that I'll let his hand go, but I don't. I drag his fingers to my neck where my pulse hammers a pounding rhythm, down to my collarbones, and finally to the sliver of exposed skin on my chest. I press his palm there. *I want you to stay*, that simple touch says.

A moment later, we hear the man's heavy footsteps cross the room. The office door closes, leaving us in silence.

Lachlan cracks the closet door open enough to let me see out. But it's him I'm watching. His hand still lies on my chest. My fingers are curled around the edge of his palm as I press it to my skin. My heart sings beneath my bones. I know he can feel it. He watches that point of contact as though he can see the secrets those beats write into his skin.

An ache coils low in my belly. A need that stalks me. More and more, it lingers, ready to consume. It's there when Lachlan stumbles out of his room in the morning in a T-shirt and low-slung sweats as he heads to the coffee machine to make us Americanos. It haunts me when his gaze lingers on my lips as I smile. It possesses me when I'm alone in my room at night, staring into the dark as my hand slips beneath my sleep shorts. It's Lachlan's touch I imagine when I circle my clit, when I plunge my fingers into my pussy. I want his touch *everywhere*. I want it for longer than just a moment that feels stolen in the dark.

My breath comes faster as these images play in my mind. My pulse stutters. My eyes solder to his lips.

Just one kiss. I want more than a phantom. More than my imagination. I want *him*.

I lean closer. But Lachlan uses the pressure on my chest to keep us apart.

The rejection must be written in every detail of my face. There's no way I can hide it, not even in shadows. Lips parted. Skin crimson. I take a step back, expecting Lachlan will lift his hand away when I let mine fall to my side. But he doesn't.

"No, duchess," Lachlan whispers, his expression resolute.

I swallow. Shake my head. I want to say so many things, but only one word comes out. "Lachlan . . ."

He pulls his hand from my chest and leaves a cold ache behind, but when I think he'll back away completely he grazes my cheek with his knuckles as he holds my eyes. "Not until I know you forgive me. Otherwise, this won't work, and I want it to work."

Before I can say anything, Lachlan gives me a faint, apologetic smile, then opens the closet door and steps out.

I feel like my mind is disconnected from my body as I follow Lachlan out of the room and down the corridor.

Though Lachlan checks on me over his shoulder, we don't speak. We slip back into the bar unnoticed, and he pulls his phone from his pocket to text Conor. A moment later, I feel the buzz of a text on my watch and wonder if he included me on a chat, but it's Sloane's name that flashes on the screen. I pull out my mobile and open the message.

> Thought you should know . . .

My steps lurch to a halt as I read the headline of the news article she sent.

With an unsteady breath, I click on the link. Dr. Louis Campbell's face stares back at me. Maybe I should feel remorse. A normal person would. Wouldn't they . . . ? I don't. All I feel is a sense of accomplishment, of justice.

I'm about to read the article when another text comes in from Sloane.

> You know, if he happened to have
> exploded in a freak fireworks accident,
> I'd be proud of you.

A chill races through my veins as I raise my eyes to watch Lachlan slice his way through the crowd, weaving a path toward the bar. I take a step back then veer to the left, headed for the doors to the empty rooftop patio.

> What do you mean? Did Lachlan
> say something to you?

> No. Not at all.

An icy wind cools the heat that floods my skin as I try to work out what to say. It feels like standing on the edge of a cliff, of being afraid of falling but still wanting to jump. Before I can work out a reply, my phone buzzes in my hand with another message.

> I just figured, maybe you needed to hear
> it. Maybe I'm wrong. But if you're like
> me, I don't love you any less. Not one
> bit. And maybe you can tell me about it
> sometime.

Tears flood my vision. I try to blink them away. Relief and regret twine in my chest. The only regret I've ever felt about the things I've done is that I haven't shared them sooner with the one person who has never hidden her darkness from me.

I swipe a tear from my cheek and tap out my reply.

> I love you too, Sloaney. And I'd
> like that.

I pocket my phone and stare at the horizon, trying to force the storm of emotions away. The lingering desire for the kiss that never came. The sting of rejection. The shame and relief of secrets forced to the surface. But there's not much hope of finding any relief as I stare across the city. It's barely been five minutes before I hear the door open behind me. I don't need to turn around to know it's Lachlan.

"Hey," he says simply as he slows to a stop next to me. "Thought I might find you here. Mind if I share your perch?"

My smile is weak, ready to shatter. I train my attention on the city lights. "Go ahead."

Lachlan leans his forearms on the railing, his elbow a gentle pressure against mine. The wind gusts as though rising from the channels and tributaries of streets below us, lifting my hair from my shoulders. It's a welcome chill to the heat that lingers just beneath my skin.

Lachlan gestures toward the view and I catch the glimmer of his wedding band. "We had a very similar view when we first moved to America," he says. "Leander put us up in a condo just a few buildings west of here."

"On your own?" I ask, and Lachlan nods. "How old were you?"

"Seventeen." He gives me a bittersweet smile before looking back at the skyline. "I enrolled the boys in school, started working. Leander got me a job at a leather manufacturing factory. For the daytime, anyway."

"And for the night?"

Lachlan shrugs. "I owe him a lot. Covering up what Rowan and I did back in Sligo. Bringing us here. Setting us up."

"Sloane might have mentioned a thing or two about that," I say, giving him a sheepish smile when he rolls his eyes. I nudge his elbow and add, "But you don't need to owe him forever. At least, not if I have anything to say about it."

"If anyone could convince Leander to do something, I think it's you," Lachlan says as he chuckles and shakes his head. "He still hasn't gotten over being bested in his own home by a muffin. He loved it."

I meet Lachlan's eyes and he seems closer than I thought he'd be, somehow. There's warmth in his eyes as he gives me a lopsided grin, but the remnants of sadness remain.

Our smiles fade as we stand side by side in the biting cold. I'm the first to break our connection and look out across the city, though it takes effort to look away. I can feel him still watching in the periphery.

"I like the view here. I like to see for a distance. It feels like you can see the whole city from this high," I say. My heart pounds, every thump driving me closer to a memory that I normally try so hard to avoid. It's so heavy and loud in my chest that I'm sure Lachlan can see it thrum in my neck, but if he can, he doesn't let on. "It was a home invasion. That's how I lost my dad. That's why my mom walks with a limp. Why I don't like small spaces. Why sometimes I can't sleep."

Lachlan could say something snarky, something teasing. But he stays quiet, a steady presence next to me. He watches as I sweep wayward strands of hair from my eyes and focus on the farthest points I can see along the horizon, pinpricks of light in the black distance.

"My mom woke us in the middle of the night. She hid us in the linen cupboard. Told us that no matter what we heard, no matter what happened, if she or Dad didn't come for us, we weren't to leave that closet until seven in the morning unless we heard the police. I guess she thought they'd be gone by dawn. Stay still, stay silent. 'God save my girls.' That was the last thing she said before she went downstairs. The last time I ever heard her ask God for anything, actually."

And I prayed too that night. I asked Him to save my family. I prayed and prayed and prayed to a God who never answered. Three shots, two screams, and only a few minutes of commotion as thieves stole money and jewelry and car keys and ran. But not a word from God.

♪

"We could see the alarm clock in the next room through the crack between the doors. I remember every time we checked. Two twenty-four. Three eighteen. Five thirty-nine. Six twelve. Six fifty-two. Seven o'clock finally came and my sister made me stay upstairs as she got help for my mom. She was unconscious downstairs. Dad was already dead. And I never prayed again." I take a deep breath and clasp my hands together as though I can press the next words out of my body. "Not even at Ashborne, when . . ."

Those words float away on the wind. I don't try to catch them. They're just *gone*, not ready to be shared, no matter how much I wish I could give them away.

I shake my head. This isn't the kind of thing I can talk about with anyone, not even Sloane. It's like the concrete in our foundation that we know exists, but never acknowledge. Even when I went to therapy, I talked *around* Ashborne. I was too nervous to tell the truth, too worried about endangering my best friend. It was easier to slip into another disguise, to channel the persona I'd practiced so that other people wouldn't feel uncomfortable around me. I thought I'd end up lonelier if I wasn't who they wanted me to be. But it doesn't really work that way. You still live with your true self on the inside.

"Thank you," I whisper, unable to look at Lachlan as tears fill my eyes. "For Dr. Campbell. For doing that with me."

Maybe Lachlan is unsure how I feel about this. I guess it's hard to know when I don't look his way. But he takes a risk anyway. My eyes drift closed when he runs a knuckle across my cheek. "He did nothing to stop what happened to you. He deserved what he got."

I turn just enough so that Lachlan can't see my face and nod. As my gaze is caught on the horizon, his hand folds around mine, gently prying my palms apart so he can grasp my hand.

"Thank you," I whisper, not taking my eyes from the city lights.

My lips press into a tight line as the silence stretches on, just the wind and cars far below us, the pulse of music behind glass, the drum of my heart behind bone. And after a long while, Lachlan starts to spin my engagement ring. Back and forth. Back and forth. It's such a simple motion that he probably doesn't even think about it, and maybe that's why my heart creases like thin paper folded one too many times. His steady presence imprints in the lines left behind.

I'm not sure how much time passes. I'm not sure when it is I lean into Lachlan's side just enough that I feel the warmth of his body through my clothes, or how long it is before he lets go of my hand to rest an arm around my shoulders. But it's a long time before I say, "We should go home."

"I'll take you back."

My breath catches. "You're not coming with me?"

"No." The word is absolute and unwavering, but I think I feel Lachlan's arm tighten, his hand tense where it wraps around my arm. "I have to go to Leander's."

"I'm sorry."

"Me too."

I turn to Lachlan and place a hand on his chest. Rising on my tiptoes, I kiss his cheek. I can feel the way his heart jumps beneath my palm. "Let's go," I say, and I lead the way back inside.

Within twenty minutes, he's dropped me off. He waits at the curb until I turn on the lights in our apartment and give him a wave out the window. Within another twenty minutes, I receive a text with a photo, one of a gold star sticker on Lachlan's chest. I grin as a second message comes through.

> My first gold star! I feel like I'm getting somewhere.

My smile brightens as I pick up my guitar and open my note-book to a fresh page. When I'm settled in the round chair by the windows, I tap out my reply.

> Maybe you are, Batman. I guess we'll just have to wait and see.

I play a few chords.
And before long, I start a new song.

SPOTLIGHT

Lachlan

"I made this for you." I pass Lark a matte black box embossed with the Kane Atelier logo, a gold ribbon tied around its edges.

She's sitting crossed-legged next to Bentley on the couch in our apartment, illuminated by the setting sun. She beams at me as she rattles the box. My nerves and excitement war with every thud of my heart. She'll love it. *Thump.* She'll hate it. *Thump.* Too much. *Thump.* Not enough. *Thump.*

"It's nothing really. Just good luck for the show, I guess." I try to bank the heat that courses through my veins. My voice is gritty and raw when I say, "It's no worries if you don't like it."

I shrug like it's no big deal, but Lark sees right through it. I can tell by the way her grin spreads as she slowly tugs one end of the ribbon to unravel the bow. "And what if I don't?"

"What if you . . . what?"

Lark giggles. The ribbon unravels to fall across her lap, but she doesn't prop open the lid and just stares at me, eyes glittering. "What if I don't like it?"

Christ Jesus. What if she doesn't? What if she pulls it from the box and she loathes it? Feckin' hell, I'll want to find a hole to crawl inside to die.

"If you don't, I can just—"

"What if I hate it? Or what if I *love* it?" Lark says, her voice quiet as she pulls the leather gift from the box.

Lark sets the box on the floor and holds up the leather harness between us. I say nothing as I watch her eyes trail over the details of the black leather and the small gold buckles. My mouth goes dry when she presses it against her chest and looks down to judge the size. Her expression is unreadable as she examines the small details on the straps that are meant to crisscross her chest and frame her breasts. It's a row of tiny, evenly spaced gold stars. There's just the faint outline of metallic shimmer on the embossed angles and points, each line carefully laid down with gold foil.

Her lips part as she runs a finger over one of the strips of black leather that will rest beneath her breasts. If she puts it on. If she doesn't think it's too much. Maybe it's too far. Too soon.

"What were you thinking about when you made these?" she asks, pointing to the stars.

Lark still doesn't look up and her question hangs in the air around us, suspended.

I take a step forward around the coffee table. Another. One more. Then I let my hand drift free of my pocket and I point to a star near her thumb. "I was thinking about the time you told me not to Keanumatize you into forgiveness when I made that one."

Lark puffs a quiet breath of doubt. I can nearly hear her eyes roll. "Liar."

"No, really. I remembered it and laughed. It's why the edge of that star isn't as uniform as the others."

Lark's eyes flick to mine before returning to the strap in her hand. She brings it closer to her face and tilts it in the light to examine the details. When she glances at me again with suspicion and doubt, I pick another one. "I was thinking about the time you sang 'I Can't Give You Anything But Love.' Your voice, it . . ." I shake my head. "I had to take a minute. My mother loved that song. I'd forgotten how she would sing in our house in Sligo. Hadn't thought of her in so long."

Lark is quiet. She runs a thumb over the star I just touched, as though she can divine my thoughts from it.

I clear my throat, point to another. "This one, your face at Sloane and Rowan's wedding. Didn't know why you seemed so different when you asked me to dance."

"Different . . . ?"

"Cold but strong. Not that I knew you, but it felt like you were sharp around the edges that night in a way I hadn't seen. Didn't seem to make sense at the time. Now I know why."

I could leave it at that. Maybe walk away, let her make sense of my words however she wants to without any help from me. And Lark watches me like she expects that's what I'll do.

But maybe I see a little bit of wary hope in her eyes that I'll try. And it terrifies me.

When I first realized I needed to earn her forgiveness, I never thought about how it would change me in the process. I knew I'd have to prove to Lark that I was sorry for judging her. That I'd made mistakes. That I felt horrible for being callous, for making her feel unsafe in my presence or afraid or disrespected. But how do you show someone in a way that's more than just a handful of empty words? Because I know now that it's not only about creating a safe place for her, or crushing anyone who threatens her happiness, or looking after her health when I know she can't. It's not just a gift I can buy or an action I can take. It's not relentlessly wearing her down until she just gets in the damn car. I'm starting to realize I need to give something of *me*. I need to be a little vulnerable. Put myself in a different kind of danger than what I'm used to.

Like now.

It's the hope in Lark's eyes that keeps me rooted to the floor, even though every instinct tells me to run.

I let my hand fall back to my side, and that's the most I'll let myself pull away. "At the time, I thought it was just because you didn't like me, but that was only part of it. Now I see it was determination to go through with your plan to help someone you loved, even if it meant giving up your own happiness and tying yourself to me. That's very brave, Lark. We were in that position in the first place because of me. And knowing you had to muster up that level of courage to save me and my brother even though it was my fault . . ." I shake my head. Drop my gaze from hers. "I'm ashamed about it all, that I treated you the way I did. But that moment on the dance floor is the worst, just knowing now what must have been going through your head. I think about it every damn day. And every day it just gets worse, because it becomes clearer how wrong I was."

Lark stares up at me, giving nothing away. It feels like a challenge. A little shove, to see if I'll retreat. But I'm not going anywhere.

"I want to make this marriage into one you can be proud of, no matter what it looks like or how long it's meant to last. I don't want it to be something you regret."

A heavy tension fills the space between us. The air feels thick with the weight of all the thoughts I've let loose into the world. Then Lark's lips form a smile and the knot in my chest uncoils.

"What about this one?" she whispers as she points to the next star in the row without breaking her gaze from mine.

I run my hand over the back of my neck and give her the faint echo of a rakish grin. "Nah, you don't want to know what I was thinking about for the rest of them."

"I don't?"

"Can't imagine so, no." I hold up both hands when she gives me a teasing, skeptical grin. "This piece is pretty close to a corset, so feathers were obviously involved."

Lark laughs and I think I see her cheeks blush in the dim light. "It's beautiful, Lachlan. I'm going to wear it tonight."

"You don't have to," I say, trying not to let my chest swell with pride.

"I know I don't. But I want to. And I got you something too. Wait here."

Her legs unfold from beneath her and she rises from the couch. She pads to her bedroom, the door closing behind her with a quiet click. I wait in silence, hands shoved in my pockets, my thumb pressed against my wedding ring as I try to remember all the shit that used to come so naturally for me when I wanted a woman. Give her a lopsided smile. Maybe tease her a little bit, but only enough to make her laugh. Be confident, but not cocky—I'm not sure I ever mastered that one. Definitely don't be an asshat.

But when Lark walks out of the bedroom a few minutes later, all those thoughts of how I'm *supposed* to act suddenly evaporate.

"You, um . . . look . . . uh . . ."

Fan-feckin'-tastic. Now I have neither confidence nor cockiness. I've somehow regressed into some teenage version of myself, and even that guy had more game than me.

And Lark revels in it. *Of course.*

"That's probably the nicest thing you've ever said to me," she says with a shimmering laugh. With a small box clutched in her hand, she gestures down to the gauzy layer of the sheer black dress that flows over the bralette and opaque skirt beneath it. The harness fits tight across her upper body over the layers of fabric, looping over her shoulders and crisscrossing her torso to hug the contours of her breasts. "Imagine if I didn't have the bottom layer on and it was just the tulle."

My heart roars in my ears.

"The compliments would be rolling in," she continues. "Just one long 'uhhhhhhh.' That's some real Irish charm."

"Duchess," I growl, and she beams at me like she's walked right into my brain to shine a light into every hidden corner, even the one where I keep my need for her stored in darkness. *Especially* that corner. No matter how much shit I pile up around it, she finds that feral desire and feeds it.

I swallow and try my best to stack the blocks of my crumbling walls back into place. "You look great. Really great."

Lark smirks. "'Great.'"

"Yep."

"Cool. Thanks. You also look fine. Just fine."

I snort.

Lark bites down on her grin. "I must admit, I was expecting maybe *stunning*, or *beautiful*. Or, God forbid, *feckin' sexy*."

Chrissakes. Lark is all those things and more. She's *everything*. She's fierce and unique and surprising and so goddamn gorgeous it sometimes feels like my heart is trapped in a vise when I just *look* at her. There isn't a single word I can think of that captures what Lark has become to me. And when I try to open my mouth to say any of them, they dissolve on my tongue. So the only thing I can do is tell her the truth. At least, maybe a little bit of it.

i step closer to where she stands next to the couch, her hand resting on Bentley's enormous head as she strokes his ear. When I stop, I'm just within her reach, but I don't touch her despite how badly I want to feel the softness of her skin beneath my fingertips.

"You're always stunning, Lark. Always beautiful. Always feckin' sexy." My voice is a husky rasp that coaxes a fleeting blush into her cheeks. "But I don't want you to feel as though I'm trying to compliment my way into forgiveness. I know it won't fix us."

Lark's smile fades. "What do you think will?"

"Time."

"How much time?"

"That's not up to me." Before I truly realize what I'm doing, my hand is out of my pocket. Lark doesn't break her gaze away from mine when I let my knuckles graze her bare arm, a slow sweep that goes from her shoulder, past her elbow, all the way to the edge of her hand, where it's wrapped tight around the box. "It's up to you. But I don't want you to ever think I'm pushing you into it because of the way I feel."

Lark swallows, her pulse a steady hum in her neck. "And how do you feel?"

"You don't know?" I let my hand fall away from hers. She shakes her head. "Probably not the same as you. Let's just leave it at that."

"You sure about that?" Lark holds my gaze for a long moment before she drops her attention to the box in her hand. When she extends it in my direction, there's very little I can tease from her expression. Her voice comes out quiet and a bit breathless when she says, "This is for you. But you can't open it until I'm on stage, not until I give you a signal."

"What kind of signal?"

Lark rolls her eyes and grins. "The bat signal. Duh."

"Christ Jesus."

"But the budget version. I'll use a cheap flashlight with a half-dead battery."

"You're almost as big of a pain in the arse as Fionn, you know."

"Oh stop. You love him and his teasing."

I bite down on my tongue and taste blood.

When Lark rattles the box, I finally take it from her hands. There's a small envelope fixed to the glittery black ribbon that secures the lid. The moment my fingers begin to tug the card free, she lays a hand over mine to stop me, just like I hoped she would. "I said *no*. Not until the gig." She might appear annoyed, but I notice it takes her a moment longer than necessary to pull her hand away from mine.

"All right, I promise," I say as I slide the box into my jacket pocket and raise my hands in surrender. "Whatever my duchess wants."

Lark turns away to gather her coat, bag, guitar, and cello, but I pick up the instruments before she can sling the cases over her shoulders.

And then we're off, leaving Bentley on the couch, where he faces the door to guard this space, one that feels more like ours with every day that passes.

When we pull up to the venue, there's already a line out the door despite the shitty weather. People in the queue burrow into their coats and bounce on their heels to keep warm. A sense of pride floods my chest when I steal a glance at Lark. She looks out at the crowd with no evidence of worry or stage fright.

"You sure you don't want me to drop you off while I find a place to park?" I ask as I slow the old Charger to a crawl, earning some appreciative glances as we roll down the street.

"No, you might have trouble getting in. I'll take you in the back."

My mind immediately empties of rational thoughts and refills with vivid images. "Take me in the back . . ."

"Yeah," Lark says, giving me a confused, sidelong glance before I resolve to keep my eyes glued to the road. "The back entrance."

I swallow.

"You know . . . ? The back door . . . ?"

I nod and shift in my seat.

"Are you okay? Do you have a thing about back doors?" Her hand shifts in my periphery and I snatch my arm away, narrowly avoiding her attempt at a reassuring squeeze. If she touches me, I'm damn well sure I'll feckin' combust. "Are they like, triggering for you or something?"

"*No*, Christ," I hiss. I'm squinting. Why am I bloody squinting? I can see the road perfectly fine. I shake my head, trying to reset my senses. My clarity lasts just long enough to zip into a spot along the curb right after another vehicle pulls away.

"You could have parked it in the back," Lark says, her tone quiet and innocent as I cut the engine and drape us in stark silence.

I drag a hand down my face but it does fuck-all to wipe my blush away. Lark opens her door with a creak of old steel. Since I don't trust any words to reliably roll off my tongue, my only response is to shake my head.

A long, loud, dramatic sigh leaves Lark's lips. "Lachlan Kane is an ass man. Good to know."

With a snicker, all Lark's innocence is swept away. She shuts the door behind her.

Fucksakes.

My forehead thunks down on the cold, unforgiving steering wheel. I'd melt into the footwell if I could, maybe ooze out onto the road or better yet, into some other dimension. But Lark, of course, has other plans, and whips my door open. "Let's go, Batman. The back door awaits," she declares as she skips away to wait on the sidewalk.

When I grab the instruments, slinging their straps over my shoulders before I join her, I'm pretty sure my skin is melting from the raging blush that heats my flesh.

"What? Nothing to be ashamed about, liking a bit of butt stuff," Lark chimes as we walk toward Amigos Cantina, dipping down an alley to our left toward a metal stage door. "Anal is great. I like anal. This one time, I was on the road touring, and—"

Before I even realized what I'm doing, I've grabbed Lark's waist and caged her against the brick wall of the building. A spike of fear hits my veins that I could have hurt her, but it's washed away by the look she gives me as I loom over her. Even with the blur at this distance, I can still see it. Flushed skin. Blown pupils. A pulse that pounds in her neck.

Desire.

I lean in slowly, every heartbeat driving me closer until I can feel the heat of her unsteady exhalations against my cooling skin. "I am not ashamed, duchess."

Lark holds my gaze and issues a dare when she whispers, "Are you sure?"

Consuming the little space that remains between us, I press my hips forward and thread one hand into her hair. Lark's breath hitches when she feels my hard length against her stomach, my need for her painful, my cock begging to sink into her tight heat. "I cannot bear to hear about the way some other guy fucked my wife. Or the way she might have fucked him. Please. Not right now."

Her lips part. Her brow furrows. Her grip on my arm tightens.

I lean closer still, touch my lips to her ear. With one long, slow thrust of my hips, I grind my erection against her. Lark presses into me in return. A whimper escapes her control. "It is agonizing, Lark. It is fucking torture to imagine. To know it's not me. Don't you understand . . . ?"

When I pull away, I let my lips graze her cheek. Not a kiss, but a caress. A promise. That I'll let her go. I'll back away.

Except she doesn't let me.

Lark moves with me, both hands gripped tight to my arms. She doesn't let the space between us widen. There's a plea in her eyes. *Don't back away.*

"Lachlan," is all she says, her eyes fixed to my mouth.

I should pry myself free. Maybe I've gone too far. I just can't seem to make myself do it, even though I'm determined to earn Lark's forgiveness before we start down another path. I gave her my word. But when she inches closer and my hand caresses her face, a touch she leans into, I'm afraid it's a promise I'm about to break.

Lark rises on her tiptoes. Her scent envelopes me. Every breath she takes mixes with mine, becomes part of me.

I'm about to beg. For what I don't know. For anything she'll give me. For her to back away. I'm not sure what will come out of my mouth when I open it. "Lark, I—"

The door next to us swings open and crashes against the brick. Two men engrossed in an animated conversation stride into the alley. A third man remains in the doorway, his eyes shifting between me and Lark. A faint grin spreads across his lips, but there's confusion in his eyes he can't quite hide. A bit of jealousy too, I think.

"Hey, Lark. Right on time," the guy says. His head tilts as he regards us. We still haven't moved, and I realize how this must appear, Lark with her wide eyes and her mask of innocence so perfectly crafted, me with my leather jacket and Lark's blond waves twisted in my tattooed hand. I probably look about ready to fuck her right here against this wall. I would do it too, if she asked me. Lift this dress and slide into her with a single thrust, and then—

"You okay?" the guy asks, and with an unsteady breath, I release my grip on Lark and take a step away. A crease notches between her brows and a flash of pain seems to flare in her eyes when she lets my arms go, but only because I leave her no choice.

"Yes," she says, and clears her throat when that confirmation comes out breathless. "I'm great."

"You sure?"

"Of course. Xander, this is my husband, Lachlan." An electric charge bursts through my heart at the word *husband*. "Lachlan, this is Xander. He plays bass guitar and sings backup for KEX."

I swallow my spiteful feckin' glee and manage to trap it in a smirk that might come off as welcoming to someone who doesn't know me. But Lark knows better. I can feel her warning glare drill into my temple as I extend a hand.

"KEX. Cool." That's it. That's all I can manage. Anything more and I won't be able to contain myself.

"*Husband?* That's a wild turn of events, Lark," Xander says as he releases my hand and pins his attention to her. "When did that happen?"

"October."

"Huh. Didn't hear about it at all."

Lark shrugs and tugs me toward the door as Xander turns to lead us into the dark corridor. "Guess I was too busy making promotional posts for KEX to splash it all over social media," Lark says.

I nearly fail to repress a snort as Xander gives her a questioning look over his shoulder. Lark just smiles innocently in reply, and I can tell he's flummoxed. He strides a little farther ahead down the hallway and Lark squeezes my arm.

"What is it with you and KEX anyway?" Lark hisses.

I lean in and whisper, "Irish slang. Means *underwear.*"

She puffs out a little laugh as Xander pushes open a black door and heads into the shared dressing room. Lark stops at the threshold and I relinquish the instruments for her to set them aside. "Well, that's ironic, seeing how I usually prefer to not wear any."

She winks. I feckin' *die.*

"Go on," she says, amusement a flare behind her eyes. "Anyone gives you trouble, just say you're married to the chick who likes to go commando and digs ass play. Bye."

She wiggles her fingers as she waves and shuts the door in my face.

I'm still standing in the hallway like a feckin' dumbass when the door opens again. She pokes her head into the hallway. "Oh, and don't you dare open that present until I give you the bat signal or I swear to God, I will make your balls into snow globes. Okay, bye."

With a sardonically blown kiss, Lark shuts the door.

And I still haven't moved an inch.

I mutter a string of hushed swears as I drag a hand through my hair. "Christ Jesus. I need a feckin' whiskey."

"Ooh, get me a Diet Coke, please," Lark chimes from the other side of the door, and with a demonic little cackle, I know she's finally leaving me to my suffering this time.

I weave through the labyrinthine passageways and exit next to the stage where the opening act is setting up. If they give me suspicious looks, I don't notice. My thoughts are only on the bar ahead and the images of pantyless Lark.

I send a Diet Coke back to the dressing room for Lark and down my first drink as the opening act starts up, managing to somehow pace myself as they play out their set. When they finish an hour later, a couple of guys transition instruments to and from the stage for KEX, and I feel a brief flood of adrenaline in my veins when I spot Lark's cello. Finishing my drink doesn't dull the sensation. Nor does it help make the wait more bearable, a wait that feels decades long.

I'm nursing another whiskey at the bar when cheers finally erupt. Then shouts and whistles. Arms raise, hands clapping in the air. I pocket my glasses so I can see her clearer in the distance and watch as Lark leads the way on stage. The band files in behind her. She places a water bottle on a chair toward the left but stands before a microphone positioned near the front of the stage. Her guitar strap is slung over her shoulder and she grins and waves at the audience as the other musicians take their places. Her eyes roam the audience.

Until she finds me.

She beams. Her smile is so bright and warm that when she turns away to tune her instruments with the band, I feel a chill in the air. When they're done, she finds me again, and I give her a salute with my raised glass and grin right back at her.

"Welcome, everyone," Xander says. A round of cheers and hollers erupts around us but my connection with Lark remains unbroken. "That's Kevin on drums, Eric on guitar, I'm Xander, and we are KEX." Lark tries to hide a laugh behind her mic, but I can see it in her eyes. "And we have a special guest with us tonight. Please give a warm welcome to Lark Montague."

The cheers and whistles and claps are deafening. If there was any doubt who the audience is truly here for, it's erased by the outpouring of love for Lark.

The band starts and Lark fits their vibe effortlessly. She's supportive but not overshadowing, her voice a perfect balance to her counterparts'. They play out the first set, and Lark spends time during the short break to speak with the opening act and fans who approach. Though part of me wants to push through the throng of people and bask in the warmth she radiates, I stay at my table instead, convincing myself I'm content to watch Lark in her element.

I take a sip of my whiskey and watch as she lights up that stage. But I fail to pull myself back from the woman in the spotlight. I'm caught in the current of Lark and her music. I take it all in: the way she pours herself into every note with her eyes closed. The way her fingers slide across the fretboard. The way her lips press so close to the mic it looks like a kiss. Her voice is buoyant above the band, cheers, and audience, who sings along.

I'm still spellbound when Xander speaks to the crowd between songs.

"Lark is going to give us a new original song," he says.

Lark's shoulders seem to relax. She's fluid, shifting her weight from one foot to the next in a slow wave of motion as she says, "I wrote this song over the past few weeks. It took me a lot longer than usual. Of all the songs I've ever written, it was the hardest, but it's also my favorite."

A round of cheers and whistles rises from the audience, drinks held aloft in salute.

"I want to dedicate this to someone in the audience," Lark says as her eyes find mine. She smiles, and things I thought I'd never feel, never *let* myself feel, rise from the darkness. "It's called 'Ruinous Love.'"

I've never wanted more with a woman than to satisfy cravings. Nothing deeper than superficial need. But when I look at Lark, a woman who is so brave, so fierce, so beautifully complex, the only thing I crave is her. I feel just like the man in the story she told me that day in her craft room, like I'm falling from a cliff with nothing but a rope around my waist, hoping to capture something elusive. It's an insatiable need for the one thing I never wanted, an inescapable obsession for the one woman I thought I'd never have.

And then Lark starts singing.

> *I've been cold for a long, long time*
> *Dreaming of flames in the night*
> *I've been living a dark and delicate lie*
> *Oh what a sweet, strange, dangerous surprise to find*

All the lingering glances that feel like heat beneath my skin, the teasing jokes, the way she smiles when I give in and play along— I'd convinced myself they were just ephemeral moments. Products of familiarity.

It's the first time I've really let myself believe that I might be wrong.

> *Your touch, hot coals*
> *Your scent, like smoke*
> *Your eyes burn holes, looking back*
> *Sparks crack so loud*
> *Light falls on your mouth*
> *Your hands reach out, holding a match*
> *As if to ask*
> *"Baby, would you burn down the world for me?*

Cause I'd burn it down for you."
Ruinous love's all I know how to do
I'm not scared of damnation, I'm just new to this desire
I do believe the best things come out of the fire
I do, I do, I do

I set the glass down. Everything in the room disappears. Lark's song invades my senses, like it's seeping through blood and bone.

Ashes out the window
Moonbeams catching dust
Lay me down, baby, don't let me rest too much
The end of life as we know it is a beautiful view
Here I am, looking at you, you, you

It aches. Feckin' burns in my veins. That's my wife. And she's singing to me. Holding my eyes the whole song. Reaching right into my chest and tearing back the layers until I'm sure she can see my soul.

I do believe the best things come out of the fire
I do, I do, I do
You've been forgiven, got my permission to carry on
    sinning
You've been forgiven, got my permission to carry on
    sinning . . .

I never wanted to be in love, afraid of the decimating power of its loss. So I buried it. Starved it. Tried my best to keep it out. But Lark has blasted through every defense, a supernova in my life.

And now as she sings about pain and longing and the fire that I now know burns us both, I can't fathom my world without her. The only thing more powerful than my fear of losing Lark is my consuming need to be with her.

The song ends. The crowd cheers. Lark is luminous. Her gaze traverses the audience as she nods in thanks, even blows the occasional kiss to people she recognizes. But she always returns to me. Always smiles most brightly at me.

Xander starts talking into the mic as Lark pulls the guitar strap over her head and sets the instrument aside. She settles on the chair and lifts her cello from its stand to center it between her legs, taking a moment to quietly tune the instrument while Xander introduces the next song. My eyes are fixed on every motion she makes. There's no way I'd miss it when she looks at me. Her brows quirk. Leaning the bow against her legs, she hooks her thumbs together and crosses her hands to make a flapping motion with her fingers, a little bat in flight. I snort a laugh.

Open it, she mouths.

I pull the box from my pocket and open the small card. "Turn me on," it says in Lark's handwriting. When I meet her eyes briefly, she grins, and then I refocus on the box to tug the ribbon free and set it next to my drink. When I lift the lid, there's a small, oval-shaped remote control inside, the center constructed of soft black silicone. There are only three buttons—a plus sign at the top, a minus sign at the bottom, and a power symbol in the center.

I tilt my head, my question met with a smirk as the song starts and Lark slides the bow across the strings.

Power on, she mouths.

Guided by her reassuring nod, I press the power button and Lark closes her eyes, just the same as she often does when she loses herself in a melody. Nothing is happening. It's not like glitter confetti is raining from the ceiling, or pyrotechnics start shooting from the edge of the stage. I'm about to dismantle the battery casing when Lark catches my eye and shakes her head.

Turn it up.

I press the plus sign, over and over until Lark's eyes go wide and she shakes her head. Her cheeks blush as she bites down on a grin.

Down down down.

Oh. My. Fucking. Christ.

I press the minus sign a few times until Lark's head drops in relief, and then she keeps her gaze shuttered, swaying gently to the melody as she balances notes with sensations.

My blood froths in my veins. My heart is a riot in my ears. I look from the remote in my hand, to my wife on the stage, and back again.

"I am going to feckin' *die*," I mutter to myself.

I press the plus sign once. Twice. On the third try, Lark's brow furrows and she shifts in her seat. My cock hardens as I watch her squirm, desire spiraling through my thoughts, pulling me down into near madness.

She's given me control to a toy she must be wearing. And she wants me to watch her come on that feckin' stage.

I turn it up by two. The crease deepens between her brows. She doesn't miss a note, but maybe I want her to. A bounce of the bow across the strings. A stuttering melody.

My thumb stays pressed down on the minus button until she meets my eyes with a petulant sulk.

Lips curled, I give her a dark smirk in reply before I turn the vibration she's feeling down one more notch. The glare I receive is incendiary, burning so brightly that I grip the edge of the table to keep myself from storming to the stage.

I press the plus sign four times and relief washes through Lark's expression.

I leave her there, watching as she draws the bow across the strings, her weight shifting from one hip to the other. For a long moment, she seems to feel the balance between music and pleasure, as though she's lost in a void beyond the reach of the world that surrounds her.

But she's not so far from my control.

I press the plus sign two times. Lark's eyes snap open and she finds me without delay. There's a dare in the way she watches me. She wants to see if I'll take her further, with all these people watching. Maybe they won't notice the blush that creeps up her neck, or the way she bites her lips as her lashes flutter closed.

Or maybe they will.

I turn the remote up three more times.

Lark's lips part. Even from this distance I feel attuned to every minor change in her body. The rise and fall of her chest. The tension in her forearm, the way she strains to stay with the music. I'm right there with her, like a note in her melody.

I press the plus sign three more times.

Lark's eyes fly open and fuse to mine. The look she gives me is pleading.

Two more pushes of the plus sign and she can barely sit still.

One more and her head drops. The orgasm must be within reach, but I want her eyes on me. I *need* them.

When I deliver five hits to the minus button, the look Lark gives me is desperate. She's about to toss that cello on the floor. I would give my right arm to see her stride off that stage and drop to her knees at my feet. I want her begging for my cock, to feel the fluttering desperation of her fingers as she fumbles with my belt to free my erection. It strains against my zipper in a painful demand as I picture her stripping me down. I'm desperate to sink into her, to feel how tightly her cunt can grip my cock as she takes me deep into her pussy. I need to see my cum dripping down her thighs so everyone here will know. She is *my* wife. *Mine.*

But for now, Lark's unwavering attention will have to do.

One. Two. Three presses to the plus button. Lust floods Lark's expression, but I know it's not enough as she shifts her weight, searching for friction.

She doesn't need to say a word to beg for release. It's written all over her face.

I press the plus symbol more times than I bother to count.

Lark's brow furrows and her mouth drops open on a moan no one can hear. But I can feel her break apart. The swell of music. The notes of longing. The way she watches me, pleading, desperate, taking everything and wanting more. She needs me. To touch her. To want her. To fuck her. This is not enough.

When I'm sure she's come, I lower the strength of the vibration before I press the power button. The song ends, the audience clapping and cheering as Lark smiles for me, sweat misting her brow in the bright lights.

She sets the cello and bow on the stand.

And by the time she's looked up, I've disappeared from view.

EXPOSED

Lark

I scan the audience.

But Lachlan is gone.

I don't catch sight of his dark hair or his tattooed skin or that fucking smirk. I don't know why, or how, or when it happened, but I *need* his teasing, cocky smile. Just like I need that soulful look in his eyes when he desperately wants to share but can't bear to. Just like I need his growls and grumbles and the zombie grumpiness he can't shake until he's had his first coffee. But what I don't need, what I can't bear, is him disappearing. Was the vibrator thing too much? Did I cross a line? I thought he would find it sexy. But maybe . . .

I smile through the encore, because I'm good at that. I push every atom of hurt to the bottom of my guts where it burns. Then I wave and pack up my shit. I ask Kevin to look after my instruments until tomorrow, though I don't say what's on my mind. I don't tell him that Lachlan—the man I finally called my husband out loud and *meant* it—has left me here.

He left me here.

I leave the stage before anyone can pull me aside, then jog down the hallway toward the backstage bathroom to cry my fucking eyes out.

The tears are streaking down my skin before I even make it to the door.

As soon as it's closed behind me, I rest my forehead in my palms, lean my elbows on the counter, and fucking *sob*.

I want him. I want him so badly it's a crushing ache. It's as though my bones are folding in on themselves, breaking into splinters and shards. The more I see who Lachlan really is—all the things he does for the people he holds close—the more I want to be near him. I want to be part of his tight embrace. I thought I was.

I thought wrong.

"What is wrong with you?" I hiss as I press my eyes shut.

I'm trying to muster the strength to face my reflection when the door bursts open and crashes against the wall. I spin around and meet the incandescent eyes of my husband.

Lachlan fills the doorframe, sucking the energy from the room as though he's made of dark matter. "What the fuck are you doing?"

I let out a watery laugh and flap a hand toward my face. "Crying, clearly. What the fuck are *you* doing?"

Every step Lachlan takes toward me is menacing. Predatory. And though my makeup is probably smeared down my cheeks and I think I lost another fake eyelash because *why the fuck won't they stay on around this man*, I don't back away.

Lachlan doesn't stop until he's looming over me, his eyes dark and filled with a vicious heat, but he doesn't touch me when he says, "I was pacing in the dressing room, duchess. I was waiting for you so I could give you the keys to drive us home and then fuck you until you can't walk tomorrow."

Everything in my body grinds to a halt. Everything except my heart. It hammers my bones with a staccato rhythm until I'm sure the bruised organ will wedge its way between my ribs and tear free of my chest.

"I . . . well . . ." I take a step back, but Lachlan moves with me. Another step and my ass hits the bathroom counter. I square my shoulders and try to tilt my chin in defiance, but I feel too exposed to scramble into my armor. "Well . . . I . . . you . . ."

"You're never at a loss for words, Lark Kane. Spit it out so I can say what I want to say."

His eyes fixate on mine, lethally dark in the dim light. It's like every cell in his body is trained on me. My stomach flips as he steps farther into my space, just enough that he grazes my body with his.

Dear God.

"You should have bat-signaled me," I finally say.

There's a brief, suspended moment where neither of us moves, and then Lachlan laughs—really laughs. The corners of his eyes crinkle with delight. "All right, you feckin' catastrophe. Next time I'll just use *this* instead of the phone, since you didn't think to check your texts," he says as he holds up the remote control.

"I left my phone in the dressing room." I tear my attention from Lachlan's unwavering stare and open the text notifications on my watch.

> Dressing room. Now.

"Oh. That's, um . . ."

Lachlan raises a single brow.

"Bossy."

"*Bossy*," he echoes.

I nod and try to resurrect my confidence. "But if you're going to use the remote instead of the phone moving forward, you should probably test it. See if it still works."

"I did test it. In front of an audience of what, three hundred—"

"Five hundred."

"—*five hundred* people. My wife. On stage. Having an orgasm. In front of five hundred feckin' people."

My wife. The possessive edge in it cuts through my thoughts. Echoes in my head. Ricochets in my chest. I try to shrug it off and give him a haughty look, but those two words rattle around in my mind. "You're the only one who noticed."

"I doubt that very much, duchess."

"And that bothers you?"

"You meant what you said in that song? That you forgive me?"

"You didn't answer my question."

"Answer my question first." Lachlan leans closer, his eyes never straying from mine. Every word is slow and distinct when he says, "Did. You. Mean. It?"

I swallow. "Yes."

Lachlan eases back just a little and I try not to move with him even though my body is burning for his closeness, begging for his touch. His eyes break away from mine to drop down the length of me, from the sweat that dots my hairline to the tips of my boots and back again. When he meets my eyes, there's fire and need and longing staring back at me.

"Does it bother me?" he says, returning to my question. "To see you on that stage and know I'm the one making you come and yet I can't touch you?" Lachlan edges closer. He leans forward to cage me between his arms as he grips the counter, but he's careful not to touch me. "Yes, it feckin' bothers me, duchess. It bothers me very feckin' much. In the best and worst of ways."

I bite my lip and Lachlan watches the motion as though it's the only thing he can see, like nothing else exists in the world except for that small display of need. "What are you going to do about it?" I whisper.

A slow, feral, ravenous smirk tugs at one corner of his lips as his eyes turn lightless, the color consumed by desire. He raises the remote clutched in his hand and turns it on. Even at its low setting, the vibration shocks my swollen clit.

"You're going to show me that toy," he commands, "and then you'll find out."

With a flash of motion, Lachlan lifts me by the waist and sets my ass on the bathroom counter.

We stare at each other. Lips parted. Breaths ragged. We're separated by mere inches of air and thin layers of fabric and the determination to not be the first to bend so far they snap.

It's Lachlan who makes the first move, Lachlan who slowly leans forward. Lachlan who bridges that gap to graze my cheek with his lips and summon shivers through my flesh, his plea a caress against my ear.

"Duchess," he whispers. His voice is a lush, luxurious spell. "Show. Me."

Lachlan pulls back just enough to solder his eyes to mine. He never breaks eye contact as he folds his hand around mine and guides it to the tulle that covers my legs. He curls my fingers into the fabric before he lets his hand drift away.

I take two shallow breaths and then bunch the fabric in my fist to drag it up my leg. The more fiercely the need burns in his eyes, the slower I move, drawing out both his torture and my own. The hem inches up my skin. Only once the edge skims Lachlan's hand where it rests against my thigh does he look down. His thumb follows in the wake of the fabric. Tension radiates from his coiled muscles. I slow to a crawl of motion as the fabric climbs higher until it finally reaches the lace edge of my panties.

And then I stop.

Lachlan's eyes snap to mine, dark with a dare. His thumb traces the hem. "Thought you didn't like to wear these," he says, his voice low and husky.

"Special circumstances." I press my hand over his when he grips the edge of scalloped lace. "I want you," I say before doubt can blossom in his thoughts. "You know things about me and my past that I don't tell anyone."

His face creases with pain. He takes a breath to reply, but I press my fingertips to his lips.

"Just don't go thinking I want you to play nice." A slow smile creeps across my lips. "I'm not your demure little duchess. I'm your fucking whore, understand?"

I slip my thumb into his mouth. Lachlan groans as he wraps his lips around my flesh and sucks. When I move to pull my thumb free he bites down, his teeth bared, his eyes hooded as he drinks in my reaction. I'm caught in the balance of pain and pleasure. The push and pull of power. Lachlan lets me go and turns up the vibration on the toy and I suck in a tremulous breath.

"Then lift that dress up and fucking prove it." Lachlan leans closer. His fingers trace my thighs, spreading them wider without lifting the fabric that pools between them. His breath floods my face as his lips stop a thread's width from mine. "Show me how soaked those goddamned panties are from coming on that stage in front of all those people. Show me how desperate you are to be fucked."

My chest grazes his as I take a shallow breath. With my eyes fused to Lachlan's, I lift the dress to my waist and lean back until my shoulders rest on the mirror where I feel the ridges of the leather harness against my spine.

Lachlan's hands are gentle on my skin even though every other muscle seems coiled to strike. Tension radiates from his body. He takes one step away and holds my eyes for a moment that feels eternal before he finally drops his gaze to the apex of my thighs.

With one long, slow stroke of his thumb, he runs his touch across the damp fabric and the vibrating toy beneath it.

"Tell me," I whisper as his thumb passes in another stroke.

His eyes are dark. Deadly. Merciless. "Tell you what? That you're my fucking whore?"

"Yes."

The vibration increases and I gasp as he presses the toy to my clit. "I didn't lock the door, Lark. Someone could walk in here at any moment. Does that scare you?"

I shake my head and bite my lip and moan.

"Good, because any one of those assholes that watched you on that stage could walk in here and I don't give a fuck. I won't stop until you scream my fucking name so they know *exactly* whose whore you are."

In a flash of motion, something metallic slides across my hip and my panties go slack. Lachlan tugs them away and with another slice of his knife they're off completely. The toy is gone, and my feet hit the floor. He grips my waist and spins me to face the mirror. The blade he used falls into the sink as Lachlan wraps the panties around my throat but doesn't tighten them, his eyes fused to my reflection.

With the vibrating toy clutched in his grip, Lachlan drags a knuckle down my cheek as the other hand holds the fabric around my neck. "Red means . . . ?"

"Stop."

"Orange means?"

"Slow down."

"Green means?"

"Fuck me and fill me with your cum."

Lachlan chuckles against my ear before he gives it a nip, letting his teeth rake across the flesh. "Only if you beg," he whispers.

Please barely leaves my lips and he tightens the panties with a twist of his fist, then presses the toy to my clit with his other hand. The vibration skates across my nerves in slow circles and I roll my hips, seeking friction. The veins in my neck strain against the pressure of the fabric. My makeup is smeared in streaks beneath my eyes. But when I let out a low and husky moan and see Lachlan's jaw clench with restrained desperation, I feel powerful. Beautiful. Like I can be the woman I want to be.

"More," I whimper. "Please, *more*."

Lachlan's smile borders on menacing. He takes a long moment to answer me, pressing kisses and nips along my jaw. "Try again, duchess. And make it pretty."

An ache to be filled clenches deep in my core as Lachlan kicks my feet out a little wider and rolls the toy across my sensitive nerves in long strokes. He doesn't turn it up or make any moves to give me what I crave. But denial is its own reward.

"Lachlan, *please*, I need more. I need *you*," I whisper. The panties tighten around my throat, just enough that I can breathe in a thin stream, but not without my skin flushing crimson. "I need to be filled with you."

Lachlan leans close to my ear. He holds my eyes with an unwavering stare as every exhalation tickles my skin. "The first time I fuck my wife is not going to be in the bathroom of some bar. So if you want to be filled, you'd better use your imagination and come with what I give you."

I whimper at the sudden need to leave with him, to go anywhere but here.

I'm disheveled. Desperate. Imperfect. But Lachlan looks at me in the mirror as though he sees through every tarnished layer, every broken mask. It's the thought of going home with this man who always searches for the real woman beneath it all that propels me into action.

I press Lachlan's hand over my clit. I grind my hips. I beg for him to tighten his grip over my throat. And then I come in blinding stars as Lachlan's name tumbles from my lips, over and over, a chant that doesn't stop until he's wrung every moment of pleasure from my body. It washes through me but leaves a hum of need behind. It's not enough. It won't be until I feel his skin against mine and the weight of his body and the planes of muscle beneath my palms.

My head drops to my chest and Lachlan lets the fabric fall from my throat. The vibration of the toy lowers and then he turns it off. He wraps his arm across my waist and holds me close. I relish his heat, the languorous kisses he layers across my neck, the pressure of his muscle and bone against my trembling flesh.

The door creaks behind us and my eyes snap open to Xander's wide-eyed reflection in the mirror.

"*Get the fuck out,*" Lachlan snarls as his arm tightens around me and he shelters my body with his. Xander disappears with a shocked apology, but Lachlan's eyes stay fused to the door in a vicious glare. "I feckin' hate that guy."

"You don't even know him." Though I bite down on the edge of my grin, it erupts when Lachlan turns his fury to me. "Are you jealous?"

"Fuck off."

"You *are* jealous."

Lachlan's deep sigh cools the beads of sweat on my neck.

"Let's get out of here so I can prove you have no reason to be." I turn in Lachlan's arms and pull his glasses from his front pocket. Slowly, I slide them on and fluff up my hair as I give him a smirk. "How do they look?"

"*Christ Jesus,* why is that so hot?"

"Now imagine them paired with a corset and feathers." My laugh is the freest it's felt in a long while as Lachlan grabs my hand and pulls me toward the door. I tug back, not ready to go yet desperate to leave. "Wait, Lachlan. I look like shit."

Lachlan looks at me over his shoulder, his eyes warm. "You look beautiful, Lark." When I still hesitate, he turns to face me fully and steps closer. He pulls the glasses from my face. Puts them on. Sees me clearly. He smiles and drags a thumb across one cheek, and then the other. "There. Less like tears. More intentional. See?"

He takes my shoulders and turns them until I meet my reflection. Maybe I still look a little crazy with my trash panda mask and flushed, freshly-fucked blush and my sweaty, wild hair. But he's right. I look beautiful too.

With a swift kiss to my cheek, Lachlan takes my hand and resumes his campaign to pull me from the bathroom, his steps purposeful. "Now let's get out of here. I meant what I said earlier about you driving us home so I can fuck you until you can't walk."

"Then let's grab my stuff quickly," I say before he can stride toward the back exit. "I'd rather not leave it with the band if I don't have to."

Lachlan groans but pivots to follow behind me as I lead the way to the stage. Xander looks up from where he packs up our equipment next to the far wall. He gives us a sheepish smile, and I motion to my cello and guitar to let him know I'll be taking them.

"Can you carry that for me, please, Lachlan?" I ask with a nod to the guitar in the black case. Lachlan squeezes my shoulder and strides toward it, progress that Xander pretends not to watch with trepidation, though he fails. Lachlan mutters something to Xander I don't hear. I try not to laugh as I lift my cello from the stand.

"A wonderful performance," a voice says from behind me. Something about the accent is familiar. "The cello is my favorite instrument."

I turn. It's the man I met in Lachlan's shop. "Mine too," I reply. "Abe, right?"

"Yes, good memory." Abe drops an appreciative glance to the instrument in my hands. "Been playing a long time?"

I nod before bending down to lower the cello into the case. "Since I was seven."

"Seven," he echoes. He squats to stay within my eyeline. "What a wonderful tool music is to escape from darkness. Don't you agree? *Make a joyful noise unto the Lord, all the earth. Break forth into joyous song and sing praises.*"

My smile is polite, yet brittle. Abe scrutinizes me, but I'm not sure that he interprets my discomfort—or maybe he just ignores it. There's a flatness in his eyes. A disconnect with his gentle smile.

Abe passes me the bow. He holds on when I grip the frog, waiting for me to meet his eyes. That smile returns, void of light. "Have a lovely evening, Miss Montague. Thank you for the inspiration."

He lets go of the bow.

By the time I set it in the case and Lachlan joins by my side, Abe is already gone.

CRAWL

Lachlan

The drive home is the longest fifteen minutes of my life.

I want to touch Lark, but I won't do anything more than look at her, not until we've made it home. And she makes it bloody agonizing, the way she bites her bottom lip when she concentrates, the way she shifts in her seat, her torn panties burning a hole in my pocket. I'm dying to run my fingers across her skin. To taste her. To sink inside her. To feel the weight of her body over mine as she rides my cock and grips me tight. But I'm determined to savor her. Even if it's torture the whole way home.

And Lark *loves* torture.

"So," she says as she takes a left at the light when it would be faster to take a right, "when you said you were going to fuck me until I couldn't walk tomorrow, what exactly do you have in mind?"

My molars clamp shut so tightly they might break.

"Like . . . are there toys involved, or is this strictly a marathon situation?"

I press my head against the headrest.

"Do you have a mood board? Pinterest?"

I turn slowly to level her with a menacing glare.

"Are we talking cold baths here? Should I stop for ice? I can pull into Power Pump. Irony and ice, it's a double win." She turns the signal light on to pull into the gas station.

"Take that turn and I swear to Christ I will make you beg on your hands and knees for me to let you come."

Lark grins at me.

She takes the turn.

I say nothing until she rolls into a parking spot and shuts off the engine. She pulls the keys from the ignition and spins them around her finger. My menacing glare does nothing but brighten her smile. "You are going to regret this, duchess."

"Oh good," she says as she opens the door. "I'll get two bags then."

She hops out of the car. When she's at the entrance, she turns and winks at me over her shoulder before she disappears inside.

My cock aches and I drag a hand down my face. I put all my effort into tearing my thoughts away from Lark, but it doesn't work.

She takes her time in the shop. And just like she promised, she comes out with two bags of ice and a magnetic, shit-eating grin, one that stays pinned on me as she saunters past the passenger door to put them both in the trunk. Lark slips back into the car looking quite pleased with herself, and it only makes my erection that much harder. Just like she probably planned.

"Quite the smirk you have there, duchess. Think you got away with something, do ya?"

Lark laughs and turns toward me to look out the back window as she reverses. The harness tightens across her breasts with the twist of her body. "Oh I know I didn't, but it still brings me joy."

"Won't be so feckin' funny when you're gagging on my cock."

A giggle escapes her lips as she throws the car into first gear but keeps her foot on the brake. She pins me with her crystalline gaze, and though she might be teasing me, I know what my words have done to her. It's in the slow pass of her tongue over her lips. The dark expanse of her pupils. The way her nipples harden to firm peaks beneath the delicate fabric of her dress.

I lean closer and her breath hitches. My eyes fuse to her mouth as a smile sneaks across my lips.

"You like that, don't you? You want me filling your throat. You want to swallow every drop of cum like my good fucking whore. Don't worry, you will. And then you're going to beg me for more, won't you?" I chuckle as her lips part and the sweet scent of her breath floods my senses. She nods. "That's what I thought."

I lean a little closer, just enough for my lips to graze Lark's as I whisper, "*Drive.*"

I sit back in my seat with a satisfied grin. My cock is so painfully hard that I'm convinced my entire body is as furious about the near kiss as she is. Finally, she takes her foot off the brake. The tires squeal against the asphalt as we pull out of the parking lot.

The moment she parks, I'm out of the car. Lark's barely gotten a foot on the garage floor before I haul her out of the vehicle and throw her over my shoulder to the sound of her shocked laugh. I grab the ice from the trunk, and a moment later I'm striding up the stairs with her body still hanging off my back. Her half-hearted protests echo across the factory floor. It's not until we're in the apartment and I've put the ice in the chest freezer that I set her down, but it's only long enough to capture her lips in a brutal kiss.

Lark melts into me. Her moan vibrates in my mouth as her tongue sweeps across mine. She fists my shirt and tugs me along with her, not breaking the kiss as she stumbles into a side table and the dog and the couch as she leads me toward the bedrooms.

The moment we're in her room, I pick her up and toss her on the bed. Lark is panting, kneeling on the crumpled covers, her eyes hooded. Her expression is ravenous as I reach over my head and pull my shirt off.

I take a step back toward the armchair in the corner of the room. "I meant what I said."

"I'm counting on it," she breathes. Her eyes rake over my body, coasting over scars hidden beneath ink. She drinks in every inch of my skin, the fabric of her dress balled in tight fists as she leans back onto her heels, her lower lip trapped between her teeth. "I want to touch you."

With a final step backward, I sink into the chair. I lean back and regard her for a long moment, reveling in the desperation painted across her face. "Then you'd better show me how much you want it, duchess."

A shiver wracks through Lark's body before she starts to climb off the bed.

"No."

Lark stops immediately. She waits for instruction, but there's frustration in her eyes. My blood turns to fire, possibilities and fantasies racing through my mind. Just like the time I spoke to Lark on the balcony, she ignites a spark in the dark. But I don't know if I've ever been the hunter with Lark, or if I'm the one who's been ensnared.

Either way, there's no stopping it now. I wouldn't want to if I could. Not when Lark is *right there*, nearly within reach, so desperate for friction that she's nearly squirming on the bed.

"Take that dress off, but leave the harness on," I say.

Lark pauses as though the words take a moment to cut through the haze of lust that's descended between us. Then she guides one of the thin straps off her shoulder, slipping it beneath the leather that loops toward her back. She does the same on the other side. With balletic flexibility, she pulls each arm free, careful not to tear the delicate fabric. Then she holds my eyes to drink in my reaction as she slowly pulls the layers down beneath the harness, exposing her breasts and pebbled nipples, the smooth expanse of skin around her navel, the narrow strip of hair leading to her pussy. She drags the dress down her legs and holds it up before she lets it drift to the floor.

Every breath she takes is unsteady as I take my time to just look. The black leather lines and tiny stars. The way they trace the contours of her breasts, the ridges of her ribs. My art embracing her flesh.

It takes everything in me to stay in the chair.

We exchange a silent conversation with no more than a glance, and I know Lark understands that she can say whatever she wants. Whatever she feels. She can be whoever she wants to be. I will take her in any version of herself she's willing to give.

My voice is as dispassionate as I can manage when I ask, "What are you?"

"Your whore."

"Then get down on your hands and knees."

Lark slides off the bed, gets down on her hands and knees, and waits. And waits. And *waits*.

I take the blade from my pocket and unhook my stropping belt. As I slide the sharp edge across the leather, I watch her tremble with the chill of anticipation. When she can't take it any longer, when I think *I'm* about to give in to my desires, she finally whispers a single word. *Please.*

I close the blade and flip it over in my hand. "You're not my wife," I say, and there's a flash of panic and hurt in her eyes. "You're just *mine*. Now *crawl*."

Relief flickers in Lark's face.

One hand and one knee after the other, Lark crawls toward me. Her eyes never stray from my face. When she stops at my feet, she doesn't touch me. Instead, she waits for my next command. There's not a single thing in this world that's more intoxicating than seeing her kneel before me but knowing that she's still the one in control. It's so clear in her willing gaze, the way she folds her hands in her lap and pushes her breasts together against the leather straps, encouraging our little game. She wants to be ordered. To be used. To be filled and denied and degraded. To be rewarded when she's ready. She's in control. And I will give her anything she wants and more.

"Belt," I say, and I let go of the strip of leather so she can free the buckle and open it wide. "Zipper." She pulls it down. "Now take my cock out."

I lift my hips so Lark can lower my pants and briefs, freeing my erection. It's painfully hard, ready to plunge into the heat of her mouth, a bead of pre-cum gathered at the head. Lark stares at it with ravenous desire. She bites her lip and wraps her hand around the base.

"Spit on it and stroke it."

Lark does as I ask without hesitation, spitting on the head before she starts languid passes of her hand from the base to the tip. The pace is slow, her grip strong. A moan rumbles in my chest as I sink farther back and resist the urge to close my eyes so I can watch her lavish my cock with her attention. I've dreamed of her touching me like this so many times, and it's a thousand times better than I imagined.

And it will never be enough.

I trace my knuckles across her cheek and thread my hand into her hair to gather it into my fist. "You remember the traffic lights?" I ask, and Lark nods. "Good. Tap my leg twice for orange. Three times for stop. Otherwise, you'll swallow every fucking inch I give you, understand?"

Lark gives me a single nod and a flash of a dark smile before I push her mouth down onto my cock and fall into heaven.

"*Christ feckin' Jesus*," I hiss as Lark swirls her tongue over the crown and firms her lips around my flesh. The wet heat of her mouth sends my blood roaring in my ears. A held breath burns in my chest until I finally let it go. I let her take a few shallow passes to get acclimated to my length before I firm up my grip on her hair. "I thought you said you were my wicked little whore, duchess. You can do better than that."

I push to the back of her throat and Lark gags as tears shine in her eyes. I do it again and she moans. A third time and she moans again, the tears streaking down her skin, the sight of her ruined makeup and her swollen lips and that fucking harness making me feral with need.

"There's nothing like turning a perfect princess into a fucking slut," I grit out as I pick up a rhythm of deep thrusts. "I bet your pussy is so wet it's dripping down your thighs."

Lark whimpers.

"Take your fingers and show me."

Lark drags her hand down her body as I continue the cadence of thrusts, each one hitting the back of her throat as she moans and whimpers. Her eyes flutter closed as she touches herself and then she brings her hand between us, the proof of her desire glistening across her fingers.

With my free hand, I capture her wrist and bring her fingers to my waiting mouth and suck.

Sweet and salty, her flavor coats my tongue and I nearly lose my goddamn mind.

I pull Lark's mouth off my cock and with a swift motion, I band an arm around her middle and hoist her into the air to deposit her on the bed. She barely has a moment to orient herself before I've pushed her onto her knees, pitched her forward onto her hands, and kneeled behind her to bury my face against her pussy.

Lark lets out a desperate cry as I swirl my tongue over her swollen clit and lavish her pussy with licks and kisses. Every sound she makes leaves an indelible mark on my mind, as immutable as the ink in my skin. Her taste burns itself into my memory like a brand. *This woman is* mine.

And I devour her like I'm going to consume her soul.

Lark writhes and moans and fists the sheets, but I don't let her out of my grip. One hand tightens around her thigh, the other grips the harness strap across her back. I take her to the edge of an orgasm and leave her there, stalling whenever she gets close to her climax and resuming my efforts when it starts to subside. And once she starts begging, that's when I let her go. I kneel back and allow the cool air to chill the saliva and arousal gathered at her entrance.

"No," she whispers, casting a desperate look over her shoulder. "Please."

The panic subsides when she sees me pull my pants and briefs the rest of the way off and kick them to the side.

"I didn't say you could move."

Lark gets back into position on her hands and knees, but it looks like it takes great effort to tear her gaze from my body, a detail that makes my heart surge beneath my bones. "I've been tested," I say as I shift one knee onto the bed and then the other, the motion eliciting a shiver of anticipation through Lark's nearly naked body. "I'm clear. Are you on contraception?"

"Yes," she breathes, her voice barely more than a whisper as breaths heave from her chest. "I want you, Lachlan. *Please.*"

I roll the head of my cock across her clit in slow circles, then notch it at her entrance as she trembles, only to bring it back to her clit again in a maddening tease. "You can beg for me better than that."

"*Please*, Lachlan. I need to feel you. I need you inside me. I need you to make me come." There's a moment of pause, a held breath. Uncertainty hangs over her and I roll my cock over her pussy, waiting her out. "I need to be fucked by my husband."

My motion slows as her words sink in and settle in my chest. And then I position my cock at her entrance and push in, just the tip, and relish the relief in Lark's responding moan.

"It's a damn good thing you got that ice, duchess, because I'm going to fucking ruin this tight cunt of yours." I push in a little deeper and tremble as her pussy grips my erection. "When I said I was going to fuck my wife until she couldn't walk, I meant it."

I slam to the base of my erection and we both cry out as pleasure and need consume us. I pull back to the tip and do it again. And again. And again until I pick up a rhythm of long, deep strokes that glide through Lark's heat.

Lark whimpers and moans and begs for more. She chants my name. I push her upper body against the mattress and grip the harness. I piston into her, every stroke deep and merciless, just like she asks for when she begs for me to go harder, deeper. And when I sense the orgasm building at the base of my spine, an electric tension that hums through my nerves, I reach around and circle her clit until Lark screams, her back bowed, her body trembling as she unravels. Her pussy tightens around my erection. I can't hold back, spilling ropes of cum as deep as I can inside her until I'm shaking and barely able to kneel, my heart a deafening hum in my ears that blankets all other sound.

I pull out and collapse next to Lark and gather her to me. Her body trembles in the aftermath of her orgasm, my breath unsteady against her back. Euphoria and relief settle in the silence that lies over us and cools our sweat. We don't talk for a long while as my heart settles into a steady rhythm and her breathing slows. Lark traces patterns on my arm, melodies in my skin, and before long she's humming. Her voice is soft and content. It's the first time I really realize how much we say to each other without words. How we've started to grow together. This was never meant to be permanent, but suddenly when I picture my future, I can't see it without the presence of her notes in the dark.

I turn her over beneath me and stare down into her face. She smiles, her skin glowing in the dim light.

"Hey," Lark whispers. Her finger traces a line across my chest, following patterns of black ink.

"Hi." I press a kiss to her forehead. One to her cheekbone. One to the side of her nose. Her fingertips trace my back as I follow the line of her jaw, then her neck. With her lips at my ear, she shimmies a hand between us and grips my length, my cock hard again and already desperate for more of her touch, her heat.

"I thought you said you were going to ruin my pussy," she coos in my ear as she runs the tip of my erection through our cum gathered at her entrance.

"Duchess," I warn as I push into her heat to the sound of her wanton moan. "You're not going to be able to sit down tomorrow without thinking of me."

"That had better be a promise."

And it is.

I lose track of the hours. Lose count of how many times she breathes my name, or screams it, or begs with it. I don't know how many times she comes. The sky beyond the curtainless windows is turning from black to indigo when we finally stop. Lark's body is a boneless, exhausted, beautiful ruin of sweaty skin and tangled hair and trembling flesh. But she smiles at me when I back off the bed and stare down at her. It's the most relaxed I've ever seen her.

"What are you doing?" she asks as I slide my briefs and jeans on.

"Taking Bentley out. I'm sure he could use a break."

"You coming back?"

"Of course I'm coming back," I say as I fold the covers down for her to slip beneath them. "I think you'd murder me and sew my skin into a chew toy if I permanently left with your dog."

"I meant here." Lark taps the free pillow.

I hesitate for a moment before I pull on my shirt. There's conflict in Lark's eyes as she watches me, as though she's not sure she should have asked. "Do you want me to?"

Lark nods. "Yeah. I think I do."

"Want me to bring back some ice?" I ask with a wicked smile, and she giggles.

"I think I'll survive, unless you're planning on fucking me in the ass when you get back. In that case, yes."

I grin like it's a joke, but my blood instantly heats and my cock hardens.

Lark settles in beneath the covers and I place a kiss to her temple before turning to leave. Her eyes are still on me when I pause at the threshold of her door and look at her over my shoulder.

I take my time around the block. Though part of me is eager to get back, I want to give Lark space to process and allow my own thoughts to settle. And predawn quiet is the perfect time to do that. The streets are dark between the lamplight, and the cold air refreshes my sweaty skin. There's hardly anyone on the street, just the occasional car and a lone man dressed in hospital scrubs, his hood pulled up against the morning chill. He leaves the building across the street and walks in the opposite direction. So I let

Bentley take his time to sniff every post and piss on every fire hydrant as we walk around the block.

When we get back inside, Lark is fast asleep.

I hesitate for a moment, unsure if I should just go to the other room to let her rest. Maybe it's selfish, but I strip down to my briefs and slip beneath the covers next to her. She wakes as soon as I do and my regret is immediate, but she reaches for my wrist to drag my arm across her body then settles against me.

"Who knew," she says, her voice hazy with exhaustion. "All I needed to get to sleep was a thorough fucking from my husband. Could have saved money on that sleep retreat."

"I think we can still make use of that yoga sleep pose. I feel like that alone is worth the investment." I kiss her shoulder as she breathes a laugh, and I wrap my arms tighter around Lark's body. "Try to get some rest."

"No trying this time," she replies with a yawn. "Only doing."

With a final kiss, I fall asleep with my wife in my arms.

When I wake a few hours later with the sun streaming through the leaded glass, Lark is gone.

Within a few slow-moving moments, I've gotten myself together enough to be semipresentable. I follow the scent of coffee and toast in the kitchen. Lark is there, humming to music that plays quietly from her speakers as she flips eggs in a pan. Bentley sits at her feet, waiting for scraps to drop in his direction.

"You know, he wouldn't be so bad about getting in your way if you didn't toss him bits of bacon. I saw that," I say, trying and failing to give Lark a chastising look as she tosses another piece of meat to the dog and grins.

"It keeps his coat shiny."

"Right. Sure." I lay a quick kiss on Lark's lips before grabbing the coffee she's already set aside for me. "What do you have planned for today, aside from giving your dog more gastro troubles?"

Lark laughs more than I thought the joke deserved. "I forgot about that."

"I didn't. That was the feckin' worst. I'm serious—you should look at changing his food. No animal should emit smells like that."

Bentley glares at me from his seat.

"It wasn't his fault," Lark says as she takes two plates to the dining table and we settle into chairs across from each other.

"I know. It's yours, for feeding him bacon and cheese."

"No, I mean I blamed it on him, but it was the dead guy in the coffee table."

I blink at Lark. Then at the coffee table. Then at Lark again. "*What?*"

Lark takes a slow sip of her coffee. "I sanded the tip of his nose a little when we were talking. That was the smell. Nose bits and resin, I guess." She shrugs and starts cutting into her bacon and eggs.

"Sometimes, I forget that I'm married to a serial"—Lark glares at me and I catch myself—"*multiple deleter.* And then you conveniently remind me that you've made your victims into crafts. Crafts which I've apparently been setting my drinks on while watching *Constantine,* or *Speed,* or basically any other Keanu movie ever made."

"About that, you should probably start using my coasters."

"I've seen your coasters. I'll take a pass."

"Anyway, crafting is a soothing hobby. I could start selling things on Etsy," Lark says with a charmingly sardonic smile. "How's your contract killer gig going by the way, *dear husband*?"

"About that . . ." I pull my phone from my pocket and set it next to me, opening the messages from Leander that came through while I was asleep. "Leander needs me to head over there this afternoon. Naturally, he's asked if his favorite muffin murderer could come with. Conor said the payments we found in Pacifico were legit, so I was thinking we should go back to the drawing board and search for some new options on who the killer might be. What do you think?"

"I'd be delighted. And I'll make some muffins."

We exchange smiles and slip into a routine that feels so easy and familiar that it's hard to reconcile our marriage with the circumstances of its beginning. We talk and laugh as we finish our breakfast and then bake together. We enjoy comfortable silences and long, weighted glances, slow smiles and crimson blushes. We take a shower together and I fuck my wife against the tiles, her legs wrapped around my back and her mouth pressed to mine.

And then we head to Leander Mayes's estate.

Visiting Leander sets me on edge as it always does, especially with Lark at my side. But he's welcoming this time, though maybe suspicious of the muffins until Lark and I each have one. He's taken with Lark in a way that a gem collector might obsess over a rare diamond. He hangs on to her words like they're precious facets of light. Polishes her with compliments. I'm halfway convinced that he only called me over here so he could learn more about the woman who waltzed into his home and left him on the floor of his man cave with a splitting headache and a bruised ego. He only asks me a few mundane questions about an old job and then his focus is back on Lark. I finally manage to pry us away and lead Lark into Leander's office.

"We need to start branching out," I say when we settle at a workstation. I'm trying to get down to business but my eyes almost instinctively linger on Lark's mouth. I clear my throat and turn back to the screen. "Let's think of people you and your family know—even people who you don't think of as enemies. Could it be someone in your inner circle? Someone trying to cause disarray among your family for their own advantage?"

Lark shrugs and leans forward, resting her chin on the heel of her palm. "Maybe. Most people in that circle have been with our family for years, though, and nothing like this has ever happened."

"Now that your aunt is so ill, maybe they're seizing their chance. Who's closest to her? Is there someone who holds sway with both the Montagues *and* the Covacis?"

Lark types a name as a little shudder rolls through her arms. "Probably not worth digging too deeply on him, but Stan Tremblay is my aunt's enforcer, for lack of a better term. He's the one who always handled our dirty work, for the Montagues, anyway. My stepfather keeps him at arm's length but respects him, particularly after the way he handled things with the school."

"Ashborne?"

"Yeah," she replies as she enters Tremblay's information into the advanced search. Though I'm sure she can feel the heat of my gaze warm her face, she doesn't glance my way. "He cleaned everything up when Sloane . . ."

Lark's sentence tapers off, and she gives a little shake of her head as she swallows.

"Leander did that for me, like Stan," I say before she can claw her way through an explanation she's not ready to give. "He waltzed in just moments after Rowan and I killed my father. My father owed debts everywhere, and eventually, he fucked with the wrong people. *Leander's* people. Leander came to collect for some of his extended family while he was visiting Sligo. Guess he did collect a soul, just not the way he thought he would." When Lark raises her eyes to mine, I give her a warning look. "Leander covered our crime. Got us to America. Set us up. He's been one of the closest people to me for more than fifteen years. I owe him my freedom, my brother's freedom. But I don't feckin' trust him. So don't discount anyone from your inner circle, no matter what they've done for you. Trust your instincts. Can you see this guy being the one?"

"Maybe. At the very least, he keeps meticulous records about the family business. He might know more than he's letting on."

"Then that's enough to spend time on him. We'll see what comes up," I say with a tip of my head toward the screen. Lark nods and enters the last fields of information on Stan Tremblay and then presses enter.

Tremblay's contact card appears, but it's surrounded by a red border, with the word WARNING next to his name.

Lark's head tilts with a question, but I'm already pulling the keyboard and mouse toward me. I click through several options before a transcript appears.

Code 2. Code 4100. Tremblay's address. A physical description that Lark confirms matches the man she knows.

A new entry appears on the screen, knocking the others down the list. Code 100.

"What is this?" she asks as I lean back in my chair. I see her eyes widen when she looks at me. She must see the faint wisp of fear on my face. "What does this mean?

"Code one hundred is a homicide," I say. "Stan Tremblay is already dead."

ENUCLEATE

Lark

Thoughts of Stan Tremblay consume me as Lachlan and I walk up the metal staircase to our apartment in silence that lingers even when we open the door to Bentley's excited footsteps, his nails clacking against the hardwood. With a pat to his head, Lachlan passes me before he heads toward the kitchen, and I haven't moved an inch.

I watch as Lachlan focuses on his phone, his thumbs rapidly tapping the screen. I know he's most likely texting Conor to solidify details of the plan we started with him on the drive home. When he seems satisfied, he pockets the device and then busies himself in the kitchen, grabbing a glass of ice water before he turns to watch me, until the silence must linger too long even for him. There's a fleeting look of worry in his eyes when he saunters closer.

"You okay there, duchess?" he asks.

I nod. His eyes skim over me as he offers me the water. I take a long sip and pass the glass back.

"I'm scared," I finally admit.

Lachlan's shoulders fall, not in disappointment, but in worry. I can see it in the way his brow creases. He takes my wrist and leads me toward the couch, setting the glass down on the gold coffee table as he gently pulls me down next to him.

"Scared of what?" he asks.

"Lots of stuff," I say with a shrug as I evade his gaze. "I knew Stan better than anyone else who's been targeted so far. It's becoming more real, you know? Like . . . *everything*."

When I look up, he watches me as though he knows this is about more than just Stan or the changes in my family that no one can stop. It's about us, too. And I wonder if it scares him as much as it frightens me. It seems like he's spent so long trying to ensure he had no one else to care about but his brothers and his business. So how do I fit into that? It's not like we had much of a choice to be together—we were a product of circumstances. So what happens if those circumstances are taken away?

A deep inhalation fills Lachlan's chest and he leans a little closer. "You know what I like most about you?"

I shake my head.

"You're brave." Lachlan squeezes my hand when I drop my gaze. "You're afraid you'll lose someone? You dive headfirst into a crazy plan to marry a broody asshat you hate just to save them. You're afraid of my crazy boss? You give him drugged muffins and make him fall at your feet, wanting to be your friend. You're afraid of the dark elevator? You sit in it for an hour so your dog won't be alone." Lachlan sweeps a lock of hair back from my shoulder with a faint smile. "You're the bravest person I know, Lark. And I love that about you."

♩

I swallow a breath that catches in my throat.

He loves that about me? Does he love other things about me too? Maybe there are things I love about him. Like the way he puts the needs of others first. Or the way he looks at me when I laugh. I love his teasing smirk. His touch. His kiss. The way his body fits mine like it was made to. Maybe I love a lot of things about Lachlan Kane.

I look away, but he tightens his grip on my hand and I'm sure he can see the sudden shine in my eyes. "You're wrong," I whisper. Lachlan's lips part on a sharp inhalation as though he's about to protest when I say, "I don't think I hated you. I think I might kinda like you, actually. Just a little bit."

Surprise is a momentary burst of light in his eyes and then Lachlan's teasing smile takes over. "Yeah, I kinda gathered as much this last little while. Not sure what gave me that impression. Might have been the remote control situation." Lachlan draws me into his embrace. His heart drums beneath my ear and I sink into his warmth. "Bravery has nothing to do with not feeling fear, and everything to do with facing it. You know that better than anyone. We'll figure it out together, yeah?"

I nod against his chest and Lachlan runs his hand up and down my back, a motion he probably doesn't think much about. But I do. Soon it's the *only* thing I think about. His fingers running down the ridges of my spine. The way they slow at the waistband of my leggings and then return up my back. An ache builds with every pass of his hand, a need that slowly coils deep in my core, a need for more than just a reassuring touch.

I pull away and meet Lachlan's eyes. His hand stalls on my back. He looks right into me, the *real* me. There's need and fear and desire and longing staring back at me. Maybe he does love more than just my bravery. I think that's what I see when I drift closer, when our breath mingles, when he frames my face in his hands.

"My feckin' catastrophe," he says as his thumb coasts across my cheek. "You fucking destroyed me. And now I can't imagine being anything but the man that I am with you."

"Lachlan Kane," I whisper. "You'd better kiss me and prove it."

One last breath. One look. And then he presses his lips to mine.

It starts sweet. A gentle sweep of our lips. A sigh. A stroke of my fingers across the short stubble on his jaw. And then the kiss deepens. The need for more seeps into every caress of his tongue across mine. I press my lips harder to his. I break away just long enough to pull his shirt off and then I take more from every moment that passes. A suck on his lip becomes a nip. The graze of my fingertips becomes a long scratch of my nails down his chest. A sigh becomes a moan.

In a flash of movement, I'm on my back on the couch with Lachlan's weight bearing down on me.

"You sore, duchess?" Lachlan says between kisses and bites to my neck. One of his hands trails down my body until it slides beneath the waistband of my leggings. I nod my head as he circles my clit with a light touch. "Good." I let out a soft, incredulous laugh that turns to a gasp as he bites my nipple through my shirt. "Do you want me to stop?" he asks when he raises his lustful gaze to me.

"Fuck no," I whisper. He dips a finger into my soaked pussy, pumping it in slow strokes.

"Then I'll make it better."

Lachlan pulls his touch away and reaches for the water glass, fishing a cylindrical ice cube from the liquid. With it gripped in his hand, he tugs my leggings down as I pull my shirt off. His smile is wicked as he centers himself between my legs and lets the cold drops hit my breasts. My breath hitches as the water slides across my skin. He brings the ice down to my nipple and circles it until it's a firm peak, and then he soothes it with the heat of his mouth as he teases the other. It's a wave of sensation. Cold then warm. Warm then cold. And all the while I'm increasingly desperate for more of him.

"Lachlan," I breathe. I run my touch down the ink that covers his arm until I grip his bicep. "Please."

He pulls away just enough to stare down at me, his eyes dark and serious. "Tell me who I am."

A crease flickers between my brows as I try to work out what he means. "Lachlan Kane," I say, smoothing my hand up the tense muscles in his arm. My reply doesn't seem to satisfy him. "My husband." The relief in his eyes is instantaneous. He nods once. I lay my hand to the side of his face. "You're my husband."

"And you're my wife. Don't forget it when I'm fucking you like a whore." He holds my gaze as he moves down my body and slips the ice into his mouth. And then he descends between my legs. He keeps the ice beneath his tongue as he sucks on my clit, swirling his caress over the sensitive nerves. The mix of cold and warm has me squirming. Desperate. My breath comes in pants. Lachlan pulls the ice from between his lips and rolls it over my clit as he thrusts his tongue into my pussy. I shudder as I near release, then he switches, rolling the ice over my pussy, his tongue over my bud of nerves. When the sensation becomes overwhelming and I buck from the couch, he pushes my stomach down with a flat hand and holds me there. There's no getting away. And I don't want to. He drives up the pleasure until I'm ready to unravel.

And then with a motion so sudden I barely have time to process it, he flips me over. He enters me with one swift stroke that has me gasping. I'd been so consumed by pleasure I didn't even realize he'd undone his belt or lowered his jeans and briefs, and now his cock is buried as deep as he can go, his hips pressed against my ass, his body shuddering behind me. He thrusts into me again to the sound of my shameless moan. And then he picks up a rhythm, one that starts with long, slow strokes. He runs the ice up my spine as he grips my hip with his other hand.

"So fucking perfect," Lachlan says as he gives my ass a gentle slap. When I cry out with need he does it again and then soothes my skin with a gentle caress. He separates my ass cheeks and groans. "That fucking perfect ass. That tight little hole." The ice slides down my ass crack and I swear under my breath as he runs it across the pleated rim. "You're *mine*, duchess. Every curse. Every moan. Every scream. *Mine*. My wife. Understand?"

I nod. "Yes."

"And I'm yours."

"Yes," I whisper.

There's a droplet of warmth as he spits on my ass. Lachlan runs the ice through it and around the rim of the hole, never breaking the cadence of his thrusts. When it's coated in a mix of water and saliva, he gently pushes his finger inside.

"Oh my *God*," I hiss as the new but familiar sensation adds to the fullness of his length in my pussy.

"*Husband*," he corrects as he buries his cock to the hilt and leans over me to lay a quick bite on my shoulder. He passes me the ice cube before he straightens behind me. He pushes a second finger into my ass and I tremble beneath him. "Use that ice and come on my cock, duchess. And I want to hear you fall apart with my name on your lips."

I guide what remains of the ice to my clit and shudder with the burst of sensation. And then Lachlan picks up his rhythm, the thrusts harder, the pace faster, his fingers pumping in their own tempo. I chant his name. I lose my mind. My thoughts unspool until I'm only sensation. All I can feel is the way he stretches me. The way his cock passes over the flesh that clenches around him. The cold caress on my clit. The strain of my throat as I call out his name. And then it starts, the burst of pleasure that erupts in my core. My muscles tense. My back bows. My heart roars in my ears and dampens the sound of Lachlan's moan as he releases inside me. I press my eyes closed and stars flood my vision and I unravel, trembling, covered in a thin film of sweat. And when I think it might never end, the orgasm starts to subside and leaves me little more than a boneless, breathless mess.

Lachlan takes a long moment to let us both come down, time that he takes to run his free hand across my back in a gentle caress. But when I shiver, he starts to pull out of me, first his fingers, then his cock. It's a slow motion, as though he's still savoring every sensation. And when his cock is free, he separates my ass cheeks to admire the mess of his cum with a low growl.

"I think you should just not shower before we go tonight," he says as he slides a finger across my entrance to gather the cum. He pushes it into my ass and I whimper with the slow glide of his finger.

"I think that Conor would probably appreciate if I don't smell like sex in the cramped van."

More cum is pushed into the tight hole and I try to suppress the growing desire already building in my core. "I couldn't care less what Conor thinks." With one more stroke of his finger, Lachlan's touch then disappears. "But you're probably right. And I need everyone on their game tonight, especially if you insist on being there."

Lachlan shifts off the couch and gives me a dark look before he heads to the kitchen to wash his hands.

"And I do insist on being there, by the way," I say, and Lachlan shakes his head, the resignation weighing on his shoulders as he stands at the sink. "So if you're hoping you were going to fuck me into submission, it didn't work."

Lachlan laughs and turns to face me as he dries his hands. "I had no illusions about that, duchess." He walks toward me where I sit on the couch, my legs gathered beneath me, my body still shimmering with a glow of sweat. He doesn't stop until he's right in front of me, and then he leans down to press a kiss to my forehead. "You're stubborn," he says as he pulls away. "It's one of the things I love about you. Now let's get moving. We only have a couple of hours."

With a worried smile, Lachlan leaves me for the kitchen to start dinner while I gather my things and have a shower. When I come out, dinner is ready, and we talk about Stan, and his vault, and everything we have to do next. And within another hour, we're heading to Conor's garage, where we leave the Charger and exchange it for his van, the three of us silent as we drive into the night.

♪

We roll to a stop within sight of the medical examiner's office, an austere redbrick building. There are only four cars in the parking lot, a benefit of the late hour. Lachlan throws the van into park and we both turn around in our seats to watch as Conor types commands on his laptop in the back of the vehicle.

"I'll wait to trigger the fire alarm when you're ready at the emergency door on the north side of the building. The standard response time of the fire department is only five minutes and twenty seconds," Conor says without taking his eyes from his work. "I'll disable the automatic emergency call from the alarm, but any more than ten minutes will start raising questions from security, so you'll need to work fast. You remember where you're going?"

"Cooler two, east side of the building."

"Perfect."

"You're sure this is going to work?" I ask, hoping that I don't sound too eager to bow out of this clearly insane plan to break into the medical examiner's office.

"It's the best shot we've got. Stan's home vault is top-of-the-line, nearly as good as Leander's. If we want to get into his records fast, we're going to need a bit of Stan to come with us." Conor gives me a sympathetic cringe. "Otherwise, it could take me weeks to hack into it, if someone else doesn't get in first."

"Right . . ."

"Try to have fun, kids. You know what they say—couples who play together, stay together," he says with a wink. Conor passes Lachlan a pair of earpieces before he returns to his laptop. "I'm ready when you are."

Lachlan and I exchange a determined glance. As much as I try to appear confident, my stomach still twists uncomfortably. Lachlan can see right through me. His expression is grim as he positions his earpiece, a deep crease notched between his brows. "You sure about this, duchess? It's not going to be pretty. I can do it myself."

"Not in ten minutes you can't," I reply. My tone is more even than I expect it to be considering I'm positive all my internal organs are now lodged in my throat. "If we want to get to the bottom of this before it happens again, this will be our best shot. Besides, it's my family issue. I want to be involved in fixing it. I don't want to just sit back while other people do it for me."

A long sigh empties Lachlan's chest as his focus drops to the device that rests on his palm. "I respect that, Lark. I really do. But things like this can go sideways. You need to be careful."

I can see it in Lachlan, all the things he refuses to say but is desperate to. So I lean forward and rest my palm against the warmth of his stubbled cheek and press a lingering kiss to his lips. He captures my quiet sigh of comfort at his familiar taste. Before I pull away, I press my forehead to his and whisper, "I promise I'll follow your lead. Just once though. Don't get used to it."

Lachlan plants another kiss on my forehead. "All right, duchess. Let's go."

With a determined nod to Conor, Lachlan exits the vehicle after me, and we stride through the dark toward the far side of the medical examiner's office. When we get to the corner of the building, Lachlan pulls me behind him and peers around the wall. He turns around and gives me a final, assessing look, a last opportunity to ditch the plan and run back to the van. A lift of my brows is all I need to give in reply.

"We're ready," Lachlan says.

"Got it," Conor replies, his voice clear though our earpieces. "There are only four people in the building right now, so stay where you're at until I give you the green light, just in case they head out the back."

My heart surges as Conor counts us down.

Three.

Two.

One.

The fire alarm startles me, even though I expected it. But Lachlan remains focused and confident in front of me, seemingly at ease with the warning that blares from the building. His gloved hand hovers next to a gun holstered at his side. I can picture the ease with which he'd wield his weapon, the grace and precision of his muscular body, the unerring focus in his eyes.

"Have you ever killed anyone with a pencil?" I blurt out.

Lachlan gives me a brief, suspicious glance over his shoulder before he refocuses on the emergency door. "No. Why would I kill someone with a pencil?"

"Because you could," I reply with a shrug. "What about slicing someone's jugular with a card?"

"What kind of card?"

"A playing card. A tarot card would be badass though. Have you ever killed anyone with a tarot card?"

"No."

I let out a disappointed sigh.

"What is it?"

"I was going to say you look a bit Keanu-y right now, but I take it back."

"Christ Jesus." Lachlan's eyes narrow into a petulant glare. "I killed a guy with a Himalayan salt lamp once. Has Keanu done that?"

I shrug.

"*No*, Keanu has not done that, because he is a bloody *actor*, ya feckin' catastrophe."

My grin ignites as Conor's laugh travels through the earpiece. "Time to go, kids. You'll have to duke it out later because the last person has just exited the building. The north door should be open."

The levity I just felt evaporates as we stride toward the door. The ten-minute countdown begins.

Lachlan leads us through the wide, arterial corridors. We pass offices and laboratory rooms. Flashing red lights pulse above us and the noise is almost deafening. We take two turns to the left and reach a hallway of silver doors. I can tell by the chill that cuts through every layer of my clothing that we've made it to the coolers. Lachlan stops before the door of cooler two and watches my reaction as his thumb stalls over a blue button.

"Let's do it," I say before he can ask.

He presses the button and the door slides open. We're hit by a rush of icy air.

We enter the room where a series of fans hum above us and swirl our fogged breath in currents and eddies. The scent of industrial cleaning solutions can't mask the human decay that lingers like a malevolent memory. Mobile stainless steel autopsy carts line two of the walls, and though there are at least twenty tables, only five contain body bags. The fire alarm still blares around us with an urgency that propels Lachlan forward toward the carts where he starts checking the name tags on the bags.

"You have eight minutes," Conor says through the line.

Lachlan has already pulled a cart forward. Before he opens the body bag, he turns to me, concern written across his expression as he scans my face. "Ready?"

"Ready."

He unzips the bag to reveal the corpse of Stan Tremblay.

I've seen bodies before, of course, but always so soon after death that they look like they could be sleeping. I've never seen someone I've known well who's been dead for a few hours. Stan's skin is chilled and bloodless, his face slack, as if he's a wax figure that's an imperfect replica of the person I once knew. There's a long gash across his throat, the edges of the wound congealed and dry like a slice of uncooked meat left too long on the counter. I know I should be moving faster and getting to work, but I can't help but stall for a moment as I try to reconcile what I see now with the formidable man I once knew.

But even with the seconds ticking along and the alarm blaring, Lachlan doesn't rush me. He carefully sets a small case on Stan's chest and passes me a pair of bone-cutting forceps.

"Index and thumb, when you're ready," he says as he pulls out a resealable plastic bag and lays it between us. "Then we'll do the other . . . thing . . ."

I take Stan's left hand and get to work with the forceps. I fit their sharp edges at the second knuckle of his index finger where it should be easier to separate along the joint. Even with the brand-new forceps, it takes a lot of pressure and a bit of repositioning to make headway, but before too long it snaps free and I deposit the severed digit into the bag with the finger Lachlan has just removed from Stan's right hand.

"You're doing good," Lachlan says, and I meet his eyes across the body. It's not just a declaration of my ability but an observation that despite knowing this dead man lying between us, I'm not hampered by familiarity.

"Yeah," I say, flashing him a smile as I saw at Stan's thumb with my forceps. "This is kinda therapeutic, actually."

Lachlan's brow furrows as he snaps the right thumb free, his eyes not leaving mine.

"Stan was helpful to me and my family, for sure. After what happened to my dad, Stan was the one tasked with teaching me some 'life skills,' at least until Damian took over. The difference between a hammer strike and an elbow strike, for example." I grit my teeth, squeezing the two handles of the forceps together until the joint finally succumbs to the pressure with a crack. "So even though I'm grateful he taught me a few useful tricks, he wasn't what you'd call the most empathetic instructor. And it's not like his presence was due to things going right with life, you know?"

"Yeah. Makes sense," Lachlan says as he holds the plastic bag open so I can drop the severed thumb inside. Once sealed, he places it in the interior pocket of his jacket. "Regardless, I'm proud of you, yeah?"

"You're my husband, sweetie. You're kind of supposed to say that."

An adorable blush creeps into Lachlan's cheeks before he clears his throat and gruffly asks Conor for a time check.

"Three minutes."

"Shite." Lachlan takes out the next set of tools and lays them on Stan's chest. There's a syringe filled with some kind of solution and a plastic jar of formalin. A scalpel. A pair of scissors. A set of dainty tongs. And something that looks disturbingly like a little ice cream scoop. "You ready?"

Bile churns in my stomach. "Probably not."

"Me neither."

We move closer to Stan's face and Lachlan passes me the tongs. "Conor, are you one hundred percent sure his security system has the iris scanner?"

"One hundred and *ten* percent sure. Enjoy."

"Fucksakes." Lachlan looks about as green as I feel when he pinches Stan's lashes between two fingers and pulls his top eyelid upward. "Hold this with the tongs."

I do as he asks and slide the instrument into place to hold the eyelid back from the prize beneath. Lachlan saturates the surface of Stan's eye with the liquid in the syringe before he takes up the scalpel with a deep, unsteady breath.

"I take back what I said earlier about leaving Sloane out of this," I say. "We should have gotten her to do it. This is fucking disgusting."

"You're not the one who has to dig it out of his face," Lachlan says as he leans over Stan's head with the scalpel. He starts slicing along the upper ridge of bone to cut the thin muscle that adheres to the eyeball. Just one glance at his progress and I have to turn away to gag. "Feckin' hell, don't you start."

"I can't help it."

"You're going to make me sick."

"Please go faster."

"Yes, go faster," Conor says, "because someone's just jumped on the delay and called dispatch for the fire department."

"*Shit*," I hiss into my sleeve.

Lachlan taps me on the wrist. "Switch lids."

As soon as I grab the bottom eyelid a surge of blood pools across the gelatinous white surface and I wretch. With a shaking hand, I manage to pinch the skin with my tongs before my stomach flips and I gag.

"Keep it together, Lark," Lachlan barks, his voice as much a plea as it is a command.

"*How?*"

"Think about Keanu."

"*No*, don't you dare ruin him for me with the power of eyeballs."

"Feckin' hell, okay. *Shite*." A little wretch comes from Lachlan, and I bury my sweaty forehead into the crook of my elbow. "How the fuck does Sloane do this?"

"Just imagine it's a marble," Conor chimes. "Or one of those Trolli Glotzer marshmallow gummy eyeball candies. Have you seen those? Gabs loves those things. They're filled with red sour liquid shit."

I gag again as Lachlan releases a string of expletives, some of which might be in Irish, though I can barely make out his words over the blaring alarm and the heartbeats roaring in my ears. "Don't bring up *food*, ya feckin' gobshite. Bloody hell."

"Yeah, fuck off, Conor. Leave my man alone."

"The spoon thingy, Lark. Pass me the spoon."

I heave. Lachlan gags. Conor cackles.

♫

I manage to pull myself together long enough to grab the mini scoop and shove it into Lachlan's hand. "Get that thing out, for the love of God."

"This sounds like a window into your sex life—"

"*Shut up*," Lachlan hisses. "Hand me the scissors, duchess."

I pass him the scissors and a moment later, there's a victorious sound of triumph. I find the jar of formalin and hold my breath as Lachlan drops the severed eye into the liquid. I don't even have the lid screwed tightly shut before Lachlan has the bloodied tools packed away, hushed expletives still spilling from his lips.

The earpiece crackles with Conor's laugh. "I was kidding, by the way. We don't need the eye."

"*Fuck you, Conor*," we snap in unison as I pocket the eyeball. Lachlan zips up the body bag, wheeling Stan's cart back into position along the wall.

"No, really, we do need the eye. But we also need you out. Fire trucks are a minute or two away."

We take off running, retracing our path through the building and into the cold November night. As we sprint toward the van, we hear the wail of sirens in the distance. I can barely catch my breath, but the adrenaline exploding through my veins gives me a sense of power. I feel invincible. I don't know if Lachlan feels this way after every job he does, this addictive rush, but I feel fucking amazing.

So amazing that I almost forget why we're really here.

Lachlan smiles as though he can divine my conflicting thoughts from my wide-eyed, manic gaze as he passes the bag of fingers to Conor. I do the same with the jar, and Conor places both items in a small cooler.

"We should have everything we need to access Stan's records. But if something happens and it doesn't work, this could take weeks. The clock is ticking. If the killer stays on their schedule, they're due to kill again in forty days. It might not be enough time."

I nod and Lachlan reaches across the center console to give my hand a squeeze. There's muted hope in the way he watches me. I can tell he wants to believe these pieces of Stan will unlock the mystery of the hunter that haunts us, but it's as though he's unwilling to put much stock in what feels like little more than witchcraft.

"Whoever is doing this, we'll find them," he says. He raises my hand to brush his lips to my knuckles. It's as much a reassurance to himself as it is a promise to me. "And once we do, I'm going to show them what hell on earth looks like."

WANDERER

The Phantom

It's been two weeks since I delivered Mr. Tremblay to God, and now He has rewarded my diligence. My servitude. He has moved the pieces across the board and cleared my way to righteous victory.

For I know the plans I have for you. Plans to prosper you and not to harm you. Plans to give you hope and a future.

And my plans are ready to come together.

I stand for a long moment at the door and watch the woman as she sleeps. The light casts lines of shadows across her body as it passes through the slatted window blinds. It illuminates every miniscule movement, every breath. I can almost smell the failure of her organs. The sterile environment and the industrial cleaners can't mask the smell of impending death.

Almighty God, the shadow of death is upon her.

The tempo of her breathing changes. Perhaps a nightmare. Fluid collects in her chest and rumbles. She coughs, and when she opens her eyes, they pan across the room until they land on me.

"Who are you?" she asks. Her vision must be hazy with sleep and old age, but I still catch the suspicion in the milky depths of her eyes. I take a purposeful step into the room and pull the door closed behind me.

"Today, I'm known as"—I point to the stolen ID card I've pinned to my chest pocket—"Steve."

"Today, I'm known as Bertha, so if you're looking for Ethel, I'm afraid you have the wrong room."

I grin at the old woman as I pull a pair of latex gloves from the pocket of my scrubs and slip them on. "You are not what I expected, Ethel."

"I've been told that before. But men like you have been underestimating women like me since the dawn of time, so your surprise is not at all refreshing. In fact, it's a little stale, if you'll forgive the muffin pun."

The old woman gives me a sharp and dismissive glare. Then she presses the button to adjust the incline of her bed. I stride forward, determined to stop her if she attempts to call for the nurse, but she only sneers at me. I know with that glance that she has either accepted her fate, or that she intends to attempt to fight me off herself.

"So," she says over the whir of the bed's hidden motor. "I assume you're here to kill me?"

"I'm here to deliver you to God," I correct her as I draw to a halt at the foot of her bed.

"On the behest of Bob?"

My head tilts.

"You know," she continues, waving her crooked fingers in the air as though imploring me to catch on. "Bob Foster. It seems like his kind of thing, sending someone like you. So uncreative and boring. Much like his muffins. He was always a one-trick pony."

I withdraw a black case from my pocket. Though I don't open it, the woman follows the motion of my hands. "I'm afraid I don't know Mr. Foster."

A rumbling cough builds in the old woman's chest until bloody phlegm spills out of her lips. I offer her a handkerchief and she takes it, holding it to her mouth. Her attention remains on me.

I nod, understanding everything she doesn't say. "It is good to accept death. Do not fight the will of God." I step to the side of the bed and open the case to pull the first of three prefilled syringes from within. "Do you repent before the judgment of the Lord?"

"I do have regrets," she says. Her eyes drift away to the corner of the room. I wonder if she feels Him here with us. I do. I feel the Lord's will in my hand. He keeps the syringe steady in my grip. His presence whispers to me, guides every beat of my heart.

"Tell me," I demand. "Confess your sins before His angel of death."

The old woman sighs deeply. "I regret . . ." She trails off as her gaze shifts back to me. It is fierce with resolve. "I regret not having stolen the recipe for Bob Foster's banoffee muffins when I had the chance. Fucker took twenty percent of my market share when he launched Bob's Banoffees."

My eyes narrow.

"I regret not having gone home with Spencer Jones after Marcie's party when I was twenty-three. Jenny Bright took him home instead and said he ate her ass six ways to Sunday. She wouldn't shut up about it at brunch at the country club for a solid month—"

"Lord thy God, I seek refuge in you from the devil—"

"—I met my Thomas shortly after and in sixty-two years of marriage he never once ate my ass. Took me nearly a year to convince Tom there were more positions than just me lying flat on my back like a dead fish."

I give her a heavy sigh. A cluck of my tongue.

And then I turn to the IV pump and pause the medication drip. I pinch the tube to keep the solution trapped.

I stare at the old woman. *"Let marriage be held in honor among all, and let the marriage bed be undefiled—"*

"Define 'undefiled'—"

"For God will judge the sexually immoral and—"

"Define 'sexually immoral'—do threesomes count? Because there was this one time with Jenny—"

"Enough."

My hand trembles with the urge to hit her. She grins, a devil satisfied. Satan has stoked my sin to consume it. But he shall have no more.

"By the power of God, cast into hell Satan and all the other evil spirits who prowl through the world seeking the ruin of souls."

I twist the protective cap from the port in the IV tube and push the saline from the first syringe into the port. I expect Ethel might try to fight. Perhaps she will pull the cannula from her hand. Though it would be futile, she could try to save herself. But she doesn't try.

She only smiles.

Her eyes don't leave mine. I feel them on my skin, even when I focus on the work of my hands as I remove the first syringe and exchange it for the second. This one contains lorazepam. Three times the dose for what I estimate her weight to be.

A thrill spikes in my veins. This is my calling, my mission from God Himself. He has granted me the means to avenge my brother, Harvey, and then He found for me a greater purpose—to kill the corrupt who protect His murderers and to destroy those who stand between me and the justice I seek. My God led me to stay in the same hotel as the Butcher and the Spider when I arrived with the hope of searching the wreckage of the house I grew up in. The police were so busy exhuming the bodies of Harvey's victims that they didn't put much effort into searching for who had killed *him*.

It didn't take long. Not with a fake badge and a tight smile and God's will.

A stolen blanket. An extra credit card charge. With a handful of questions, I had a fake name. And before long, I found a real one. Rowan Kane.

And now, as I remove the second syringe from the port and replace it with a final flush of saline, I feel Him within me, flooding my soul with peace.

"Some would say that my mother was a difficult woman," I tell Ethel as I close the cap on the port and turn the IV pump back on. I replace the empty syringes in my case and pocket it. "But the truth is, she showed my brother and me the depths of the world's darkness. She showed us its unforgiving nature. And she taught us how to survive. She showed us the other side of God. The reckoning before the light."

"That sounds pretty ass-backwards, boy."

I smile, then recite the words to the hymn I always sing to my offerings in their final breaths. My parting gift, one to usher their souls to judgment. *"Abide with me—"*

"I'd rather not."

"—fast falls the eventide—"

"It would fall a bit slower if you hadn't drugged me," Ethel says, her speech slurred.

"The darkness deepens, Lord with me abide. When other helpers fail and comforts flee, help of the helpless, O abide with me."

I slowly pull the bloodied handkerchief from Ethel's clenched fist. It's like a magic trick. It will be the only material evidence of our encounter that I will take from this room. A reminder that magic is an illusion. Death, an illusion. Life, a fleeting moment of time in God's will.

My eyes lock with the old woman's. Her rasping exhalations are desperate, but she shows no fear. Only defiance.

"Touch my Lark and he'll kill you," she whispers.

I smile as I fold my handkerchief and slip it into my pocket.

"I'm sure hoping he'll try."

And then I watch until the last breath leaves her lips like a final, unanswered prayer.

LAST DEFENSE

Lark

"I'm happy for you," Rose says. My eyes lift from the two plates of pastry crumbs that sit between us and Rose's grin widens beneath my scrutinous gaze. "I can tell things are different."

"What do you mean?"

"With Lachlan. You just seem different from a couple of months ago. You looked like you wanted to murder him at Sloane's wedding. And look at you now." Rose's arms spread wide and she nearly gut-punches a barista who strides past our table. "You were murdery before and now you're all sexed-up and glowing."

I cough around a sip of coffee. "Um . . . yeah. Thanks."

"Is it good?"

"Is what good?"

"The sex. Duh."

My cheeks heat as a memory from last night flashes through my mind: Lachlan's face buried between my legs, my fist gripped tight in his hair as I pushed his sinful mouth against my pussy. It's been just two weeks since our lives and desires finally aligned, and now each day we're stitched closer together. Every night he fucks me until I'm ready to collapse, exhausted but sated. Every morning I wake up less able to imagine the days before Lachlan's presence in my life and my bed. Sometimes his touch is all I can think about. His hands on my flesh. His kiss on my neck. His cock buried deep—

"That good that you can't sit still, huh?" Rose asks as I shift on my seat. She grins as my blush grows hotter. "I'm happy for you, Lark. You deserve it."

Though I give her my thanks, there's an edge of sadness to my gratitude. I know I can't say the same to Rose. And with the way we both look down at the table, she knows it too.

"How am I going to keep track of you?" I ask as Rose sips the last of her coffee and sets the empty mug down as she leans back to regard me with a melancholy smile.

"I do have a phone. Silveria Circus might have a nostalgic vibe, but it also has modern technology."

"I know, but you'll be all over the place. It's going to be a little harder to meet up. But I'll come see you as much as I can, whenever you're nearby."

"I'd love that. You and Sloane." Rose shakes her head and swallows, her smile faltering. "You're my girls. My bally broads."

"I still have no idea what that means, but I kinda like it." I smile and take a sip of my coffee. "How long before you meet up with Silveria?"

Rose glances down at her watch and gnaws at her lip. "About an hour."

"And Fionn?"

"He'll drop me off. And then I guess that's that." Rose shrugs. Sadness etches itself deeper into her features, even though she tries to hide it. I reach across the table and take her hand in mine. I know how it feels to try to maintain a mirage for someone else's benefit while you crumble behind the illusion. But Rose wears her heart wide open for everyone to see, and it's only a second or two before tears well in her eyes.

I don't tell her it will be okay. I don't know if that's true, and I don't want to pretend that comments like that are anything more than platitudes. Not anymore. Not for myself nor for anyone else. So instead, I hold Rose's hand across the table and tell her what I really feel. "I'm going to miss you."

Rose nods. "I'm going to miss you too," she whispers. Her smile is brittle and my chest aches in reply. "You know what they say about the circus."

"What, that the show must go on?"

"No," she says. "That the show can't begin until you jump."

I'm caught in Rose's words and her shimmering dark eyes when her phone vibrates with a text to break the spell between us. With a glance at the screen, she slides the device off the table and pockets it.

"Doc's here. Guess I'll see you around. Don't be a stranger."

We both stand and crush each other in a hug. The tremble in Rose's shoulders cracks my heart and fills it with both pain and anger on her behalf. I know whatever is happening with Fionn is none of my business and she doesn't seem willing to get into it in detail, but I can't help but make a dig at him. "Maybe Lachlan wasn't the asshat of the Kanes after all," I whisper, and Rose laughs in my arms.

"Yeah. Maybe not," Rose says as she places a kiss on my cheek. "Take care of yourself, Boss Hostler."

With a final, weak smile, Rose turns away and leaves the coffee shop. I watch as she opens the door to a car waiting at the curb and disappears inside.

It's a short walk home and I use most of it to text back and forth with Sloane. She and Rowan are spending a weekend in Martha's Vineyard to bask in their newlywed bliss, something I guess I'm starting to feel too, even though it's all been a little backward for Lachlan and me. But does that really matter? There's a worn path in life that most people take when they wind up married. Fall in love first. Make your vows. But maybe I was never meant to be on it. It surprises me more than anyone when I realize that I'm happy where I am.

I'm thinking about that epiphany as I enter the apartment and send Lachlan a text to let him know I've arrived home. I set my mobile down to spend a little time playing with Bentley, who grabs the stuffed squeaky skull that Lachlan bought him last week. We're playing tug-of-war when my phone vibrates on the coffee table with an incoming call.

The rush I just felt expecting to see Lachlan's contact on my screen is washed away when it's my mother's details that appear instead.

"Hi, Mom."

"Honey."

I already know what she's going to say next.

There's a vortex in time right before the words come that feels even worse than the moment you hear them spoken aloud. It's like waiting for the anticipation of a needle—you know the hurt will come, but imagining it is sometimes worse than the moment it slides into your skin.

"Auntie Ethel passed away."

That pain still hits me like an ax to the chest. Tears fall freely down my face. We all knew this was coming. I thought about it every day. And yet it still feels like a hole has erupted inside me, a void that seems gravitational. Unfillable. Like it was made to only consume.

The tears don't stop as my mom gives me the details. That Ethel passed in her sleep. It was peaceful. She says all the things that are supposed to be a minor comfort in the aftermath of loss. And then she talks about the practicalities that don't stop for grief, not even for a moment. Mom sounds tentative when she asks if I want to meet them at Shoreview before the funeral home comes to take Ethel's body away. She barely gets the question out before I tell her yes, to wait until I get there. And though my mom doesn't ask outright about Lachlan, he's the first person whose presence I crave. His quiet countenance. His steady shadow to my faltering light. There's comfort knowing he's seen more of me than I've been willing to share, and yet he doesn't back away.

As soon as my mom hangs up, I select Lachlan's number from my list of favorites. I try to compose myself, but the room seems to pulse with every beat of my heart, a watery film obscuring my vision.

Lachlan answers on the first ring. "Hey, duchess. I was just thinking about you."

"Hi."

That's it. That's all I need to say. Just one short word. A breath of sorrow.

"What's wrong? Did something happen? Are you okay? Where are you?"

For a man who doesn't say more than he has to, the barrage of questions almost makes me smile despite the pain that fills every crevice of my chest.

"Ethel," I say around the stone lodged in my throat. "She passed."

"Oh, Lark, I'm so sorry, love. I can come get you. What do you need?"

"It'll be faster if we just meet at the nursing home." I start gathering my belongings into my bag and head to the kitchen to refill Bentley's water as he trails behind me. "My parents should be nearly there. I'll grab an Uber."

"You sure?"

"Yeah. I'll be okay. It's just . . ." I pause and press my lips together, trying to trap the grief that invades every bone, every drop of blood. It takes a few unsteady breaths and twisting a loose thread of my sweater around my finger until it aches before I can speak again. "It's just that she was my anchor," I say as I head to my bedroom. "She was steady in every storm. It's not like I didn't know it was coming, but I still feel . . . adrift. Expecting it doesn't make it easier, you know? I was hoping we'd have a little more time."

"I know. I was too, duchess. I'm sorry, I know how much she meant to you." Lachlan's heavy, worried sigh permeates the line. "Is there anything I can do?"

A breathy, mirthless laugh leaves my lips before my throat closes once more. "Probably. But right now I just need a hug."

"I can do that," Lachlan's says. I clutch the phone to my ear and let the tears fall again. I feel solace in his silence. I know he's there, giving me time, another steady anchor in a storm. I stand in the bedroom that's become ours and stare at the floor, caught in my torrent of thoughts and realizations when his quiet voice finally pulls me free. "Lark . . . ?"

"Yeah?"

"I love you."

A breath stalls in my lungs. That quiet confession echoes in my mind until it brands itself there. *I love you*, an indelible ink written in memory.

Every big and bold moment with Lachlan seems to roll through my mind. The first time we met. The second. That kiss in the city clerk's office when we said our vows. The way he whispered to me just before our lips met. *Geallaim duit a bheith i mo fhear céile dílis duit, fad a mhairimid le chéile.* I didn't know what it meant—I still don't. But I felt it. That this man would be there with me in my darkest times. And if I let him, he'll be there in the light too.

The show can't start until you jump.

I press my hand across my eyes, but it doesn't stop a fresh wave of tears from flooding my eyes and sliding down my skin. Bentley whines at my feet and I drop to his level, gripping an arm around his thick neck to cry into his fur as I hold the phone to my ear with an unsteady hand. "I love you too, Lachlan."

"Get an Uber, duchess," Lachlan says, relief and a smile in his voice. "I'll meet you at Shoreview soon."

With a deep sigh, I say goodbye and try to reconcile a world that feels like it's turned upside down. Ethel is gone. Everything in my family will change. I'm in love with my husband.

An incredulous laugh bursts from my lips despite the tears that still cling to my lashes. I press my forehead to the soft fur between Bentley's ears. "I'm in love with my husband, Bentley. I guess that means we have to keep him." My eyes lift to the ceiling with a bittersweet smile. It doesn't take much to imagine Ethel's reveling in a final plan coming together just the way she wanted. "Hear that, you scheming hell-raiser? I'm in love with Lachlan Kane. I'm pretty sure that's what you were after, right?"

I rise to my feet. Before I order an Uber, I head to the bathroom to splash water on my face. My flesh feels too hot with all this emotion coursing beneath my skin. But when I look at my reflection, I see the beauty of being stripped down to my core. It has nothing to do with the makeup that still clings to my eyes or the foundation that's been washed away. It's got everything to do with the person I see in the mirror matching the woman I feel like inside. One who doesn't hide behind what the world wants to see. There's no practiced smile, no facade to keep others from being inconvenienced by my emotions. I'm in pain and I look like I'm hurting. I'm in love and I look like I'm living.

I like the woman looking back at me. I think my aunt would be proud of her too.

I'm just wiping the final drops of water from my face as Bentley gives a warning bark from the living room. *Maybe the Uber was closer than I realized and I missed the bell*, I think. But when I pick up my phone and check the app as I start toward the living room, the Uber is still ten minutes away.

Bentley barks again as I enter the living space. And then he growls.

"What is—" I start, but then I see what it is—*who* it is.

Abe Midus is standing in my living room.

Predatory eyes. A hungry smile.

All at once we are hunter and prey.

I take off running for the kitchen. Something hits my legs and I smack into a lamp on my way to the floor. A lightning strike of pain blinds me when I land. My palm finds the side of my head and comes away sticky with blood. Bentley growls behind me. There's a thud and he yelps. Something pierces my neck, sharp and inescapable before it's pulled away.

I reach for my phone. My fingers slip across the glass when it's kicked from my grasp. My groan is muffled by the roar of my heart as I try to pull myself across the floor. Power leeches from my muscles with every second that passes. I have just enough strength to turn on my back and breathe.

Breathe. Breathe. Breathe.

Stay awake.

The edges of my vision darken and blur.

Abe Midus stands at my feet and slides a cap onto a syringe before slipping it into his pocket. A slow smile stretches across his face. Light reflects off something clutched in his grip. A black-handled tool with a brutal silver edge. Tears leak from the corners of my eyes. I try to beg but my mouth won't form the words.

Bentley squares himself over my legs, head lowered, hackles raised. His vicious growl burns through my last moments of conscious thought. Abe bends, his eyes pinned to my snarling dog.

"Hello, you."

APPARITION

Lachlan

I stride through the doors of Shoreview Assisted Living and check in with the reception desk, the staff regarding me with somber smiles. When I get to Ethel's room, Lark's parents are already there. Damian's hand gently caresses Nina's back as she smooths Ethel's silver-white waves. I scan the room but find nothing of Lark's on the chair in the corner where she usually leaves her bag and jacket.

"Lachlan, thank you for coming." Though Damian tries to keep his tone even, I still catch the wary notes in his voice. I can't blame him for it either. I wish it could be different for Lark's sake, though, at least on a day like today.

"Of course. I'm so sorry for your loss. Ethel was . . ." I find that my throat grows tight as I picture Ethel at the brunch when I met Lark's family for the first time. She was so wicked and funny and sharp. So full of life. And I respected the hell out of her. Even knowing how sick she was, it seems inconceivable that she's simply *gone.* "Ethel was a force of nature. I'm grateful to have known her, even for a little while."

"Thank you." Nina gives me a weak smile, her eyes shining. Her brow furrows. "Where's Lark?"

"I thought she'd be here already. She was at home when she called to give me the news. She said she'd be coming straight here."

With a glance toward the door, I pull out my phone and type a text.

| Everything okay?

"Maybe it was the stress of losing Stan," Nina says as she runs a tissue beneath her lashes and straightens her shoulders. "They were close friends for many years. Maybe it was just too much for Ethel to handle."

Damian says something reassuring but I lose track of what it is as I pace toward the door and back again, the phone clutched in my hand. The message was delivered, but there's no response from Lark. Something grips my guts and twists.

"I'll be right back," I say to Damian and Nina, willing my voice to remain steady.

I leave the room and head down the corridor toward the reception desk. I look out the sliding glass doors hoping to catch a glimpse of an Uber dropping Lark off, or her mass of blond waves catching on the breeze, or that giant feckin' bag that weighs nearly as much as she does bouncing against her hip. But there's nothing, just an empty sidewalk and cars that pass by on the road.

I select Lark's number and ring it as I head back toward the room. It goes unanswered. I hang up when it gets to Lark's voicemail.

"Has Lark contacted you?" I ask as I step back into Ethel's room. Nina and Damian both shake their heads. My pulse quickens and

I open my messages again as I hope for the dots of an incoming reply, but they don't come.

> Let me know you're okay,
> duchess

My plea is as much to the universe as it is to Lark. But still there's no response.

"*Fuck.*"

I can feel the tension erupt in the room like a malevolent phantom. Damian takes a step closer. "What's wrong? Is Lark all right?"

"I don't know, she hasn't responded. She should have been here by now. Even with waiting for an Uber she was still closer than me."

I'm about to call her a second time when my phone rings in my hand, but my momentary relief is cut short when I see Conor's name on the screen and not Lark's.

"Is Lark with you?" I ask by way of greeting.

"No, man. Sorry," he replies with confusion in his voice. "But I've got something from Stan's videos. Paranoid old fucker had everything encrypted and I just got past it about ten minutes ago. Sending you a screenshot now."

I pull the phone from my ear and place the call on speaker as I wait for Conor's text to come through. When it does, I see an image of a man standing over Stan's body. His features are obscured by the angle of the camera and the ball cap he wears, the brim pulled low. He clutches a weapon in his hand, not a normal knife but something small and irregularly shaped. Something familiar.

"Can you—"

"Already on it, bro."

A second text comes in from Conor, this time a zoomed-in image of the tool. The man's palm covers most of the black handle, but not the ring of gold that attaches the sharp head of the edge beveller. I can see the brand name—WUTA—stamped on the stainless steel.

"Fuck, *fuck*." Blood freezes in my veins as my heart tumbles into my guts. "That's *mine*."

"Bro, what the fuck? He was in your shop?"

Images click together like pieces of a puzzle as Nina and Damian ask questions that I don't answer. "Get me a better picture of the hat."

A handful of heartbeats later, a new image of the man comes through, his face still mostly in shadow, but the Carhartt logo clearly visible on the front of the cap.

"*Motherfucker.*" I scroll through my recent appointments until I find the last name that suddenly escapes me as disbelief and panic creep through my flesh. "Get me everything you can find on Abe Midus. I'm going home to look for Lark." I disconnect the call and face Nina and Damian, their eyes wide with confusion and concern. "Abe Midus. Do you know that name?"

"No," Damian says. Nina shakes her head next to him. "What the hell is going on?"

"We've got him on video, the man who killed Tremblay. And he did it with a tool from my shop." I try ringing Lark's phone

one more time as her parents pepper me with more questions, but again my call goes unanswered. "Something isn't right. I'm going to find Lark."

Nina clamps her hand over her mouth, muffling a strangled cry.

Damian surges forward. "I'll come with you."

"No. Stay and text me if Lark shows up." I stride down the corridor, Damian's footfalls an echo behind me as we head into the lobby. "Texan accent, short gray hair, five-foot-eleven, medium build, tattoo of a Bible and cross on his right forearm. Call me right away if you see him."

"Oh, you lookin' for Steve? I think he left about an hour ago," one of the nurses says from where she sits at the reception desk.

"*What?*"

"Steve. The temp guy. Likes his Bible quotes." Confusion deepens in the nurse's expression as her eyes dart between me and Damian. "We had a few people out sick yesterday so we called the staffing company for a temp worker to cover."

Damian and I turn to each other. His face crumples. I try to swallow the lump in my throat.

"My daughter—"

"I *will* find her. Even if I have to kill every person in this goddamn city to do it."

Damian gives me a single nod and I take off at a jog, calling Fionn as I run to my car on the off-chance Lark might still be with Rose. I'm speeding through a red light when he says he hasn't seen her, but he tells me they're in their rental and not far from our building, ready to help. By the time I reach our street, they're already parking next to the entrance.

My heart races. My hands shake. I try her phone again as Fionn and Rose meet me at my car, but Lark still doesn't answer.

"We called Rowan but he and Sloane are in Martha's Vineyard for the weekend. They're on their way home but it's gonna take a while." Rose's face is creased with worry as I withdraw my gun from the glove box. "What's going on? Where the fuck is Lark?"

"I don't know. She called me to say her aunt died. She was supposed to meet me at the nursing home, but she never showed." I lead the way to the main door and grab the door handle only to find it unlocked. It swings open to the textile production floor where there's no sign of anything amiss. "Conor just found information about the man who's been targeting her family. And now Lark won't respond to any of my calls."

I stride toward the stairs, taking them by twos, Fionn and Rose close on my heels. The worst fears I never could have imagined suddenly pile up around me with every step I take.

"The guy was *right fucking there*. He was in my goddamn shop. He spoke to Lark, shook her hand. He's been around us this whole time and I had no fucking clue."

By the time we reach the apartment I feel like I might vomit. The desperation and panic are so foreign they're overwhelming. I keep hoping my phone will suddenly ring, that Lark's smiling face will pop up on my screen. But it stays silent. And I'm not sure I can survive what I might find on the other side of the door.

I hesitate for just a moment, letting Rose and Fionn know with a nod that they need to stay behind me. And then I twist the handle and push it open.

Blood coats the floor and my knees buckle. It's my brother who holds me up long enough to stumble into the room and regain my balance.

"*Lark.*" My despondent plea receives a pained whine in reply. I surge forward into the living space and find Bentley lying on his side near the table, blood coating the white patches on his fur. He whines again, a sorrowful cry that incinerates my crumbling heart.

"Save that fucking dog," I order my brother as I scramble for tea towels from the kitchen and toss them to Fionn.

"I'm not a vet—"

"*I don't fucking care, save that goddamn dog.*"

I stalk toward the corridor where the bedrooms are, calling to Lark as I go. My efforts are unrewarded. I check the bedrooms and bathrooms, but there's no sign of Lark, nothing out of place except her absence. I return to the living room with a bottle of isopropyl alcohol and clippers clutched in one hand and my gun in the other. Rose has bloodied towels pressed to Bentley's side as Fionn threads a needle.

"I'll do what I can to stop the bleeding now and get him to the vet," Fionn says. I hand him the clippers and he shaves off a line of fur next to what looks like a deep stab wound. When he glances up at me, Fionn's expression is grim. "Do you have any idea where Lark could be?"

"No." I scan the room and spot her phone near the coffee table, a broken lamp nearby on the floor. There's a bloody streak across the screen. My missed calls and texts and notifications from the Uber she never took flash on the backlit glass when I pick it up.

Lark needed me. And I wasn't there.

An anguished scream fills the room. It comes from *me*.

Tears fill my eyes as I toss the phone on the couch. I want to pace. To *run*. But there's nowhere to go to escape the way I feel.

"I wasn't here," I whisper.

A hand wraps around my forearm and squeezes, and I look down to meet Rose's fierce determination.

"*Think*," she demands as the dog whines behind her. "There's got to be *something*. Something weird. Something out of place."

I press my eyes closed and search the darkness. At first, all I see is Lark's face. How beautiful she is when she's trying to get under my skin. How she looked on that stage, singing to me. Her body beneath the sheets the first night we spent together, the way she smiled when I turned for one last glance from the doorway.

And then it strikes me, an image that burns brighter than lightning.

"Across the street. He was *across the fucking street*."

I stride toward the door, Rose right on my heels. "I'm coming with you," she says.

"Rose, don't," Fionn says, his voice breaking. "*Please*."

We stop just long enough for Rose to turn and face him. He's kneeling on the floor, a hand still placed on Bentley's side. "Lark is my girl. I'm going to get her back."

"But—"

"I love you, Fionn Kane."

Shocked silence fills the room. I expect Fionn to say something, anything, but he doesn't. It's as though her words are so unexpected that he can't process them.

Rose takes a step backward toward the door. Fionn stares at her like he's frozen. Rose takes another step away. "Save the dog or this asshat will kill you."

Then Rose strides past me, pulling a huge hunting blade from a sheathe hidden beneath her shirt. When I turn toward my brother, there's anguish in his eyes.

He swallows, but his voice still comes out uneven when he says, "Keep her safe."

"I will. I promise."

I jog to catch up with Rose. When we reach the bottom of the stairs we burst into the cold air, heading for the building across the street.

"So who is this guy?" Rose asks as we get to the locked door. I'm about to try shooting it when she pulls out a small black case from the bag slung across her shoulder and fits a pin and snap gun into the lock. With a few clicks and turns, it's open and we step inside. The former industrial building has been converted to small offices on the main floor with apartments on the second.

"He said his name was Abe Midus. He booked an appointment at my studio and brought in a saddle for repair. But I know nothing about him aside from he's a religious guy. Conor is working on it."

We run up the stairs to the second floor and head to the apartments that face our building, of which there are only three. We stop at the door at the end of the hall, the one most likely to align with our windows, and listen for sounds within. Nothing comes. I keep my gun pointed to the wood as Rose fits her tools into the keyhole. When the bolt gives, I motion at her to stand aside. Then I turn the handle and push the door in.

"Well," Rose whispers as I lead the way over the threshold. "I think we got the right place."

There's no one here. But the evidence of his obsession is everywhere.

Charcoal drawings line the walls, images of crosses with quotes scribbled in margins, sketches of houses and unfamiliar places and people. There are several drawings of an older woman with a Bible spread open on her lap. Handwritten notes are piled on every surface. Times and dates and locations. A colorful strip of paper sticks out among the white ruled sheets, and I pick it up. *KEX, with Lark Montague*, the ticket says.

Fire fills my chest with a burning ache.

My phone rings and I scramble to pull it from my pocket. It's Conor.

"Anything?" I say.

Rose watches from where she stands next to a scope mounted on a tripod, the lens pointed to our apartment.

"Nothing for an Abe Midus. He's a ghost."

"Did you check records for Texas?"

"I checked records for *everywhere*. There's no one who's feasibly within the range of your description."

I let out a string of swears as Rose shoots me a worried look. She starts searching through a pile of syringes and vials arranged on a tray on a side table. Conor is rattling off different iterations of Abe's name and everything that he's searched as Rose opens a Bible that lies near the table's edge. Her eyes go wide as she whips it off the surface and thrusts it toward me, pointing frantically at the name.

"We found something. It's Abe *Mead*," I say to Conor. The realization hits me right in the chest. "Oh *shit*. Mead. Harvey

Mead is that bloke Rowan and Sloane killed in Texas. He must be related."

Conor's fingers tap furiously over the keyboard. There's a brief pause that feels like an eternity. "It's his brother," Conor finally says. "I'm coming up with an address for Oregon. I'll need to get to Leander's and search from the office for anything more than the basics."

"His history isn't going to tell me where he's taken Lark," I bite out.

"No," Rose says as she points to the closed front door behind us. There's a map taped to the wood. "But maybe *that* will."

We step closer.

Portsmouth, the title says.

I rip the map from the wood and throw the door open. Then I run down the hallway, feeling like I'm being burned alive, one cell at a time.

SCORCHED

Lark

I wake to darkness.

No sliver of light. No sound. Nothing to orient my brain as to where I am or how I got here.

Only a familiar smell, a vague recognition my brain can't pull from the haze of whatever drug still swirls in my veins.

I slide my arm across a cold metal floor and tap my wrist to check the time. But my watch is gone.

"Fuck," I whisper. The word is too thick on my tongue. I roll onto my back and blink at the dark, willing any filament of light to appear, but nothing comes. All I see is a blackness.

Every heartbeat pushes me to a cliff edge of panic.

My breath quickens. Bile roils in my stomach. I pat my pockets down for my phone. Nothing.

Memories surface through the haze of drugs. A man in my apartment. My dog snarling. Blood on my throbbing head. I touch my hair and there's a crust of it clumped in the strands. I remember a pinprick of pain in the side of my neck. My trembling fingers drift down to the mark.

I press my eyes closed. I will myself not to cry. The drug still lingering in my veins is both a blessing and a curse, dulling the memories of another darkness. Even still, I see the red numbers of the clock through the slats in the door as I huddled with my sister in the closet. Those glowing lines are so clear in my mind despite the many years that have passed.

Five thirty-nine. "How much longer?" I'd whispered to my sister. It had been hours since we'd heard any sounds from the house, but we refused to disobey our mother. We saw the desperate fear in her eyes when she closed us in and demanded we keep our promise to stay hidden.

Ava held me close. Kept me warm. "Figure it out, Lark," she said.

Figure it out, Lark.

My fingers land on a small circle of metal embedded into the floor. I push myself up to sit and trace it, looking for a latch. But there isn't one. There's just a smaller, raised metal circle with eight screws near its perimeter beneath me. The surface of the circle feels slicker than the surrounding floor. I try every inch of the circle, hoping for a solution, some kind of button or clue. Nothing. Just the roar of my heart and the tremor in my hands as I fight to keep my fear at bay.

I crawl forward with one hand reaching into the darkness and hit a wall. The metal is the same as that beneath me, but there are small slats in rows, precise openings in the wall just wide enough to stick my finger in. I can't feel anything inside. After trying a few of the holes, I trace the length of the wall and reach the next one, then the next. Halfway through my progress to map the metal in the dark, my fingers land on glass.

A window.

I press my face close to it and try to look out, but there's nothing on the other side. Just darkness.

My fist is weak when I ball my hand tight to pound on the narrow strip of glass. "Let me out." My voice is gravelly, barely more than a rasp. I try again, putting as much strength as I can into my fist as I bang on the window. "Somebody let me out—"

Something is pulled away from the window and I take a startled step back. Suddenly, bright light flicks on behind the glass. In the window, there's a man looking back at me with a lethal smile.

Abe Midus.

I fall back on my ass. The light goes off.

On. Off. On. Off. His silhouette is illuminated only to disappear in darkness with the metronomic pulse of light. My heart pounds so hard it feels like it's crawling up my throat. But I put my hands on the floor and force myself to rise.

When I'm standing straight and facing him, Abe leaves the light on, a remote control clutched in his raised hand.

My eyes dart to my surroundings now washed in light.

I know exactly what this is. A rotary batch oven.

"And we know that in all things God works for the good of those who love Him, who have been called according to His purpose," Abe says, his voice muffled by the heavy steel and thick glass. His lightless smile is triumphant. "It was God who provided me with the idea to bring you here. Through *you.*"

"Let me out." Furious tears well in my eyes. I hold Abe's unwavering gaze as I grip the handle I can now see on the inside of the door. I jostle it, but it doesn't budge.

Abe rotates his arm to display bloody marks that weep through white gauze taped across his forearm. "Your dog made an admirable effort to defend you. So loyal." Abe's head tilts as his eyes scour my face. I curl my short nails into my palms. "Do you think your husband will be as loyal to you? Or do his loyalties lie elsewhere, I wonder?"

I say nothing. Fear is a spiral that coils tightly around my thoughts and traps them. I might not know what Abe's plans are, but I can already tell they're designed to test every boundary and burn through them. And if he's asking this question, there's a good chance my heart will be the first thing to break by his design.

"Why are you doing this?"

"A tooth for a tooth."

My brows knit together. I try to draw a connection between this man and anything I've done but I can't find one. For him to go to this effort to sow chaos in my family and orchestrate an elaborate plan, there must be only one reason.

"I killed someone important to you."

Abe's expression clears and then fills with wonder. *Excitement*, almost. He lets out an incredulous laugh before he raises a hand to the heavens in praise. *"But let justice roll down like waters and righteousness like an ever-flowing stream."* His smile transforms as his arm falls to his side, and I realize that what I confessed is not at all what he expected. "You know, I almost gave up on my plans for whole-scale retribution in favor of simply killing you and Kane, and then

God put you together in marriage. A second time, I nearly strayed from my path when I went to Kane's studio, intent on indulging my weakness and bringing my vengeance to him, and God stayed my hand when you walked through the door. You delivered His wishes for the final notes of my masterpiece. The Lord knew what I did not, that your wickedness deserved to be punished. Divine inspiration indeed."

"*For in the same way you judge others, you will be judged, and with the measure you use, it will be measured to you,*" I say, and Abe's eyes narrow. "You can cherry-pick from the Bible all you want, but I still know what kind of man you are. *Let me out.*"

"That's not up to me."

"Yes it is."

Abe shakes his head. "It's not." He turns with a sudden motion as though he's heard something in the distance. When his gaze returns to me, it's bright with the kind of exhilaration that comes from watching your intricate plans come together. It's a look I know, because I've felt it too. "It's up to Kane."

Abe presses a button on the remote and the room beyond the narrow window is plunged into darkness. His silhouette disappears.

As soon as he's gone, I try the door handle again, desperately tugging at it. I resort to a few kicks that accomplish nothing. I head to the back of the oven where there's a second door, but that handle doesn't budge either, and the window on this one is covered so I can't see out. I'm still jostling the door handle when the lights flick on in the window behind me.

"Put down your weapon and you'll have a hope of saving someone you love." Abe's voice booms from beyond the door, directed at someone I can't see. "If you don't, they all die."

My eyes narrow as I try to work out what he means. His words tear at my chest, claws that rake across its depths and leave venom in the wounds. Someone else is at risk here, and I don't even know who.

A new wave of desperation floods the chambers of my heart. I search the perimeter of the door for a hidden release.

"Isn't technology wondrous?" Abe says, pulling me from my efforts to think my way out of a steel box and a situation where I know I have no control. "I can program all of these ovens with an app. For example, I can set a simple timer to start baking in five minutes. Just like I can follow Rowan Kane's car with an app and see that it's on the road, driving in our direction on I-95. I can even use my phone to set a timer that will detonate the bomb I placed beneath his engine, all with the touch of a button. With one tap of my finger, I can press send on the pre-drafted email I wrote to the authorities, the one that contains damning evidence pointing to none other than Lachlan Kane as the man responsible for the murders of Stan Tremblay, and Cristian Covaci, and Kelly Ellis, and all the other serpents in that nest of snakes who have recently wound up dead. And then I just have to lock my phone, and you won't be able to stop it from happening."

I feel a choked sob bubbling in my chest. But before I fall apart, I hear a derisive laugh coming from somewhere beyond Abe. The tone is instantly familiar. *Lachlan.* I press my face to the glass and look to the left, but I can't see him.

"A *bomb*?" He might try to sound skeptical, but there's no mistaking the worried undertone in his voice. "I don't believe you."

"Have I proven myself incapable? I do have your wife here, after all. Taken from your very own home. I've watched you for months.

Slipped right beneath your world to shape it. So, believe what you want to believe, but is it a risk you're truly willing to take?"

There's a pause, silence beyond the door.

"Your gun. Or they all die now."

I hear the clank of metal as it falls on the floor.

"Smart decision. But the next one you can't make with your head. You must make it with your heart."

Abe crosses in front of my window, a gun in one hand, a phone in the other. He backs away slowly until he disappears from view, and the next thing I see is my husband.

Lachlan tries the handle but it doesn't release for him either. "Lark—"

"It's locked, I can't get out," I say, slapping the steel with my palms even though I know it won't get me anywhere.

Lachlan makes a move toward where the control panel must be, but Abe warns him off with a threat and he refocuses on me. "Are you hurt?"

I shake my head, though his eyes fixate on the blood in my hair. He looks at me with the kind of terror that I never imagined he could possess.

"I'm okay," I say, and though it might sound impossible, it's true. There's no lie in it, even though I'm terrified too. Maybe it's because I already know what's coming. I can see my path ahead, even in the dark.

But Lachlan, I know he's not ready. He's caught in a riptide, trying to swim his way free. He still tries the door, still glances at Abe as though there's some other solution to get me out. And there's so much pain in his eyes, so much distress in this man who I once believed could never be anything but callous, even cruel. I thought for so long that he was jagged and sharp. But in time, I saw the soft edges of old wounds. And now I see the broken shards of dwindling hope. Of impending loss.

I can barely see through my tears. The only thing I want is to embrace this man who stands right outside this door, and I can't. This trap is designed so that I never will.

"It's time to right the wrongs done to my brother." Abe's voice booms, rich with both menace and victory. "An eye for an eye. A tooth for a tooth. You have one minute left. You can stop the timer to the oven and save your wife. Or you can stop the timer for the bomb and save your brother. But you cannot have both."

Lachlan shakes his head. "No," is all he says, a whisper I can see but can't hear.

"Your wife, or your brother. Choose."

Lachlan doesn't break his gaze from me. Tears shine in his eyes.

This is meant to make us suffer. And the only thing I can do is try to lessen Lachlan's pain.

"I love you, Lachlan. Let me do the choosing." I press my hand to the glass. And then, loud enough that Abe can hear me above Lachlan's anguished pleas, I say the two words that feel like a betrayal even though I know they're the right decision. "Save Rowan."

Lachlan cries out as I take a step back from the window. He hits the glass over and over until his knuckles bleed. He calls my name. "Stop the oven. *Stop it now*—"

Abe's voice is clinical and detached in the periphery. "She made the choice for you. It's done."

I take another step back. Tears gather at my lashes as Lachlan desperately tries to break in. My shoulders square up even though they shake. I raise my chin and give him a smile so full of sorrow and apology and love and pain that my heart shatters when Lachlan's eyes meet mine through the glass.

An alarm goes off.

"Lark, *no*—"

"Tell them I love them."

"*No, no, no.* Stop the fucking oven, goddammit—"

"I love you, Lachlan. I'm sorry."

It all happens so fast—just not fast enough.

There's a sound of metal falling on concrete. A determined cry. A yell of frustration, then one of pain. A gunshot that echoes beyond my steel walls.

And then the oven fans start.

Air blows through the slats in the walls. The circle in the floor turns clockwise, the rotary function spinning me in a slow dance as the current of air grows warm. There's commotion outside the door. When I turn in that direction, I see Rose with Lachlan at the window.

"He locked it somehow," Lachlan says. "Hit the emergency stop—"

"*Where?*"

"*There.*"

"It's not working—I don't know why it's not working."

"He fucked with it. *Get her out*—"

The air is already hot, getting hotter with every heartbeat that knocks against my ribs. My skin is slick with sweat. I drop to the spinning floor in search of a cooler breath that never comes. When I look up to the window, I see Lachlan with a gun pointed to the door handle.

Rose pushes his hand away. "*No*, you could make it worse. Shoot the window."

I try to keep hold of Lachlan's eyes as I spin. The heat becomes nearly unbearable as the fans pick up speed.

"Get down, Lark."

I fold my slick arms over my head.

With a deafening bang, glass shatters into my enclosure and rains down around me. Some of the heat is released and I'm able to fight back the wave of darkness that threatens to knock me unconscious.

A moment later, I hear Rose's sound of triumph and feel a rush of cool air. Two hands wrap around my ankles to drag me from the steel and onto the concrete.

The cold floor. I've never felt such relief as when I press my hot skin against it. I blink. Breathe. I try to control the nausea roiling in my belly as shock and adrenaline and the remaining sedative swirl in my body. With my pulse raging in my ears, I lift my head just enough so that I can meet Abe's lifeless eyes. A hole sits between them, a rivulet of thick crimson trailing toward a growing pool of blood on the floor. A discarded tool lies at his side. It's the same one Abe had in my apartment; the silver end now painted crimson.

I pull my attention away to reach out a hand and Rose takes it with a squeeze. "What about Sloane—"

"I contacted them as soon as that fucker said he knew they were driving. They managed to pull off the road and get out of the vehicle." Rose kneels beside me, heavy, unsteady breaths heaving from her lungs as she looks down at her phone. There's a tremor in her hands as she taps out a message. "They're fine, the car hasn't blown up but it's not like they really wanna check it, you know?"

I let out a long sigh and close my eyes. When I open them Rose's tired smile is waiting. "I might call in a contract for that one. Anyone here know if Leviathan does bombs? I bet I've got a guy."

With Rose's help, I push up enough to look at Lachlan where he sits near my feet. His forearms rest against his knees. His dark hair, slick with sweat, hangs over his brow. He tilts his head up to look at me. In his eyes, I can see all the pain and fury and fear rising to the surface.

"You feckin' catastrophe. Don't you ever. *Ever*. Do that to me again," he grits out as a tear slips from his lashes to fall down his cheek.

"Getting kidnapped by a psychopath? I'm not planning on any do-overs, Batman," I whisper through an unsteady smile.

Lachlan shakes his head. "No. Forcing me to not choose you." Though he grasps for control of his emotions, he's as powerless as I am to stop them. "You're brave as hell. But you're my person, Lark. I can't do this without you."

And this is one of my favorite things about Lachlan. I can look at him and that one glance tells me everything that words can't. It shows truths that are locked away, about how hard it is to love. How much it hurts to let go of the armor we wear, to peel it back and show the most damaged layers of ourselves, to bear all our wounds.

Lachlan opens one arm toward me and I launch into him like a crashing tide.

His arms wrap across my back, powerful even though they tremble. He lifts me from the floor. This is the feeling I thought we would never have again. The feeling of being entwined with each other. To stitch together and know it's not the last time. It's just the beginning.

"You're my wife, Lark Kane," Lachlan whispers, his breath hot against my neck before he presses a lingering kiss to my skin. "And I'm not letting you go."

Lachlan's arms tighten around me. And he keeps his promise.

He doesn't let me go.

RENEW

Lachlan

"How can I be sure Damian has authorized you to sign the contract on his behalf?" Leander asks as he watches Lark read through the paperwork laid out on the coffee table of the basement pub of his home.

Lark shrugs, not looking up as she flips to the last page and picks up the waiting pen. "I guess you'll just have to trust me. Have I ever given you a reason not to?"

Leander laughs but still shifts his attention to me as though I might give him a hint of reassurance. When I don't, he looks even more delighted. Blimmin' nutjob. He loves chaos almost as much as he loves money, two concepts that don't seem compatible, and yet he makes it work.

Lark signs the final page of the Covaci contract and slides it across the coffee table. Leander leans back in his chair and feckin' beams at the both of us. If I didn't know better, I'd think he's actually happy for me. I'm not sure he has that capacity to feel genuinely happy for anyone but himself, but he at least *looks* the part. Or maybe it's not so much the end of my tenure with Leviathan that has him looking so pleased. It could just be Lark, who has been the source of his admiration ever since the muffin incident.

Plus she's also just given him a six-pack of beer.

"It's from my brother-in-law's craft brewery. Buckeye Brewery pale ale," she says as she passes him one of the glass bottles. "An apology for drugging you with muffins."

Leander smiles as he motions to the other bottles in a bid for us to take one. "Don't apologize. I like to be surprised." He reads the label with an appreciative nod and pops the cap. "Speaking of surprises, I never thought I'd see the day, but Lachlan Kane is officially retired. That deserves a toast."

Lark passes me a beer and grabs one for herself. When they're open, we raise our bottles in the air.

"To you, Lark, for sorting out this asshole."

"Asshat," she says.

"Yeah, somehow that works better. *Asshat*," Leander says with a sage nod. "To me, for finding these Kane boys and taking them home. Best decision I ever made was not killing them."

I roll my eyes and Leander laughs before he gives me a slap to the shoulder. But the teasing light in his grin fades to something that seems real, at least as much as a man like Leander Mayes can manage. "And to you, Lachlan. You raised those boys and started your business and managed to somehow find the perfect wife despite being an asshat. You've done good. I'm going to miss you around here, kid."

I nod, an unexpected pang of gratitude and nostalgia hitting my chest as I raise my bottle. "*Sláinte.*"

We clink the necks of our bottles and take a long sip of the honey-brown liquid.

"So," Leander says after downing a third of his beer. "What's your first plan for retirement, Lachlan? Gonna take up gardening, maybe? Throw pickles at neighborhood children and yell at them to get off your lawn?"

I grin and drape an arm across the couch behind Lark as I settle into my seat. "We're going away for the weekend."

"Whereabouts?"

"Cape Cod," Lark says at the same time as I tell him it's none of his business.

"Don't even think about showing up there asking me to do some batshit-crazy job." I shake my head as Leander gives me a devious grin before he takes another long pull from his bottle. "I am *retired.*"

Leander waves me off and sways a little on his seat as he turns his attention to Lark. "Speaking of jobs, got anything new lined up for me yet?"

A smile sneaks across Lark's lips as Leander sets his beer down on the coffee table and gives the bottle a long, befuddled look. "Maybe let's talk about it after you have a little nap."

"Ahh *shhhhit.*"

Leander's body swings in an unsteady circle before he passes out in a heap on the floor. We stare down at him where he lies crumpled between the sofa and the coffee table, a gentle snore already rumbling from his throat.

"Lark . . ."

"Hmm?"

"Didn't we have a talk about this . . . ?"

"I don't think so, no," she says. She rises from the couch and dusts off her jeans before flashing me a brilliant smile. "Not that I recall."

"That's funny. Because I remember saying something about letting me know before you drugged my feckin' psycho boss next time," I say as I stand and fold my arms across my chest. "He looks pretty drugged to me, duchess."

"You told me to let you know if I gave him drugged *muffins*. I gave him drugged beer."

I shake my head. But any attempt I have at stoicism falters as Lark approaches.

She folds her hands around my wrists. I drop my arms at her command and let her close in on me, her eyes fused to my lips. "Take me home," Lark says as she rises on her tiptoes. One of her hands wraps around the back of my neck to draw my lips close to hers. "Since you're officially retired, I think we should celebrate."

My hand threads into Lark's hair. I breathe in her scent of sweet citrus and let my lips graze hers when I whisper, "What exactly do you have in mind?"

"I can't tell you that. It would ruin the surprise."

Lark presses her lips to mine. My tongue sweeps across hers and I pull her closer, deepening the kiss. I'm carried away by my insatiable need for her that only grows more intense with each day that passes. I forget where I am and the world that spins around us as I lift her in my arms.

At least until Leander snorts a rumbling snore on the floor.

I set Lark on her feet with a disappointed sigh. "Christ Jesus. Let's get the hell out of here."

"Deal," she says. She presses a kiss to my cheek before she steps away. With a devious little grin, Lark shrugs on her jacket and grabs my hand.

We leave Leander untouched as we head upstairs and out the door. A message dings on my phone as we slide into the Charger, a text from Rowan. I start up the car and let it warm up as I tap out a reply. I feel Lark's eyes on me as I pocket my phone and shift the car into drive.

"Everything okay?" she asks.

"Yeah, just Rowan asking about Christmas morning, if we want to do their place or ours."

"Maybe ours for Bentley, since he's still feeling sorry for himself. He's really milking this 'injured savior' bit." Lark fiddles with the hem of her jacket, unspoken words hanging in the air. "Do you think Fionn will come?"

Even though I knew that was what she was going to ask, it still feels as though she's reached around my heart and squeezed. "I don't know," I reply as I keep my focus on the winding driveway. When I don't glance her way, Lark lays her hand over mine where it rests on the gear shift. "I hope so."

"Me too."

We don't talk much for the rest of the drive home. Though it would normally be a comforting quiet with Lark, my heart beats too quickly for me to feel relaxed. It only gets worse when we park. I try to take a deep breath as I walk over to the passenger side to open her door. With every step we take, I think she's going to notice the way I hold her hand just a little too tightly, or the way I can't seem to stop biting my bottom lip. But if she does catch on to those details, she never says so. She's seemingly content to walk up the stairs side by side in silence. By the time we get to the landing, I'm nearly vibrating with nerves and anticipation.

"I got you something," I say. I barely give us time to greet Bentley and take off our jackets before I tug Lark along to the living room. She looks at me with scrutiny and I shrug. "Early birthday present."

"My birthday is in February. We haven't even made it to Christmas yet."

"*Extra* early."

Lark's gaze pans across the room before it lands on me. "Where?"

"Gotta figure that out for yourself, duchess."

"Do I get a clue?"

I tap my finger against my lips to draw out her suffering before I finally say, "What kind of conduit is universal?"

A crease appears between Lark's brows. She pivots on her heel, her focus roaming toward the kitchen until her expression suddenly clears. With the most feckin' adorable grin, she grasps my arms and bounces on her toes. "Water. *Constantine.*"

And then she's gone.

I trail in her wake as Lark heads to the *Constantine* poster and lifts it from the wall to reveal a safe. The smile she beams my way lights up every dark crevice in my heart.

"I don't need to pry out an eyeball to open it?" she says as she spins the dial.

"Appears not."

"What's the code?"

"Go with the theme."

I watch as Lark thinks on this for a minute then tries a few options. Her frustration mounts when nothing seems to work. It's a valiant effort, and she seems determined to keep going until she finally lets out a dejected sigh and looks to where I stand with my hands shoved deep in my pockets. "Give up yet?"

"No," she says with a scoff. She tries three more combinations before her shoulders fall. "Yes."

I saunter up behind her, only stopping when my body is flush with her back. With a lingering kiss to Lark's neck, I reach over her shoulder to spin the lock. "Well, well. Look who's more up on their *Constantine* trivia now. Three, three, nine, three. The number on the back of Chas Kramer's taxi."

With the final number in place, I unlock the safe and stand back.

"Don't gloat yet, Batman. I . . ."

Lark trails off as she opens the door, revealing her trophies. The snow globe. The coaster. The maracas were trickier to salvage, so I made her a new pouch from cowhide for the teeth of the broken one. There are a few other things I found hidden in the apartment, like a bookmark made of charred fabric and a beaded bracelet made of bone. And behind all those trophies, there's something she's never seen before.

"What's this?" she asks as she pulls a cube of clear resin from the safe. She twists it side to side, examining the heart suspended in gold wire, frozen in time.

"That's maybe the wrong question."

"*Who* is this?"

"Dr. Louis Campbell."

Lark stiffens. She stares at that heart. She doesn't take her eyes from it, not even when they well with tears that she struggles to blink into submission. Her pain stokes the rage that lingers like venom in my veins. But there's satisfaction too, in the hope that this trophy will give her some measure of closure to questions that have haunted her sleepless nights.

"Are you serious . . . ?"

I nod.

Lark's lip wobbles, and for a moment I wonder if this was the wrong thing to do. But when she looks at me, a smile breaks through the pain that creases her brow and floods her eyes with tears.

"This is the best present I've ever gotten," she squeaks out. She feckin' *sobs* as she wraps her arms around the cube and hugs it to her chest. Relief washes over me as I pull her into my embrace. Her body trembles as she lets go of at least some of this pain that's haunted her for so many years. And I know this isn't just something she wanted. It was something she *needed*.

When we finally separate, I pull the box from her arms and set it on the coffee table so I can take her shoulders and turn her away. "There's one more thing," I whisper as I nudge her toward the safe.

"More . . . ?"

"You heard me."

With a wary glance over her shoulder, Lark focuses on the items left inside, where I know there's a manila envelope with her name on it. She keeps her back to me as she opens it. There's a gasp as she withdraws the documents and reads the itinerary for a prebooked honeymoon trip to Indonesia I printed earlier today.

And then she flips to the divorce papers.

"What the fuck is this . . . ?"

When I say nothing, she turns to face me, and finds me down on one knee.

A fresh wave of tears cascades down Lark's cheeks in shining rivulets. She can't seem to land on furious, or elated, or purely overwhelmed, but they all seem to combine when she says, "What the hell are you doing?"

"Proposing, by the looks of things," I say with a glance at the diamond band I hold between us.

Lark looks around us as though the explanation can be found on the sofa, or out the window, or on the floor. Her gaze lingers on Bentley, who looks as confounded as she does. Then her eyes land on the papers that waver in her unsteady hands. I'm pretty sure a feckin' eternity passes before her attention returns to me. "Why?"

"Because you never really had a choice in this marriage."

Lark shakes her head. Her lips press into a tight line and her brow furrows. And I'm feckin' terrified. I'm *terrified* to let her go. But I made a promise to protect her. From anyone, even herself. Even *me*. And the only way I can do that is to be sure she can live the life she wants. Otherwise, I'm not a protector. I'm a cage.

Lark's expression is so hard and so pained that I can't tell what she's really feeling, but I know I need to keep going.

"You made this vow to save me. My brother. Your best friend. But I want you to *choose* the future you want, Lark. You can dissolve this marriage. Or we can do things another way. Maybe we start over and pretend we'd first met at Rowan's place. Or we can stay married, have the honeymoon we talked about. You said it would be Indonesia, if this were real." I take a steadying breath, but my throat burns when I swallow. It's so hard to keep my eyes on her as I break open my heart to let her look inside. "This is real to me, Lark. I know I promised I wouldn't let you go, but I was wrong. Because this decision is more important than me keeping my word. And for what it's worth, I hope you choose me, in whatever way that needs to be. I'm asking you to stay with me. But I want you to choose what's right for you."

Lark holds my eyes.

And she doesn't look away. Not as she tosses the itinerary over her shoulder, a move that incinerates my heart in a beat of panic. Not as she holds the divorce papers up and rips them apart, one after the next until each one is torn. Then she points at me with a trembling hand.

"I am madly in love with you, Lachlan Kane," she says, jabbing her finger in my direction as though punctuating each word. "And I am also just madly *mad*. Don't you *ever* give me divorce papers again."

"I promise, duchess." A burst of hope and relief and joy floods my chest. They are feelings I thought I'd never have, a life I never thought I'd live. Not until I made the choice to let Lark in. "I love you, Lark Kane."

Lark's anger dissolves. Her smile ignites. It's the most beautiful she's ever been, her happiness an unstoppable dawn.

"Good, you 'feckin' catastrophe,'" she says, and then she crashes into my arms. "Because I choose you."

I slip the ring above the set on her finger.

And I choose her, like I have every day since I found the bottom of the chasm between us and decided to do whatever it took to claw my way into her light. I choose her like I will every day to come.

I kiss my wife. And I choose love.

MAGIC TRICK

Rose

My grandma used to say that the best magic tricks are performed by the ones who believe.

It's true. I see it all the time at Silveria Circus. The best magicians are always the ones who understand that the true magic at the heart of a trick is *possibility*.

Maybe that's why no one looks my way now. Because I believed in magic too.

Abe Mead lies dead on the factory floor. That fucker. Wouldn't mind having another shot at killing him if I could. Maybe I'd have done a few things a little differently.

I pull my attention away from his cooling body. I don't want him to take another second of my time.

So I put all my focus on something beautiful instead. Lachlan and Lark. They hold each other in a crushing embrace. They sway like two trees that have twisted together and weathered storms side by side. Maybe this will be the last big one. A thunderstorm that leaves clean air and vibrant colors behind. I'd like to think the weather will always be fair for them now, the skies always clear. I think that's what I'll choose to believe.

I glance down at my shirt. There's almost nothing to show for everything that's happened. Just a small hole in the flannel fabric on my side, right beneath my ribs. There's no more than a few drops of crimson to stain my shirt. A little trick. Nothing to see.

But I can feel it.

It burns *right there*, while the rest of me feels cold. No one notices when I lie down on the floor.

Lachlan and Lark are still wrapped together when a door flies open somewhere nearby. Running footsteps echo against machines and concrete walls.

"*Rose*," Fionn calls out. There's panic in his voice. He repeats my name over and over. It sounds like it's growing more distant. Not coming closer.

It feels like the first time I flew through the metal cage on my motorcycle. The terrifying roar of the engine. The flip of my stomach when I realized I didn't know which way was up. I just pulled back on that throttle and sped through the sphere until everything else faded away except the headlight in front of me.

"She's here," Lark calls back when I don't answer, but she sounds far away too. "Oh my God—"

"*Christ Jesus.* Fionn, help—"

The world doesn't go dark. It goes bright white. In the final moment before the light washes the shadows away, I see Fionn in the distance. And I know he's my home. My person.

My love.

Maybe magic is real after all.

STRAPPED

LARK

Funny thing about marriage.

Sometimes I look at my husband and think, *I can't imagine having loved anyone as much as Lachlan Kane.*

And other times, I just want to make him *suffer.*

In a loving way, of course. Most of the time.

Like now.

I watch from the hammock as Lachlan checks his gear and lays his wet suit out to dry in the sun on the porch of our beach hut. I give him a saccharine smile as he bends to place a kiss on my forehead and then heads inside, leaving the door open. He can't see the way my eyes narrow behind my sunglasses, or the way my smile turns menacing as I roll out of the hammock and follow behind him.

"How was your dive?" I ask as he picks up his wedding band from the dresser and slides it onto his finger where the tattoo of a gold star is recently healed, the pale yellow and black lines vibrant.

"Good. Saw a couple of manta rays. Lots of fish. A ribbon eel. Really cool."

"Cool, yeah. Cool." Lachlan gives me a suspicious glance over his shoulder, but my waiting smile is flawless. I lay a reassuring hand on his arm. "Why don't you get in the shower? I'll join you in a sec."

Lachlan's eyes sweep down my body, lingering on my bikini top, dropping to my navel and the waistband of my jean shorts, trailing an electric current down my bare legs. A slow, ravenous smirk spreads on his lips.

"Sounds like a good idea to me, duchess," he says as he runs a hand over my hair and presses a kiss to my forehead. "See you in a minute."

My smile becomes lethal when he turns his back. As soon as I hear the water turn on, I get to work.

By the time I enter the bathroom, the steam has started to gather at the ceiling and across the surface of the mirror. Lachlan stands beneath the spray of water with his head bent, his eyes closed. Water sluices down his thick bands of corded muscle and inked skin. An ache fills my core as I take a moment to just watch.

"You gonna get in, or are you just gonna stand out there and admire my Keanu-ish hotness all afternoon?" he asks without opening his eyes.

I roll my eyes and unbutton my shorts to slide them over my hips. "You're way hotter than Keanu."

"I know."

Lachlan's self-satisfied smile turns heated when I pull the string at my back and let the bikini top fall to the floor. He pushes the glass door open and offers me a hand to step inside, and as soon as I take it he wraps me in a wet embrace.

"So beautiful," he murmurs in my ear as he runs a hand down my back, following the contour of my spine. His palm stops at my ass and he presses me closer, his length hard against my stomach. "Maybe we should extend our stay here. It's good to see you so relaxed." My breath catches as he bites the junction between my neck and shoulder. He soothes it with a kiss. "I take back what I said that one time about beaches being boring. It's a hell of a lot more fun when I get to fuck my wife morning, noon, and night."

Lachlan kisses a line that follows my collarbone and then down to my right breast. He sucks my nipple and my hand twines into his hair to grip the short strands. I press him to my chest and he groans. "Maybe we *should* stay a little longer. I'm not ready to go home."

Lachlan moans his agreement into my flesh before he kisses his way to my other breast, teasing my nipple into a firm peak. Before he can kiss his way lower, I pull away and let my hands trail down his chest and the rippling muscle of his abs to anchor to his tapered waist. I keep my eyes on his as I slowly drop to my knees. He blows out a long breath as I take his erection in a firm grip and spit on the tip.

"You sure you won't get bored?" I ask with feigned innocence. I blink up at him as I stroke his length then run my tongue along the underside of his erection. He shudders when I skate the crown across my lips.

"One hundred percent sure." His hand threads into my hair and my lips envelop the crown of his erection. I suck hard on his cock and let him free of my mouth with an audible pop. "Lark . . . *Christ Jesus.*"

I work his erection. My motion is slow, my grip firm. I cup his balls and take him deep. I swallow his length. My tears mix with the water that pelts my face every time he hits the back of my throat. I moan around his flesh, let the vibration push him closer to the edge, closer and closer until he's shuddering and cursing and chanting my name like a prayer. I feel every muscle in his body tensing. I hear his impending release in the desperation that colors every whispered word.

And in the moment before he's ready to fill my throat, I let go of my husband and back out of his reach.

Lachlan's confusion meets my waiting smirk. He's trembling with the release I just denied him. His eyes scour my face, his brow creased with worry. "Did I do something wrong?"

I drag the back of my hand across my lips and open the shower door. "Dry yourself off and come out," I say as I step out and tug my robe off the hanger to drape it over my arm. I don't bother with a towel. I nod to his watch where it sits on the counter. "Give me five minutes exactly. Not a single one more or less."

I shut the shower door and leave the bathroom with the sound of Lachlan's confusion following on my heels.

When Lachlan exits the bathroom a few moments later with a towel wrapped around his waist and a wary look on his face, I'm waiting, sitting on the edge of the bed.

"What's going on?" he asks as his eyes dart from me to the bed and back again. "What is this?"

I pat the surface of the bed, stirring the torn strips of paper that litter the surface. "Come and have a look."

The crease between Lachlan's brows deepens and then he approaches, stopping next to me. He picks up a piece of paper but sets it back down when he can't glean anything from the few words typed on it. When he takes a second strip, a deep blush flames in his tanned cheeks. He meets my eyes and I slide the shoulder of my robe down to reveal a black leather bra strap.

"You know," I say as I pull the tie on my robe, "every time you take off that wedding band, I feel compelled to get vengeance for those divorce papers you gave me as a 'present.'"

Lachlan's throat bobs with a swallow. "I was trying to give you a choice."

I shrug.

"I . . . I tattooed it on my finger," he says as he holds up his hand as though I'm seeing his ink for the first time. "I don't want to lose the band in the ocean."

"And yet, I don't really care." I give Lachlan a sardonic smile as I pull the other shoulder down to reveal the leather and lace bra that I made myself. It's not perfect, not like it would be if Lachlan had made it, but he stares at my chest as though it's a beautiful work of art.

I stand, letting the robe fall to my feet to reveal the rest of my work. Lace panties. Leather straps. And a glittery black dildo attached to the harness I'm wearing.

Lachlan's eyes turn black with desire.

"Like I said. Never again. And now I'm going to fuck you on those papers. I'm going to fuck you until you never forget who you belong to. Get on the goddamned bed."

Lachlan holds my eyes for a long moment before his hand moves to the bunched fabric where the towel folds at his waist. He tugs it free and lets the towel drop to the floor. His erection twitches as his eyes drop to the dildo, feral need consuming his gaze.

Lachlan moves toward the bed with predatory grace, his steps slow and purposeful. He passes close enough to me that I can feel his body heat, his eyes not leaving mine, not even as he places his fists on the mattress.

"What does red mean?" I ask as his first knee presses down on strips of torn paper.

"Stop."

"Yellow means?"

"Slow down."

I watch as the mattress dips beneath the weight of Lachlan's muscular body. He positions himself on all fours in the center of the bed, his back tense, a shudder rolling through his powerful frame. I smile as I pick up a small bottle of lube and crack open the lid. "Green means?"

"Fuck me until I'm spraying my cum all over these feckin' papers."

I run my palm across Lachlan's ass before I give it a sharp slap. "Such a good boy," I coo as I tilt the bottle of lube to let the first thick drops land on his ass crack. With my hands on his smooth skin, I separate his ass cheeks and maneuver my hips to drag the tip of the dildo through the viscous liquid. "Are you *sure* you're a good boy, though?" With one hand, I grip the toy and press it to the puckered hole, massaging the tight ring of muscle, circling it until the lube spreads and I feel him start to relax.

"Yes," he hisses.

"Really? Or are you my fucking whore?"

I press the tip of the dildo to the pleated hole, keeping the pressure on until it slips past the resistance. Lachlan cries out with the sensation, dropping his head to his arm as I move with him, keeping the end of the dildo lodged in his ass. He takes a few deep breaths and I caress the thick planes of muscle that bracket his spine.

"Color?" I ask.

"*Feckin' hell*," he whispers.

"Last time I checked, that wasn't a color—"

"Green, fuck. *Green.*"

I flip my wet hair from my eyes and keep my gaze on the sight before me as I push the toy deeper into Lachlan's ass. My back arches as I keep the pressure on, steadily moving forward until I'm stretching and filling him, my powerful, lethal husband reduced to shuddering, unraveling, animalistic need.

"Don't forget the part about you screaming my name as you spray your cum on these bullshit papers," I whisper.

And then I pick up a rhythm of thrusts.

Slow and steady at first. Long strokes. I pull out all the way to the tip of the dildo, then push back in until I fill him completely. Lachlan growls with pleasure. Moans as I pick up a faster cadence. Shudders when I scrape my nails down his back and slap his ass. And just watching what I do to him stokes an ache deep in my belly. I seize the power of every rocking motion and I know that I'm the one pushing him to the brink of madness. That there are billions of people in the world but I am the only person he trusts to throw him off that cliff and still give him a safe place to land. I know it in every thrust of my hips. Every tremble in his arms. Every curse and unsteady exhalation. I revel in every moment of pulling Lachlan Kane apart.

Sweat coats Lachlan's skin in a glistening film. He grips the sheets with bleached knuckles. Torn papers rustle on the bed as I thrust with a quickening pace.

I drape my body over Lachlan's back and reach around his hip to grip his cock. He hisses with pleasure as I coat my palm with the pre-cum gathered at the tip and stroke his length.

389

"Come for me, baby," I whisper in his ear. "Say my name loud enough that the whole damn island knows whose whore you are."

A gravelly moan escapes Lachlan's lips as I ramp up the pace of my thrusts and pump his erection. "Christ, Lark. *Lark*," he grits out. And he says it again. And again. And again. My pace is unrelenting. I'm merciless. I want him mindless with pleasure. I want him to be ruined. To know my name is the only word he can remember.

And my name is the only thing Lachlan says as he comes.

His spine locks. His cock pulses in my hand. Ropes of cum spray across the bedding. Across ripped paper. Across words like *divorce*, and *irreconcilable*, and *final decree*. They're all stained with the proof that we are unbroken. My husband and I chose a different path. We choose it every day.

I wrap my arm around Lachlan's waist and press my cheek to his back where I can hear his heartbeat riot through muscle and bone. And he lays a hand on mine, holding me close. It's a long moment before I start to slide my touch away and pull out. I take my time, reveling in every shudder and shiver he makes as I slip free.

The second the dildo leaves his ass, Lachlan flips me over and I laugh as he pins me beneath his knees. He fumbles with the buckle for the harness as though he's desperate for a taste of my pussy. When it's finally undone, he tosses it to the floor and then pulls the lace panties aside as he settles between my legs.

"Your turn," he whispers, and with a devious grin and a dark wink, he feasts.

ACKNOWLEDGMENTS

First and foremost, to YOU, dear reader, for spending some of your time with Lachlan and Lark, and their friends and family, and curmudgeonly Bentley (I promise he's living his BEST fictional dog life!). I hope you enjoyed the crazy journey. The experience of writing *Leather & Lark* was unlike any book I've written so far. Much like Lark and Lachlan's story, life is full of joy and heartbreak and love and perseverance. This book was both incredibly challenging and rewarding in equal measure, and I hope you love it.

Huge, enormous, endless thanks to Kim Whalen from the Whalen Agency. You've changed my life in ways that are still difficult for me to fathom. I absolutely love working with you and I'm so grateful for everything you have done and continue to do for me. Thank you also to Mary Pender and Orly Greenberg at UTA; I'm so excited to see what comes next for these stories! Thank you for helping to open these characters to a whole new world.

To Molly Stern, Sierra Stovall, Hayley Wagreich, Andrew Rein, and the entire team at Zando, thank you for taking a chance on my work and not only asking me to jump on the pirate ship, but then making the pirate ship into a superyacht, and now we're zooming around the seven seas! Next stop: SPACE.

In the UK, huge thanks to the team at Little, Brown UK, particularly Ellie Russell and Becky West, who have been so wonderful to work with and who were some of the very first folks in the publishing industry to rally behind the Ruinous Love series. Thank you also to Glenn Tavennec from Éditions du Seuil for being such a huge supporter of me and these characters. And I will always be so grateful to András Kepets in Hungary, who set in place the first domino that brought these partnerships to life.

Big thanks to Najla and the team at Qamber Designs, who created the stunning covers for all three books in this series. It has been an absolute pleasure to work with everyone on that team—they did an amazing job bringing the essence of these stories to life! To my lifesaver PA and graphics wizard, Val Downs. Thank you for keeping me afloat whenever I fall off the pirate ship, HAHA. You keep the sails up and I'm so thankful to work with you.

I am enormously grateful to the amazing ARC readers and social media supporters of *Butcher & Blackbird* for taking time out of their day to read, promote, and talk about these stories, and their willingness to come on these crazy journeys with me. It means the world to me that you love the characters as much as I do, and that you take the time to let me know. I absolutely love your drawings, edits, videos, messages, and comments. Being on this adventure with you makes the carpal tunnel worthwhile, AHAHA.

Super special thanks to Arley and Jess, who so kindly vibe-check things for me when I'm in the "I want to BURN THIS" phase of writing. You save my sanity and for that I'm enormously grateful. I love you ladies. And to Kristie, huge thanks for the gift of "multiple deleter," but most of all, thank you for your love and support.

To T. Thomason, who when I said, "I have a crazy idea," was like, "Sign me the fuck up!" As I write this, our wild little plan is still under construction. Please know that I am so thankful for your friendship and your willingness to entertain such a weird and fun idea out of the blue!

I have been so lucky to become friends with some incredibly talented authors on this writing journey, and their help and guidance has been so critical for me, particularly during this series. To Avina St. Graves, thank you for letting me include a little snippet of *Death's Obsession*. Lachlan loved it, haha! And thank you for being my deadline buddy. I could not have survived without you (for reals). "I'm going to wax my legs to feel something other than stress" should be on a shirt. To Abby Jimenez, thank you for your sage advice (and the bottle of moonshine in the sketchy alley, it went down a treat). And Lauren Biel, who is always up for a batshit-crazy brainstorming session, I'll get that boxcar romance out of you yet!

Last but certainly not least, to my amazing boys: my husband, Daniel, and son, Hayden. Daniel, thank you for always taking the time to help me make sense of the glittery brain soup, and for your patience, love, and support. Definitely also the wine and the olive and cheese plates—those really saved my soul. I love you, my boys. (Hayden, when you asked how old you'd need to be before you could read this, the answer is 245.)

ABOUT THE AUTHOR

New York Times and *USA TODAY* best-selling author and TikTok sensation with works sold worldwide in over fifteen languages to date, **Brynne Weaver** has traveled the world, taken in more stray animals than her husband would probably prefer, and nurtured her love for dark comedies, horror, and romance in both literature and film. During all her adventures, the constant thread in Brynne's life has been writing. With eight published works and counting, Brynne has made her mark in the literary world by blending irreverent dark comedy, swoon-worthy romance, and riveting suspense to create genre-breaking, addictive stories for readers to escape into.

Instagram: @brynne_weaver

TikTok: @brynneweaverbooks

Facebook: facebook.com/groups/1200796990512620

Goodreads:
goodreads.com/author/show/21299126.Brynne_Weaver